RACHEL VINCENT

STRAY

MIRA®

MIRA®

Recycling programs
for this product may
not exist in your area.

ISBN-13: 978-0-7783-2907-7

STRAY

For questions and comments about the quality of this book please contact us
at Customer_eCare@Harlequin.ca.

www.MIRABooks.com

Printed in U.S.A.

ACKNOWLEDGMENTS

Writing a book is a very solitary pursuit. Publishing one is not. It's a group effort, requiring contributions from many people, with many different areas of expertise. With that in mind, I'd like to thank everyone who worked on *Stray* during its development: editorial director Dianne Moggy and executive editor Margaret Marbury; in marketing, Ana Movileanu and Stacy Widdrington; art director Erin Craig and designer Sean Kapitain; editorial assistant Adam Wilson, whose contributions behind the scenes should not go unnoticed; and everyone involved in production and sales. Thank you all.

Also, thanks to *Ohh,* who double-checked my Spanish, without laughing at my mistakes.

Thanks to my editor, the fabulous Mary-Theresa Hussey, whose patience with me and faith in my story are directly responsible for putting this book on the shelf.

Thanks to literary agent extraordinaire Miriam Kriss for being so incredibly good at her job. For answering my questions and calming me down. For giving me confidence and pride in my work. In short, thanks for selling my books.

And finally, I owe a huge debt of gratitude—and a big hug—to Kim Harrison, the world's greatest mentor, for lending her wisdom, her experience and her time to a newbie writer in need of guidance. For teaching me more than I ever thought possible, and more than I could ever express. And most of all, thanks, Kim, for taking me seriously.

To my # 1 fan, the love of my life, for endless support and encouragement. For providing me with the time and the space I needed to make my dream come true. And most of all, for daring me to finally put my hands on the keyboard, and the words on the page.

This never would have happened without you.

One

The moment the door opened I knew an ass-kicking was inevitable. Whether I'd be giving it or receiving it was still a bit of a mystery.

The smell hit me as I left the air-conditioned comfort of the language building for the heat of another north-central Texas summer, tugging my backpack higher on my shoulder as I squinted into the sunset. A step behind me, my roommate, Sammi, was ranting about the guest lecturer's discriminatory view of women's contributions to nineteenth-century literature. I'd been about to play devil's advocate, just for the hell of it, when a shift in the evening breeze stopped me where I stood, on the top step of the narrow front porch.

My argument forgotten, I froze, scanning the

shadowy quad for the source of the unmistakable scent. Visually, nothing was out of the ordinary: just small groups of summer students talking on their way to and from the dorms. Human students. But what I smelled wasn't human. It wasn't even close.

Absorbed in her rant, Sammi didn't realize I'd stopped. She walked right into me, cursing loud enough to draw stares when her binder fell out of her hand and popped open on the ground, littering the steps with loose-leaf paper.

"I could use a little notice next time you plan on zoning out, Faythe," she snapped, bending to gather up her notes. Grunts and more colorful words issued from behind her, where our fellow grad students were stalled by our pedestrian traffic jam. Lit majors are not known for watching where they're going; most of us walk with our eyes in a book instead of on the path ahead.

"Sorry." I knelt to help her, snatching a sheet of paper from the concrete before the student behind me could stomp on it. Standing, I took the steps two at a time, following Sammi to a brick half wall jutting from the porch. Still talking, she set her binder on the ledge and began methodically reorganizing her notes, completely oblivious to the scent, as humans always were. I barely heard her incessant chatter as she worked.

My nostrils flared slightly to take in more of the smell as I turned my face into the breeze. *There.* Across the quad, in the alley between the physics building and Curry Hall.

My fist clenched around the strap of my backpack and my teeth ground together. He wasn't supposed to be here. *None* of them were supposed to be here. My father had promised.

I'd always known they were watching me, in spite of my father's agreement not to interfere in my life. On occasion, I'd spot a too-bright eye in the crowd at a football game, or notice a familiar profile in line at the food court. And rarely—only twice before in five years—I caught a distinctive scent on the air, like the taste of my childhood, sweet and familiar, but with a bitter aftertaste. The smell was faint and tauntingly intimate. And completely unwelcome.

They were subtle, all those glimpses, those hints that my life wasn't as private as we all pretended. Daddy's spies faded silently into crowds and shadows because they wanted to be seen no more than I wanted to see them.

But this one was different. He wanted me to see him. Even worse—he wasn't one of Daddy's.

"...that her ideas are somehow less important because she had ovaries instead of testes is beyond chauvinistic. It's barbaric. Someone should...Faythe?"

Sammi nudged me with her newly restored notebook. "You okay? You look like you just saw a ghost."

No, I hadn't seen a ghost. I'd smelled a cat.

"I'm feeling a little sick to my stomach." I grimaced only long enough to be convincing. "I'm going to go lie down. Will you apologize to the group for me?"

She frowned. "Faythe, this was *your* idea."

"I know." I nodded, thinking of the four other M.A. candidates already gathered around their copies of *Love's Labours Lost* in the library. "Tell everyone I'll be there next week. I swear."

"Okay," she said with a shrug of her bare, freckled shoulders. "It's your grade." Seconds later, Sammi was just another denim-clad student on the sidewalk, completely oblivious to what lurked in the late-evening shadows thirty yards away.

I left the concrete path to cut across the quad, struggling to keep anger from showing on my face. Several feet from the sidewalk, I stepped on my shoelace, giving myself time to come up with a plan of action as I retied it. Kneeling, I kept one eye on the alley, watching for a glimpse of the trespasser. This wasn't supposed to happen. In my entire twenty-three years, I'd never heard of a stray getting this far into our territory without being caught. It simply wasn't possible.

Yet there he was, hiding just out of sight in the alley. Like a coward.

I could have called my father to report the intruder. I probably *should* have called him, so he could send the designated spy-of-the-day to take care of the problem. But calling would necessitate speaking to my father, which I made a point to avoid at all costs. My only other course of action was to scare the stray off on my own, then dutifully report the incident the next time I caught one of the guys watching me. No big deal. Strays were loners, and typically as skittish as deer when confronted. They always ran from Pride cats because we always worked in pairs, at the very least.

Except for me.

But the stray wouldn't know I had no backup. Hell, I probably *did* have backup. Thanks to my father's paranoia, I was never really alone. True, I hadn't actually *seen* whoever was on duty today, but that didn't mean anything. I couldn't always spot them, but they were always there.

Shoe tied, I stood, for once reassured by my father's overprotective measures. I tossed my bag over one shoulder and ambled toward the alley, doing my best to appear relaxed. As I walked, I searched the quad discreetly, looking for my hidden backup. Whoever he was, he'd finally learned how to hide. Perfect timing.

The sun slipped below the horizon as I approached the alley. In front of Curry Hall, an automatic streetlight flickered to life, buzzing softly. I stopped in the circle of soft yellow light cast on the sidewalk, gathering my nerve.

The stray was probably just curious, and would likely run as soon as he knew I'd seen him. But if he didn't, I'd have to scare him off through other, more hands-on means. Unlike most of my fellow tabby cats, I knew how to fight; my father had made sure of that. Unfortunately, I'd never made the jump from theory to practice, except against my brothers. Sure, I could hold my own with them, but I hadn't sparred in years, and this didn't feel like a very good time to test skills still unproven in the real world.

It's not too late to call in the cavalry, I thought, patting the slim cell phone in my pocket. Except that it *was*. Every time I spoke to my father, he came up with a new excuse to call me home. This time he wouldn't even need to make one up. I'd have to handle the problem myself.

My resolve as stiff as my spine, I stepped out of the light and into the darkness.

Heart pounding, I entered the alley, tightening my grip on my bag as if it were the handle of a sword. Or maybe the corner of a security blanket. I sniffed the air. He was still there; I could smell him. But now that I was closer to the source, I detected something strange in his scent—something even more out of place than the odor of a stray deep inside my Pride's territory. Whoever this trespasser was, he wasn't local. There was a distinctive foreign nuance to his scent. Exotic. Spicy, compared to the blandly familiar base scent of my fellow American cats.

My pulse throbbed in my throat. *Foreign. Shit.* I was in over my head.

I was digging in my pocket for my phone when something clattered to the ground farther down the alley. I froze, straining to see in the dark, but with my human eyes, it was a lost cause. Without Shifting, I couldn't make out anything but vague outlines and deep shadows. Unfortunately, Shifting wasn't an option at that moment. It would take too long, and I'd be defenseless during the transition.

Human form it is.

I glanced quickly behind me, looking for signs of life from the quad. It was empty now, as far as I could tell. There were no potential witnesses; everyone with half a brain was either studying or partying. So why was I playing hide-and-seek after dark with an unidentified stray?

My muscles tense and my ears on alert, I started down the alley. Four steps later, I stepped through a broken tennis racket and stumbled into a rusty Dumpster. My bag thumped to the ground as my head hit the side of the trash receptacle, ringing it like an oversize gong.

Smooth, Faythe, I thought, the metallic thrum still echoing in my ears.

I bent over to pick up my bag, and a darting motion up ahead caught my eye. The stray—in human form, thankfully—ran from the mouth of the alley into the parking lot behind Curry Hall, his feet unnaturally silent on the asphalt. Pale moonlight shined on a head full of dark, glossy curls as he ran.

Instinct overrode my fear and caution. Adrenaline flooded my veins. I tossed my bag over my shoulder and sprinted down the center of the alley. The stray had fled, as I'd hoped he would, and the feline part of my brain demanded I follow. When mice run, cats give chase.

At the end of the alley, I paused, staring at the parking lot. It was empty, but for an old, busted up Lincoln with a rusty headlight. The stray was gone. How the hell had he gotten away so fast?

A prickly feeling started at the base of my neck, raising tiny hairs the length of my spine. Every security light in the lot was unlit. They were supposed to be automatic, like the ones in the quad. Without the familiar buzz and the reassuring flood of incandescent light, the parking lot was an unbroken sea of dark asphalt, eerily quiet and disturbingly calm.

My heart pounding, I stepped out of the alley, half expecting to be struck by lightning or hit by a runaway train. Nothing happened, but I couldn't shake the feeling that something was wrong. I took another step, my eyes wide to let in all of the available light. Still nothing happened.

I was feeling foolish now, chasing a stranger down a dark alley at night, like some bimbo from a bad horror film. In the movies, this was where things always went wrong. A hairy hand would reach out of the shadows and grab the curious-but-brainless heroine around the throat, laughing sadistically while she wasted her last breath on a scream.

The difference between the movies and reality was that in real life, I *was* the hairy monster, and the only screaming I ever did was in rage. I was about as likely to cry for help as I was to spontaneously combust. If this particular bad guy hadn't figured that out yet, he was in for a very big surprise.

Emboldened by my own mental pep talk, I took another step.

The distinctive foreign scent washed over me, and my pulse jumped, but I never saw the kick coming.

Suddenly I was staring at the ground, doubled over from the pain in my stomach and fighting for the strength to suck in my next breath.

My bag fell to the ground at my feet. A pair of black, army-style boots stepped into sight, and the smell of stray intensified. I looked up just in time to register dark eyes and a creepy smile before his right fist shot out toward me. My arms flew up to block the blow, but his other arm was already flying. His left fist slammed into the right side of my chest.

Fresh pain burst to life in my rib cage, radiating in a widening circle. One hand pressed to my side, I struggled to stand up straight, panicked when I couldn't.

An ugly cackling laugh clawed my inner chalkboard and pissed me off. This was *my* campus, and *my* Pride's territory. *He* was the outsider, and it was time he learned how Pride cats dealt with intruders.

He pulled his fist back for another blow, but this time I was ready. Ignoring the pain in my side, I lunged to my right, reaching for a handful of his hair. My fingers tangled in a thick clump of curls. I shoved his head down and brought my knee up. The two connected. Bone crunched. Something warm and wet soaked through my jeans. The scent of fresh blood saturated the air, and I smiled.

Ah, memories…

The stray jerked his head free of my grip and lurched out of reach, leaving me several damp curls as souvenirs. Wiping blood from his broken nose, he growled deep inside his throat, a sound like the muted rumble of an engine.

"You should really thank me," I said, a little impressed by the damage I'd caused. "Trust me. It's an improvement."

"Jodienda puta!" he said, spitting a mouthful of blood on the concrete.

Spanish? I was pretty sure it wasn't a compliment. "Yeah, well, back at 'cha. Get your mangy ass out of here before I decide a warning isn't enough!"

Instead of complying, he aimed his next shot for my face. I tried to dodge the punch, but couldn't quite move fast enough. His fist slammed into the side of my skull.

I reeled from the blow, fireworks going off behind my eyelids. My head throbbed like a migraine on steroids. The whole world seemed to spin just for me.

At the edge of my graying vision, the stray fumbled for something in his pocket, cursing beneath his breath in a Spanish-like language I couldn't quite identify. His arm shot out again. Not steady enough yet to move, I braced myself for impact. The blow never came. He grabbed my arm and pulled trying to haul me away from the deserted student center.

What the hell? When confronted by a Pride cat, any stray in possession of two brain cells to rub together would take off with his fur standing on end. After what I'd done to his face, this one should have run screaming from me in terror. It was because I was a girl, I knew it. If I were a tomcat instead of a tabby, he'd already be halfway to Mexico.

I hate it when men aren't afraid of me. It reminds me of home.

Backpedaling to keep from falling, I tried to yank my arm from his grip. It didn't work. Angry now, I swung my free fist around, smashing it into his skull. He grunted and dropped my arm.

I rushed toward the alley and snatched my bag from the ground. The stray's footsteps pounded behind me. I tightened my grip and whirled around, swinging the pack by its straps. It smashed into his left ear. His head snapped back and to the side. More blood flew from his nose, splattering the parking lot with dark droplets. The stray fell on his ass on the concrete, one hand covering the side of his head. He stared at me in astonishment. I laughed. Apparently the complete works of Shakespeare packed quite a wallop.

To think, my mother said I'd never find use for

an English degree. Ha! I'd like to see her knock someone silly with an apron and a cookie press.

"Puta loco," the stray muttered, digging in his pocket again as he scrambled to his feet. Without another word—or even a glance—he took off across the parking lot toward the Lincoln. Seconds later, tires screeched as he peeled from the lot, heading south on Welch Street.

"Adios!" I watched him go, sore but pleased. *Surely after that, Daddy will have to admit I can take care of myself.*

Panting from exertion, I threw my bag over my shoulder and glanced at my watch. *Damn.* Sammi would be home from study group soon, and she'd be horrified by my bloody jeans and brand-new bruises. I'd have to change before she got in. Unfortunately, keeping bruises hidden from Andrew would be much harder. Dating humans could be a real pain in the ass sometimes.

Still picturing the intruder's mutilated face, I turned back toward the alley—and came face-to-face with another stray. Well, face-to-head-shrouded-in-shadow, anyway. He stood five feet away, just out of reach of the pale moonlight, and I could see nothing but the hands hanging empty at his sides. I knew at a glance that they could do serious damage, even clenched around nothing but air.

I didn't need to smell this stray to know who he was; his scent was as familiar to me as my own. *Marc*. My father's second-in-command. Daddy had never sent Marc before—not once in five years. Something was wrong.

Tension crept up my back and down my arms, curling my hands into fists. I gritted my teeth to hold in a shriek of fury; the last thing I needed was to call attention to myself. Human do-gooders were always out to save the world, but few of them had any idea what kind of a world they really lived in.

I stepped slowly toward Marc, letting my backpack slide down my arm to the ground. I fixed my gaze on the shadow hiding his gold-flecked eyes. He didn't move. I came closer, my pulse pounding in my throat. He raised his left hand, reaching out to me. I slapped it away.

Shifting my weight to my left leg, I let my right foot fly, hitting him in the chest with a high side kick. Grunting, he stumbled into the alley. His heel hit the corner of a wooden crate and he fell on his ass on a damp cardboard box.

"Faythe, it's me!"

"I know who the hell you are." I came toward him with my hands on my hips. "Why do you think I kicked you?" I pulled my right foot back, prepared to let it fly again. His arm shot out almost too fast to see, and his hand wrapped around my left ankle. He pulled me off my feet with one tug. I landed on my rear beside him, on a split-open trash bag.

"Damn it, Marc, I'm sitting in this morning's fresh-squeezed orange peels."

He chuckled, crossing his arms over a black T-shirt, clinging to well-defined pecs. "You nearly broke my ribs."

"You'll live."

"No thanks to you." He pushed himself awkwardly to his feet and held out a hand for me. When I ignored it, he rolled his eyes and pulled me up by my wrist. "What's with the kung fu routine, anyway?"

I yanked my arm from his grip and stepped back, glaring at him as I wiped orange pulp from the seat of my pants. "It's tae kwon do, and you damn well know it." We'd trained together—alongside all four of my brothers—for nearly a decade. "You're lucky I didn't kick your face in. What took you so fucking long? If you guys are going to hang around without permission, you might as well make yourselves useful when I'm in mortal peril. That *is* what Daddy's paying you for."

"You handled yourself fine."

"Like you'd know. I bet he was halfway to his car by the time you got here."

"Only a quarter of the way," Marc said, grinning. "Anyway, I was the one in real danger. I got cornered by a pack of wild sorority sisters in the food court. Apparently it's mating season."

I frowned at him, picturing a throng of girls in matching pink T-shirts giggling as they vied for his attention. I could have told them they were wasting their time. Marc had no use for human women, especially silly, flirtatious trophy wives–in–training. His dark curls and exotic brownish-gold eyes had always garnered him more attention than he really wanted. And this time they'd kept him from doing his job.

"You're a worthless bastard," I said, not quite able to forgive him for being late, even though I didn't want him there in the first place.

"And you're a callous bitch." He smiled, completely unaffected by my heartfelt insult. "We're a matched set."

I groaned. At least we were back in familiar territory. And it was kind of nice to see him too, though I would never have admitted it.

Turning my back on him, I grabbed my book bag and stomped to the other end of the alley, then into the empty quad. Marc followed closely, murmuring beneath his breath in Spanish too fast for me to understand. Memories I'd successfully blocked for years came tumbling to the front of my mind, triggered by his whispered rant. He'd been doing that for as long as I could remember.

My patience long gone, I stopped in front of the student center in the same circle of light, and whirled around to face Marc. "Hey, you wanna drop back a few paces? Did you forget how spying works? You're supposed to at least *aim* for unobtrusive. The others pretty much have it down, but you're about as inconspicuous as a drag queen at a Girl Scout meeting." I propped my hands on the hips of my low-rise jeans and scowled up at him, trying to remain unaffected by the thickly lashed eyes staring back at me.

Marc smiled, his expression casual, inviting, and utterly infuriating. "It's nice to see you too." A wistful look darted across his face as he glanced at my bare midriff, his gaze moving quickly over my snug red halter top to settle on the barrette nestled in my hair.

"Go home, Marc."

"There's no reason for you to be rude."

"There's no reason for you to be here."

He frowned down at me, thick brows shadowing his eyes, and my mood improved. I'd gotten rid of his smile. Was I really that petty? Hell, yeah.

"Look, if Daddy's mad because I didn't invite

anyone to graduation, he can tell me himself. I don't need an emissary to let me know he's pissed."

"He sent me to bring you home." My expression hardened, and Marc held up one hand to cut off the argument he knew to expect. "I'm only following orders."

Of course he was. That's all he ever did.

I adjusted my bag on my shoulder, shaking my head. "Forget it. I'm not going." I started to walk away, but he grabbed my arm. I jerked free of his grip, but only because he let me.

"Sara's gone," he said, his face carefully blank.

I blinked, surprised by what seemed to be a random comment.

Sara had left? Good for her. But if they thought they could blame me because she wanted more out of life than a husband and half a dozen babies, they had another think coming. Sara had a mind of her own; all I'd done was dust a few cobwebs from it. If she'd decided not to get married, so be it. That was her choice.

"She didn't run out on the wedding, Faythe." Marc's eyes burned into mine like amber fire, and his meaning was unmistakable. It was always the same old fight with him, no matter where we were or how much time had passed. Some things never changed, and the rest only grew more irritating.

"You can wipe that smug look off your face," I snapped. "You only think you still know me well enough to read my mind." So what if he'd been right? That wasn't the point.

Marc gave an exaggerated sigh, as if talking to me was exhausting, and not really worth the effort. "She didn't leave. She was taken."

My pulse jumped, and I shook my head, giving in to denial as it surfaced. All around us, crickets chirped, filling the silence during my pause as I tried to formulate a coherent thought. "That's impossible. No human could take a…" There was no need to finish the sentence, because that was one thought he most definitely *could* read. Sara might have been petite, but she was far from weak. She would have shredded any man who laid a hand on her. At least, any *human* man.

But she hadn't been taken by a human, which was why Marc had come for me.

The stray, I thought, my hands curling into fists around the strap of my backpack. He wasn't just trespassing; he was *collecting*. Daddy had sent Marc to make sure I didn't become the stray's next acquisition.

I knew then that there would be no arguing, and no negotiation. Marc would take me home if he had to carry me over one shoulder, scratching and hissing all the way. As much as I would have loved to resist, I would spare myself the indignity, because ultimately, he would win a physical fight, no matter how dirty I played. It was just one more of those things that never changed, like Marc himself.

By the time I'd changed out of my citrus-scented pants and packed what clothes and books I couldn't do without, Sammi was back from the library. She dumped her books on the counter in our tiny galley-style kitchen, already chattering about her latest misogynistic conspiracy theory. She hesitated when she saw Marc, and her words sputtered to a stop. It was kind of funny; I'd finally found something to shut her up. Too bad I couldn't stick around and enjoy the silence.

Marc laughed from behind my desk, where he'd made himself at home. Beneath him, the straight-backed chair looked no more substantial than a stack of toothpicks, as if it might collapse into a pile of kindling at any moment. "I'm impressed, Faythe," he said, leaning the chair back on two legs. "I didn't think you could find someone who talked more than you do, but I've obviously underestimated you. Again."

Well, he did make a habit of it.

"Sammi, this is Marc Ramos. Marc, my roommate, Samantha."

Sammi's mouth opened and closed soundlessly as she tried—and failed—to come up with something intelligent to say. I rolled my eyes. Yeah, he looked good, but her reaction was a little over the top. But then, Sammi had a flair for melodrama.

Marc laughed again and the chair thumped to the ground as he rose to shake her hand. When Marc came toward her, Sammi took a step back, bumping her leg against the edge of an end table before she took his hand in brief, wide-eyed greeting.

"What's going on?" she managed to say, eyeing the suitcase open on the couch. I'd packed more books than clothing, which meant the bag would weigh a ton, but Marc could probably lift it with a single finger. He wouldn't, because that would draw attention. But he *could*.

"Daddy pulled the plug," I said, snapping the latches on the front of the suitcase. "I'll be back in the fall, but he won't pay for grad school unless I spend the summer at home." It was the closest I could come to an explanation Sammi would believe.

"And Marc would be...?" She left the question open-ended, glancing at him during the pause.

Good question. There was no easy way to describe Marc's role in my life, because he usually had none. He was no longer my bed warmer, my confidant, or even a fond memory, and he didn't fit any definition of "friend" she'd understand, so how to explain…?

"My ride." That should do it. Marc had been demoted to chauffeur, and his only reaction was a wink and an I've-got-a-secret grin. Great. He thought it was funny.

Sammi nodded slowly, as if she didn't believe me, but that was her problem, because I was done thinking up explanations. At least until the fall term.

"You're leaving now?" She fingered the hem of her blouse, glancing around the apartment at several piles of my belongings that hadn't made the single-suitcase cut.

"Yeah, sorry about the mess. We're paid up through the first, and I'll send you a check for my half of next month's rent. Can I leave my stuff here till I get back?"

"Sure," she said. "What about Andrew?"

I felt Marc's focus shift to me, and I bit my lip to keep from saying something I'd regret. I hadn't told him about my new boyfriend, and obviously neither had any of my father's spies. No doubt their silence was out of respect for him, rather than me.

Marc stiffened, and only the slight flaring of his nostrils betrayed him as he tested my scent. He scowled, and I stifled a groan, suddenly thankful that Andrew and I had had…um…*lunch* in his apartment rather than in mine. Smelling a man's scent mixed with mine was one thing, but smelling it on my sheets would have been quite another.

The lingering smell of stray on me was probably the only reason Marc hadn't already noticed Andrew's...um, *place* in my life. And in my bed. The stray's heavy mix of earthy musk and mixed blood easily overpowered Andrew's simple blend of light sweat and untainted humanity.

I would have told him, eventually. Really. However, I pride myself on having marginally more tact than Sammi. But then, I hadn't been honest with her about who my ride actually was, so what did I expect?

"I'll call him," I said, zipping up my suitcase.

Marc snatched the bag from my grip and stomped out the front door, leaving it open into the hallway.

I hugged Sammi, breathing in the floral fragrance of her shampoo. If my parents had their way, it would be a while before I smelled my roommate's wholesome femininity layered with Herbal Essences and cherry Bubble Yum. Assuming I ever made it back to school at all. And where my father was concerned, there were no guarantees.

"Study enough for both of us," I said, releasing her reluctantly. She smiled, more confused than sad, and I returned the look. I didn't really know what was going on, either.

In the corridor, Marc said something rude to my neighbor across the hall, just loud enough for me to hear. Sighing, I plucked my keys and cell phone from the coffee table, glancing around the apartment one last time. Why is it that goodbyes always feel so final? Except when I leave home. I always know I'll be back at the ranch eventually, not because I want to go home, but because they keep dragging me back. It's a small difference, but an important one.

I followed Marc down the wide hall to the stairwell, and neither of us said a word. Outside, I stayed several steps behind him, trying to gauge his mood as he marched down the sidewalk. He gripped the handle of my suitcase with knuckles white from tension. His stride was long, each step firm and heavy. But most telling was his posture as he wove between the cars in the parking lot. Head high and shoulders squared, his bearing was stiff and formal, as if he were truly nothing more to me than my chauffeur.

And in case I missed any of those more subtle signs, when I moved up to walk alongside him, Marc favored me with a growl, low and angry, and too soft for anyone else to hear.

Great. Nothing beats several hours in a car with a pissed-off werecat. Welcome to my life.

Two

The drive home from the University of North Texas seemed interminable, even with Marc driving. He took out his anger at me and Andrew on the car, and by the time we merged with the highway traffic, he was going twenty miles an hour over the speed limit. At that rate, the drive from Denton to Lufkin—220 miles across the Texas prairie into the lush eastern woodlands—would take him two and a half hours. It should have taken more than four.

When we left the interstate loop around Dallas for state highway 175, the traffic noise ebbed, leaving an awkward silence. Marc glanced at me, his mouth set in a grim line. "Tell me about Andrew."

"Not for all the money in the world." Although freedom was the currency I truly valued. I stared out my window at moonlit fields and defunct oil wells. Northeast Texas had few trees, fewer hills and way too many miles of empty highway.

"Why not? You ashamed of him?" Marc's eyes flashed with smug satisfaction.

Damn him! Five years, and he still knew exactly how to piss me off. My fist clenched around the "oh shit!" handle built into his car door. The plastic casing cracked, falling apart in my hand to expose the steel frame inside. *Oops*.

I brushed shards of plastic from my lap onto the floorboard, but a few slivers protruded from my palm like spines from a cactus. I plucked them out one by one, dropping them at my feet with the rest.

My palm was dotted with several tiny spots of blood and one long, shallow cut. Such minor wounds would likely heal during my next Shift, if not before. That was one of the advantages to spending half your life on four paws, along with increased metabolism, strength and hearing. No superhuman lifespan, though, as cool as that would have been. In fact, in some places, many toms die young, in fights over territory or mates.

Marc glanced at my hand, his face impassive. He didn't care about the broken handle. His driver's seat was missing an armrest and his steering wheel resembled a dented hexagon more than it did a circle. My little accident couldn't begin to compare with the damage he'd done to his own vehicle in past fits of anger.

"I'm not ashamed of him, Marc." I snatched a tissue from the box he kept on the center console and wiped the blood from my palm in short, angry strokes. "I just don't want to talk about him."

"To anyone, or just to me?" His voice was strained, and his eyes flicked to my face quickly, then back to the road before I could read his expression.

To anyone with fur and claws. But I couldn't say that. "Does it matter?"

"I guess not." However, the tense lines around his mouth argued otherwise. "Aren't you going to call him?"

I flipped my phone open and closed, considering. As much fun as it might have been to make Marc listen while I spoke to Andrew, it certainly wouldn't make the ride home any more bearable. "I'll wait till we stop for gas."

"We won't be stopping for a couple of hours. Won't he worry before then?"

I almost laughed out loud. As if he gave a damn whether or not Andrew would worry. "No, he won't. He's my boyfriend. Not my conscience, my conjoined twin or my father."

Marc frowned, and I looked away, dabbing at my palm again, though the bleeding had already stopped. His question was typical of Pride mentality. A tomcat's strongest instinct was to protect the women at any cost, with no consideration for our desires for privacy or independence. Or for whether we wanted, or even *needed* to be protected.

As I'd demonstrated an hour earlier, I did *not* need his protection. What I needed was a life of my own, which was exactly what I'd found on campus. My decision to live outside the Pride confounded the entire werecat community. Including my parents, which I'll probably never understand. After all, *they* taught me to think things through and to defend myself. Then they seemed genuinely surprised when I fought for the very independence they'd prepared me to handle.

While a tomcat would be labeled strong and self-sufficient for pursuing his own interests, I was considered stubborn and selfish for abandoning my Pride in favor of an education and a life of my own.

My parents had decided to humor my "phase," indulging me on the assumption that I would either grow out of it or come home after graduation. They thought they would lose, at most, four years of manipulation and micromanagement. They were wrong.

I'd intentionally spent an extra year as an under-grad, then applied to the graduate program without telling anyone. The day after graduation, I enrolled in two summer classes. The only notice my father got that I'd completed my B.A. was the bill for grad school tuition. He'd underestimated me. Like Marc.

I scanned the car for somewhere to put the blood-smeared tissue but couldn't find anyplace that didn't involve making Marc bend over. Stifling a laugh at the thought of where I'd *like* to shove the tissue, I dropped it on the floorboard, making a mental note to clean up my mess when we got home.

"What about you?" I asked, thinking of the sorority girls in the food court. "Have you been dating?"

"No, I haven't been *dating*." He spat the word as if it tasted bad, and I suppose it did. Marc had never been one for casual relationships, which had been a big part of our problem. Everything he did, he did with his whole heart and soul. Including me. It was sweet for about the first ten minutes. After that, it got old quickly.

"Do you really think that's healthy?" I asked, still irritated by his prying questions. "It's been years, Marc. You can't be my father's hired muscle forever. You need a plan for your life, something to give it meaning." Like I was one to talk. My grand scheme, which consisted of avoiding my family for as long as possible, had already failed. But that didn't stop me from dispensing advice I couldn't follow.

"I *had* a plan." The gold specks in Marc's irises flashed at me in the glow of passing headlights. I started to respond but he cut me off with a look. A very angry look. He was mad enough that I almost felt sorry for the steering wheel. "My personal life is none of your business, Faythe. Not anymore."

"That's a two-way street."

"No, it really isn't." He glared at me, ignoring the road long enough that I wanted to grab the wheel. "Your personal life is the business of the entire Pride, by custom and by necessity. You can't change that, no matter how long you hide out at school pretending to be human."

I growled, deep in my throat; it was a sound no human could have made. Some people think only dogs growl, but cats growl too, mostly in warning. For once, Marc took my warning and shut up.

For the next two hours, I faked sleep, beyond caring whether or not he bought the act. Just as my eyes were starting to close for real, Marc jerked the wheel to the right and veered across two lanes of highway—both empty, fortunately. He sped down the off-ramp and swerved into an all-night service station, sliding in front of another customer in line for the only available pump.

I twisted in my seat to see the unfortunate driver—a chunky man in ill-fitting slacks and a dress shirt—burst from his Volkswagen Passat and slam the door. His face was comically red in the fluorescent light from the awning overhead. He was yelling before he'd taken two steps, his gestures becoming more and more animated with each word.

Marc watched in the rearview mirror. His grip on the steering wheel tightened. The metal began to groan.

"Play nice with the other boys," I warned, watching his jaw tense and relax.

He ignored me. Without a word, Marc opened his door and set first one foot, then the other on the concrete. He stood slowly and smoothed his black T-shirt, giving the other man a chance to realize that he lacked both the size and the build to back up his big talk. When that didn't work, Marc took a single step forward.

The other man dove into his car, pulled the door shut, and slammed his hand down on the lock.

Satisfied, Marc nodded politely at the man, as if in greeting. The Passat pulled out of the parking lot as Marc lifted the nozzle from the pump.

Shaking my head at the near-toxic level of testosterone, I headed for the convenience store. While Marc pumped, I called Andrew from the one-man restroom, standing to avoid any contact with the filthy toilet seat.

"How 'bout pizza?" Andrew said by way of answering his phone. He never bothered to say hi, but spoke as if continuing the same ongoing conversation we'd been having for the entire four months of our relationship. I thought it was cute, but also wondered how he answered when someone else's number showed up on his caller ID. Did he ask the guy selling magazine subscriptions whether he wanted mushrooms or pepperoni?

I glanced at my watch: 11:04 p.m. "It's too late for dinner, and too early for a midnight snack."

"It's never too early for pizza." He sounded a little stuffy, as if he had a head cold.

"You okay?" I eyed the scum-coated cinder-block walls for a spot clean enough to lean against. No such luck. "You sound a little nasal."

"I think I'm getting a cold. It's not affecting my appetite, though. I'm starved. I'll pick up a large with everything. Unless you're afraid of catching my germs."

I smiled. "No, I don't mind your germs." I probably couldn't catch them anyway. "But it'll take you a while to get here."

"Why, where are you?" he asked, sniffling. Over the phone, loud grunge music echoed with a reverberation apparently unique to thin apartment walls.

"Twenty miles north of Waco."

No pause, and no questions. "Okay, but it'll be cold by the time I get there."

The grimy concrete seemed to absorb the sound of my laughter as soon as it left my throat. Andrew's sense of humor was contagious. It made him very easy to be around, which had become my only prerequisite for boyfriends lately. Not that he couldn't set the jokes aside when he needed to. But his smile was genuine, and it was always lurking on the edge of his other expressions. Talking to him never felt like work, as it did with *some* people. Andrew knew how to take things in stride, such as my sudden departure from campus.

I glanced at my face in the grease-streaked mirror. I looked tired, but it was probably just the thick layer of dirt. On the mirror, not on me. "I think you'll have to eat without me tonight. And tomorrow. And maybe for the rest of the summer."

"Why, what's up?"

"My dad's mad 'cause I didn't invite my family to graduation. He threatened to yank my funds unless I spend the summer at home."

Andrew laughed. "So the mysterious Faythe Sanders does have a family. And where is home?"

I hesitated long enough that anyone else would have commented on my reluctance to answer. Not Andrew. He never acknowledged an uncomfortable situation, unlike Marc, who wallowed in tension like pigs roll in the mud. "A ranch near the Louisiana border," I said finally.

For years, I'd carefully avoided any conversation that might have led to questions about my childhood, because it had always been easier for me to pretend I hadn't had one than to try to explain the Sanders family dynamic. From a human perspective, we didn't make sense, and struggling to explain it only made things worse.

As children, humans learned to compromise, share and make friends. I learned to identify animals by scent and to stalk them without betraying my presence. While normal parents discussed political elections and spiking interest rates, mine discussed expanding territorial boundary lines and how harshly to deal with trespassers. Humans just didn't understand my childhood, so I generally avoided the subject altogether.

Andrew coughed, but the sound was muffled, like he'd covered the mouthpiece. "So you withdrew from school?"

"Not yet." I cringed at the very idea of withdrawing, as if my absence from school wasn't real as long as I was still enrolled in a class. "I'll do it over the phone tomorrow, but it's only for the summer. I'll be back in September. Maybe earlier. It depends on how long it takes me to talk some sense into my father." Yeah, right. Like my father and I had ever had a sensible discussion. Or even a calm one.

"No problem. I'll come see you during the break between summer sessions."

My stomach lurched at the thought of introducing Andrew to my parents. And to Marc. "Um, let me talk to my dad first, okay?"

"Sure. But don't worry, parents always like me."

Not my parents, I thought, leaning against a sink jutting from the wall like a porcelain ledge. *Not unless you're hiding fur and claws beneath your Abercrombie khakis.* But he wasn't. I didn't know every cat in the country personally, but I'd know one if I met one, and Andrew was one hundred percent certifiably human. Which, of course, was the attraction.

"I have to go now, but I'll talk to you later, okay?" I glanced in regret at the bathroom door. If the facilities had been nicer, I might have considered staging a sit-in, in protest of being taken home against my will. But one glance at the filthy floor drove that thought right out of my head.

"Sure. I'll give you a wake-up call before my first class," he said. "Or do you farm girls get up with the roosters?"

"Not this farm girl," I said. "We don't have roosters." *Or any other livestock, for that matter.*

"Good to know," Andrew said. "I'm going to go eat now, all by myself. Talk to you tomorrow."

I said goodbye, and my stomach growled as I hung up. I thought of Andrew's pizza with envy. Maybe I could talk Marc into swinging by a drive-thru on the way back to the highway. But I'd probably have to say please.

Suddenly I wasn't that hungry.

Back at the car, Marc was nowhere in sight. I was searching the glove box for a spare key when I noticed him walking toward me from the burger joint next door. He carried a grease-stained paper bag in one hand and a cardboard tray of drinks in the other.

Damn. Now I'd have to say thank-you.

"Four double cheeseburgers, extra pickles," he said, sliding into the driver's seat with a creak of leather. "But two of them are mine." He dropped the bag in my lap and settled a drink into each of the cup holders in the center console.

I opened the bag and stuck my nose inside. Warm, fragrant steam engulfed my face, and my mouth watered. The meat was grilled, my preferred way to have a burger. Marc had probably chosen this particular gas station just so I could have my favorite fast food.

"Thanks," I said, feeling my cheeks flush with guilt. Maybe he'd think it was the steam.

He almost smiled. Not quite, but almost. And his

eyes practically glowed when they met mine. "So how do you manage to eat enough at school without looking like a pig?"

"The same way I did in high school." I tore into the first cheeseburger, barely bothering to chew before I swallowed. "Carry snacks, eat on the way, then again when I get to the cafeteria. And tell everyone I'm bulimic." I snorted, doing an uncanny impersonation of a pig, if I do say so myself.

His eyes widened for an instant. Then he laughed. The sound of pure amusement caught me off guard, and I smiled, leaning back against the headrest as I watched him. For a moment, that old familiarity crept in, like the comfort of my favorite well-worn T-shirt. Then I remembered I didn't want to be comfortable with him, and my smile died on my lips, even as his laughter faded from my ears.

Marc watched the change in my expression with mounting disappointment. He knew what it meant. Jaw tight with tension, he slammed the car into gear, reversing in a tight arc across the empty parking lot.

I bit another chunk from my burger, staring out the windshield as he shifted into First gear. The beef, so appetizing moments earlier, was suddenly bland and difficult to swallow.

Marc snuck one more glance at my face and tore from the parking lot as if we were being chased. And we were, but you can't outrun your own memories. Not for long, anyway.

Three

I'd fallen asleep for real by the time we got home, but the crunch of gravel and the unmistakable sway of the car on our quarter-mile-long driveway woke me. I sat up, staring out at an impressive display of stars as we pulled through the open wrought-iron gate. Marc poked at the remote clipped onto his visor, and I turned around in my seat to watch the gate close. At the top was a capital S lying on its back, as if at rest.

Ours wasn't the only Lazy S Ranch in the country, or even in Texas, but it was the only one I knew of which housed cats instead of cattle. I'd told Andrew we didn't keep roosters, but the truth was that we *couldn't* keep them or any other livestock, because when animals smelled us, they smelled natural predators and they reacted in panic.

Years ago, in an uncharacteristic burst of optimism, my father bought a horse for my brother Owen, but it took one whiff of him and went crazy, charging the gate of its stall and running into the walls. They had to shoot the poor thing because no one could get close enough to sedate it. So, ours was a ranch in name only.

I sighed, staring through the windshield at land and outbuildings I hadn't seen in years. Nothing had changed—at least, nothing I could identify in the dark. Waist-high grass grew in fields to the east and west of the main house, destined to become hay when the season changed. I smiled as we passed the barn in the eastern field, empty but picturesque in the moonlight with its peeling red paint and gabled roof. As a child, I'd spent entire summers playing in there, hiding from life in general and my mother in particular.

And directly ahead lay the main house, stretched across the yard like a lion at rest.

Marc parked in the circle driveway, behind the Volvo my mother hardly ever drove. I got out and looked around, glancing at the guesthouse, where Marc lived with three of my father's other enforcers. All the lights were out. No one was home.

Gravel shifted beneath my feet as I passed the cars lining the drive, trying to identify the owners. I'd been gone a long time, having spent vacations at school for the last two years, and I could no longer say for certain what each of my brothers drove. But I could guess.

The Porsche—solid black and gleaming in the glare of the floodlights—had to be Michael's. No one else was that ostentatious, except maybe Ryan, who would never come home voluntarily. He'd left when I was barely thirteen and wouldn't be back, because for him, that was an option.

Ethan drove the convertible, no doubt about it. But if I needed further evidence, there was plenty to choose from in the front floorboard, littered with fast-food wrappers and empty plastic soda bottles. I grinned, staring through his driver's-side window at the collection of CDs, ranging from nineties grunge to the latest hip-hop.

The truck, a three-quarter-ton Dodge Ram, as clean on the inside as it was dusty on the outside—that was Owen's. I hadn't seen this particular model, but it was close enough to the last one to make me smile. Owen was a frustrated cowboy at heart, and only he would drive a work truck.

Marc led me through the front door and into the foyer, where I turned left out of habit, surprised to find the kitchen dark and empty. *Huh.* Usually all the guys hung out around the tiled peninsula, snacking and talking over one another with full mouths.

48	*Rachel Vincent*

"Go wait in the office," Marc said, pointing the way as if I could possibly have forgotten. "I'll tell your father we're here."

That wasn't necessary, of course, because just as I could hear them speaking in whispers in one of the back bedrooms, I knew they could hear us. They'd probably heard the car from a mile away.

I considered arguing with Marc but couldn't think of a good reason, so I complied. See? I could play nice when I wanted to. I just didn't want to very often.

My shoes squeaked as I walked across the kitchen tile to the dining room, and back into the foyer. To my left, across from the front door, was a long straight hallway, dividing the house in half and ending at the back door. In front of me was my father's office.

I crossed the hall and entered my father's haven, savoring the darkness of a room with no windows. The air smelled like my father, like leather furniture, polished wood, and expensive coffee. To my right was a sitting area arranged around a rectangular rug: a love seat across from a couch, with Daddy's armchair at one end, facing them both. In one corner sat a massive oak desk, covered—though not cluttered—in neat stacks of paper, notebooks and ledgers, arranged at perfect ninety-degree angles.

On one side of the desk, its flat-screen monitor turned toward the desk chair, was a state-of-the-art computer, equipped with the latest in drafting software. On the other side sat an antique lamp with a pewter base. I turned the knob on the base, and soft light washed over the room, leaving the corners thick with shadows.

Behind the desk, the glass display cabinet caught my eye, and I moved forward to examine it. My mother had ordered it for my father, to showcase his awards. I opened the right-hand door and flipped a tiny hidden switch on the end of the last shelf. Fluorescent light flickered to life inside the case, and I closed the door, pressing gently until I heard the latch click.

Each shelf was lit from above, so that the trophies and plaques shined, the words glaring almost too brightly to be read. Most were in appreciation of his charity work, but those on the top shelf were in recognition of his buildings, his best ones. My father's buildings graced the skylines of five different U. S. cities, and in my opinion—admittedly biased—they improved the view from every angle.

Wood creaked behind me. I froze, trying to interpret the blurred reflection in the glass. Another creak as he came closer, and I smiled, in recognition and in breathless anticipation.

"You still have the sweetest ass this side of the Rio Grande." Hot breath caressed my neck, and lips brushed my earlobe.

I spun around to find my body pinned between the glass case and someone tall, hard and tauntingly masculine. *Jace*. I inhaled his scent. Bar soap, fabric softener, and something meaty, maybe beef jerky. But under those was something more, something wild, and pungent, that woke up my instincts and made my heartbeat echo in my throat. It made me crave things my human form couldn't accommodate, things my brain couldn't even articulate, but my heart and my nose recognized instantly.

I tilted my face up to look at him. "What about the other side?"

He grinned, showing two rows of perfect white teeth, framed by lips that would have been wasted on mere speech. "I've never been south of the river, but I bet you could hold your own down there, too." Jace bent his face toward my ear. I closed my eyes as he sniffed the length of my neck, trailing the tip of his tongue along my skin as he came back up. I shivered and gasped, and he responded with a moan as he pressed his hips against mine, nipping the flesh at the base of my neck.

"Get *off* my sister."

Jace hissed in my ear, and cool air brushed my

stomach where his body had been a second earlier. I opened my eyes. My brother Michael stood in front of me, holding Jace at arm's length by the back of his neck.

"I was only saying hello," Jace purred, his lazy smile still aimed at me.

"Do it without your tongue." Michael enunciated each word carefully and slowly to make sure he was understood. He shoved Jace to one side, a little too hard to be playful.

Jace stumbled, catching himself on the edge of Daddy's desk. "If I were Marc you'd let me greet her properly," he said, a hint of resentment in his voice.

"There was nothing proper about that." Michael frowned, but I glimpsed amusement behind his stern, I-mean-business face. "And if you were Marc, she'd have tossed you off herself. But you're not Marc."

"If I were, she wouldn't have left us in the first place." He turned his back on us both, slinking to the door with a fluid grace no human could have duplicated.

I blushed, thinking of the carnal promise in his casual words. No one else would have gotten away with such a comment, much less the intimate greeting, but I took a lot from Jace that would have lost anyone else an ear. Or worse. Jace got away with it because I secretly suspected he was right, that his body could really do what his teasing kisses and caresses hinted at. And because he'd never really tried. Our relationship had always been fundamentally platonic, a safe zone for playful flirting, which Michael either couldn't or wouldn't understand.

High heels clicked briskly on the tiles in the hallway, and I turned toward the door, steeling myself to face my mother. She stepped into the office, pausing for effect in the doorway as she spread her arms in greeting. "Faythe, we're so glad to finally have you home." As if I'd returned for a friendly visit, instead of for a command appearance.

My mother looked exactly as I remembered, down to her gray pageboy and charcoal-colored slacks. She had a closet full of them, hanging right next to a collection of novelty kitchen aprons, printed with not-so-funny sayings, like "I'd give you the recipe, but then I'd have to kill you."

She came toward me, pausing almost imperceptibly when she realized I wasn't going to rush forward to meet her. Michael and Jace stepped back, making way for my mother, a tiny life raft of estrogen bobbing amongst the waves of testosterone.

She hugged me, her embrace bringing with it the scent of homemade cookies, with cinnamon and nutmeg. Who cooks with nutmeg in the middle of the summer? Only my pretty-kitty version of a mother, a remnant of the June Cleaver days of intact families and repressed emotions.

Over her shoulder, I watched Marc come in, followed by my father, who pulled a handkerchief from his pocket to polish the lenses of his glasses while he waited patiently for my mother let me go. Daddy was always the last man to enter any room, so he could take charge of everyone all at once. Tall, and still firm at fifty-six, my father commanded respect everywhere he went, and it was all innate. He could never have explained why people did what he wanted, but his authority was undeniable, and unless I was at home, unquestioned.

I frowned at him, preparing to argue my case. "Daddy, what—?"

He smiled, cutting me off with a wave of one thick hand. "Give me a hug first, before we let business get in the way of family."

I hugged him, but was bothered by his statement, because the business *was* family. Always. No matter how much he loved creating beautiful buildings, and how many days a year it took him away from home, his true passion—his life's calling—was the Pride. We were his family, some by blood and others, like Jace and Marc, by association and employment.

Daddy released me, leaving one heavy hand on my shoulder as he turned to Jace. "Go unload Marc's car, please, and let everyone know the prodigal daughter has returned."

Again, this was unnecessary; everyone knew I was home. It was just Daddy's polite way of getting rid of Jace. I took it as a good sign. If my father had been mad or upset, he wouldn't have bothered with tact. He'd have merely started shouting orders.

Jace nodded and left without complaint. Marc closed the solid oak door behind him, cutting off the masculine buzz of conversation coming from the back of the house.

Suddenly nervous, I wiped sweat from my palms on my pants. I'd never been comfortable in Daddy's office when the door was closed. Unlike the rest of the house, the walls of the office were made of solid concrete, which made them virtually soundproof, even for us. At least in human form. Most families use rooms like that as an indoor tornado shelter, or as safe rooms in case of home invasions. My father used it for privacy, a hot commodity in a house full of people gifted with a cat's hearing.

Marc leaned against the door frame with his hands in his pockets, apparently relaxed. I wasn't fooled. Daddy hadn't forgotten to post a guard at the door since the summer I turned eighteen, and considering how long it took them to find me that time, he probably never would again.

My mother sat on the leather love seat, patting the cushion next to her—not for me, but for Michael. He glanced at me for a moment before sitting, and I couldn't resist a tiny smile. Michael was what you'd get if you mixed a Chippendale dancer with a *Law Review* editor: a handsome face crowning an athlete's body, all dressed up in a hand-tailored suit, with silver, wire-rimmed glasses added for effect. Seriously. His vision was better than perfect, but he thought he looked more like an attorney in the spectacles. And maybe more like our father, who'd been fitted with prescription lenses three years earlier.

Daddy sat in his armchair, where he could see everyone. And they all stared at me.

Shrugging, I plopped down on the couch, all alone. I glanced back at Marc, but he wouldn't meet my eyes. Once again, it was me against the world. Or at least against the Pride, which, unfortunately, was *my* world.

I took a deep breath and held it for a moment, then let it out all at once. *Time to get it over with.* "So, tell me about Sara."

"We don't know much yet," my mother said, crossing one ankle over the other. "She went shopping in downtown Atlanta, and never came back. Your father sent Vic home to help with the search, and he's promised to keep us informed." Vic was Sara's brother, and one of my father's enforcers.

"That's it?" I ignored my mother and frowned at my father. That couldn't be all they knew.

"So far." Daddy nodded, and I noticed absently that the gray streaks at his temples had broadened since I'd seen him last. "From the credit card bills, they know where she actually made purchases, and her brothers have been in all the stores, discreetly questioning the salespeople. Most of the clerks remembered her, but no one saw anything unusual. Bert has his men out looking, but so far they haven't found anything."

Bert was Umberto Di Carlo, Sara's father, Alpha of one of the neighboring territories. And one of my father's closest friends.

"How long has she been gone?" I asked.

"Since the night before last."

"I assume they've questioned Sean."

Daddy shook his head.

"No one can find him," Marc added, and I twisted around to look at him. "He was staying near Chattanooga, right outside the southeast territory, but now his apartment's empty. The landlord said he moved out a couple of weeks ago."

I shrugged, turning back to face Michael and my parents. "So, what are we going to do?"

"Nothing." Disapproval traced deep lines on my father's face; I was intimately familiar with that expression. "Bert hasn't asked for our help. We only have details because Vic called last night."

I frowned at my father. "If we're not going to help, why drag me home from school?" Silence greeted my question, and I glanced from face to face, anger building in a slow, hot crescendo. My mother looked away, but Michael stared right at me.

"What would you suggest?" he asked, narrowed eyes daring me to answer. "You want us to go in uninvited?"

Did I?

Bert and Donna Di Carlo controlled the southeast territory, encompassing everything east of the Tombigbee River in Alabama, and south of the Tennessee River and the southern edge of the Smokies. My father was Alpha of the south-central territory, which was south of the Missouri River and east of the Rockies, running all the way to the Mississippi. The unclaimed portion of Mississippi between the two territories was considered free range, where strays and wildcats of any lineage could live and run without having to secure permission.

My father and Umberto Di Carlo were friends—very old friends. But in the werecat community, even the strongest of friendships was defined by strictly observed boundaries, both geographical and personal. Breaching a territorial boundary, even with an offer of assistance, would do more harm than good, because the Di Carlos—and likely the rest of the werecat community—would see it as an insult. Our interference would undermine Umberto's authority and call his leadership into question. We might as well announce to the world that we don't think the southeast Pride can handle its own problems. No Alpha could afford to let such an insult go unpunished.

Did I want my father to breach another Pride's territorial boundaries and risk breaking the peace, just to reassure me that everything possible was being done? Just so I could return to my life as soon as possible?

Hmm. Tough call.

Though my father was clearly disappointed by Umberto's failure to seek his aid and advice, without being invited to help, he would take no action. Our boundaries were older than the U. S. Constitution and written in stone—almost literally, in the case of several mountain ranges.

According to tradition, werecats preceded the European colonists to the new world by several hundred years. Of course, we migrated on foot from the jungles of South America, rather than crossing the Atlantic by boat. Out of instinct, we formed territories, and out of necessity those territories overlapped areas occupied by the already-native humans. As is often the case with human boundaries, our borders followed naturally occurring lines of division: mountain ranges, rivers and large lakes.

Over the centuries, our boundary lines shifted slightly along with the evolving landscape, but they remain much as they were originally. Those lines are the basis for the fragile structure which keeps us civilized. To preserve that civilization, Daddy would not breach a territorial boundary line without permission for anything, even a missing daughter.

I turned back to my father, preparing to state my case. "If there's nothing we can do, let me go back to school. The term just started."

His frown was impenetrable. "You're not going back until we're sure you're safe."

"I *am* safe," I said through clenched jaws, praying Marc hadn't already told him about the stray on campus. Yes, my father would find out eventually; there was no stopping that. But hopefully he wouldn't find out until I was back on campus and out of the direct line of fire.

"Sean took her," I continued. "He's mad because she accepted Kyle's proposal, and he's either trying to change her mind, or get back at her." Like most tabbies, Sara'd had several suitors to choose from when her parents decided it was time for her to marry. Unfortunately, one of those she turned down hadn't taken the news very well. Sean had thrown an embarrassing public fit, then left the territory in protest. "It's horrible, and scary, and infuriating. But it has nothing to do with me."

I was starting to panic at the idea of sitting home all summer with nothing to occupy my time but chaperoned runs into town for groceries. If I was lucky. I'd been free far too long to ever go back to the way things used to be.

"Faythe, give it a rest," Marc said. Everyone turned to look at him, including me. I stared at him, begging him with my eyes to keep his mouth shut. As usual, he ignored me. "You know it wasn't Sean."

"How would she know that?" My father's voice was deep with anger. He clearly realized he'd been kept out of the loop.

I watched Marc, still pleading with him silently to keep his mouth shut. Just this once. Daddy would never let me out of his sight if he knew.

Marc gave me the slightest shake of his head. "A stray tried to grab her on campus."

"Yeah, but I kicked his trespassing ass!" I whirled around to face my father.

"Faythe!" my mother cried, horrified more by my language than by what had actually happened.

"What? It's true. Tell them, Marc," I demanded, turning on him angrily. "I can take care of myself."

Marc shrugged. And he conveniently forgot to mention where he was while I was kicking serious ass. I briefly considered ratting him out, as he'd done to me, but decided my secret might be worth more to him down the line.

"You're not leaving," Daddy said, completely unmoved by the news of my first victory in battle.

"The hell I'm not." I clenched my hands together in my lap to keep them from curling into fists, which he would see as a sign of aggression. "I'm never alone anyway, so what does it matter? I know you have the guys watching me, even though you promised me privacy. I'm just not sure whether it's to protect me or to spy on me."

"Faythe, your tone is unacceptable." My mother never raised her voice, because she never needed to. Until I came along, it had apparently never occurred to anyone to disobey. As children, my brothers were typically loud and raucous, managing to find trouble in the most benign places, but none of them ever thought to openly defy either of our parents. No, rebellion was my sole territory to explore, and I'd pushed the very limits of what would be endured.

"That's old news, Mom." Claustrophobia constricted my throat at the very thought of being confined to the ranch for an unknown period of time. "I'm old enough to vote, I'm old enough to drink, and I'm damn well old enough to make my own decisions. And I've decided to go back to school."

My father nodded to Marc, who stepped in front of the door and leaned against it, both arms crossed over his chest. It would take a bulldozer to move him, and heavy machinery I was not. "Don't make threats, Faythe," Daddy said. "We're only trying to protect you."

One look at his face told me things were going downhill. Fast. If I couldn't keep my cool, I'd wind up stuck in my room until I was thirty. "I'm not making threats, Daddy. I swear I'm not. But I truly don't need your protection. I proved that tonight."

My father sighed and met my eyes. "I know you think you can take care of yourself, and I think that with a little more training, you just may be right. If you'd like to take advantage of this opportunity to get in some more practice with the guys, I'm sure they'd all be happy to oblige. But you are not going back to school. At least not now."

Furious at being patronized, I stood, and so did my father. He stared behind me at Marc and nodded again. They thought I was going to run and were prepared to stop me. Wonderful. "How long?" I asked, trying to keep defeat from my voice. It was too late for my face.

"Until they find Sara and whoever took her. You can speed up the process by giving us a description."

"Get it from Marc," I snapped, daring him to admit he'd barely seen the stray.

I took a step forward, and Michael stood, preparing to stop me. I rolled my eyes. "Relax, I'm just going to my room. Otherwise known as my prison cell."

He glanced at my father. Daddy nodded, and Michael sat back down.

Spine stiff and chin high, I marched toward the guarded exit. Marc averted his eyes as he held the door for me, but I could feel his gaze on my back as I plodded down the hall.

In my room, I slammed the door and leaned against it, my eyes roaming walls I hadn't seen in years. I crossed the floor in an instant, using speed I hadn't had the nerve to display in front of my father. When I pressed the power button on my stereo, music blared to life through speakers Marc had mounted for me on my seventeenth birthday. My hand hovered over the volume knob as I considered turning it down. But then footsteps clomped down the hall outside my door. I turned the music up instead and flopped down on my stomach on the bed.

Welcome home, Faythe, I thought, eyeing the brand-new security bars on my window. *For now.*

Four

A soft scratching sound came from the hallway. I rolled onto my back, staring at the door. The scratching came again, and I sat up on the bed, sniffing the air. My nose works much better in cat form, but even on two legs I could identify each of my brothers' scents.

"Go away, Ethan," I yelled, not bothering to screen irritation from my voice. My misery didn't want company.

The knob turned, as I'd known it would, and I leapt to my feet as the door swung open. A dark head appeared in the gap, and I found myself looking into eyes barely a shade greener than my own. "Damn it, Ethan!" I propped both hands on my hips, in unconscious imitation of my mother's angry stance. "You can't waltz in here anytime you want, just because my door doesn't lock." Daddy had snapped the lock the time I shut myself in and tried to sneak out the window. And he'd steadfastly refused to replace it.

"I didn't waltz. And I'm not technically in." Ethan leaned against the door frame, naked from the waist up, a half-eaten Granny Smith apple in one hand. He wore his typical lopsided grin, the one that said nothing in the world could ever really bother him. When we were kids, his inescapable optimism had frayed my nerves, but now I found myself welcoming that distinctive smile with one of my own. I couldn't help it. His attitude was contagious.

"You still mad, or can I have a hug?" he asked. I shrugged. It wasn't his fault Marc had dragged me home.

Ethan set his apple on my dresser, and before I could blink he'd enveloped me in his long arms, my cheek resting on a chest smooth enough to be mistaken for a boy's, if not for an obviously mature physique. And it wasn't just his chest. Ethan was two years older than I was, but you couldn't tell it from his cherubic face, all dimples, wide eyes, and long, gorgeous lashes.

He squeezed just a bit too hard, to show me how much I'd been missed. Then he swung me in a complete circle as I squealed, taking me back to my childhood, when I'd spent every summer tagging along behind him and Jace, just in case they decided to let me play.

He set me gently on the floor, then plopped down on my bed and leaned back, propping himself up on his elbows. The pose was familiar enough to send a pang of nostalgia ringing through me. As children, we'd spent hours sprawled across my bed, making fun of Michael's latest girlfriend and laughing at Owen's most recent attempt to sneak a terrified pet past our mother.

"So," he said, still grinning. "Got your escape planned yet?"

"Like I'd tell you if I did." I curled up at the head of the bed and pulled a small, frilly pillow into my lap. It was one of those worthless, decorative things that do nothing but get in the way. My mother bought it, assuming I'd like it because I had ovaries. She was right, but for the wrong reason. I used it when I needed something to punch.

"You think I'd rat you out?" Ethan asked, his eyes twinkling with mischief.

"I *know* you would. That's your job." He didn't deny it, and I couldn't work up any real indignation. Trying to hold a grudge against Ethan was like trying to catch a fish with your bare hands. Not impossible, but damn near.

A soft shuffling sound from the doorway drew my

attention. At the threshold stood Owen, my third brother. He was just tall enough that a chunk of his perpetually tousled hair brushed the top of the door frame. Dark eyes met mine and a smile spread across his face, slow and sweet as his Texas drawl. "Hey, sis, I heard you were home."

"Owen!" I crawled off the bed, tossing the pillow aside, and ran toward him. He met me in the middle of the room, scooping me up into a hug to shame all others, the kind that pops your spine and steals your breath, all in the name of brotherly love. Owen was our resident farm boy, cowboy hat and all. He smelled like the land, like dirt, fresh water and hard work. His jeans were torn and permanently stained, which meant he hadn't changed out of his work clothes yet. But then, he hardly ever did. Or, more accurately, he hardly ever stopped working, which eventually turned all his clothes into work clothes.

"Aren't they feedin' you up there?" he asked, holding me at arm's length for a better view. "You're lookin' kinda skinny."

"She looks good to me," Jace said from the doorway. He dropped my suitcase on the floor and snatched Ethan's apple from the dresser. Grinning, he took a big bite and sank backward into my desk chair, his arms crossed over the arched back.

"She *is* thin." Ethan sat up to scratch one tanned

shoulder. "But it wouldn't be quite so noticeable if you'd wear actual clothes, Faythe."

"I *am* wearing actual clothes." I glanced down at myself, trying not to see his point. Okay, maybe my shirt was a little low cut. And tight. And my jeans didn't quite reach my belly button, but that's how everyone on campus dressed in the summer. We lived in Texas, for crying out loud. It was hot. "Besides, it's not like you have any room to talk," I said, eyeing his bare chest.

He shrugged, as if to say he didn't make up the rules. "It's different for guys."

A double standard. Shocking, really.

"Leave her alone before you scare her off again," Owen drawled. "You know how sensitive women can be about their clothes." He put his arm around my waist and squeezed me affectionately, a gesture as smooth and gentle as his temperament.

"She's no woman, she's our sister," Ethan said. I twisted in Owen's embrace to stick my tongue out at him. Ethan reciprocated and moved to sit on the edge of my bed, feet brushing the thick taupe carpet.

"She's not *my* sister," Jace said around a mouthful of half-chewed apple. His easy grin spoke of casual teasing, but his eyes met mine with enough heat to make me pause with uncertainty for a moment before replying.

I smiled to soften the coming blow. "I'm not your anything."

"Ouch!" He leaned back against the desk with one hand over his heart, covering an imaginary wound. Then his smile reached his eyes, and he took another bite of the apple. Clearly I'd dealt him a fatal blow.

Owen hugged me one more time, brushing the top of my head with his chin full of prickly stubble, then let me go, backing up to lean against my wall. On the radio, the first notes of "Miss Independent" played, and I smiled at the irony of listening to it from inside my tumbleweed prison. *Lucky bitch,* I thought, turning it up to give my father every opportunity to hear the song through the walls.

I sank onto the bed next to Ethan and leaned my head against his bare shoulder. "What's this about you fighting a stray at school?" he asked, draping one arm around my waist. "Didn't your mother ever tell you it's not ladylike to pick on boys?"

Had she ever. "It was nothing. Just a scuffle."

Jace tossed the apple into the air and caught it behind his back. "Marc thinks it was the same guy who took Sara."

Like he'd know, I thought. But what I said was, "Couldn't have been. He was too easily frightened. It was just some asshole intruder looking for a little excitement."

"Sounds like he found it." Owen drawled.

I grinned. "Damn right."

"Looks like you found a little too," Jace said, his gaze focused on my stomach.

Shrugging out from under Ethan's arm, I looked down at the gap between the hem of my shirt and the waist of my jeans. An amorphous purple blob had taken shape on my left side, over the lowest of my ribs. "Beautiful," I said, standing to get a better view in the mirror. "Just lovely." It hadn't looked anywhere near that bad when I'd left campus. Sammi hadn't even noticed.

"Where's everyone else?" I asked, tugging my shirt down to hide the bruise as I sank back onto the bed.

"Vic's out looking for Sara," Jace said. He tossed the apple core into my trash can and held both fists up in victory. I rolled my eyes. Guys may get bigger, but they never really grow up.

"Yeah, I heard." I pulled away from Ethan, rolling my head on my shoulders, trying to ease the tension that had been building since the moment I'd smelled the stray on campus. It didn't work, but it did give me a pretty good crick in my neck. "What about Parker?"

"He's around," Ethan said. "Marc has him out playing foot soldier."

"On our own property?" My eyebrows arched in surprise as I rubbed my neck. Then the implication sank in, and my hand fell into my lap, my discomfort temporarily forgotten. "Daddy must be really spooked by all this."

Ethan and Owen exchanged looks, but I wasn't fast enough to interpret them before their expressions were gone. Something else was up, but they weren't talking. *Wonderful.* I hate secrets I'm not in on.

"We better go," Owen said, shooting Ethan a stern look. "We're supposed to help Parker."

"Yeah, yeah." Ethan mumbled, pulling himself off the bed with one hand wrapped around the corner post.

Owen slapped him on the shoulder and shoved him toward the door, turning back to look at me from the threshold. "We're going huntin' later, if you wanna come."

"We'll see," I said, careful not to commit myself. I loved hunting, and he knew it. But if I appeared too eager to go, they might think I was glad to be home, and I certainly couldn't have a dangerous rumor like that floating around unchecked.

Owen gave me a leisurely, knowing smile and disappeared into the hallway. I listened until I heard the back door slam shut, then turned to look at Jace.

He smiled back at me from my desk chair, showing no inclination to leave. Big surprise. I considered kicking him out so I could pout in private, but then he turned those bright blue eyes on me—the playful sparkle mingling seamlessly with a hint of that earlier heat—and I couldn't do it. I couldn't kick him out and watch the light fade from his eyes.

Instead, I returned his smile, running my hand over the bed to smooth out wrinkles I didn't really mind in the first place.

Jace leaned back in my desk chair, his Kentucky Wildcats T-shirt stretched across broad shoulders. He was descended from the original Kentucky wildcat, which, of course, was more than just a mascot. "Don't be mad at me," he said. "None of this was my idea."

"I know." I tilted my head to the left, still trying to work out the muscle cramp. "You can stay. Until you start to bore me."

"Why, thank you, Your Highness." He stood to perform a deep, highly sarcastic bow. But instead of returning to the chair, he sat down behind me on the bed, brushing my hand away from my neck. Careful not to tug, he gathered my hair and laid it over my shoulder, then began massaging my neck at the base of my skull.

His touch was firm and warm, and his fingers

moved with confidence, seeking the tensest muscles. I moaned with relief, then stiffened and flushed from embarrassment. Jace only laughed and rubbed harder until I relaxed again.

"So, how ya doin', kid?" he asked, moving down to work on my shoulders.

"Not too bad, for a prisoner."

He chuckled, sounding distinctly unsympathetic. "Could be worse."

"How?"

"You could be a hostage."

I huffed, plucking imaginary fuzz from my comforter as he moved lower, kneading the muscles between my shoulder blades through the thin cotton of my shirt. "At least a hostage has hope of a ransom."

His hands hesitated for a moment, his breath stirring my hair as he sighed. "Your dad's only trying to do what's best."

"For whom?" I pulled away, turning to half face him.

"For everyone."

"What's good for the gander isn't always good for the goose, Jace," I said, resorting to a mutilated cliché. It didn't help. He couldn't understand. Tomcats were immune to my particular plight, a fact I'd envied all of my adult life.

"You're not poultry," Jace said, grinning as he brushed a strand of hair from my shoulder. "And anyway, after everything that's happened the last couple of days, you have to admit us watching out for you was a good idea."

"The hell it was." I beat Jace over the head with that stupid fancy pillow as I spoke, punctuating each word with another harmless blow, even when he brought his arms up in defense. "I…watched… out…for…my… self." After one final whack, I dropped the pillow into my lap and sat frowning at Jace. "Marc wasn't even there. But don't you dare tell Daddy. I'm getting ready to try my hand at blackmail."

"A new hobby? What, you get tired of the disappearing act?"

"Funny." I smacked him one last time with the pillow. "But I'm not kidding. He has no right interfering in my life. For that matter, neither does my father."

Jace's grin faded slowly. "My father died when I was three, and my stepfather never gave me anything but a hard time. Your dad gave you five years of freedom. Why isn't that enough?" With nothing appropriate left to rub, his hands settled aimlessly into his lap, and I stared at them to avoid seeing the dejected look in his eyes. He was taking it too personally. It wasn't like I'd left *him* in particular.

"Because my life isn't his to give," I said, my

words clipped short in frustration. "It's mine, and I should be able to do whatever I want with it." *Why is that so hard for everyone else to understand?*

Jace shrugged. "So, what do you want to do with your life?"

My hand clenched around a handful of my comforter. "I don't know yet."

Instead of laughing, he nodded as if he understood. He probably did. If Jace had any long-term goals, surely he wouldn't have still been working for my father.

He ran a hand through his straight, light brown hair, and my eyes tracked the movement automatically. "Your dad never sent Marc, you know. He could have, but he didn't."

"Until today." I tried not to pout. I really did, knowing I'd never be accepted as an adult as long as I acted like a child. But old habits really do die hard.

"Today's different."

"No, today's the same." I straightened out of my slouch, drawing his gaze up with me. "It's the same as tomorrow will be, and the next day. It's the same as it was when I left."

"Not quite," he said, and the grin was back. He shifted into a more comfortable position, wrinkling my comforter, and leaned forward, blue eyes gleaming. "You're out of practice now."

Out of practice? A slow smile spread across my face. He wanted to run.

"Is that a challenge?" My pulse quickened at the thought of a race, my heart already preparing to increase the blood flow to my muscles. I leaned forward in anticipation, my breath coming fast and shallow. My aggravation was gone, overwhelmed by my love of the chase.

"It's a fact." Jace's eyes sparkled as he edged subtly toward the side of the bed. "There's no way you could have kept in shape up there, with nowhere to stretch your legs."

I flashed him a smile, brazen and cocky. "You'd be surprised."

His eyes narrowed. "I'd be astonished."

"To the tree line?" I asked, and he nodded. "Let's go." Pulling the barrette from my hair, I hopped onto the floor, kicking off my shoes one at a time. I was already halfway to the hall when Jace tackled me from behind. My knees and elbows hit the carpet with a rapid series of thuds. He fell on top of me, pinning me to the floor on my stomach, his body stretched the length of mine.

My breath whooshed from my lungs, and I struggled to replace it for a long moment, until Jace realized the problem. He propped himself up with one elbow, giving me just enough room to breathe.

Irritation blossomed, and I opened my mouth to demand that he get up. But my words were forgotten at the first tentative brush of his fingers against my bare skin.

Jace and I had always enjoyed a very casual physical relationship, trading chaste smooches and the occasional rump pinch with no more significance than a hug from a brother, which he practically was. However, this was a new kind of touch, different even than his boldly seductive greeting in Daddy's office. Before, he'd acted with confidence, almost arrogant in his certainty that I enjoyed his attention. But now he was hesitant, his touch featherlight and slow, as if he expected me to stop him at any moment.

I probably should have.

"No head start for you," he whispered, running one hand over my hip and up my side. His fingers tickled, sending promising shivers all over me. I squirmed beneath him and heard his breath catch.

"I don't need a head start," I breathed, my cheek pressed into the floor. His stomach was warm against the curve of my lower back, bare between the seam of my shirt and the low waist of my jeans. On the radio, a new tune played, intense, and heavy on guitar and drums. My heart raced along with its rhythm, and my legs ached to run. But instead of glorying in the freedom of speed, I was trapped, immobile. "I've always been faster than you, and a few years with limited practice time isn't enough to give you an advantage." I twisted my neck, trying to see him. "Besides, you can't run while you're holding me down."

His fingers eased beneath the edge of my top, brushing the sensitive skin over my ribs and beneath my breast. I gasped, fascinated by the curiously delicate sensation and my own conflicting impulses. One was to fight, to claw at the carpet in a bid for freedom. But the other was to lie still in anticipation of what might come next. Because whatever it was, knowing Jace, it would be good.

Okay, maybe today was a little different after all, I thought, more puzzled by my body's reaction to him than by anything he'd done.

"I'm just slowing you down to give the guys a chance," he whispered into my ear.

I froze, listening, and heard laughter and footsteps coming from the backyard. They were already heading for the trees.

Damn it! How could I have forgotten? As teenagers, Ethan and Owen had taken turns "delaying" me by tripping me or distracting me through even less honorable means. Apparently they'd now recruited Jace to do their dirty work. If I couldn't get out from under him, they would start the hunt without me.

Fueled by impatience and mounting aggravation, I bucked, trying to throw him off, but he rode me with ease. I couldn't help being a little impressed, in spite of my frustration. I hadn't been near another cat in ages and had forgotten how good our balance really was. "Whatever liberties you take now, you'll pay for outside," I panted, winded by my own struggle.

"Oooh," he purred, his nose skimming the surface of my skin. "Say that again." His fingers brushed the wire edge of my bra cup, but went no farther.

"You're all talk," I said, trying not to squirm. But my voice was throatier than I'd intended, and the hitch in his breath told me he'd noticed.

"Is that a challenge?"

"It's a fact." I threw his own words back at him, and he laughed, his body shaking against me.

"How 'bout a bet?"

"You'll lose," I warned, still listening for the others. I could barely hear them now; they'd already disappeared into the trees, their laughter blending into the chorus of sounds that defined the night. And as interesting as Jace's distraction was proving to be, I was eager to join the hunt.

"Maybe," he said. "But if I don't, you owe me."

"Owe you what?"

His voice deepened, and he grew still against me. "The chance to prove I'm not all talk."

Five

My heart thumped in surprise, accompanied by a tiny, treacherous spark of curiosity. I'd expected him to ask for something typically lecherous—like me washing his car in a tiny bikini—but I was completely unprepared for his actual request. I was tempted to laugh it off as a joke.

But Jace wasn't laughing. He wasn't even breathing. He lay on top of me, heavy and completely motionless, his pulse racing as he waited for my answer.

I strained again to look at him over my shoulder, trying to see if he was serious. Surely he was only teasing. But no matter how I twisted, I couldn't see his face. I saw dust bunnies under my desk and the edge of a long-lost CD case jutting out from beneath my dresser. But all I could see of Jace was his shadow, stretching in front of me and into the hall through the open doorway.

"What's the matter?" he asked, soft lips brushing my ear again. "Afraid you're going to lose?"

Was I? I'd never lost a race to him, but I'd never bet on one either. And my body was a high price to pay for a stumble at the wrong time. But if I won... My reward would have to be huge to match the one he'd named. I could ask for practically anything.

Did he have anything I wanted?

An inkling of an idea formed in my head. I smiled, my decision made. Jace didn't know it, but he'd just given me an opportunity I couldn't pass up—assuming I won. And if I lost? I'd worry about that when and if the time came.

"What do I get if I win?" I asked.

Jace purred in anticipation, trailing a finger slowly across my neck as he brushed back a strand of hair. "Anything you want. Name it."

"First, let me up."

He started to get up, then hesitated, considering. "Promise you won't bolt?"

"I don't make promises." *Anymore*, I amended silently.

Jace chuckled. "Glad I asked." He wrapped one hand around my right wrist, holding tight as he got to his knees, in case I made a dash for the hall.

Pulling my arm forward with him, he knee-walked three steps to the door and swung it shut, then sat down and leaned against it, pulling me toward him by the arm he held captive.

I let Jace tug me down into his lap, my back resting against his chest. He moved my hair to one side and propped his chin on my shoulder, making a small sound of contentment deep in his throat. "So, what am I wagering?" he asked, wrapping his arms around my waist.

Okay. No big deal, I thought. *I've been in his lap before.* We'd wrestled on mats in the basement and fallen asleep on the couch watching old horror movies. We'd even shared a sleeping bag once, on a camping trip. This was just more of the same. Friendly cuddling. *Riiight.*

I took a deep breath and held it, preparing to set my newly hatched escape plan in motion. "I want you to take my side. Convince Daddy to let me go back to school."

Jace stiffened against me, lifting his chin from my shoulder. The back of his head thunked against the door. "Faythe…you know I can't do that." His arms were gone, as was the heat in his voice, drenched by the cold wash of reality.

I smiled, glad he couldn't see my face. Ask for the impossible, then settle instead for what you really wanted in the first place. My father had taught me that lesson years ago. He probably never suspected I'd put it to good use.

"Are you afraid?" I asked, daring Jace to say yes and own up to a weakness.

"Of you or your father?"

I laughed. *Good question.* "Of losing."

"Yes." He didn't even hesitate. "Pick something else, anything you want. But I can't go against orders."

"You mean you won't."

"It's the same thing." His tone pleaded with me to understand. "I swore myself to him."

I nodded, and his arms snaked around my waist again, a gesture of relief that I'd accepted his decision. I'd counted on him saying no, and he hadn't disappointed me.

Like all adopted Pride members, Jace had sworn allegiance to my father when he joined the Pride, and again when he became an enforcer shortly before I left for college. Any violation of his oath would end his association with the south-central Pride, and without endorsement or acceptance from another Alpha, he would not be welcomed into any of the others. He would become a wildcat—a natural-born werecat who either left his birth Pride or was exiled from it, usually for the commission of a crime. Such as breaking an oath of allegiance.

Wildcats have no recognized territory, no companionship, and no protection. They are vulnerable and alone. Wildcats are rare, because unlike the adolescent-rebellion version of freedom I'd claimed—the kind where Daddy still paid my tuition and rent—true independence is difficult to achieve in total social seclusion. Isolation from the Pride is most tomcats' worst fear, and Jace was no exception.

I sighed for effect, and my eyes roamed my room as I pretended to try to think of an alternate prize, something worth risking my body for. After passing over my desk, bed, and dresser, my gaze settled on an old family photograph hanging on the wall. It was the last we'd ever taken. In it, a thirteen year-old version of me stood between Ryan and Owen, looking shinier and happier than I remembered ever actually being. After Ryan left, my mother refused to pose for another family picture. She took his absence very personally. I think she felt guilty for something I didn't understand.

Ryan was one of those rare toms who wanted independence badly enough to leave the security of Pride life for the freedom of an existence with no supreme authority figure. He considered the rewards to be worth the risks, and more often than not, I thought he was right. But not Jace. He'd known since before his tenth birthday that he wanted to serve my father, if for no other reason than to be near Ethan, who would never consider leaving. Ethan and Jace were two halves of the same coin, and as such, could not be separated. Even by me.

Jace had sworn his oath to my father, but he kept it for Ethan.

Leaning my head against his chest, I took another deep breath, as if an idea had just occurred to me. "Fine, if I win, I get your keys."

"My house keys?"

I tilted my face up, rubbing my cheek against his shirt as I tried to look at him. "No, Jace. Your car keys."

"Why do you want—?" He stopped, shaking his head in sudden understanding. "No. I can't help you run away again."

"You wouldn't be." I removed his arms from my waist gently and turned around to sit facing him, still encircled by his long legs. "I'd say I took the keys. All you'd have to do is leave them lying around where I could grab them."

From the hall came the creak of hinges and the whisper of wood sliding across carpet. Someone had just opened a door, probably to better hear our conversation. I tensed, listening for some sound with which to identify the eavesdropper, but heard only the quiet, steady rhythm of Jace breathing as he considered my proposal. If he heard the door open, he gave no sign.

I was a little surprised by how sincerely he considered my request. I could almost hear the argument between the devil atop one of his shoulders and the angel hovering over the other. As an enforcer, Jace took his vow to my father very seriously, and for him to even consider endangering his connection to the Pride meant that he wanted…what he wanted from me very, very badly. That realization was almost enough to make me reconsider my plan. Involving emotions added a dangerous edge to our little game. I didn't want anyone to get hurt. I just wanted a little liberty.

"We'd catch you," he said finally, meeting my eyes as he brushed a strand of hair from my face with warm fingertips. "You know we would."

His words faded into silence for a moment, as I debated how to answer in front of the secret listener. In the end, I decided it didn't matter. Daddy was the only person I was worried about, and he was above spying, even on me. "Yeah, but I might get a long weekend out of it." I smiled up at Jace. "And even if I don't, I'll be making a statement."

He snorted. "Saying what, that you're stupid, or just plain crazy?"

"That I'm an adult."

"You want to prove you're an adult by stealing my car for a joyride?"

I sighed. He would never understand, but at least he listened, unlike the others. "I'll take what I can get. What are you driving these days, anyway?"

"A Pathfinder, and it's new."

"Great, so we're on?"

He hesitated, searching my eyes, and I used the opportunity to practice my innocent look. He smiled. It was working. He was going to say yes. I knew it. And finally he nodded. *Yes!*

"You'd better come through if I win," he said, his hand just above my elbow.

"About that…" I tugged on the hem of my shirt, avoiding his eyes.

He took my chin in one hand, lifting my face until I had to look at him. "Backing out already?" His tone was casual, but again his eyes didn't match. He was disappointed and trying to hide it.

"No." I jerked my chin from his grasp. "I'm not backing out. Just…clarifying." But *man,* I didn't want to clarify, because that meant stating out loud what I was agreeing to, which would make it official, with no room to wiggle out of my promise. And I just couldn't look at him while I promised to sleep with him.

I'd never considered myself shy until that

moment, but our wager had made me reconsider several things, including Jace himself.

"Okay, clarify away," he said, running his hand slowly up and down my bare arm. Goose bumps popped up all over, reminding me that even if I lost, I wasn't really losing. This was Jace, and if I was truly honest with myself, I'd have to admit I'd always kind of wondered…

That was enough honesty for the moment. I was much better at manipulation. It was a natural gift.

I made myself meet his eyes, strengthening my resolve to win the race. If I had trouble looking at him, how was I ever going to go through with anything more? "If I lose… Well, I mean…" I glanced away, trying to gather my thoughts, but again he tilted my chin up. He grinned, clearly flattered that thinking of him along forbidden lines had me so flustered.

"You're talking about one time, right?" I asked, blurting it out all in one breath, before I could chicken out again. "A one-night stand, of sorts."

"Standing, huh?" he teased. "What are they teaching you at that school?"

I flushed, and could actually feel my cheeks burn.

He ran one knuckle down the side of my face, leaving a cold trail in its wake. "I was just kidding, Faythe," he said, but his wistful tone made me doubt his words. I cringed inwardly, wondering how I always managed to bury myself so deep in trouble. Daddy would kill me if I started something with Jace. Ethan's best friend was a great enforcer and practically a member of the family, but my father had made it clear early on that Jace was not suitable husband material for his only daughter. And neither of my parents understood a relationship, for me at least, that led to anything less than marriage and lots of babies.

Jace's knuckle followed the line of my jaw, then trailed down my throat to the hollow between my collarbones, sending a fresh wave of shivers through me. "Once it is, if that's what you want. After that, it's up to you." He paused, tilting his head down to catch my eyes. "It's up to you anyway. We can forget the whole thing right now, if you want."

I seriously considered it. Really. But if I said no, I'd be turning down my best chance of escape. Daddy wouldn't let me have a car, for the same reason he'd installed bars on my bedroom window: I was a flight risk. So, if I wanted freedom, it would have to come behind the wheel of someone else's car, and everyone knew better than to leave their keys unattended.

Digging deep inside myself, I recovered my determination to win. I needed those keys. "No. I'm still in."

Jace's smile brightened his whole face, turning his eyes into blue stained glass, lit from within. "Great. Let's get the race out of the way so we can get down to the good stuff."

I blushed again, and something low and sensitive clenched. I couldn't help it. I had no intention of losing, but I was only human—well, mostly human, anyway—and subject to the same temptations as the rest of my gender. And what a temptation Jace was.

Could Marc's overwhelming presence in my life be the real reason I'd never seriously considered Jace before, even though dating him would have seriously irked my father?

Marc. Shit. Marc would throw a fit if I lost and held up my end of the bargain. And there would be no way to hide it from him. Not in a house like ours, where we were lucky to shower in private. *Screw Marc*. I no longer cared what he thought. Really. Yet I was suddenly terribly eager to be on my feet, earning Jace's keys and absolving myself of any obligation to him.

"The good stuff, huh?" I teased with newfound confidence, already backing out of his lap. "Then you'd better catch me."

"You're on." He jumped to his feet with a speed and dexterity that would have shocked a human. But he was too late. Despite pausing to open the door, I was already halfway down the hall and looking back over my shoulder when Marc stepped out of the den to block Jace's path. He'd intentionally let me go by.

"Move, Marc, she's getting away," Jace groaned. I slowed enough to turn around and jog backward, watching them uneasily as I went.

"Yes, she is." Marc lunged to block Jace's dart to the right.

"But if she wins—"

"I'm more worried about her losing."

I cringed, but kept going. I should have realized the eavesdropper was Marc. Anyone else would have shown himself. Cats have amazing ears, and we were lucky my parents hadn't heard us. How was I sure they hadn't? Because my father would have already locked me in the basement and ground the key into steel powder.

Spinning in midstep, I shoved the back door open and raced for the trees, letting the screen slam shut behind me. I ran at top speed, glorying in the taste of freedom, temporary as it was. Grass tickled my bare feet, and the sultry night air caressed my skin. If I hadn't been racing, I would have stopped to look at the moon. It was full, which wasn't necessary for Shifting, but made for a very scenic run.

Standing at the tree line, I could still hear Jace and

Marc arguing in the house behind me, but more interesting was what I heard in the woods.

Our ranch and its adjoining twenty acres of woodland backed up to the north side of the Davy Crockett National Forest, with nothing more than an imaginary boundary separating the two. What that meant for me was a freedom unlike anything I could ever gain in civilized society. It was the freedom of grass, and trees, and fallen leaves, and pinecones, and most important, the freedom of speed. With speed and our natural stealth came the power of life and death. It was an intoxication alcohol could never match. And it was my birthright.

Obviously, prudence demanded the use of caution during the tourist season, which included all three summer months, as well as most of the fall. But we could hear and smell humans long before we saw them, and we could see them before they saw us, so it really wasn't difficult to avoid contact. In fact, it was kind of fun, like a one-sided game of sight-tag.

Deep in the forest, I heard the guys weaving among the trees, occasionally pouncing on one another, or on a rodent or small rabbit. Behind me, at the front of the house, Michael's car growled to life, followed by the crunch of gravel beneath his tires and the biting odor of exhaust. He was going home.

I spared a moment for disappointment that my

homecoming hadn't meant more to my oldest brother, but only a moment. I sympathized with his obligations and respected them. Michael had a wife. He was the only tomcat I knew who'd married a human woman, and even though Holly was a model—an honest-to-goodness runway model who spent most of her time in New York, L.A., or Paris— maintaining his marriage when she was home required a delicate balance of secrecy and creative planning. Even better than most, I understood. Though I'll admit to being curious about how he interacted with her normal, human family.

Jace burst through the back door with Marc on his heels while I was still unzipping my pants. I let them fall to the ground as I pulled my shirt over my head, then dropped my underwear on the small heap of clothing on the grass.

Both men ran toward me, pulling their shirts off as they came. I paused for a moment to enjoy the view as generous moonlight highlighted every hard plane on their chests and cast shadows beneath each ripple of their abs. Very nice. Almost worth being dragged home for.

The guys never bothered with neat piles. They left their clothing scattered all over the yard, draped across bushes and sometimes hanging from tree branches. It would have been quite a sight for the unaccustomed eye. Fortunately, we had no close neighbors and never had human visitors, other than Michael's wife, who visited rarely enough that it was easy for us to keep our inner cats on their leashes. So there was seldom anyone around to be scandalized by our behavior.

Naked, I ducked beneath the branches of the nearest tree and into the forest, twigs and thorns scraping my bare skin. Relief rushed through me to ease tension I hadn't even realized I'd felt. My impulse to rush was gone now; in crossing the tree line, I'd won the race. Jace's car was mine, if and when I had the nerve to take it. I'd have to remember to thank Marc. *Yeah, right.*

My means of escape secured, I was ready to relax and stretch my legs in the forest, a luxury I'd sorely missed at school.

As soon as the guys were out of sight, I dropped to all fours and closed my eyes in concentration. Shifting always begins for me with a moment of quiet relaxation or meditation. It sounds like a page from *Zen for Dummies,* but it really helps and only takes a couple of minutes. It's just a moment for my mind to acknowledge and submit to what my body wants.

Shifting is possible during moments of extreme stress, but I wouldn't recommend it. If your brain hasn't had a chance to adjust to what's coming, it responds by sending your body more pain signals than necessary. No one wants to experience avoidable pain. Okay, maybe masochists do, but I harbor no fondness for pain. No fondness for *experiencing* it, anyway.

Dimly, I heard leaves rustle as Marc and Jace entered the woods, but I made no effort to acknowledge them. I didn't need to. They dropped to the ground, one on either side of me, and began their own Shifts.

On my knees, with my nose less than two feet from the ground, I breathed in the fragrances of the forest, letting the pine-scented air trigger my Shift. Just as certain notes played on the piano can bring to mind an entire melody, so the smell of last year's pine needles and leaf mold called forth the cat from inside me. An undulating wave of pain and change, the Shift rolled through me, tensing and relaxing my muscles with no pattern I could discern.

As a teenager, I'd struggled to try to prepare myself for each phase as it came, determined to master the art of Shifting. It didn't work. In the end, Shifting mastered me. When I gave up trying and relaxed, I realized that while I couldn't control my discomfort, I could anticipate it, from the first sharp stab of pain to the last nagging bone-ache. With anticipation came acceptance, and that turned out to be enough.

My spine arched and joints popped. I ground my teeth together as my fingernails hardened and grew into claws, remembering to unclench my jaw before the first ripple of pain lapped at my face, announcing the arrival of the tidal wave just behind it. Mouth open, I stretched my chin as far forward as I could, gasping as my jaw buckled and bulged with the ingress of new teeth, pointed, slightly curved, and very sharp. My tongue itched briefly but unbearably, as hundreds of tiny, backward-pointing barbs budded from it in a prickling surge from the base to the rounded tip.

And finally, just as I was starting to catch my breath, my skin began to tingle as fur sprouted across my back, flowing to cover my limbs and stomach, before moving on to my face.

The only good thing about the pain was its brevity, and the worst by far was its intensity. It was like being ripped open and rearranged, without so much as a capsule of Tylenol. Immediately following a Shift, I felt like all my bones had been broken and allowed to heal wrong, like I didn't quite fit into my new body. Fortunately, it only took one good stretch to improve the fit. I extended my front paws, claws piercing ground cover to grip the fragrant earth while I presented my rump to the sky, my tail waving slowly in the air.

There was a time when Shifting on a regular basis was a normal part of my life, just something else I did, like I slept, showered, and ate. Along with other, normal physical changes, my initial Shift was brought on by puberty. But unlike other biological processes, it could be repressed or initiated, though I'd pay a severe physical penalty for doing too much of either.

Away at school, I Shifted when I had to, or when an irresistible opportunity presented itself, like my yearly camping trip with Sammi's family. While slinking undetected through a forest swarming with humans is exciting in a forbidden kind of way, it can't compare to the sense of belonging I felt each time I hunted with the members of my Pride.

And it's been so long, I thought, watching Marc and Jace writhe, each in the grip of his own Shift. *Far too long.*

Six

By the time Marc and Jace stood, their Shifts complete, I was ready to greet them on four legs. I weighed a healthy one-hundred-and-thirty-five pounds, which is slim, with ample allowance for curves on a woman my height. As a human, that's not very impressive. But a one-hundred-and-thirty-five pound cat always gets a second glance—and usually a panicked scream.

But if I was impressive as a cat, Marc was downright scary. Including his tail, he was just over six and a half feet of sleek black fur, sharp claws and jaws powerful enough to split the back of a deer's skull with a single bite. He was a two-hundred-and-forty-pound mass of graceful, rippling muscles, just waiting to pounce. And few things pounced on by Marc ever got back up.

My father theorized that in cat form we have occasionally been mistaken for so-called "black panthers," a term used to refer to melanistic jaguars or leopards. In short, black panthers don't exist, but we do. All of us, regardless of our coloring as humans, have, as cats, the same short, solid black, glossy fur, completely devoid of stripes or rosettes. Length and weight vary with each individual, of course, but in general we are somewhere between the size of a jaguar and that of a small-to-medium lion.

Finished with his own Shift, Marc circled me slowly, stopping several times to sniff my fur in specific places, and once to give my nose a quick lick. Finally satisfied that all was well with me, he rubbed his cheek against mine and nipped tenderly at my neck. I let him. Social guidelines were different in cat form, when it no longer mattered who'd left whom, and why. As cats, we were part of a whole, like littermates.

Jace stood back, letting Marc have his way, because just as some rules changed, others stayed the same. Marc walked the length of my body, letting his tail drag across my back. Then he sat on the ground in front of me and roared.

My heart leapt to hear it. I hadn't heard a roar other than my own in years. Ours is not the distinctive roar of a lion, though it's nearly as deep and clearly feline. It sounds like a series of low-pitched bleats, rising and falling in volume, each blending into the next.

Deeper in the woods, the playful romping stopped as the others froze in place to listen. Marc had called, and he was their leader in my father's absence. As the last of Marc's roar faded from my ears, it was replaced with the sounds signaling their approach: snapping twigs, crunching leaves and deep breathing. Cats could be absolutely silent when they chose, but rarely bothered when there was no need. The guys weren't stalking; they were responding to a summons.

In moments, Parker burst through the brush, followed by Owen and Ethan, three dark blurs soaring through the air in front of me to land with delicate, easy grace. Except for one. Ethan landed not on the ground, but on Jace, who rolled over onto his back at the last second. He caught Ethan's throat between enlarged canines and the vulnerable flesh of his attacker's stomach with exposed rear claws. They were only playing, so Jace neither bit nor slashed, but had it been for real, it would have been bloody. And it would have been over in a heartbeat. But then, if it had been for real, Jace would never have heard him coming.

Jace tossed Ethan to the ground, where he landed on his feet, hissing with his fur standing on end.

They both joined the others in greeting me. In cat form, even more than as humans, our greetings were very physical. I found myself at the center of a writhing, purring mass of black fur and whiskers, tails curling over, under, and around me. The mingling of personal scents was both comforting and invigorating, as were the memories tumbling over one another in a bid for my attention.

When my patience dwindled, I nipped at whatever came near my mouth. I got a whiff of hay and dry soil as I bit down gently on Owen's tail. Jace's ear came with the faint scent of the Granny Smith he'd finished for Ethan. But no one paid any attention to my warnings until I growled, and even then they were slow learners. Marc came to my rescue, which I thought was the least he could do, since it was his fault they'd converged on me in the first place. And since even the smallest of them— Ethan—outweighed me by forty pounds.

Marc hissed, and I turned to look at him across someone's back. He stood several feet away with his neck straining forward and his jaw open to expose a mouthful of sharp teeth, ears flat against the top of his skull. He wasn't really mad; he was just posturing to get their attention. It worked.

All eyes were on Marc, and since I was never one to pass up an opportunity, I launched myself over Parker and through a thin clump of brush. The chase was on.

I heard them behind me, pursuing me for the thrill of speed, and not because they had any hope of catching me. Surely they knew they had no chance. Maybe in a car on a long stretch of highway, but not in the woods where I'd grown up. And never on four paws.

My pulse racing, I darted between trees and vaulted off fallen limbs, sending small creatures fleeing ahead of me. Everywhere were the sights and sounds of the woods. The undergrowth grew thick and green, and pine trees soared to over one hundred feet high, with the red birches not far behind. My ears were on alert, catching and instantly cataloging the various nocturnal forest creatures as I passed them. Mice squeaked, owls hooted, and possums waddled off in search of safety. I ignored them all.

For fun, as my heart beat a syncopated rhythm against my rib cage, I climbed a broad oak tree, gripping the trunk with my claws over and over again, leg muscles tensing and relaxing as they propelled me upward until I gained a low, thick branch. With a glance at the ground below, I leapt onto a limb extending from a neighboring trunk. From there, I worked my way along, leaping from branch to branch, tree to tree, until I finally thumped to the ground, already running.

My eyes were perfectly suited to roaming the forest at night. They made good use of generous pools of moonlight pouring through gaps in the canopy of leaves and heavily laden pine branches above. Light reflected from the eyes of potential prey, and I could easily distinguish the dark coats of nocturnal animals from the shadows nestled in every niche and crevice, and hiding beneath curtains of fern and blankets of poison ivy. Dry leaves crackled beneath my paws and thorns tugged at my fur as I sprinted, my lungs relishing the luxury of such fresh, fragrant air.

Our forest was home to any number of woodland creatures, the largest of which were deer. But we were the biggest predators around for miles. Dogs— and especially cats—knew to avoid our territory thanks to Marc's obsessively organized system of scent marking. We had the run of the forest, and we liked it that way.

On my right, something slithered beneath a pile of leaves, but I didn't pause to identify it as I ran. The only things I chased that night were my personal demons. Or rather, they were chasing me. For the first time in years, I felt the hot breath of my past on the back of my neck. It was the carnivorous spirit of everything tradition demanded I become, and the only way to escape was to run, to beat the ground with my paws, in a furious race for the right to control my life. And I would not lose. Not again.

Finally, when my lungs burned, my legs ached, and every muscle in my body insisted that I must stop or collapse, I had to admit that at least for now, the demons were only in my head. My pursuers were my fellow Pride members, and they only chased because I ran. It was a cat's instinct to try to catch anything that moved, like a kitten pouncing on a piece of string trailed across the floor. And I'd trailed my string all over the forest, practically daring them to come get me.

I slowed to a stop, listening between ragged pants as I calmed my racing heart. The guys had fallen far behind, and the evidence of their pursuit faded into the symphony of shuffles, rustles, cracks, hoots and squeaks that defined the forest at night. Satisfied that I'd proven my point, that I could outrun them all, I sank to the ground to rest at the base of a pine tree. I glanced around, taking in even the most minute shift of leaves in the warm night breeze. The night was mine for as long as I wanted it, and I finally had the privacy I'd sought for so long at school. It irked me that I'd found what I wanted in my own backyard, when I'd searched for it fruitlessly for years, hundreds of miles from home.

Content, I licked the dirt from my paws, giving my ears a good swipe while I was at it. Grooming was always relaxing. It gave me a chance to think, which I could never do without something to occupy my hands. Or paws, as the case may be. As I set to work on my whiskers, a gurgling sound caught my attention, and my ears perked up—literally. I'd paid little attention to direction as I ran, more intent on escaping the tomcats and my personal demons, which became harder to tell apart with each passing moment. But the sound of running water was unmistakable. I was near the stream.

Unlike house cats, we swim very well and love to fish. And unless something had changed in the last two years, the stream was full of fish practically tripping over one another for the honor of filling my stomach. I stood and listened carefully, my ears rotating in unison as I searched for the direction of the sound.

There. Southeast, and not very far away. I could already smell the mineral-rich water.

Still tired from my run, I turned in the direction of the stream and took my time, batting at every firefly I saw on the way. At the water's edge, I peered down at the rippling surface. My own face looked back at me in the moonlight. It wasn't my human face, of course, with dimples and slightly ruddy cheeks, but the reflection wavering in the stream was no less familiar. My fur was solid black, with no distinguishing marks and no variation in color except for whiskers, which stood out as startlingly white against the dark background.

My eyes were the same color in either form: pale green, almost yellow in the moonlight. At school my friends said they were distinctive, but in cat form they looked normal, even average. Of course, the shape was completely different than my human eyes; as a cat, my pupils were slits, rather than circles. At least in the daylight. At night, they dilated almost all the way, leaving only thin rings of color around broad black disks.

I leaned forward and lapped at the water, quenching the scorching thirst I'd worked up during my sprint. And fluid wasn't the only thing the race had cost me. Cats have a higher metabolic rate than humans do, and we seem to have a higher rate than even most large cats, possibly due to the calories used up during the process of Shifting. Simply put, Shifting makes us hungry. Immediately.

Motion from the stream caught my eye. Something darted just beneath the surface of the water, too big to be a frog, and too fast to be a turtle. I hunkered low to the ground, preparing to charge into the water after my dinner. When everything felt right—a feeling I couldn't verbalize because it had no human equivalent—I jumped. But I never hit the water.

Something smacked into me in midair, ending my forward momentum and driving me to the right. I hit the ground on my side. A crushing weight pinned me down. I saw nothing but black fur, but even with my eyes closed I would have known who it was. On two legs or four, I knew his scent better than I knew my own and had every inch of his body memorized, in both forms. I knew every line, every scar, and even every striation in his irises. As a teenager, I'd gazed into those eyes for hours at a time, wondering if they were as bright by moonlight as they were in the sun. It turned out that they were.

But those days were behind me, by my own choice.

Get off me, Marc! I thought, but what came out was a growl. It was a damn fine growl, in my opinion. Low and threatening, and very serious. But he ignored it with a blatant disregard for my will that would have been uniquely his, if not for the fact that he'd learned it from my father.

Marc lowered his face to mine slowly. He rubbed his cheek against my whiskers and my head, making his way slowly to my only exposed shoulder.

Great job, Faythe, I thought, as furious at myself as I was at Marc. *You've been pinned twice in less than an hour.*

Marc bit me softly each time I tried to throw him off or get to my feet, and I never stopped growling. He was marking me with the scent glands on either side of his face.

I hate being marked.

He would go no farther; we both knew that. And he was being very gentle, even seductive for a cat, but that couldn't have been further from the point. The point was that he had no right to mark me. None at all.

Marking was an overt declaration of possession. Of territorial rights. Werecat instinct led us to mark our personal possessions, our kills, and the boundaries of our property. By rubbing his personal scent on me, Marc was claiming me for himself like he might claim the front seat or the biggest slice of pizza. The implication was that I *belonged* to him. Which was far from the truth.

His behavior would have been perfectly acceptable, even expected, if I were his mate—a wife, or even a long-term girlfriend. In that case, it would be appropriate for me to reciprocate. But I was *not* his mate, therefore I was not his to mark. Not anymore. Not ever, if we were being completely honest.

Trapped in a cage formed by his legs and pressed to the ground by his weight, I could do nothing but wait for him to finish. That, and feed the rage mounting in every bone in my body. In every shadowed corner of my soul. I passed the seconds with thoughts of retaliation, of the pain and humiliation I would unleash on him at the first available opportunity.

Yep, that's me. Sugar and spice, and everything nice.

Finally he made a mistake. He moved lower to reach my rib cage, but wasn't willing to back off of me for fear of my escape. Instead, he turned, placing his left hind leg within reach of my muzzle.

I lunged. My teeth sank into his leg, an inch above his paw. I withheld nothing, giving in to my instinct to bite through to the bone. Marc deserved only my best effort. After all, that's what I was getting from him, in a bizarre, gently insistent kind of way.

Marc yowled and tried to jump away, hissing in pain and anger.

I refused to let go. It took every ounce of self-control I had to keep from snapping his bone. My canines met around his leg. My back teeth sank through fur and into muscle. I growled, my claws gripping the ground for stability. Blood flowed into my mouth, threatening to choke me if I didn't swallow. Still, I held on.

Marc turned on me, with that peculiar feline flexibility, and roared almost directly into my ear.

But I didn't let go until he nipped my shoulder just hard enough to draw blood. I'd had a potentially crippling grip on his leg, and he'd held back from hurting me. Some might call that sweet. I called it poor judgment. I only played for keeps, and if Marc wanted to play with me, he'd have to do the same. I was finished making exceptions for him. I'd moved on, whether he realized it or not. And hopefully he would now.

Four more shapes burst through the thick undergrowth, all large and black, the edges of their fur melting into the shadows. Daddy's other loyal tomcats had come to rescue his right-hand man from a tabby half his size. If I could have, I would have laughed. As it was, I could only huff, but that was good enough to make my point. Marc hobbled off, settling on the ground several feet away to clean his wound, pausing to glare at me periodically and to growl.

As I washed Marc's blood from my face, Ethan approached me warily, his head hanging low. He sniffed the air as he came, as if he wasn't quite sure it was actually me. If my scent didn't convince him, one look at my eyes would. Cats can communicate anger through their expressions just as people can, and I was really good at looking pissed off. I'd had lots of practice.

My appetite was gone, along with any peace I'd gained from my run in the forest. I shot one last contemptuous glance at Marc, then turned my back on them all and jumped over a tangled clump of brush and vines, landing silently on a bed of pine needles on the other side. I was too tired to run, and the walk back to the house took much too long to suit me. The sights and sounds I'd rejoiced in half an hour earlier now grated on my last nerve. Each owl's hoot seemed to scold me; each rodent's squeak mocked my plight.

At the edge of the trees, I sank my teeth into my neat pile of clothes, managing to get everything but my panties. I hesitated, uncomfortable with leaving my underwear exposed on the lawn, but abandoned it in the end because I didn't have any hands and was too pissed off to try Shifting immediately.

Luckily, I didn't need hands to open the back door, because it was equipped with an oblong handle, easily depressed by cat paws. As long as someone was home, we never locked the doors, because a cat has no place to carry keys. Also, we figured that anyone stupid enough to trespass deserved to be eaten and probably wouldn't be missed.

I'm kidding, of course. Mostly.

Pawing open the screen-door latch, I trudged into

the back hall. The tiles felt cold and smooth against my paws, and the air-conditioning ruffled my sensitive facial whiskers. The only sound other than the whistle of air through the vents was the hum of the refrigerator. It sounded oddly mechanical to my cat ears.

I padded into my room through the open doorway and dropped my clothes on the carpet. Still fuming, I jumped onto the bed and curled up with my tail wrapped around my body. I was hungry and thirsty, and too mad to Shift. Great.

And it only got better when Jace leaned around the door frame, waving my panties from one finger like a white flag. I growled at him, but he only laughed. He knew I wouldn't hurt him in human form, because that wouldn't be playing fair. But then, neither was waving my underwear around for the whole world to see.

"You want them back?" he asked. I bobbed my head, and he laughed again at my approximation of a very human gesture. "Come and get them."

He stepped into the doorway, wearing nothing but a pair of black bikini briefs, and I was suddenly glad to still be a cat. Anyone else might have looked ridiculous in so little material, but Jace was temptation personified. If I'd been human, he couldn't have mistaken the look in my eyes for anything less than lust. But as a cat, while I had a healthy appreciation for what lay, rather obviously, beneath that tiny triangle of cloth, I was distanced from it by the boundary of species. Jace was much less a possibility than he would have been had I not been sporting fur and claws.

"Come on, if you want them," he repeated, and I cocked my head, trying to look curious since I couldn't just ask why he wouldn't bring them to me. It worked. "Marc said he'd use me as a scratching post if I ever went into your room unchaperoned again."

Aah. Yes, that sounded like Marc, though he would never have said it in front of me.

Jace grinned, eyes glinting suggestively. "He didn't say anything about you coming into *my* room."

I snorted air through my nose at him and thumped to the floor, landing more delicately on four feet than I ever could have on two. He held out my panties, and I padded over to him, taking the waistband between my teeth. I blinked up at him.

"You're welcome," he said. "You really did some damage to his leg, you know."

I bobbed my head again. I did know. I'd meant to.

"Your father's going to be pissed. Marc was supposed to make a run up to Oklahoma tomorrow to check out a report we got yesterday about a stray."

I blinked again and yawned, dropping the underwear on the floor. *So Owen would go instead. Or Parker.* I didn't really care about my father's plans to patrol the territory, unless they meant taking prying eyes away from me. Of course, by injuring Marc, I'd inadvertently guaranteed that he'd be around to watch me for a while. *Great job, Faythe.* That was me, always careful to plan ahead.

"Shift back," Jace said, smiling down at me. "I'll get you something to eat." He closed the door without waiting for my response. Not that I could have said no. But it would have been pretty satisfying to nudge the door closed in his face.

The Shift back to human was harder than it should have been, and took longer than normal because I couldn't help thinking about Marc and dwelling on my own anger. I could still taste his blood, which made me simultaneously hungry and furious, a decidedly bizarre combination.

Jace's last comment ran through my head as I Shifted. He'd said a stray had been reported in Oklahoma, well within the boundaries of our territory. That made at least two such reports, that I knew of, in the last two days. What was going on?

Strays are humans who became werecats after being scratched or bitten by one of us in cat form. Not every bite or scratch produces a werecat, but in spite of centuries spent observing the process, no one seems to know for sure why. Or why not. But there are plenty of theories.

Some werecats believe the size or severity of the wound is directly proportionate to the chances of "infection," if that's even the right term. Others, mostly the older generation, believe that transmission is more likely to occur under certain phases of the moon. I'd even met one sweet old dam years earlier who believed that fate determined who would join our ranks and who would not—that those meant to Shift would, and those who were not meant to would not.

According to her theory, human women were not meant to be werecats. Ever. In my entire life, I'd never heard of a female stray. Naturally, nearly everyone had a theory explaining the trans-formation's apparent gender bias, and the reasons were just as ridiculous as the prevailing theories about conduction in general. The most popular of these was the conjecture by an elderly former Alpha that women—as the weaker sex—weren't strong enough to survive the initial Shift.

I thought that particular old man was full of shit. My personal theory was that something in a woman's physiology, maybe in her immune system, kept the werecat "virus" from getting a grip on her body. But until I could prove it, which wasn't likely to happen anytime soon, no one gave a damn what I thought. As usual.

Either way, the only thing we know with any certainty about contamination is that humans can only be infected by one of us in cat form, just like with werewolves in the movies. Hollywood got the transmission part right but missed the species altogether. By a long shot.

As a child, I once saw two thunderbirds, flying in tandem across a brilliant blue sky too large to hint at their actual size and strength. And we'd all heard my father recount his infamous run-in with a bruin— a werebear, if you will. But to my knowledge, werewolves are pure fiction. Stray cats, however, are undeniably real, and they posed a constant problem for the rest of us.

Since they were not born into any Pride, most strays could claim no territory of their own and had no system of support. Along with wildcats, who either left their birth Prides or were kicked out, strays lived their lives in seclusion from the rest of us, wandering within the free territories, struggling to either accept or end a life they never asked for or even imagined.

From all accounts, strays lived a miserable existence, so it was no wonder they sometimes crossed the border into our land looking for companionship, and sometimes for answers. When that happened, our enforcers were glad to fill in the many blanks— as the strays were escorted back to the border. Unfortunately, most strays who crossed our boundaries were looking for something else entirely: revenge, or even a slice out of the territorial pie. As a result, the territorial council had long since passed laws forbidding strays from crossing Pride borderlines. Marc was the exception. But then, Marc was exceptional, so that was really no surprise to anyone who knew him.

And now I'm back to thinking about Marc... Damn it.

By the time I stepped back into my pants, I could smell beef cooking. Hamburgers. It had to be, because Jace's culinary skills were limited to burgers and spaghetti, and I didn't smell tomato sauce. Oh well, a girl can never have too many burgers, right?

I padded down the hall on bare feet, my steps silent as I passed several closed doors on the way to the kitchen. Jace's off-key whistling met my ears, accompanied by the sizzle of meat on the stove. I paused in the doorway, glad to see that he'd donned a pair of jeans, if nothing else.

A smile slid into place as I watched him. Jace was comically out of place in front of any household appliance, particularly my mother's six-burner, stain-less-steel behemoth of a stove. He subscribed to the Jackson Pollock theory of cooking, which had somehow led to the creation of an abstract master-piece out of the formerly spotless, white-tiled kitchen.

As I watched, he turned from the stove toward the peninsula, dripping grease in an arc across the floor from a plastic spatula gripped loosely in one hand. He dropped the spatula on the countertop—without the benefit of a spoon holder—and began slicing tomatoes with a six-inch smooth-bladed butcher knife. I covered my mouth to stifle a giggle as tiny seeds and red juice spurted across the countertop tiles, mingling with a tangle of discarded onion skins and outer lettuce leaves.

"Shit," he mumbled under his breath, still oblivi-ous to my presence. Grinning, I slipped silently into a chair at the breakfast table. I inhaled deeply, tempted by the aroma of beef and onions. Beneath those were the usual kitchen smells: disinfectant, most notably, mingled with the faintly lingering scents of lemon and rosemary, my mother's favorite ingredients.

Jace turned back to the stove, still whistling as he piled seasoned beef patties on a plate lined with paper towels. Then he spun gracefully on one foot, the plate balanced on the fingertips of one hand, and stopped in midstep, his eyes wide with surprise to find me watching him. Laughter bubbled from my throat; I couldn't stop it. The look on his face was almost enough to cure my bad mood.

"I'm glad you're pleased with yourself," he said, his voice full of self-deprecating amusement. He set the plate on the table in front of me and went back to the counter to finish butchering the tomatoes. "Why were you spying on me, anyway?"

"Goldfish syndrome," I said, pinching a chunk from the nearest beef patty.

Jace paused in midslice to glance at me quizzically.

"You guys have been watching my every move for years, and I couldn't resist the novelty of being the observer for once, rather than the observed."

"Oh." He resumed hacking apart vegetables with the butcher knife. "I wouldn't say we watched your *every* move…"

"Oh, please." I rolled my eyes at him. "I'm surprised my father didn't commission a big glass bowl for me to move into."

He laughed, scooping a double handful of smooshed tomato slices onto a clean plate.

"Speaking of which, where are my mighty sire and dam hiding out tonight?" I asked, my voice thick with sarcasm. "Have I already scared them into submission?"

"Hardly. It's late for old folks. They went to bed an hour ago, with orders for us to keep an eye on you."

"Oh." Of course they had. And wouldn't my father *love* to hear himself described as old.

In the silence that followed, Jace's ham-fisted sawing captured my attention, and my eyes narrowed in suspicion. He was slicing *way* too many tomatoes. I glanced from the plate of condiments on the counter to the huge stack of burgers in front of me, my smile fading quickly. "You can't fatten me up in a single meal, Jace."

"I'm not trying to." Finished with the tomatoes, he began fishing pickle slices from an economy-size jar. The combined scents of dill, garlic, and vinegar made my mouth water. Jace turned, a pickle slice halfway to his mouth. "You're going to have to share and play nice." He popped the slice into his mouth and crunched into it.

I gripped the tabletop in irritation as his meaning sank in. "The guys aren't invited." I wouldn't have minded eating with Parker and my brothers, but they'd bring Marc, and I didn't care if I didn't see *him* again for another five years.

Jace shot me a stern look, catching me off guard.

It was my father's expression. "They're giving you time to cool off, but they're hungry too, and you ruined the hunt. So, we're all going to sit down like civilized adults and enjoy a meal together. Fresh deer would have been nice—" he glared at me pointedly "—but burgers will have to do."

I scowled, but he turned around to keep from seeing it. I hadn't ruined the hunt. Marc had, but it would do no good to explain that to Jace, so I kept my mouth shut. When the battle lines were drawn, the guys would stick together, and I'd be left with only my thick skin to protect me from testosterone-laced barbs and daggers. Unfortunately, the nearest tabby other than my mother was several hundred miles away.

No, wait. Sara was missing, which was the reason for my unscheduled trip home.

Tense laughter and the shuffling of bare feet on tile preceded the guys as they filed into the kitchen, in varying degrees of undress. As usual, Owen was the only one who did justice to the phrase "fully clothed."

Marc limped in last, his hair damp and smelling of shampoo. I glanced at his left ankle but couldn't see the wound because his foot was wrapped in a clean white gauze bandage, extending beneath the cuff of his jeans. He crossed his arms over his bare chest and leaned against the wall, staring past me with flushed cheeks. He was either embarrassed or mad, and probably both.

So what? Screw him. He'd brought it on himself.

The other three stood clustered around him, avoiding my eyes. "Grab a plate, guys," Jace said, ignoring the obvious tension. He set a stack of my mother's everyday plates on the table, but I made no move to take one. The guys came forward one by one, beginning with Ethan, who had half of his first burger eaten before he settled into the chair next to me.

While the others filled their plates, all except Marc, who still scowled from the doorway, Parker knelt next to my chair, smiling up at me. "How long has it been, Faythe?" he asked. We'd already greeted each other as cats, but it was hard to catch up on lost time with a purr and a lick on the cheek. "What, two years?" His eyes twinkled at me, daring me to disagree.

"More like two months." I swatted his shoulder fondly. "I saw you at the concert, you know. You don't exactly fit in with the college crowd."

He smiled and shrugged, running one hand through prematurely graying hair. "I had my orders. You know that."

I did know. Everyone always had orders, and for some reason the guys felt honor-bound to follow theirs. I felt no such obligation. But then, I wasn't getting a paycheck, either.

Parker stood and leaned down to give me a chaste kiss on the cheek before going to fill his plate. Marc followed him, limping past me without so much as a glance in my direction.

Looking around the room, I took in the familiar faces one at a time. It was just like old times, pigging out on junk food after my parents went to bed and arguing about who had to clean up. Even the tension between me and Marc felt familiar; we'd been one of those couples for whom one kind of passion was as good as another. We'd fought as often as we'd made love, and one often led to the other.

"So, Jace," Owen said from his seat at the bar. "Did Burger King blow up in here, or what?"

"I didn't see *you* sweatin' over a hot stove," Jace said around a mouthful of food.

"He was sweating?" Ethan glanced at me for confirmation.

I shrugged. "I didn't see any sweat, but I did see some dancing."

Parker raised an eyebrow, bemused. "There was dancing?"

"No. There was no dancing." Jace scowled at me.

I grinned. "Not only was he dancing, he was *twirling*."

Parker snickered, and Ethan laughed outright, nearly choking on the last bite of his first burger.

"Okay, I may have taken a graceful step or two," Jace admitted, a barbecue-flavored chip halfway to his mouth. "But it's not like I was doing Vic's rain dance." He crunched into the chip, and for a long moment his chewing splintered a tense silence.

It was a harmless reference to a very funny night several summers before, when Vic had danced naked in the backyard, appealing to the heavens for some much-needed rainfall. But mentioning Vic had brought to mind his sister, which reminded me forcefully of just what I was doing there, surrounded by my brothers and lifelong friends.

I was home because my parents saw a strike against one North American Pride as a strike against us all. They were closing ranks, circling the wagons to protect the women and children, and as insulted as I was to be included among those in need of protection, I seemed to be the only one who considered their precautions unnecessary.

Could I be wrong? I'd assumed my parents had seized upon Sara's vanishing act as an excuse to bring their stray sheep back into the fold, where they thought I belonged. But what if they were right? What if someone *had* taken her?

That one thought changed everything.

All at once, the gravity of Sara's disappearance hit me like a fist in the gut. Air whooshed from my lungs, and I gasped, trying to draw more in. Doubled over, I panted, near panic. I'd been convinced that she had run away, but what if I was wrong? What if Sean *had* taken her? If he was crazy enough to snatch her from her own territory, there was no guarantee he wouldn't hurt her.

A hand settled on my shoulder, heavy and warm. I looked up, fighting back tears. Marc stood in front of me, with a plate in his other hand and concern in his eyes where there had been only anger moments earlier.

Embarrassed by my near collapse and still furious with Marc, I slapped his hand from my shoulder. The sound echoed throughout the room for much longer than I thought it should have. His eyes widened in shock as his arm dropped to hang at his side.

"Don't touch me," I whispered through clenched teeth, glaring at him. He had no right to try to comfort me after the stunt he'd pulled in the woods.

Marc's cheeks flushed with humiliation as his expression hardened into anger.

The others stared openly, their food apparently forgotten.

My chair made a harsh scraping sound as I shoved it back from the table. All eyes were on me as I stood. I turned away from them, letting my hair fall to shield my face. The only thing worse than having the guys witness my little breakdown would be having to accept their comfort. I didn't want comfort. I wanted solitude. I had to get away from them all, but especially from Marc. "Excuse me, guys," I mumbled. "I've lost my appetite."

I'd taken two steps toward the doorway when a warm, strong hand closed around my wrist. I glanced back at Marc, trying to jerk free. His fingers tightened around my arm, grinding the bones together. I whimpered, hating the sound of weakness even as I made it.

Owen stood, and I thought he'd intervene on my behalf, but one look from Marc stopped him in midstep.

Marc's plate crashed to the table. His pickle spear landed on its side on my mother's floral tablecloth. A tomato slice dangled from the raised edge of his plate. He stomped out of the kitchen with one hand clamped around my arm, and even with his limp I had to jog to keep up. He pulled me down the hall, past a half dozen closed doors, then tossed me into my bedroom with one hand.

I stumbled and kept putting one foot in front of the other to keep from losing my balance. My momentum took me all the way to the bed, where I banged my thighs against the footboard, and fell forward on my face.

I came up hissing.

Seven

I spun around to face Marc and found my bedroom door closed. Anger, already scorching a path through my veins, blazed all new trails in the face of his audacity. Beyond the capacity for rational thought, I stormed toward him, my right hand curling into a fist.

Marc limped backward, bringing his arm up to ward off the blow. He was too late. My fist slammed into his jaw. His head snapped back and to the left. But before I could even consider taking a second shot, he'd wrapped a hand around each of my forearms, the gold sparks in his eyes glittering in fury.

I tried to pull free, but his fists tightened around my arms. He took a step forward, pushing me ahead of himself. Then his left foot hit the ground, and he grimaced in obvious agony.

The pain seemed to clear Marc's head, and his eyes regained focus. He struggled visibly to get control over his temper, his gaze shifting back and forth between my eyes. I tried to jerk my arms away again, and he blinked. Then he shoved me. Hard.

I staggered backward, all the way to my bed. Again.

"What the hell is wrong with you?" I spat, gripping the footboard to recover my balance. Since my claws were temporarily unavailable, I scrambled for words sharp enough to wound him. "Don't you *ever* lay another finger on me," I said, the calm surface of my voice hiding a churning current of rage. "You lost the right to touch me a long time ago."

Hurt flickered across his face, and for an instant, my inner bitch was pretty happy. But then his expression hardened into anger once more as his hands formed fists at his sides. "If you have a problem with me, by all means let me know. In private. Throwing fits in front of the entire Pride was one thing when you were fifteen, but you're an adult now, so start acting like it."

I clenched the bedpost at a narrow section of the spindle, carving fresh grooves amid a tangle of older scars etched in the grip of a very different kind of passion. "You're in for quite a shock if you thought *that* was a fit," I said through teeth clenched hard enough to hurt. "Besides, four toms hardly make up the entire Pride. And there is no 'in private' around here, in case you haven't noticed. They're probably listening to us right now." In fact, I knew they were because no one was talking.

Marc sighed, and eased his weight onto his good leg. I couldn't resist a little silent gloating as he winced. "It's been a long time, Faythe," he said, his features twisted in pain. He probably wanted me to think his ankle was the only thing bothering him, but I knew better. This was a different kind of hurt, older and far more acute. "I was just trying to get reacquainted," he continued. "Looking for a way to reconnect with you." He stared at the floor, curling his toes in the carpet. "I made a mistake, and I'm sorry."

I blinked, surprised by both his apology and the sudden change of subject. Weren't we just talking about my "fit" in the kitchen? How had he made the leap to his forest faux pas?

Anyone else would have just accepted his apology and moved on, but did I? No, because I can't see an emotional scab without picking at it to see if it will bleed. "What do you want me to say, Marc? That I'm sorry, too?" I paused, and he shook his head. "Good, because I'm not. You had no right to mark me. I'm not yours. I'm not *anyone's*."

The pain in his eyes bled into anger with frightening speed, and he clutched the top of my dresser for support. "I messed up, and you called me on it. Nearly took my foot off, in fact, so we're even as far as I'm concerned."

I started to tell him we would never be even as long as I was under house arrest while he was free to come and go as he pleased. But for once, his words came faster than mine. He was learning—and only five years too late.

"You can pretend you're one of the guys all you want, but that means I outrank you. We *all* outrank you. And no tomcat would get away with punching me."

Marc was right, though I would never admit that to him. And though he would never say it, he wasn't just angry about being punched. I'd insulted and embarrassed him in front of his subordinate Pride members. Anyone else would pay for that. But I wasn't anyone else.

"What do you want to do, drag me out back and beat the shit out of me?" I stuck my chin out and crossed my arms over my chest, daring him to come teach me a lesson.

He looked tempted for an instant, but then he

exhaled softly and shook his head, leaning against the closed door. "You know what I want, Faythe."

Closing my eyes, I counted to ten silently, hoping that when I looked again, I'd be back in my apartment at UNT, far from Marc, the emotional black hole. I opened my eyes. Nothing had changed. He was still watching me, waiting for my response.

Maybe I should have counted to fifteen.

"No," I said, wincing as his face fell. Scarring him physically was one thing, but I'd decided long ago to keep my claws off his heart, which he typically left undefended.

"It doesn't have to be like it is with your parents," he said. "We could start from scratch. Make up the rules as we go."

My heart thumped painfully, and I hated the fact that he could hear it, that he could discern temptation in the rhythm of my pulse and hesitation in the hitch in my breath. We'd only been together for two years, but they were a very intense two years, and at one point, I thought we'd be together forever. Then reality smacked me in the forehead and I realized that I certainly *could* have Marc for the rest of my life if I wanted. Him, and his children, and nothing else.

But now he was offering me more than he ever had, compromising on things he'd always sworn could never be changed. But it still wasn't enough, and it never would be. If nearly biting off his foot hadn't made that clear, I didn't know what would.

"I don't want to make up the rules," I said, suddenly tired. This was the point where our old argument lost its vitality. The part where I turned him down. Again. "I don't want any rules at all."

Marc swallowed, and I could almost taste his disappointment on the air, bitter as unsweetened tea and painfully tart.

"There are rules for everything," he said. "You follow the rules at school without a second thought, but you won't bend to the few that could make you truly happy."

He'd summed up my problem exactly. I wouldn't bend. Not for him. Not for anyone.

"We are *not* having this argument again," I insisted. Yet we seemed incapable of discussing anything else. No matter how our conversations began, they always came back to what went wrong with us and why I wasn't willing to try again.

He continued as if I hadn't spoken. "You could run things however you want, with no one to tell you what to do. I don't have to be in charge. I don't even *want* to be." He paused and I shook my head slowly. "Come on, Faythe, just think about what I'm saying."

I didn't have to think about it; I already knew what he was saying. According to traditions that were already well in place when the first colonists came to America, it was my responsibility to mate a man qualified to become the new Pride Alpha, someone capable of getting all the toms in line and keeping them there.

Marc was saying that if I married him, I could be in charge—that when Daddy turned the Pride over to him, he would hand it over to me. I would be my own boss, and his too. Sure, I would have the independence I'd always wanted, but it would come at a steep price: I'd be responsible not just for myself but for the entire Pride.

Not counting his enforcers, my father had more than thirty loyal tomcats spread across Texas, Oklahoma, and parts of Kansas, Louisiana, and Arkansas, each living his own life in his own way, just like Michael. They'd sworn loyalty to their Alpha and to the south-central Pride, and they would be available for more active duty should the need arise. But until then, they lived in relative peace under their Alpha's protection, secure in his ability to lead and protect them.

And protect them he did—Daddy was a damn fine Alpha. But if Marc was right, and my father got his way, every tom in the territory would one day depend on *me* to lead him and keep him safe. Unfortunately, unless the job description included a translation of the prologue to *The Canterbury Tales,* I was dreadfully underqualified. And completely unmotivated to remedy the situation.

Marc thought he was offering me a deal I couldn't refuse, but he didn't understand. Giving me the Pride wouldn't be giving me freedom. It would be chaining me hand and foot to a responsibility I didn't want, and probably couldn't handle.

Or maybe he *did* understand. Maybe he wanted me tethered to him and to a life I'd already rejected.

In the foyer, my mother's antique grandfather clock chimed, and I counted along with the tones. Both of them. It was two o'clock in the morning, and I saw no end in sight for what had already been one of the longest evenings of my life.

"You'll have to give them a leader one day, whether you like it or not," Marc said on the tail of the last chime. "You can't lead them by yourself."

"The hell I can't."

Damn it! I stopped, squeezing my eyes shut in frustration. I'd been so ready to argue with him that I hadn't actually listened to what he was saying.

Wood creaked as I leaned against the bedpost and rubbed my forehead, trying to clear away a thick mental fog. "I don't want to lead them—with or without you." Opening my eyes, I stared at him, letting him read the conviction on my face. "I don't know anything about defending a territory, and I'm not interested in learning."

Marc favored me with a patronizing smile, yet another of my many pet peeves. "You know, for a smart girl, you sure can act dumb."

I frowned, unsure how to take the combination compliment/insult. "What is *that* supposed to mean?"

"You already know most of what you need to know. All you need now is some experience."

"I have no idea what you're talking about," I snapped, clenching the footboard behind me. I rubbed my fingertips over the polished grain of the wood, using the sensation to ground myself in reality, in the world where I spoke with poise and confidence, and Marc spouted his usual nonsense with the fervor of a true fanatic. My mind rebelled against the idea that Daddy had been cultivating me as his replacement for years and I'd never even noticed. That wasn't possible. Was it?

"Shut up and think about it for a minute." He pulled out my desk chair and sat, staring at me with an irritatingly smug confidence. "Have you ever taken dance lessons?"

"Is there a point to this question?" I put my

hands on my hips, tapping my foot with exaggerated impatience.

"Just answer me. Have you ever had a dance lesson? Or a shopping spree? What about a manicure?"

My decidedly unmanicured hand clenched around a handful of denim, one finger snagging in my belt loop. "If this is a joke, it isn't funny. You know me better than that." *Unfortunately*.

"So does your father. He never encouraged your interest in anything frivolous, but he made sure you had a say in every decision about the Pride from the time you were twelve years old, even if he didn't actually use your input."

Marc let his gaze slide to the floor, clearly searching his memory for another example to support his harebrained theory. "He taught you how to fight." His eyes snapped back to mine, as fast as a flash of lightning. "Why would he do that? None of the other Alphas teach their daughters to fight. You've never worn a tutu, but how many afternoons have you spent in sweatpants, sparring with the guys?"

I studied my fingernails, bitten to short, jagged edges. "Too many to count." The sparring sessions had started when I was ten and wanted to take karate with a girlfriend from school. Daddy wouldn't let me. He was afraid I'd really hurt someone. My first face-off against Ethan had proven him right, to my simultaneous horror and delight.

"Who taught you to control your breathing when you sprint and how to pounce from the trees?"

My father. There was no need to say it aloud because, like any good prosecutor, Marc never asked a question unless he already knew the answer.

"What about council diplomacy?"

I groaned and glanced at the clock on my stereo. Apparently time really could stand still. "What about it?" I asked, turning back to him reluctantly. My father had dragged me to at least one Pride council meeting a year until I left for school. After listening to two Alphas negotiate interterritory traveling rights for their college-bound sons, staving off boredom in Advanced Grammar class hadn't even been a challenge.

"You know the details of every treaty negotiated by the council since you had your first Shift."

"So what?" I tossed my hands into the air in exasperation. "What's the point?" But understanding came even as I asked, and his next words only confirmed it for that last, stubborn part of my brain.

Marc stood straighter, barely pausing this time when his full weight hit his injured ankle. "Those are the things you'd have to know to lead a Pride. Your father doesn't just want you to marry the next Alpha, Faythe. He wants you to *be* the next Alpha. To succeed him." He searched my eyes, trying to gauge my reaction.

It struck me all at once, as if hearing it spelled out in small words made it real.

I'll be damned. Daddy wasn't teaching me to be independent. After all, how would that benefit the Pride? He was teaching me to be *responsible*.

Still staring at Marc, I sat down on the bed—not because I wanted to, but because my legs refused to support me any longer. Numb with shock, I let my gaze drift down from his face to the Berber carpet. I studied the familiar design, tracing the overlapping diamonds one at a time, as if the answers to every question floating around in my head must lie hidden somewhere within the pattern. But if they did, I couldn't find them.

"All this time, I thought you understood," Marc whispered. I glanced up to find him staring at me with wide eyes, the surprise in his expression bordering on disbelief. "I thought you knew what he wanted and were refusing on general principle. I can't believe you never realized."

"Yeah. Me neither." I barely recognized my own voice. I sounded dazed, or maybe drugged. But then a deeper understanding hit me like a slap in the face. Everything he'd said was true, but it wasn't the *whole* truth. Not by a long shot.

My eyes returned to him slowly. "You have all the same qualifications, Marc." The stunned quality in my voice had been replaced by an unsettling calm, and as I watched, his face flushed. "You know everything I know, and you already have the experience."

Yet without me, he would never be Alpha. And we both knew it.

Marc studied the collection of CDs lined up next to my stereo. "My training as an enforcer was very thorough, and my areas of study often overlapped yours." He was hedging, covering up the truth with a thick layer of bullshit.

"How long?"

He met my eyes, his own carefully blank. "How long what?"

"How long has Daddy been grooming you? How old was I when he chose you for me? Eight? Ten?"

He had the decency to blush. "He didn't choose me, Faythe. You did."

I considered reminding him about a woman's prerogative to change her mind, but didn't think it would help. "I'm not an idiot, Marc. Daddy picked my boyfriend to be his top enforcer, and I'm supposed to believe that's just a coincidence?" I heard my voice rise in pitch but couldn't seem to stop it. "He wasn't training you to defend the boundaries. He was preparing you to take over for him as Alpha."

"No." His denial was earnest and simple. "I've been trained to help and support you. To be your top enforcer, like I am for Greg."

But I couldn't believe it. Of *course*, that's what Marc would say. He'd say anything to get us back together, and so would my father, but he had an ulterior motive.

I'd always known my father wanted me to marry Marc, but I'd assumed he was trying to make me happy, misguided though his efforts were. It had never occurred to me that because I was his daughter, Daddy was stuck with me. But he'd *chosen* Marc. My father wanted Marc as his heir, and the only way to accomplish that was through me.

Marc saw my thoughts on my face and shook his head at me slowly, as if I should have known better. "It wasn't like that. You can't train someone to be an Alpha. You know that."

Of course I knew. You couldn't teach a cat to utilize strengths and instincts he didn't possess. But inherent talents could be molded if they were caught early enough, and that was exactly what Daddy had done with Marc.

An Alpha had to be fast, strong, and very good under pressure. He had to be able to make critical decisions quickly, with little information to go on. And most important, he had to have that indefinable something—akin to charisma, but infinitely stronger— which drew loyal tomcats to him and kept them true under even the worst circumstances.

Marc had all of that and more. He was decisive and evenhanded, but ruthless when he had to be. He'd been born to lead, and Daddy had guaranteed that his talents would never go unnoticed, especially by me. He'd made sure that the man closest to me— the only eligible man in the house during my formative years—was one he approved of and had, in fact, handpicked.

Staring into those gold-flecked eyes, I realized that my father had steered me toward Marc not to make either of us happy, but for the good of the Pride. Because everything Daddy did was for the good of the Pride, even if it wasn't good for any one individual. Including me.

"You know he set us up," I whispered, anger lending a bitter taste to my words. "You know neither of us ever really had a choice."

Marc frowned, never taking his eyes from mine. "I had a choice, Faythe, and I made it years ago. I told you I'd never change my mind, and I haven't. You're the one who left."

He had *that* right. I'd left, and spoiled all of my

father's careful planning. After all, even the best Alpha male was no good without a mate.

Unable to hold his gaze anymore, I let my eyes wander. They fell on a framed photograph on my dresser: Marc and me at my senior prom. My mother must have put it there, because I certainly hadn't. That was the night he'd asked me to marry him. It was also the night I'd run away for the first time, terrified not by anything that went bump in the night but of growing up to be just like my mother.

Centuries ago, according to legend, our ancestors lived like true cats, with the biggest, strongest toms fighting for the right to mate the available tabbies. Unfortunately, there were very few tabbies. As I understood it, the problem lay not with the women but with the men. As with humans, the gender of our offspring is determined by the sex chromosome donated by the father. But in tomcats, the gametes carrying the Y chromosome are more motile than those containing the X chromosome. Simply put, the sperm cells that would produce male fetuses swim much faster than those that would produce females. This results in an average of five toms born for every one tabby.

To say that the competition for mating rights was fierce and bloody would be like saying the universe is pretty big. There are no words to describe an understatement of such magnitude.

Fortunately, in order to maintain the secret of our existence, most Prides were long ago forced to abandon instinct for the civilization of human society. In our modern Prides, each tabby chose her own husband. And almost invariably—whether through instinct, or deep-rooted social conditioning—she chose someone capable of leading her Pride.

However, even with civilized customs in place and a support system of enforcers, the Alpha had to be a strong leader in order to keep the respect and loyalty of his Pride. A weak Alpha wasn't Alpha for long, even in the modern world. By contrast, like my father, Marc would have been a great Alpha.

Marc-in-the-picture looked so young, so happy. He was a triple threat: strong, charismatic and beautiful. Helen's face may have launched a thousand ships, but Marc's had sunk at least as many hearts, one of them mine.

When I'd asked him to choose, he'd picked the Pride over me. He wouldn't get a chance to do it twice.

As he'd pointed out, I'd left, and just because he'd dragged me home didn't mean I would stay there.

I turned from the photograph to the live version, for the first time noticing tiny age lines in the outside corners of his eyes. "I'm sorry, Marc," I said, suddenly compelled to apologize, in spite of refusing to do so earlier. "I'm sorry about the way I left. And I'm sorry about your leg. But nothing's changed, so please don't make this any harder by refusing to believe me."

He stared at me for almost a minute, as if waiting for me to break down and admit I was lying. Then, finally, he nodded, his face hardening with resolve. "Fine." His eyes glazed over with the unreadable expression he wore at work, the one that reflected my own feelings but revealed none of his own. He'd cast me out and put up his defenses.

It was about time.

Marc pushed my chair back up to the desk. "You've always been stubborn, and I don't know why I thought that might have changed."

I smiled, more comfortable on familiar terrain. "I don't know either."

"Let's just try to be civil to each other."

"I've never been less than civil to you, Marc."

He snorted, pulling his hands from his pockets in feigned exasperation. "What do you call slapping away my hand when I tried to comfort you?"

"Bad judgment?" I admitted, flushing with embarrassment.

"Damn right." He didn't smile, but the line of his

jaw softened just a little; it wasn't often I admitted to being wrong. "Let's go eat." He opened the door and gestured for me to go in front of him.

"You go ahead." I picked at the edge of my comforter. "I'm not hungry anymore."

"Yes, you are. Stop pouting. You're hungry, so go eat."

"You gonna make me?" I asked, trying to make it sound like a joke.

"If I have to." Marc limped toward me with a determined edge to his lopsided gait. He reached for my arm again, but this time I dodged his grip. I was learning too.

"Okay, okay. I'm going."

I smiled as I marched down the hall, convinced I was going of my own volition, in spite of the large tomcat walking at my back. Like I said, I find comfort in the familiar.

Eight

I polished off two burgers in spite of the tension. It takes a lot to get in the way of a cat's appetite, and even Jace couldn't screw up a hamburger. When the food was gone, we flipped a quarter to see who had to clean up. Owen lost a coin toss to Jace and got stuck doing the dishes. Ethan lost to Parker and wound up wiping down the cabinets and cleaning the stove. Marc was excused because of his injury.

No one asked me to lift a finger. I think they were afraid of losing a foot to my temper. It was kind of nice to be feared for once. Almost as nice as being respected. From what I can imagine, anyway.

I left the guys in the kitchen and wandered into my father's office. In spite of our strained relationship, I was more comfortable in his sanctuary than anywhere else on the ranch. It was dark and kept just a little cooler than the rest of the house, and always made me think of evenings spent playing Candy Land or reading the Sunday-morning funny pages from my father's lap.

As a little girl, I'd known of no more comfortable place to sleep than on Daddy's love seat, and that was where I found myself, curled up with my knees touching my chest and my head resting against the cool leather cushion. The scent of leather conditioner brought to mind countless times I'd sat there in years past, listening in as my father conducted council business over the phone. I'd dripped jelly from my biscuit onto the cushion once when I was seven, and he hung up on the Alpha of the midplains territory to help me clean it up. I remember being awed by how important he'd made me feel.

But that was years ago, and a lot had changed since then.

I was almost asleep when the soft click of the door latch brought me instantly alert. My eyes flew open, frantically searching the dark room as my heart raced. Still lying on my side, I arched one arm over my head, fumbling on the glass end table for the lamp switch. My fingertips brushed over a notepad and a small, heavy statuette of a cat reared to pounce. But I couldn't find the lamp.

Wood creaked beneath someone's bare feet, but my human eyes couldn't make out more than a man's vague silhouette against the dim moonlight spilling in from the foyer.

Still feeling around on the table, I twisted silently onto my stomach, hoping for a better reach. Instead of the lamp, my fingers swept a path across my father's marble-and-jade chess set, knocking off most of the hand-carved playing pieces.

"Shit," I muttered, still stretching for the lamp as the last figures clattered to the floor. I held my breath, trying to determine from the sound whether any of them had broken. I couldn't tell.

Another footstep whispered across the floor as the silhouette approached. I froze, sniffing the air. I identified his scent even as he spoke.

"Relax, it's just me."

Marc. Of course. "I'm not sure that's any reason to relax," I said, sagging with relief anyway. I let my head fall to rest against the arm of the love seat, my hand dangling above the chessboard. In two long steps, Marc was there, turning on the lamp.

I squinted against the sudden glare. "Why the hell were you sneaking up on me like that?" I demanded, frowning up at him. I pushed myself into a sitting position and glanced at the clock over the door. It was nearly three in the morning, and I couldn't clearly remember why I'd come to Daddy's office instead of just going to bed.

"I wasn't sneaking up."

"The hell you weren't," I snapped, swinging my feet onto the floor. My right foot came down on a chess piece, and I bent to pick it up. It was a jade rook, shaped like a traditional castle turret. And it was whole, thank goodness. I had no idea how to go about replacing one-of-a-kind chess pieces carved especially for my father by an associate in China. The artisan whose handiwork I'd sent crashing to the floor had died a decade before I was born.

"I need to talk to you."

"Not now, Marc." My voice was sleep-gruff and groggy. "I can't deal with you anymore tonight."

"It's not about us."

"Good, because there *is* no us." The rook still nestled in my palm, I slid off the love seat and onto the floor to pick up the other pieces. Marc knelt across from me with the scattering of jade and marble figures between us, like slain soldiers on a miniature battlefield.

"I was supposed to go to Oklahoma tomorrow."

"I know. Jace told me." I set the rook on a corner square of the chessboard, next to a jade knight, a horse frozen in the act of tossing its mane.

"What did he say?"

"Just that you were supposed to check out a report about another stray." I held a white marble bishop up to the light, looking for cracks. "Why?"

"Did he tell you who called it in?"

I shook my head slowly, suspiciously, my focus shifting from the bishop to Marc. *Why should it matter who made the report?*

"Danny Carver."

I froze, my hand clenching around the cold marble, and met his eyes in dread. *Dr. Carver. Shit. That means there's a body.*

Dr. Danny Carver was a tom born into one of the western Prides. When I was a kid, he worked as a part-time enforcer for my father as part of an agreement allowing him to complete his fellowship in forensic pathology at a school in our territory. He'd been a kind of last-minute backup, just for emergencies. After his fellowship, he'd taken a job as an assistant medical examiner in Oklahoma and my father had gladly accepted him as an adopted member of our Pride, just as he would later accept Jace, Vic, Parker, and several other toms now scattered across the territory.

After nearly ten years in the same office, Dr. Carver was promoted to senior assistant to the state medical examiner, which gave us a conveniently placed set of eyes and ears. We'd hoped never to have to use his position, and we'd been lucky for the most part. Until now.

"What happened?" I asked, my hand hovering over the prone form of a white pawn. I desperately didn't want to know the answer, but I'd long since learned that ignorance was not really bliss. Not ever.

"They brought in a partially dismembered body yesterday morning," Marc said.

I groaned, and let my hand fall into my lap, empty. I was supposed to be at school studying the classics, not at home hearing about abductions and dead bodies. This was the worst summer vacation ever.

When I realized he'd stopped talking, I glanced at Marc. He hooked one eyebrow at me like a facial question mark, and I nodded for him to continue as I picked up the pawn and set it on an empty square in the second row.

"The cops can't figure out what happened to her, but their best guess so far is that she was attacked by some psychopath and left to die, then actually killed by a large wildcat. But it won't take them long to measure the claw and bite marks and realize there shouldn't be cats that big roaming wild in suburban Oklahoma. Or anywhere else in the U.S."

My eyes were glued to his face as I waited for the rest, but nothing more came. "What happened to her?" I asked again, my hands tangled together in my lap. He was avoiding the details of the crime, probably hoping to spare me from the specifics. Far from finding that considerate, I found it annoying. If I needed to know, I'd rather get it all over with at once.

"There were finger-size bruises on her thighs and more mixed in with claw marks on her neck. Danny thinks he raped her, then Shifted to tear out her throat." Marc glanced away, but I caught a glimpse of raw fear and outrage in his eyes before he could lower them. "Then he ripped into her stomach."

My breath caught in my throat as I choked on my own horror. A jade pawn slipped from my fingers. Marc's hand shot out, almost too fast to see, and the pawn fell into his palm before it could hit the floor.

That poor girl, I thought, watching as he carefully placed the piece on the chessboard in line with its comrades. I cleared my throat, drawing his eyes back to mine. "How old?"

"Faythe, you don't need—"

One sharp glance stopped him cold, and I was glad to see that at least one of my old tricks still worked. "How old, Marc?"

"Nineteen."

My eyes squeezed shut as I gave in to my need to wallow in denial. That kind of thing didn't happen in our territory. In South America, yes. But not in the States, and definitely not in the south-central territory. At least, not since it happened to Marc's mother.

I ran my thumb over the cold, smooth chess piece in my hand, noticing absently that it was the marble queen, stately in her white robes and pointed crown. She lay on my palm, the features only hinted at on her polished stone face. But the expression I saw on her was one I'd seen in a photograph once, before Marc snatched it from my hand to shove it back beneath the socks in his top drawer.

Sonora Ramos. He never spoke about her, so I knew nothing but her name, and I only knew that because I'd overheard a private conversation between my parents.

The territorial council recognized only three capital crimes. The first was murder, the second was infection of a human, and the third was disclosure to a human. The wildcat who'd invaded our territory fifteen years earlier was guilty of all three.

We never discovered his real name, but there was a note in his back pocket made out to "Jose," so that's what we called him, when we called him anything at all. Jose snuck into our territory after being run out of a Pride somewhere in Central America for crimes I couldn't stand to even think about. From what we could tell, his presence in southern Texas was reported the very day he arrived. It was an incredible stroke of luck. Pure chance. And if it hadn't happened, Marc would have died that night.

As soon as he got the call, Daddy dispatched his three best enforcers with instructions to find the intruder and escort him back to the border with as much force as necessary. Unfortunately, a simple escort proved to be much too little and far too late.

The enforcers found Jose, in cat form, in the home of a widowed Mexican immigrant. He killed two of them while the third Shifted. The remaining enforcer took out the now-wounded Jose with little more than a scratch to show for his trouble, but it was too late for Sonora Ramos.

Jose had broken into Marc's house and attacked his mother while she slept. The details of the assault were eerily similar to what happened to the girl in Oklahoma, including the fact that Jose used his victim to satisfy more than one kind of appetite. He'd had his muzzle buried in what remained of her stomach when Daddy's enforcers found him.

Marc woke up at some point during the attack and tried to defend his mother, but Jose swatted him away with a single paw full of unsheathed claws. With Jose dead, the enforcer found Marc between his mother's bed and the wall, bleeding and unconscious. The claw marks on his chest were already swollen at the edges and festering—sure signs that he would soon be one of us.

He was only fourteen years old.

Marc waved a chess piece in front of my nose, drawing my attention back to him. "Are you okay?"

I tried to smile, but my effort felt more like a grimace. "Yeah. You?"

He nodded. "I'm fine." But I found that hard to believe. How could he be fine, faced with such a graphic reminder of what had happened to his mother?

I studied Marc's face, conscious suddenly of how much he'd changed since the day we met, the morning after his mother died. He'd looked so scared, lying alone in the guest bed, a wisp of a boy with dark curly hair and deep dimples. He'd arrived at the Lazy S with nothing but a threadbare suitcase and a sad scowl. But he was a fighter. Even as an eight-year-old, I'd recognized the will to survive in the quiet defiance in his eyes and hard line of his mouth, both of which said that he'd seen the worst the world had to offer, and that nothing I put him through could possibly compare.

He was right.

Sitting on the floor across from him fifteen years later, I thought back to his first year with us. His adjustment period was long and hard, and his first Shift sent his body into severe shock. He wouldn't let anyone near him at first, and didn't say a single word until he'd been on the ranch for nearly two months. But in the end, he not only survived, he thrived, against the predictions of the entire council.

Except for having watched his mother die, Marc was probably the most fortunate stray in history. Because he was so young when he was scratched, and because his attack happened on our territory, my parents felt responsible for him. They took him in and nursed him through the initial sickness—the scratch-fever—when most other Alphas would have let him die, not out of callous disregard, but out of practicality. Survival of the fittest. In the wild, when a mother dies, her cubs die too. But my parents couldn't let Marc die. They saw in him the opportunity to try to make up for the solitude and tragedy that define the lives of most strays.

The vast majority of strays are created by other strays, then abandoned before the attacker knows his victim will not only survive but become a werecat. These attackers are perpetuating a cycle that began when they were abandoned in the same fashion, before they had a chance to learn about the werecat way of life.

Many werecat victims don't survive their initial

attack, and others die soon afterward. And while some strays do live and learn to survive on their own, many of them never learn to hide their existence from humans or to control their feline impulses, which makes it very important for us to get to them before their actions expose us all to humanity. Unfortunately, by the time we find them, few strays are happy to see us. They blame us for the destruction of their lives, and they have no interest in being "ruled" by an Alpha they don't know from Adam. It doesn't help that instincts they can't possibly understand yet tell them to be wary of and hostile toward strange cats.

As recently as a century ago, an enforcer's job consisted mainly of defending territorial borders, not from humans, who don't yet know we exist, but from other Prides intent on expanding their own boundaries. But recent history has seen an important shift. Just as the various Prides learned to get along—for the most part—in the interest of secrecy, the population of strays exploded. Pride enforcers are now mostly used to deal with these new members of our society.

My father's men track newly infected werecats as they come to our attention and administer a crash-course on werecat history, biology and law. They also monitor and control those strays who become violent and volatile. But an ever-increasing amount of their time is spent trying to keep strays out of our territory, cleaning up after them, and dealing out justice as necessary for those who refuse to follow the rules.

Even those few strays we manage to form a cordial relationship with typically have no interest in joining a Pride. Which is just as well, because most council members have no interest in letting them in. For them, it's an issue of class. Strays are considered second-class citizens. In fact, my father dealt with a lot of criticism for taking Marc in, but he never once faltered in his decision, even though the beginning was really hard on all of us, particularly Marc.

Watching him, I remembered how confused he'd been and how much he'd missed his mother. *Why would Daddy send him to investigate a case like that?* I thought, furious with my father all over again.

"I wanted to go," Marc said.

"Stop reading my mind," I snapped, pulling my feet out from under me to sit cross-legged at the edge of the area rug.

"I'm reading your expression." His lips curled up into a tight, smug smile. "It's not my fault you can't keep every fleeting thought from showing on your face." He made it sound so easy, so logical, but it was just another reminder that he knew me better than anyone else in the world. Whether I liked it or not.

Marc plucked the queen from my palm, returning her to her rightful place at her husband's side. Most of the chess pieces had landed on the rug, which kept them from breaking. But not the queen. She'd taken the full impact of her fall on the hardwood, yet remained stubbornly whole and unscathed. She was one tough bitch. My kind of gal.

I glanced at her and thought I saw the tiniest hint of a smirk among the vague features of her face. The queen was my favorite chess piece. Unlike the women I knew in real life, she was powerful. Her job was to defend her husband at all costs, because while he was weak and practically defenseless—only allowed to move one square at a time—she was the strongest player on the board, hindered by no restrictions at all.

If real life were a game of chess, I'd be calling the shots, dragging Marc's helpless ass home for his own protection.

Marc frowned at me, as if to let me know he'd read that thought on my face too. I cleared my throat and leaned back against the love seat, determined to bring the discussion back on track. "I assume Dr. Carver could smell the bastard on her body?"

"Yeah."

When he volunteered no more information, I asked the obvious question. "Well? Did he recognize the scent?"

Marc shook his head, and I wasn't really surprised. If they'd identified the killer, he would already have told me. "But Danny said it was definitely a stray. We've had two other reports of a stray from Oklahoma in the last week and a half. My guess is that they were all the same cat."

I frowned. Both wildcats and strays were forbidden to enter our territory without permission for a very good reason: they were usually unpredictable, uncontrollable and often violent. There were no exceptions to that rule, even for Ryan, in self-imposed exile.

"Couldn't Dr. Carver be wrong?" I asked. "Couldn't it have been one of Daddy's cats?" As horrifying as I found the idea of there being a murderer among us, it's always easier to fight the evil you know than the one you don't.

Marc shook his head. "Danny knows all the other south-central Pride cats, if not by name, then by scent. He said this one had a foreign smell to him. Central, or maybe South American." His eyes held mine captive, waiting for his meaning to sink in.

My heart leapt from fear bordering on terror, as I thought of the stray on campus. *He's a jungle cat. And he's collecting tabbies, but killing humans.*

South American cats were an entirely different kind of animal. They formed no councils, acknowledged no political borders, and suffered no negotiations. With the Amazon rain forest at their disposal, the Prides in most of the southern hemisphere indulged their feline instinct at the expense of their humanity, meaning they lived more like actual jungle cats than like people, as if over the past few hundred years, the world had moved on without them. Their territorial boundaries were in a constant state of flux, swelling and shrinking with the slaughter of each Alpha and the rise of his successor.

The only rules jungle cats submitted to were the laws of nature, namely that you claim only that which you can defend. They fought to the death on a regular basis for the two things that mattered most to them: the right to control a territory and the right to sire another generation of savage monsters. It was a violent and chaotic existence, defined by a lack of stability and a short life expectancy.

Jungle cats were my secret fear, my version of the bogeyman in the closet. But unlike the bogeyman, they were very, very real.

"South American?" I breathed, running my fingers nervously along the fringe at the edge of the area rug. "Really?"

"He's probably wrong." Marc stared transfixed at

the jade king where it sat on the far row of the chess-board. "It's probably the same thing as always, some new stray accidentally crossed a boundary line and wound up on our land. But this time he lost control. It happens sometimes. You know that."

I nodded. I did know that. But I also recognized Marc's quickly reversed theory for the bullshit it was. Dr. Carver knew the difference in scent—likely genetic in origin—between an American-born cat and a jungle cat. And new strays were known for losing control of their feline impulses, not their human behavior. They stalk and hunt as cats, killing only because they're hungry and have temporarily lost the control needed to Shift back and go grocery shopping. They don't attack on two legs, then Shift into cat form to rip their victims apart.

The girl in Oklahoma was killed by a human monster, who just happened to have canines and claws at his disposal. It was the work of a jungle cat, not an American stray. And Marc knew it as well as I did.

"I'm sure it's nothing, Faythe."

"Then why tell me?" I knew him way too well to fall for that.

He didn't answer; he just stared at me with those deep brown eyes, shot through with specks of gold that were only visible up close. And in the moonlight.

"You think it's related to Sara, don't you?"

He shrugged. "I don't know. It's possible, but no more possible than your theory that she ran away. I'm probably just being paranoid."

"That's what Daddy pays you for."

He frowned, staring at his own hands. "Well, lately I don't feel like he's getting his money's worth."

"You're a great enforcer, Marc." I glanced away, because I couldn't stand to look at him as I said the next part, even though it was true. Precisely *because* it was true. "You're great at everything."

"Not quite everything," he said.

I breathed deeply, in and out, wishing once again that I'd slept through the entire conversation. When I looked up, Marc was gone.

Nine

I woke up in my own room for the first time in more than two years, groaning as highlights from the day before played in my mind like a silent film in fast-forward. Burying my head beneath my pillows, I willed the morning away, but it refused to go. Instead, it greeted my ill-humored grunt with bright, irritatingly cheerful sunlight and the incessant trilling of a bird from the branches of the stunted blackjack oak outside my window.

"I haven't had breakfast yet, you know," I grumbled in the general direction of the racket. *You'd think birds would know better than to irritate a sleep-deprived cat.*

Resigned to rising at last, I sat up in bed. My eyes roamed the walls, settling on the mirror over my dresser, where several photographs were wedged between the glass and the oak frame, climbing the edge of the reflective surface like a vine of memories. I glanced over them, experiencing my life as a series of moments frozen in time, neat and orderly in their full-color, glossy splendor.

At the bottom of the mirror was a snapshot taken at the ranch the summer I was seventeen, less than two months before I left for college. It showed a group of eight girls, ranging in age from twelve to twenty, beaming bright white smiles from the front gate. That photo represented the future of the American Prides, because it showed every unmarried female cat of childbearing age in the entire country.

Ours was one of ten territories in the continental United States, each protected and governed by a single Pride Alpha. Each Alpha was the head of that territory's core family group, consisting of the Alpha's mate and their children—typically several boys and the long-awaited daughter—and a group of loyal enforcers. In addition, each Pride had between twenty and forty other loyal tomcats, mostly the Alphas' uncles, brothers, sons, and nephews, who led their own lives spread out across the territory. Unfortunately, in contrast to the surplus of tomcats, no Alpha in recent history had sired more than a single tabby to give birth to the next generation. And for that reason, we were very, very valuable.

Our ranks had shrunk and swelled since the photo was taken, as older girls got married and younger ones entered puberty. There were eight of us again, spread out over all ten territories, but now I was the oldest—by several years. In the picture, I stood in the middle of the front row, my left arm around my cousin Abby and my right around…

Sara.

My stomach growled, as usual, announcing its demands first thing in the morning, and I wondered if Sara was having breakfast, wherever she was.

With a stretch and a sigh, I threw back the covers and swung my legs over the edge of the bed into a patch of sunlight pouring through the window. *Wait, that's wrong.* Sunlight shouldn't hit that part of the room until midmorning.

I glanced at the alarm clock. Ten twenty-four. That couldn't be right. The last time my mother let me sleep through breakfast was the day my grandmother died. My mother hadn't changed a bit in the last few years, so something had to be wrong.

A search of my suitcase produced more books than clothing, but I found a pale blue stretchy tee that would work. It read It's not the length of the word;

It's how well you use it. Daddy would love it. I pulled my nightshirt over my head and tossed it onto the bed, then donned the shirt and stepped into the jeans I'd worn the day before.

I was tugging a brush through my nest of black tangles when the first polyphonic notes of "Criminal" rang out faintly from somewhere behind me. My phone. *Where did I leave my phone?* I'd been home for roughly twelve hours and had already forgotten I had a life outside of the Lazy S. That was one of the dangers of coming home. Home traps you. It swallows you whole, like a sandpit of nostalgia, sucking at you until you can neither move nor think, and you choke on your own panic.

Or maybe I was just being paranoid.

I tossed the contents from my suitcase, searching for the source of the music. The bottom layer of canvas stared back at me, empty, but still the music played. Grunting in frustration, I threw the bag across the room. Its plastic-reinforced corner left a dent in the wall. Great. But Fiona Apple's sultry, alto crooning grew louder. There it was, half an inch of shiny chrome sticking out from under my bed skirt. I lunged for it, glad I'd disabled my voicemail.

Still panting from my frantic search, I pushed the Talk button, cutting Fiona off in midsyllable. "Hello?"

"So I woke up this morning thinking something was wrong, and it took me a moment to figure out what it was."

Huh? I held the phone out at arm's length, staring at it as if it were to blame for the speaker's lack of sense.

The caller spoke again. "This is the part where you ask me what was wrong."

Ah. It was Andrew. I should have known.

"Faythe? Are you there?"

I put the phone back up to my ear, but a long moment passed before I could answer. Hearing his voice in my father's house was disorienting and vaguely uncomfortable, as if two very separate halves of my life had collided, crushing me between them and making it nearly impossible for me to think, much less speak.

"Faythe?" Concern raised Andrew's pitch, exaggerating the stuffy sound of his voice.

I swallowed, wincing at how dry my throat felt. "Yeah, I'm here."

"You okay?"

"Yeah. I just woke up." I sank onto the bed facing the mirror, where the photographs mocked me from various points in my own past.

"Me, too. That's what was wrong."

"Huh?" My eyes settled on the photo of me and

Rachel Vincent

Marc at my senior prom. Try as I might to drag my gaze from it, Marc's eyes kept pulling mine back. They seemed to follow me from the photo, glinting in amusement at my futile attempt to concentrate on what Andrew was saying. Or maybe they were just reflecting the clear Christmas lights used as prom decorations.

"I slept through my alarm and missed my first class."

"Oh, no." I turned my back on the photo, pleased at my victory over Marc's picture-self.

"Yeah, but it doesn't matter. I don't feel like learning anything today anyway. My cold's worse, and I think I have a bit of a fever. Anyway, I'd much rather talk to you than go to class."

"Thanks."

Thanks? Okay, I'm a moron. My brain just doesn't kick in until I get some caffeine, but even after a gallon of coffee, I wouldn't have known what to say to Andrew. Talking to him felt awkward, like we'd been out of touch for months instead of for a single day.

"What did your dad say about me coming to visit between summer terms?"

"Oh. Uh… I haven't had a chance to talk to him yet. But I will." I punched my fancy pillow, glad he wasn't there to see the dread on my face. I did *not* look forward to having that conversation with my father. Or any other conversation, come to think of it.

"Good. I'll be there in three weeks."

Yeah. Great. He'd never make it out alive.

I was only vaguely aware that Andrew was still talking, until the lengthening silence told me it was my turn to speak. *Crap.* "You faded out for a second there." I rolled my eyes at my own lie. "What did you say?"

"I asked you how many you have."

"How many what?" Over the phone, I heard his sheets rustle as he moved. *He really must feel bad if he's still in bed,* I thought.

"How many brothers."

"Oh. Uh, four." I saw no reason to explain about Ryan being MIA for most of the last decade. Or about anything else, for that matter.

"Four. Wow. Your parents must have really been trying for a girl, huh?"

You have no idea.

"Faythe, is anything wrong?"

"Yes. No." I frowned in confusion, one hand hovering over my face to shield my eyes from the sunlight. If only it could shield me from my life too… "Everything's fine. I'm just still half-asleep."

I sat up, glancing at my bedroom door as footsteps hurried past in the hall. "Hey, I was just about to get something to eat. Can I call you back later?" I sniffed the air, trying to identify the owner of the footsteps. No luck. I was too slow.

"Sure," Andrew said. "I was about to head out for breakfast anyway. I'm starving."

"Okay, go eat. And I hope you feel better," I said, too preoccupied with the footsteps in the hall to inject any sincerity into my reply.

"I already do, after hearing your voice." His tone was as warm and pleasant as spring sunshine, yet for my life, I didn't know how to respond. Maybe if he'd sounded more like moonlight… But Andrew had nothing in common with the night. Nothing at all. That had always worked in his favor before.

"That's sweet," I said finally, cringing at my own dim-witted response. "I'll call you later."

"Sure." Was that a tremor of doubt in his voice? Andrew didn't deserve doubt. Not because of me.

I knew I should say something reassuring, or at least friendly, but again words failed me. All except for one. "Bye."

"Bye."

Faythe, you are such an idiot! I thought as I pressed the End button. Andrew was everything I wanted, in the only place I wanted to be, but I couldn't think of a thing to say to him.

It would be better when I went back to school. It

had to be better, because it certainly couldn't get any worse.

Disgusted, I threw the phone at my headboard. It bounced off a pillow and onto the floor. As I bent to pick it up, another set of footsteps rushed past my door. I froze, sniffing the air, and caught just enough scent for identification. *Parker*. His footsteps stopped farther down the hall, replaced by the creak of hinges. Tense whispers rose over the creaking. I heard a faint click, and the whispering stopped abruptly.

Only one room in the house blocked noise that well. Daddy had called a meeting in his office. Without me.

That's just freaking great. Irritation flowed through me like the tide, cold and numbing. *He drags me back here, then lets me sleep through all the excitement.* I tossed the phone onto my dresser, where it slid across the smooth surface and off the far end. I was in the hall before it hit the carpet.

With my ear pressed to the office door, I strained to hear something. Anything. I got nothing but unintelligible mumbles. Stupid solid-oak door! I tried the knob gently, but it wouldn't turn. They'd locked it. Nice try, but it would take more than a thumbpress lock to keep me out.

I gripped the doorknob with one hand over the

other and jerked it to the right, hard. The lock snapped, and when I let go, the door swung open to reveal seven surprised faces, gathered around a picnic blanket scattered with the remains of their breakfast: two slices of French toast, a small pile of bacon, and two half-full pots of coffee.

"Is this an exclusive party?" I asked, coming in uninvited. Everything looked different this morning than it had the night before. The room was brighter, shadows cast from the brilliant overhead fixture, rather than from a dim floor lamp. Light shined in the beveled edges of the matching glass end tables and sparkled on awards in the curio cabinet behind my father's desk. Yet in stark contrast to the bright, cheery morning, every face in the room was shadowed, seemingly from within.

"We thought we'd let you sleep in, dear," my mother said from the leather love seat, where she sat next to Owen. Her eyes and nose were red from crying. Something was definitely wrong.

"Do we always have breakfast on the office floor now?" I arched an eyebrow at my father, but he just glanced at my shirt and raised one back at me.

"Remind me not to subsidize any more of your wardrobe," he said, waving a hand generously at the remaining food. I plopped down on the floor between Ethan and Jace, grabbing a paper plate from the stack. They must have come from the guest-house, because my mother never bought paper plates. She said they were emblematic of society's trend toward all things disposable, along with plastic razors, foam coffee cups and shotgun weddings.

Jace handed me a mug, and I washed down a mouthful of bacon with a gulp of tepid coffee. It was black. Yuck. "So, what's with the picnic?" I glanced at my mother, but she wouldn't meet my eyes. Neither would Owen or Parker. I lowered the coffee slowly and looked at Marc, but he only stared at the syrup-sticky crumbs on his plate. Definitely not a good sign.

"Oh, come on. I'm going to find out eventually, so you might as well get it over with the easy way."

Jace squirmed and I pinned him with my eyes. A good hunter can always spot the weakest animal in the herd. Regarding classified information, Jace fit the bill. "Abby's missing," he said, glancing at me in sympathy for an instant before staring back down into his mug.

I made myself swallow my mouthful of coffee, and then clamped my jaws shut to keep from throwing it back up. If it had just been Jace, I could have safely assumed he was playing a tasteless joke, but my parents would never go along with something like that.

Neither would Marc, no matter what I'd tried to bite off.

"Abby?" I prayed silently that I'd heard them wrong. "She's just a kid."

"Seventeen last month," my mother said. Her glass shook in her hand, sloshing coffee onto her unironed slacks. Owen took it from her gently, and she never even glanced at him.

"Since when?" I asked, my breakfast forgotten.

"She went to a party last night and never came back. The host said she left around ten o'clock, and no one's seen her since."

"Ten o'clock last night?" I glanced from my mother to my father, trying to remember what I'd been doing at that exact moment. Probably faking sleep on the drive home. "You've known since last night and didn't tell me?"

"No." My father cracked one thick knuckle. "We got the call five hours ago. Her parents wanted to make sure she was really gone before involving anyone else." Abby and her family lived in North Carolina, which was an hour ahead of us. According to my quick mental math, she could have been missing for as many as thirteen hours.

My hand clenched around my mug, and I lowered it carefully to the blanket, knowing that if I didn't put the cup down, I'd crush it. The edges of my vision blurred as the first tears threatened. I blinked them away, impatient for more information. "Why didn't you wake me up?"

"We thought you might take the news badly, dear." My mother watched me through eyes glazed with shock. Maybe they shouldn't have told her either.

Abby Wade was my mother's niece, her brother Rick's only daughter, and in a community with very few women, we were all pretty close, in spite of the distance between us. I'd always thought of Abby as my little sister, and my mother indulged her as she'd never indulged me, because she could send Abby home at the first sign of trouble. Not that Abby ever caused trouble. She was a good girl, liked by literally everyone who knew her. She was the only family member I'd kept in contact with from UNT. In fact, I'd spoken to her less than a week earlier.

And now she was missing.

"Who's doing this?" I demanded of the room in general, knowing no one had an answer.

"We're going to find out," Daddy said. I looked at him with simultaneous hope and doubt. I was way too old to believe my father could make everything okay, but I still desperately wanted it to be true.

"They asked for help?"

Daddy nodded, brushing the tip of his chin with

the knuckles of his clasped hands. "I'm convening the council. They'll need a description to start with." He watched me expectantly.

I nodded. "Shorter than Marc but taller than me. Small-to-medium build. Black eyes and dark curly hair. Foreign scent—probably a jungle cat." I glanced at Marc, thinking about what he'd told me the night before.

"Anything else?" my father asked.

"Yeah." I met his gaze, unblinking. "A broken nose."

The smallest hint of a smile teased the corner of his mouth, like a twitch. Then it was gone, but it had been enough. He was proud. I could see it. "Thank you, Faythe. I'll pass the description on."

"The Di Carlos' plane lands at one, and they need a ride from the airport," Michael said from behind me.

I whirled around, and Ethan sputtered as my hair smacked him in the face. I ignored him, surprised to realize I'd slept through Michael's arrival. I should have known that teaching myself to sleep through the incessant noise in an apartment building would come back to bite me on the ass.

"How many are coming?" Daddy asked.

"Four." Michael smoothed the front of another in his collection of nearly identical suit jackets. "Bert and Donna, and two of the boys. Vic's staying behind to help search for Sara."

"I'll pick them up in the van," Parker offered, and Daddy nodded.

"What about Abby's parents?" Mom asked.

"Uncle Rick and Aunt Melissa are coming to meet with the council, but the guys are staying behind, in case they find her."

"Fine. Thanks, Michael." Daddy stood to excuse himself, handing his mug to my mother. "I'll make the rest of the calls personally. We'll have a houseful by this evening, so I don't need to remind you all to be on your best behavior." He was looking at me. Why was he only looking at me?

"What?" I couldn't be in trouble already. I'd just gotten up.

"We'll talk about Marc's leg later."

Oh. That.

"It was an accident, Greg," Marc said without so much as a glance in my direction.

Daddy eyed Marc with one hand resting on the back of his chair, his gaze unwavering. "She *accidentally* bit your leg through to the bone?"

Marc blinked but remained silent.

"That's what I thought." Daddy turned on his heel and headed for the hall, apparently planning to make the calls from the phone in his room. He was gruff at times, but almost never truly rude, which meant that he was either really mad at me for biting Marc, or really worried about Sara and Abby. I wasn't sure which I preferred.

With my father gone, my mother fluttered uselessly around the office, clearing away food and generally getting on everyone's nerves. She couldn't help it. She was visibly upset, and the only way she knew of to deal with strong emotions was to clean everything in sight.

I hadn't inherited that particular problem. I dealt with my emotions the old-fashioned way: by tearing things apart. With my teeth and claws.

What the hell, I thought, glancing at the cold remains of their indoor picnic. *I'm hungry anyway.* I pulled my top off and dropped it on the floor. The guys stared at me as if I'd lost my mind. Okay, so I'd never stripped in my father's office before, but I'd have to be naked to Shift, unless I wanted to spend most of my time and money restocking my ruined wardrobe. Which I did not. Did it really matter whether I took my clothes off inside or on the lawn?

My mother turned toward me with a coffeepot in each hand, her jaw dangling somewhere near her collarbone. You'd think she'd never seen me naked, when I knew for a fact I'd been born that way, and she'd seen me sans clothing on countless occasions since. We'd all seen each other naked; there was no practical way to avoid it, even if we'd wanted to.

Nudity was too routine in a houseful of werecats to be considered sexual. It took a certain context— a particular kind of intimacy and erotic intent—for bare skin to cross the line between ordinary and arousing. In fact, tight or skimpy clothes were more exciting to most toms because they were intentionally sexy, whereas nudity was simply natural.

But my mother lived in some kind of 1950s fantasy world that even most human households would consider prudish. "Katherine Faythe Sanders, put your shirt back on this instant!"

Uh-oh. All three names.

"Really, Faythe, was that necessary?" Michael asked, but the glimmer of amusement in his eyes was unmistakable. I smiled. Like Daddy, he probably genuinely disapproved of most of my wardrobe, but he had no problem with nudity, so long as it served a valid purpose. Only my mother did.

I glanced around the room, taking in the guys all at once. "I'm going hunting, if anyone wants to join me."

"I'm in." Ethan's shirt hit the floor a second before Jace's. Parker laughed out loud.

"Boys, please don't encourage her," my mother

groaned, setting down one coffeepot to prop her hand on her hip. "She's wild enough on her own."

"They're just blowing off steam, Mom," Michael said. He hadn't taken anything off, but he hadn't stopped us either. Good for him.

Still fully dressed, Owen stepped over the growing pile of discarded clothes. "I'd love to go," he drawled, "but I'm coverin' for Marc in Oklahoma."

I crossed my arms beneath my bra, noticing his ensemble for the first time. He wore a T-shirt, jeans, and sneakers. No boots, or even a cowboy hat. He was going incognito, as a normal, non-western human.

"I'll be back tomorrow, and I'll hunt with you then, okay?"

"Promise?" I asked.

"I promise."

"Be careful." I hugged him, squeezing as hard as he'd squeezed me the night before.

He gave me a goofy grin. "What was that for?"

Sneaking a sideways look at my mother, I tugged him toward the hall. "I'll walk you out," I said, pulling the office door shut behind us. We ambled slowly toward the front door. "Marc thinks the stray is involved with Sara, and now maybe with Abby."

"I only said it was a possibility," Marc corrected me.

I jumped, flushing from embarrassment. He was right behind me, but I hadn't heard him slip out of the office. I was definitely going to have to work on my listening skills.

"I'll be careful," Owen said, a grin teasing the corners of his mouth. "I have to go now, or I'll miss my flight. But I'll see y'all tomorrow."

Behind me, the office door flew open, and nude men poured out into the hallway, my mother right behind them. Choruses of "Bye, Owen" echoed across the foyer, and Mom took time out from her tirade on youthful anarchy to give him a kiss. She gave me a scowl.

I smiled at her, and unbuttoned my pants.

Ten

Owen's car pulled out of the driveway as I led the parade of tomcats out the back door and toward the woods. Because of our various daytime obligations, we rarely got the chance to hunt during the day. Under other circumstances, ours might have been a jubilant excursion, but we didn't race this time, in spite of the unseasonably cool breeze and the sunlight glinting off our skin. Morning dew lingered in the shaded sections of the yard, but not one eager foot ran to trail through it. We weren't in a playful mood, and there were no jokes or good-natured boasts about speed and agility, or even the comparative length of anyone's canines. Michael was right, we were blowing off steam.

The guys emanated anger, like lightbulbs lit up

with rage. They were worried about Sara and Abby, but they were also nursing injured pride. As enforcers, they were insulted that someone feared the council little enough to invade our territory and steal one full quarter of our eligible women. They were eager for the chance to avenge the insult and rip the offender to shreds in the process. And until then, they had some destructive energy to burn.

I wasn't insulted. I didn't really care whether or not anyone feared me, because no one ever had. But I was scared, really frightened, for the first time in my life. I was afraid for Sara and Abby because no matter how hard my mother tried to delude herself, I knew the chances of us finding them uninjured were slim. They were strong, and I couldn't imagine them cooperating with their captors if they thought there was any chance of escape.

In spite of Marc's transparent assurances, I couldn't believe the human murders and the tabby disappearances were unrelated. I didn't believe in coincidence, but I certainly believed in justice. And in revenge. If either girl was hurt, the council wouldn't stop hunting the responsible party until they found him and took him out, not with a vet's peaceful never-wake-up serum, but in a manner so violent, painful and drawn-out that the mere rumor of what happened would be enough to prevent such occurrences in the future.

The thought of someone hurting Sara and Abby fueled my Shift, propelling it at a rate I'd never before experienced and dulling the pain somewhat because my brain was too busy to acknowledge discomfort. I came into my fur bursting with a furious energy and the uncontrollable urge to maul something. Or someone.

Bloodlust. My tail twitched nervously at the thought, trying to deny what my brain knew for a fact. I recognized the symptoms, though I'd never personally experienced them. I had the urge, a true physical need, as well as a psychological one, to sink my teeth into skin and shred flesh with my claws. I could already taste the blood, like a flashback for my taste buds. Only it wasn't just that I *remembered* what blood tasted like, but that I could actually feel it in my mouth, a shadow-taste, like a blood phantom haunting my tongue.

Standing with my front paws nestled in a tangled patch of ivy, I roared, which I hardly ever do. Roaring is really more of a tomcat kind of thing, but at that moment I could find no more appropriate expression for my outrage. And it felt damn good to be heard for once.

I glanced around, seeing the world in the dull greens and blues of my feline vision. Scattered throughout the undergrowth around me, the guys were still in various stages of Shifting, unable to respond to my roar. I left them behind without a second thought. My anger was different than theirs and would have to be spent differently. And alone.

When I'd gone a few hundred feet, I heard Marc's roar and knew it was meant for me. He was normally the fastest of the tomcats, but with his limp, he would never catch me, and with my head start, neither would any of the others. Thinking of Sara and Abby, I ran as far and as fast as I could, not stopping even when my lungs heaved and my pulse raced.

With my thoughts on my missing friend and cousin, and on their unidentified kidnapper, the forest took on an entirely new feel. Every whisper of wind through the leaves sounded like someone hissing, "Sara." Every bird trilling above brought to mind Abby's clear, ringing soprano. Each shadow held the threat of the unknown, where before they'd held only curiosity and adventure.

The sounds of the woods mocked my fright, turning my lifelong refuge into a waking nightmare in which every dry crack was a stranger's footstep, and each new turn took me farther from everything safe and familiar. Dread and fear were ruining my run. I was handing over control of my emotions to some sadistic stray I'd already kicked around once, and that simply wouldn't do. I had to get ahold of my-self. Fast.

Bloodlust seemed to be the solution to distracting me from my fear.

Exhausted, I stopped to rest and to drink from the creek. Shiny fish scales flashed beneath the surface of the water, and though I was hungry, I barely glanced at them. I was aiming for something bigger, something I could chase, then rip apart before devouring.

I heard just the thing.

To the south, only a few yards away, a single twig cracked, accompanied by the rustle of leaves signaling the approach of something large. I froze, listening, my nose wiggling almost imperceptibly as I sniffed the air.

Deer. Two of them. A male and a female, based on their scents. I was upwind for the moment, and they obviously hadn't smelled me yet. A dense tangle of briars separated me from the deer, blocking us each from the other's sight. They had no idea they were in danger. Perfect.

Adrenaline surged through me with the power of a hundred cups of coffee. The chemical jolt of caffeine couldn't compare to the natural high of the hunt. I looked up and around, searching for exactly the right branch. I found one with little trouble. It was low enough to jump onto without climbing, thick enough to hold my weight for at least half of its

length, and close enough to others that I could effectively walk on a path of tree limbs until I was ready
to pounce. Assuming the deer didn't hear me and
bolt.

I hunkered on my back legs, wiggling my hindquarters to find just the right position. My eyes
focused on the low branch. I jumped. My front paws
hit first, in silence, followed an instant later by my
hind paws. I fought panic as my left hind leg slipped
from the branch, threatening to upset my balance. I
clenched the branch with my hind claws, freezing in
place until I regained my equilibrium. Huffing in
relief, I repositioned myself slightly for a better view.
From my new height, I could see the deer in a small
clearing ahead: a light brown doe and her fawn, his
back sprinkled with white spots.

For a moment, I felt a twinge of guilt over my
intent to kill Bambi's mother, but such was the way
of life in the forest, and it didn't bother me for long.
Especially when I saw the fawn tugging on a low
leaf. If he was old enough to eat greens, he was at
least partially weaned and probably old enough to
survive on his own.

Heart pounding, I tensed, getting my balance just
right. I jumped up onto the next branch, pausing
briefly to steady myself before taking the next leap.
I approached my prey from behind as the wind

carried her scent to me, like a preview of coming attractions. Ahead, the doe leaned down to nibble at a blade of grass, blissfully unaware of what the next few minutes would bring. Her ignorance excited me, bringing my breath in fast, quiet pants. Her life depended entirely on my whim, and I loved the feeling of power that knowledge brought. For the first time since I'd come home, I was in control, with no one to answer to and nothing to fear.

Anticipation surged through me. I leapt onto the next limb, then the next, and the next after that. I aimed for the thickest part next to the trunk to minimize the noise and the chance that I would shake loose a leaf to drop on the deer. Close enough, I crept silently out onto a sturdy limb, watching my prey from above. I was salivating, my heart beating fiercely. Its rhythm was accompanied by the rush of anger through my veins like a second pulse, feeding my heart as surely as my blood did.

The doe was below and to my left. I pounced, angling my fall so I would land on the mother's hindquarters. As my paws left the branch, she froze, alerted to danger. She started to bolt, but it was too late; I was airborne and closing fast. Claws unsheathed, I was ready to slash.

The impact knocked us both to the ground. I lunged forward to clamp my teeth on her throat, pinning her. Blood rushed into my mouth in spurts as her heart pumped her life into me until my teeth pinched her throat closed, suffocating her.

It was over in minutes. Standing, I shook the deer by the throat, just in case. She was dead, and her fawn was gone. Good. I lapped at the blood still dribbling from her neck, then ripped open her stomach with my claws and began to eat. As the carcass slowly cooled in the shadow of a broad red oak, I concentrated on the meal at hand, shoving my lingering bloodlust to the back of my mind. Surely it would be satisfied long before my stomach was.

My appetite satiated at last, I lay down next to the still-warm carcass to clean my face and paws. It had been a messy meal, and I didn't like messes. Not the figurative ones, and certainly not the literal ones.

The smell of blood and fresh meat filled the clearing, reminding me of what still needed to be done. I stood, wondering what to do with my catch. When we hunted as a group, there was little left to worry about, and we donated the remains to the small scavengers present in any forest, nature's own recyclers. But this time I was alone, with lots of leftovers and no Tupperware. I was full and certainly didn't need the dead deer, but instinct told me to protect my meal. I paced in front of it for a couple of minutes, undecided, then froze, focusing my ears and attention on a dry rustle from some brush to the west. The guys had caught up with me, surely drawn by the smell of my kill.

The breeze had shifted, the wind now carrying my scent toward the tomcats. Though they could smell me, I couldn't smell them. But it had to be them, because any other animal would run *away* from the scent of a large cat, not toward it.

Yet when the brush parted, I came face-to-face not with a group of agitated, hungry werecats, but with a single human. He wore a hunter's vest, which I knew to be orange, though my cat's eyes couldn't identify the color, and carried a large hunting rifle propped across one arm. I had no idea what kind of gun it was. Few of us had any experience with firearms, and since we didn't need them for hunting, we didn't own any. But I had no doubt it would kill me at such close range.

At first the hunter didn't notice me; he was too busy gaping at the slaughtered deer. Then something caught his attention. Probably my tail, which I couldn't seem to keep still when I was nervous. His eyes widened in comprehension, and the skin pulsing over his jugular vein jiggled faster. He was as scared of me as I was of the gun, and maybe more so. Unless he'd been to Africa, he'd never seen a cat my size outside of a zoo, and he was clearly terrified.

I could smell his fear, sour like sweat, thick like smoke, and tangy like blood. The scent cried out to something exhilaratingly primal in me, something that answered to the proverbial call of the wild and was completely beyond my control.

All at once, I understood that stalking from the trees had been a mistake; it hadn't satisfied the bloodlust. The deer hadn't even had a chance to run from me. I'd wanted a chase, or at least a little excitement, and all I got was dead meat. But this man was *alive,* his pulse beating so invitingly in his throat. And I was confused and angry, which translates to the cat brain as something completely different. Something more like carnal aggression, intoxicating and irresistible.

I watched him carefully, wrestling with instincts I'd never been at odds with before. Excitement tingled through me. My fur stood on end and my eyes dilated. My tail whipped back and forth behind me, stirring an almost palpable cloud of danger in the air. And even as my body prepared to do what came naturally for a cat, some small human thought nagged at the back of my mind, warning me about capital crimes, of all things. I swatted it away, irritated. My feline brain was too narrowly focused to deal with more than one issue at a time. The most pressing issue at that moment was the hunter, simply because he was there. And because the bloodlust wanted him.

I took a single step forward. My whiskers arced forward as I sniffed in his direction, just to see how he would react. His eyes flicked to my tail. A bead of sweat trailed down his nose to dangle in the air above his considerable gut. His muscles tensed. He was preparing to run. *Oh goodie.*

My ears lay flat against my head. I hissed, showing off two-and-a-half-inch top canines. The pungent stench of human urine saturated the air. *Some hunter,* I thought. He'd probably been tracking my deer, thinking he was the only predator around. *Oh, well, he shouldn't have wandered onto private property.* At least, I *thought* I was still on Daddy's acreage. But maybe not. I hadn't been paying that much attention.

I settled back onto my rear paws and lowered my chest to the ground, preparing to pounce, because that's what cats did, and because I was long past the ability to think with human rationality. I wiggled my hindquarters, getting comfortable, and was seconds away from attacking when dead leaves crackled to my right, drawing my attention away from the hunter. Marc padded out of the undergrowth and growled, his eyes flashing at me in warning. He was growling at me, but the human didn't know that.

After one look at Marc, who was half again my size, Mr. Fierce Hunter remembered he had a gun. He swung the barrel toward Marc's head, in a movement much too slow to seem real. His finger wrapped around the trigger. From somewhere at my back, a dark shape flew past me. It landed on the hunter, knocking him to the ground. The gun went off. The cracking boom echoed in my head. The acrid stench of gunpowder burned my nose.

Movement on my left caught my eye and I turned to look. Leaves swung in the foliage inches above Marc's shoulder.

It had happened too fast for me to react. Another second, and Marc would have been dead. Hell, another three *inches,* and Marc would have been dead. And it would have been my fault.

I blinked and shook my head, trying to shake some sense into myself. The bloodlust drained from my body like hot water from a bathtub, leaving me cold, exposed, and in shock. Shaking, I turned toward the hunter, stunned to realize that mere seconds had passed since the gun went off. It felt like much longer.

Parker stood on the man's chest, and as I watched, he sat down, swatting the gun aside like a kitten with a ball of string. It landed with a metallic thunk in a nearby drift of leaves. Parker lowered his head slowly toward the hunter's face, sniffing as if he smelled something interesting. It was probably fear, the same aroma that had sent my common sense fleeing in the face of instinct. But Parker still had his head on straight. He huffed, blowing the man's hair back and making him blink. Then he stepped gracefully onto the ground, between the man and his gun.

Parker blinked deep hazel eyes at the hunter. When that had no effect, he roared, and Marc joined him. That got the man moving. He rolled over and jumped to his feet, tearing off through the bushes, screaming like a lunatic. You'd think he'd be grateful to be alive, but where's the gratitude?

Marc's angry growl claimed my attention from the witless hunter. He sounded pretty mad.

I whined and stared at the ground, trying to show remorse. The sound died in my throat when Marc hobbled over to me, still growling, and bit the back of my neck, forcing my head down in submission. He bit me hard enough to draw blood, which meant he was pretty pissed.

Yeah, I should've seen that coming.

With both the hunter and the bloodlust gone, I was horrified by what I'd almost done. Pride cats don't attack humans. Not even strays attack humans, if they want to live. But I'd almost done just that. I'd been a breath away from committing the unforgivable sin, and Daddy was going to skin me alive. If Marc didn't do it first.

And the worst part was the knowledge that they had every right to be furious with me. Hell, *I* was furious with me.

Marc let go of my neck and slapped my rump with his forepaw, urging me forward. I went without complaint, and he stayed close on my right, while Parker flanked me on the left. Jace and Ethan appeared out of nowhere, marching just behind me. I was surrounded, with only one way to go. So I went, my head hanging low in the proper posture of penitence.

They escorted me all the way to the tree line, where Marc signaled that he wanted me to Shift by swatting my rump again and tossing his head toward Parker, who had already begun the process.

Again, Shifting back was slow and painful. By the time I finished, the others were waiting for me, and no one looked sympathetic. Marc grabbed my arm and hauled me to my feet. "Not a word about this to anyone," he said, staring at each of the others one at a time. "I'll handle it."

"But Dad—" Ethan started.

Marc cut him off with a snarl, sounding more canine than feline for a moment. "I said I'll take care of it." His eyes were fierce. "And if that isn't enough for you, I'll owe you. Each of you. Whatever you want, whenever you want it, so long as no one gets hurt." He paused, still staring hard at Ethan. "Okay?"

Slowly, Ethan nodded, looking as if he wanted to throw up. He'd truly never been on my father's bad side, which was exactly where he'd wind up if Marc's little bribe ever came to light.

"Parker?" Marc asked. Parker nodded without hesitation, which made me wonder if he already had something in mind. *Interesting...*

"Jace?"

Jace shook his head, refusing. I stared at him in disappointment, hurt but not surprised. He was probably mad because Marc had interfered in our bet, and as pleased as I was with the outcome, I could hardly blame him.

"I don't need a favor," he said. "I'll do it to prove I'm not all talk." His eyes burned into me, though his statement was directed at Marc.

I rewarded him with a thankful nod and a hesitant smile, but it was gone in an instant when Marc nearly jerked me off my feet, backing toward the tree line with me in tow. "Whatever works," he said, shrugging at Jace. But I'd never before seen anyone look so pissed off as the result of getting his own way.

Marc dragged me across the yard toward the

house with his lips drawn tight in anger. Both of us still nude, he pulled me through the back door, down the hall, and into my bedroom. Again. I was starting to sense a pattern.

Eleven

The moment we crossed my threshold, I jerked my arm from Marc's grip and slunk across the room toward the dresser. Angry more with myself than with him, I yanked open the top right-hand drawer and pulled out a pair of panties. Slamming the drawer shut, I whirled around to face him.

Marc had his arms crossed over his bare chest, covering most of the fifteen-year-old claw marks. He stood in front of my open bedroom door, as if to block my escape. It bothered me that I was getting used to people positioning themselves between me and the nearest exit. *Was I that predictable?* I clamped my jaws shut; it probably wasn't a very good time to ask questions.

Ethan appeared in the hall and pulled the door

closed with his eyes averted, which was his way of giving us privacy. His footsteps receded down the hall, and my hope of anyone stepping in on my behalf went with them. Oh, well. Being rescued wasn't my cup of tea anyway. Especially when I knew I didn't deserve it.

I held Marc's angry gaze for as long as I could, but after less than a minute, I chickened out. I love a good argument. I've even been known to go looking for one, especially with Marc. But I hate being in the wrong, and I hate it even more when he's around to witness my screwups. Or worse, keep me from making them in the first place. And he'd certainly pulled my tail out of the fire this time.

"You'd better have a good explanation for that little lapse in judgment," he whispered from across the room. With Marc, whispering is always worse than yelling. It means he's so mad he can't trust himself to shout without saying things he'll regret. "Never mind," he spat, running one hand through his head full of thick, dark curls. "There *is* no good explanation, so don't bother. Why would you even *think* about attacking a human?"

I stepped into the panties, pulling them up in a series of angry, jerky movements. "I thought you didn't want an explanation." Without waiting for a reply, I turned my back on him, digging through a drawerful of shorts left over from high school. I hated naked arguments. They reminded me too much of when we were a couple.

"Don't get smart with me, Faythe," he said, his teeth grinding together during the pause. "I'm barely holding on to my temper right now as it is. If you were a guy, you'd be hurting already." He was right. If I were a tomcat, I might have been declawed. He'd done worse to strays who broke the rules. But since it was clearly not the time to lobby for equal treatment for women, I opted for an apology.

"I'm sorry." I spiked my voice with a heavy dose of sincerity as I stepped into my shorts, but I couldn't bring myself to turn and face him.

"You're *sorry?*" Again with the whispers. This was definitely not good.

My hands shook as they pawed through a selection of old bras, and I was glad he couldn't see how upset I really was. I'd rather let him think I didn't care, than think I was emotionally frail.

"You're going to have to do better than that."

Better than that? In my opinion, nothing was better than an apology.

Stalling for time to think, I picked a bra at random and leaned over to scoop myself into it. Hooking the bra in place, I turned to face him, forcing my hands to stop shaking and cooperate, rather than ask him for help. I grabbed a T-shirt from the floor and tugged it over my head. Fully clothed, I felt like I had an advantage over Marc for the first time since I'd come home. Nude men don't look threatening, no matter how mad they are. They just look vulnerable.

"Well?" He leaned against the wall, taking weight off his injured leg. My eyes wandered down his body, on their way to inspect his ankle, but when I got to his bare lower stomach, I stopped, jerking my gaze away as if the sight of him naked had burned my retinas.

His eyes, I thought. *Only his eyes.*

Spinning abruptly, I stomped over to my bathroom and opened the door, my hand hovering over the robe hanging on its hook. But it was lavender, embroidered with purple and white irises. Marc would never wear it. Shaking my head, I balled up a bath towel from the rack instead and tossed it to him, one-handed.

Marc shook the towel out and glanced at me quizzically, as if he didn't understand what I expected him to do with it.

"Wear it, or get out," I said, careful to look only at his eyes.

He scowled, but wrapped the towel around his waist, tucking one corner in at his hip. "Better?" he asked, arms spread for my approval.

My pulse jumped as my traitorous eyes traveled over his chest, lingering on the old claw marks. "Marginally."

"Good, now talk."

My eyes roamed the room, searching for any excuse to avoid looking at him. The empty suitcase caught my attention, lying on the carpet below the dent it left in my wall. "What do you want me to say?" I stomped past him and snatched up the suitcase. "I messed up—badly—and I'm very sorry. I'll never do it again." I opened the case on the end of the bed and turned to face him. "So hit me, or ground me, or do whatever it is you do when one of the guys gets out of line. Then get the hell out of my room."

Fury flashed in his eyes, and his voice was barely audible. "You're really tempting me, you know."

"Tempting you to what, get out?"

"To knock some sense into you."

"Go ahead. This can't be the first time you've wanted to." I snatched a lump of white nylon from the scattering of clothes I'd tossed from the suitcase that morning and swung around to face him with my arms open, inviting him to take his best shot. But the image must have been ruined by the bra dangling from my fist, because he just stared at me, his arms crossed over his chest.

Marc had never hit me, and he never would, not just because the council frowned heavily on hitting tabbies, but because he knew better. I wasn't a turn-the-other-cheek kind of girl. But mostly he wouldn't hit me because he'd never hit a woman. Even one who'd nearly bitten his foot off.

Anger at me had driven him to put his fists through walls, to rip doors from their hinges, and to pick fights with other toms out of frustration. On one memorable occasion, he threw my mother's solid-oak dinner table across the room and into a wall, leaving a dent four feet long in the Sheetrock. But the word *dent* didn't do justice to the damage. It was more like the wall buckled. The table actually snapped one of the studs, its splintered edges protruding through the wall into the next room.

As well as docking Marc's paycheck, Daddy had taken away my allowance for eight months to help pay for the repairs, though I hadn't even touched the table. He'd blamed me for pushing Marc's buttons on purpose. Like *that* was fair.

Marc sighed and shook his head slowly. "What am I going to do with you, Faythe?"

Not a damn thing, I thought. But I knew better than to dare him. If I claimed to be beyond his authority, he'd do something to prove me wrong, just to make a point. "You sound like my mother," I muttered, tossing the bra into the suitcase as I bent to grab a dog-eared copy of *Sense and Sensibility*. I was intentionally ignoring my resemblance to my mother as I tidied up to keep my nervous hands busy. When left empty, they tended to form fists.

Marc's eyes tracked me as I moved to place my copy of *Beowulf* on the shelf. "I feel more like your father," he said.

"Well, you're not my father."

"Thank goodness," he muttered, shaking his head. I had to agree. I crossed the room again with a small stack of books clenched to my chest. Marc stepped into my path. "Come on, Faythe," he said, taking the books from me. He set the entire stack on my desk without breaking eye contact. "Tell me what happened out there."

Forced back to the topic at hand, I closed my eyes as fresh pangs of guilt and confusion coursed through me. I turned away from him, sinking onto the side of my bed with my hands loose in my lap, breathing deeply to try to calm myself. "I don't know what I was thinking. I *wasn't* thinking. I was upset, and frustrated, and worried about Sara and Abby. Then, when I Shifted, it all changed. My anger felt different. It felt…productive. Almost cathartic. I thought if I could just slash something, or bite something, I'd feel better."

His eyes softened almost imperceptibly, and I knew he understood—from very personal experience. "Bloodlust?" he asked, and I nodded, holding back tears with sheer willpower. "The deer didn't help?"

"Not much." I pressed my fingertips against my eyelids, as if I could physically stop the tears from coming. "She was too easy."

Marc sat next to me on the bed, his leg brushing mine. He put his arm around my shoulder and pulled me toward him. I let him. I shouldn't have. Any other time, I wouldn't have. But as soon as my head touched his shoulder, tears blurred my vision, scorching their way down my cheeks.

Horrified, I pulled away from him, wiping furiously at my face with clenched fists, trying to erase the evidence of my emotional outburst before he noticed. I worked so hard to make everyone take me seriously, to make them treat me with the same respect they'd give a tomcat, the same respect they gave each other. And my little waterworks display would ruin it all, exposing me as the emotionally fragile little girl they'd always assumed me to be inside. Before I knew it, I'd be in the kitchen at my mother's side, wearing one of her aprons as I learned the difference between baking powder and baking soda.

That thought only made me cry harder.

"It could have been worse," Marc said, putting his arm around my shoulders again. I let him. What did it matter, now that I'd already embarrassed myself? "You didn't actually attack him, and he didn't see anyone Shift. All he has is a crazy story about huge wild panthers. No one will believe him." He squeezed my shoulders, and I sobbed out loud. I'd liked it better when he was mad. I knew how to deal with anger, but I was terrible with sympathy, both giving and receiving. "And anyway, we all know how you feel. We all wanted to shred something, and the truth is that if we hadn't been busy trying to find you, one of us might have done the same thing."

He was lying. It was a sweet lie, but a lie nonetheless. None of the guys had so little control.

"You don't understand," I sniffed, sitting up straighter as I wiped tears from my face. "I wasn't just mad. I was scared." I whispered the last word, ashamed. With the admission of fear came humiliation, and I avoided his eyes, afraid I'd find scorn in them if I looked.

But then I had to look. I had to see what he thought of me, because for some stupid reason it still mattered. A little.

I looked up into his eyes from inches away, and what I found was not contempt but understanding. Not intellectual comprehension but actual empathy.

He knew what I felt because he'd felt it too. I remembered the fear I'd seen on his face the night before and knew that he understood mine.

I took a deep breath, preparing to explain myself. The words tumbled from my mouth in an untempered surge, determined, once they were free, to keep coming. "Somebody took Abby and Sara, and if it happened to them, it can happen to me." Marc shook his head in denial, but I ignored him. "I just kept thinking that if they'd been faster, or stronger, they could have gotten away. I guess I was trying to prove to myself that I'm fast enough and strong enough. Then I just lost control."

He held out his injured leg, and I noticed the bandage hadn't survived his Shift. Luckily, he didn't really need it anymore. The wound was jagged and inflamed, but the worst of the damage had already healed, probably during his recent Shift back to human. Either that, or I hadn't hurt him as badly as I'd first thought. Even so, it would leave a thick scar. I'd permanently marked him as punishment for him trying to scent-mark me. How's that for irony?

"You're too fast for me, that's for sure," he said, eyeing his own injury.

I smiled ruefully. "Yeah, but Daddy's going to kill me for that."

"Speaking of which…"

I looked up, already suspicious. "What?"

"There's no reason to tell him about the hunter," Marc said, and I held my breath, waiting for the catch. "After all, no one got hurt or exposed, so there's really nothing to tell."

My eyes narrowed. "You trying to get back on my good side?"

"You have a good side?" He grinned, and I glared at him as he held up two hands in defense. "All I'm saying is that—assuming you can behave yourself from now on—there's no reason to mention something that only *almost* happened."

I reached up to pull a T-shirt from the bedpost where it hung like a white flag signaling my surrender. "And let me guess, you're doing this because you're such a nice guy."

"That, and because I like having you in my debt."

"Debt?" Now, *that* sounded more like Marc. "I'd say we're even. You keep your mouth shut about the hunter, and I won't mention you and the flock of airheads in the cafeteria."

He cocked one eyebrow at me, as if impressed in spite of himself. Then he frowned. "That won't make us even. I owe Ethan and Parker for you. You're at a deficit."

Damn. And Ethan was likely to ask for something big in return for his reluctant silence. I folded the shirt, mentally weighing a debt to Marc against facing my father's wrath. *Talk about a rock and a hard place.* Groaning in resignation, I dropped the folded shirt onto the bed. "Fine. Within reason."

"Agreed." He grinned again. "Should we shake?"

I shrugged; he could have asked for a lot more. He took the hand I held out and kept it for a moment, as if he might kiss it rather than shake it. Or maybe he was considering biting me. His fingers were warm against mine and comfortably familiar. I smiled, but Marc didn't notice. He was staring intently at his injured ankle, as if trying to figure something out.

He let go of my hand, and his towel gaped, exposing a wide slice of bare thigh as he pulled his wounded leg onto the bed between us, turning to face me. His eyes were somber, his frown intense. "Faythe, listen." He grabbed my arms as if to shake me, but he wasn't mad this time. He was worried.

"Sara and Abby weren't just tossed into the back of someone's car. They couldn't have been. You know how hard it is to catch a cat. We twist, and scratch, and yowl. And we bite." His eyes dropped to his ankle between us on the comforter. "Even in human form we fight. Remember when Ethan turned twenty-one? It took five of us to wrestle his keys away from him."

"Yeah." The bite mark on my left arm guaranteed I'd never forget it.

"How easy do you think it would be to subdue a scared cat, even a seventeen-year-old tabby?"

I thought about it. I really, seriously thought about it and decided it would be nearly impossible to do without attracting unwanted attention, even in the dark. We're strong, we're stubborn, and we fight when we're cornered. My hands clenched around handfuls of my rumpled comforter, my arms tightening beneath his grip. "What are you saying?"

"I'm saying they were probably disabled. Maybe shot." He let go of me but his eyes never left mine. "Faythe, no matter what anyone else says today to make the Wades and the Di Carlos feel better, there's a good chance Abby and Sara are dead."

I stared at him, numb. I was tingling all over, trying to swallow my own pulse. I'd heard what he said, and I understood it. But I just couldn't believe it, even though I'd been thinking the same thing right before my hunt. They couldn't be dead. Abby was barely seventeen years old, and Sara was only twenty. Death just wasn't an option for people that young.

But it happened to cats in the jungle every day.

"I'm not trying to scare you," he said. "I just want you to be prepared."

I nodded, but my head barely moved. It felt like it weighed fifty pounds.

Two short, sharp knocks came from the hall, and we turned to look as my door opened. Parker stuck his head in, drawing my attention away from Marc and from thoughts I didn't want to think. "Faythe, your dad wants to see you in his office."

"Now?" Marc snapped.

I glanced at him, surprised by his tone.

"Yeah. Now." Parker pushed the door open farther and tossed Marc a bundle of clothes. "I'm leaving to pick up the Di Carlos, but I'll be back in a couple of hours." He looked at me with something bordering on sympathy. I guess he thought being chewed out by both Marc and my father in the same hour was enough punishment for anyone. I had to agree. "Your mom set up a buffet in the kitchen. She says you should eat before everyone gets here."

Yeah, that sounded like my mother, more worried about my stomach than my head. Or my hide.

I glanced at my clock radio, surprised to see that it was nearly three o'clock. Marc and I had been talking for ages. Or maybe my run in the woods had taken longer than I'd thought. My stomach growled, as if to highlight the passage of time, and I realized I hadn't eaten anything since I'd Shifted. No wonder I was starving.

"Any word on who's coming?" Marc asked, reaching down to grab his jeans from the floor where they'd landed.

"Yeah." Parker leaned against the door frame. "Michael said all ten Alphas are coming. Apparently they all want a say on how we handle this. Four are bringing their wives, and Nick Davidson's bringing his daughter."

All ten? I thought, wondering if I'd heard him wrong. *Wow.* That was every Alpha from every territory in the country. We hardly ever had perfect attendance, even at scheduled meetings.

Marc stood up, one hand holding his pants by the waistband, the other on the towel around his waist. "Where are they staying?" He gave the towel a tug, and it dropped to the floor.

I jumped up fast enough to get a head rush, and scurried over to my dresser, slipping my watch over my wrist to avoid staring at him.

Parker cleared his throat, disguising a chuckle at my reaction. "Michael made reservations for everyone in town, but Mr. Davidson asked if Nikki could stay here."

"Mom will love that." I turned to face the room again, my blushing under control. My mother loved all kids, especially dainty little girls like Nikki Davidson. As a child, I was a constant source of frustration for her, with my skinned knees and torn skirts. When I was nine, I blew up a Laura Ashley doll with one of Ethan's firecrackers. That was the last time she ever tried to make a lady out of me. At least openly. She'd resorted to passive-aggressive tactics ever since.

Marc zipped up his pants, and my eyes were pulled toward the sound. The waistband of his jeans left the top curve of his hipbones exposed, and those masculine points seemed to hold me captive for a moment. When I could, I jerked my eyes away, and they landed on his shirt, crumpled at the end of my bed, abandoned. He'd been tossing shirts there for years, since long before his clothes had any business being on my bedroom floor. My theory was that he liked having me return them. He took advantage of any occasion that required me to seek out his attention. But it was hard to get mad this time. The missing shirt definitely improved the view.

Marc was one of those naturally well-built men, for whom weight training merely added definition to an already impressive physique. I could count each ripple of his abs, and had done so on more than one occasion in years past, trailing my fingers lightly down his stomach until… Well, never mind that.

But the memory came just to spite my floundering willpower. I'd almost forgotten there had ever been a time when we could touch each other without one of us tensing, but there had been, once.

I read somewhere that most girls either fall in love with or grow to hate the man who takes their virginity. For me, it was both. I hated Marc's cocky assurance that I would eventually want him back, but I couldn't imagine him not being there every time I came home. He had been my first everything. My first boyfriend, my first kiss, my first real confidant. And that was most of the reason I hated him, on those occasions when I did. He knew me too well. But I knew him, too.

"See anything you like?"

I blinked, my cheeks flaming. I'd been staring, and for a while, apparently. Parker was gone, and I hadn't noticed him leave. There was no one left to shield me from the heat in Marc's eyes.

I sighed, knowing his question was far from rhetorical. "Seeing something I like isn't the problem, Marc. It never was."

"What *is* the problem?" he asked, his voice thick with yearning. I had my hand on the doorknob, and I fought the urge to turn and look at him. I lost. And there was that expression on his face again, that fear I'd had trouble placing the day before. It still looked all wrong, like Christmas lights in June.

"I've changed, and you haven't." I left the room

before he could ask me to elaborate, because I wasn't sure I could. Not until he put on a shirt, anyway. I couldn't even think until then.

Twelve

The twenty feet of plush beige carpet between my room and my father's office might as well have been a bed of hot coals. Each step hurt a little more than the last, and the distance seemed to swell with each painful thump of my heart. Growing up, I'd feared nothing worse than being called into the office. Going on my own was one thing, but being summoned was quite another. Like Marc, Daddy never yelled, but unlike Marc, he would not be moved by my tears. Not that I planned to shed any.

My father was more than just my sire. He was my Alpha, and because I was a girl, that wouldn't change until I got married, which I'd spent the last few years avoiding. As a child, I'd owed my father obedience and respect, but as an adult and a member of the Pride, I owed him even more: lifelong loyalty. Everything I did, even away from the ranch and the rest of the Pride, had to be done with the safety of our secret existence in mind. The mistake I'd almost made in the woods might have gotten anyone else, even my brothers, expelled from the Pride. But Daddy wouldn't expel me. Ever. Tabbies are too valuable to be discarded for any reason. At least until they've borne a daughter.

No, Daddy couldn't afford to oust me, but he could take away my freedom. He'd certainly done it before.

I stared at the door, postponing the inevitable for another few seconds of torturous anticipation. Ethan used to say that waiting to be punished is always worse than the punishment itself. But Ethan had never been grounded. At least, not like I had been.

The house was a collage of sound around me; I could hear people going about their business in nearly every room. My mother puttered around the kitchen, wiping down counters and rewarming food, in blissful ignorance of my emotional turmoil. Ethan was in the shower; I could hear him humming the theme to Gilligan's Island as he lathered and rinsed. And repeated.

But in front of me was an auditory vacuum, a white spot on the canvas of chaos that was my home.

Daddy's concrete-walled sanctuary was scary in a way no dark alley could ever be. Anything could be happening in there—anything at all—and no one would know it. But then, that was the whole point.

I knocked on the door and opened it without waiting for a reply. I probably wouldn't have heard one anyway. Daddy sat hunched over his desk, talking on the phone, but when he saw me, he said goodbye and hung up. It wasn't a good sign.

"Close the door, please, Faythe."

I pushed the door shut, and took a seat on the couch. I knew the drill. I even folded my hands on my lap like a good little girl. But it had been years since my father bought that act.

Daddy pushed back his chair and stood, leaning on the desk with both hands while he looked at me with an expression I couldn't quite place. Exasperation? Dread, maybe? But it definitely wasn't the fury I'd expected.

"Tell me about Andrew."

"What?" I gaped at him, so surprised by his request that at first I actually couldn't process what he'd said.

"Your boyfriend at school."

"Yes, Daddy, I know who he is," I snapped, and he raised his eyebrows at my tone. I took a breath and tried again. "I thought this was about Marc's leg.

Or maybe…not inviting anyone to graduation." I'd
started to say "the man in the woods," or "my bet
with Jace." But then I remembered he didn't know
about either of those little errors in judgment, and I
wasn't about to tell him. Soon I'd have more secrets
on file than the CIA.

Daddy frowned, dark, heavy brows overshadow-
ing eyes the same shade of green as Ethan's. "You
know, you could avoid this kind of confusion if you
weren't always in some kind of trouble."

Shit, why didn't I think of that? I tugged my shirt
down, wishing suddenly that I'd paid more attention
to the clothes I'd grabbed. "Why do you want to
know about Andrew?"

He crossed the room in several leisurely strides
to sit in his armchair, leaning back with the ankle of
one leg resting on his opposite knee. The relaxed
pose and the long pause were both intended to make
me nervous. They worked. "How long have you been
dating him?"

"Why do I have the feeling you already know the
answer?" I asked, curling my toes in the thick rug.
Suddenly I was very conscious of my bare feet,
which was strange, considering how much less I'd
worn in the very same room only hours earlier.

"I have a responsibility to the entire Pride to
ensure your safety, Faythe."

Great, the responsibility speech. I stared at him, knowing he would respect continued eye contact. "You promised me freedom."

"I kept my promise." He cracked his knuckles one at a time, so slowly that after the first few, I leaned forward in anticipation of the next. It was psychological torture.

"You also promised me privacy." My eyes were drawn to the first finger of his right hand, as he pressed on it with his thumb.

Crack. "No," he said, his face impassive as another pop punctuated his reply. "I promised not to interfere with your life, and I haven't." *Crack.*

"Never argue semantics with an English major, Daddy."

Finished with the largest ones, he started on the middle knuckles of the same hand, ending each sentence with one, like an auditory exclamation point. "I'm not arguing anything." *Crack.* "I'm stating facts." *Crack.*

I rolled my eyes. Arguing with my father was pointless, but like one of those windup toy soldiers, I kept walking face-first into the same obstacle, over and over again. I couldn't seem to help it. Sighing, I resigned myself to the inquisition because resistance was more trouble than submission, and I was already tired of arguing. "What do you want to know about Andrew?"

He nodded, acknowledging my willingness to cooperate by folding his hands in his lap. He didn't seem to care that my compliance stemmed more from weariness than from any sense of respect or obligation. "How serious are you about him?"

Irritation flared in my chest like heartburn, bringing with it a tiny spark of courage. "Why?"

"You know why." He watched me calmly, expectantly, his age betrayed by the crinkles at the outside corners of his eyes and the gray streaks just above each ear. They were the only flaws among his otherwise strong, firm features.

"You can't just pick a tomcat at random and reserve a chapel." My head began to ache at the prospect of rehashing the argument we'd started when I was seventeen. "I have no plans to get married. If I change my mind later, that's *my* business and *my* choice. Only mine."

"I haven't even mentioned marriage."

Damn it, why did he have to sound so reasonable? And he'd made me bring up the M word! I closed my eyes, gathering my thoughts and my nerve. "Not today, but I know it's what you were thinking."

"You know no such thing," he said, still infuriatingly poised. "I wasn't thinking of you at all. I was thinking of him. If you spend too much time with this Andrew, he might think he has some kind of future with you. But he doesn't, and it isn't fair of you to mislead him."

"Maybe I'm not misleading him."

My father watched me calmly from his chair, demonstrating what I lacked and he had plenty of. Patience. He clearly expected this argument to go like all the others in years past: I would yell myself hoarse, then, when I had no more voice with which to argue, he'd speak his mind. And just like that, another choice would be gone, another path in my life chosen without my input or consent.

Not this time. I wasn't going to yell or throw a fit. I'd outgrown that. His prying questions had led me to a decision—one of the first important choices of my entire life—and I was going to announce it evenly. Serenely. Maturely.

I was leaving. But I wasn't going to sneak away in the middle of the night, as I'd done in the past. I'd learned from my mistakes, or at least learned that he'd expect me to repeat them. This time I would make my stand boldly in the light of day, face-to-face with my father and Alpha.

It was simple, really. All I had to do was tell him I was leaving—then convince him to let me go. Of course, that was the tricky part.

I shoved doubt from my mind, ignoring the voice in my head telling me that, as usual, I'd bitten off far more than I could chew. My father would fight my decision. He wouldn't bluster, or bellow, or roar. That wasn't his style. Instead, he would deny my "request" and forbid me to leave. When that didn't work—and it certainly wouldn't—he'd chase me all over the country if necessary, because he couldn't afford to lose me. I knew that intellectually, just as I knew emotionally that I couldn't stay. The Pride needed my uterus but seemed to have no use for the stubborn, opinionated parcel it came in. But I was a package deal—all or nothing.

Bolstered by anger and the intoxicating rush of rebellion, I stood and stepped into the center of the rug, standing directly in front of my father. "I want out," I said, careful again to meet his eyes. Avoiding them would look like weakness, and I couldn't afford to appear weak.

"Out?" One eyebrow rose, as if he wasn't sure what I meant.

"Out of the Pride. Like Ryan. I want to live on my own in one of the free territories. I want to be a wildcat."

He shook his head slowly, his hands templed beneath his chin, clearly trying to decide how best to crush my dreams. "That life is not an option for you."

"The hell it's not." Nervous even though I'd

known what he'd say, I took a deep breath, trying to impress him with my composed, mature stance. "I'm leaving, Daddy."

Crack.

I jumped, startled by the sudden sound. *So much for not appearing weak.*

"Don't be foolish, Faythe." His voice was low and menacing, warning me not to tread any farther onto dangerous ground. But I was pleased by his transition in tone, because it meant he was finally taking me seriously.

"I'm not being foolish." My skin tingled a little at my own nerve. "I'm just leaving. I don't need your money. I have an education and a good head on my shoulders. And *you* taught me to protect myself. I'll be fine on my own." *Of course, I could use a ride to the bus station.*

His eyes never left mine, but for a moment I thought he might stand. In fact, he seemed to be resisting standing for the same reason Marc resisted yelling. It was an issue of control. If he stood, he'd lose it, and might do something he'd regret. Or at least something *I'd* regret. "I can't let you go, Faythe," he said finally. "Even if I was willing to consider something temporary, like graduate school, I couldn't do it now. Not until we know what happened to Sara and Abby."

"I'm not asking for permission." My smile blossomed, carefully light and casual. And very calculated. "I'll be in Mississippi, if you want to keep in touch. Or maybe Nevada. There's still some free territory out there, right?"

My head seemed to float, as if it were merely tethered to my body by my neck. I was high on rebellion, an act I should have outgrown along with Kool-Aid–dyed hair and fake tattoos, yet somehow its appeal had only grown. But again that voice nagged me, insisting that no matter how much fun it was to play the escape artist, eventually even Houdini had to come up for air.

Frowning darkly, my father clasped his hands together, resting his chin on them, his knuckles white with tension. After a moment of consideration, he spoke, his response so soft I had to hold my breath to hear him. "I won't discuss this any further. If you try to leave the property, I'll have you caged."

The cage. Memories of steel bars, rough concrete, and constant darkness flooded my mind, chasing away my rebellious euphoria. I hadn't been in the cage since the last time I'd run away, the summer I'd turned eighteen. I hadn't been running from Daddy then. I'd been running from my life, but Daddy took it personally. Once they'd found me and hauled me home in the back of Vic's SUV, my father had locked me up for fourteen days, most of which I'd spent on four paws out of protest.

I stared at my father, wanting to believe he was bluffing. But I knew better. Daddy didn't bluff; he had no reason to. The business suits, ties and diplomatic demeanor were only one side of my father, and it was the other side that worried me. The other side was as strong as Marc and still nearly as fast, but Daddy's speed and strength were enhanced by an extra thirty years of wisdom and experience. Far from a figurehead, my father was Alpha in practice as well as in name. Yes, he gave orders, but he never ordered anyone to do anything that he would not or could not do himself. My father's word was final.

I was kidding myself, and we both knew it. I could make my stand and run away, but no matter what I said or did, Daddy would come after me. Personally, if he had to. Eventually he'd catch me, and I'd be back to square one, after having my spirit broken by a few nights in the cage. So the real question was, Is it worth it?

And the answer was, Hell, yeah. *I might not make it if I run away, but I definitely won't make it if I don't try.*

My feet shuffled against the soft rug as I took a single step forward, but what I felt was cold, damp concrete. I smelled Daddy's aftershave, but beneath that was mildew and the faint, metallic scent of steel, like the way your hands smell after you jingle coins in your pocket. I knew what I was risking, and I knew what would happen if I failed. But I had to give it one more shot. I owed myself that much.

"You can try," I said, my resolve reinforced by memories of the cage and determination to avoid seeing it again. "But I promise you this. Whomever you send after me will come back blind and neutered."

The phone on his desk rang, but he ignored it, eyeing me calmly. "You don't mean that. You wouldn't hurt your brothers."

Apparently he didn't question whether or not I'd hurt Marc.

"Don't make me prove myself, Daddy. I—" I never got to finish my threat because Michael nearly tore the office door off its hinges. I heard his frantic heartbeat, and smelled distress in his sweat. It was sour, and made my own heart pound harder. Something was terribly wrong.

"Owen's on the phone for you, Dad. He says it's urgent."

Thirteen

"Sit, Faythe," Daddy ordered. Then, addressing Michael, "Don't let her off the couch." He turned his back on us both with the phone at his ear.

Still standing, I watched my father, trying to overhear the other side of the conversation. If I was going to be stuck in the office, I might as well do a little eavesdropping. That was the only way I'd get any information anyway.

Michael's anxiety was contagious, and curiosity and worry for Owen had temporarily eclipsed my zeal for escape.

"Owen? What did you find out?" my father said into the phone.

Michael nudged me with his elbow and nodded at the couch. I shook my head. I was afraid to back down because once I had, I might never gather enough courage to stand my ground again. Instead, I'd be tempted to run off in the middle of the night, like I'd always done before. While that technique was pretty effective, it made me look like a coward and a child. Neither of which I was.

I caught a blur of movement as Michael's foot shot out behind my ankles. Before I could move, he swept my feet out from under me. My backside hit the rug with a bruising thud, and my teeth snapped together, the sharp click resounding through my head. Daddy turned to look at us with a raised eyebrow, but Michael just shrugged at him. He hauled me up by my arms, dropping me onto the couch like a naughty puppy onto a pile of newspapers.

Michael straightened his suit coat, smiling, then settled onto the love seat across from me as if he were sitting down to his afternoon tea. I glared at him as I rubbed the marks his fingers left on my arms, but it was just for show. I'd learned long ago that even though Michael no longer officially worked for our father, he took his orders seriously. I defied him at my own risk.

"Is he sure?" Daddy asked, turning to face the curio cabinet so that I saw him in profile. Light from the cabinet bathed his strong features, highlighting the tension on his normally unreadable face.

Leather creaked as I leaned sideways on the couch, rubbing my tailbone while I listened closely for Owen's side of the conversation. "Yeah. It was a jungle cat," he drawled. "No doubt about it."

"What about the scent?" My father glanced at me, then turned back to face the display case, as if that would keep me from hearing the answer.

"My guess would be Brazilian," Owen said. My pulse jumped, and I sat up straighter, my sore tailbone forgotten. "But he could be from anywhere in the area. He's definitely South American, though, and definitely a stray."

Strays have a distinctive scent, which is easily distinguished from that of a Pride-born cat. It's like the difference in taste between Coke and Pepsi: subtle if you never drink either, but unmistakable if you're accustomed to one and suddenly confronted with a mouthful of the other.

Marc told me once that Pride cats smell differently to strays too, which I wasn't surprised to hear. We have a family-specific identity—a base scent, if you will—threaded through our individual scent ID, which lets us classify a cat with his blood relatives with a single whiff.

This isn't possible with strays because they have no base scent. They have only the feline smell of werecats in general, and of themselves specifically.

Which led me to an interesting thought as my eyes skimmed the family photos on my father's desk: if Marc and I had given my parents the grandchildren they wanted, would they inherit my Pride-born scent, or his stray scent? For that matter, would they even be werecats at all? If Marc wasn't born with a werecat gene, how could he possibly pass one on?

It was easy for me to forget, considering how long he'd been a part of the south-central Pride, that Marc was still—and always would be—a stray. Hell, I hardly noticed the difference in his scent anymore; it was just part of who he was. But with any other stray, I would detect it immediately. And so would Owen.

"What about the police?" Daddy asked. I couldn't see his face, but the tension in his broad shoulders was obvious, even through his suit jacket.

"They don't know what to think. The detective in charge of this one is convinced that some psychopath is keeping a jaguar as a pet and letting it eat his victims."

I inhaled sharply, turning on the sofa to fully face my father. Daddy glanced at me over his shoulder, nodding to let me know he'd caught the plural ending, too. "Victims?" he asked, straightening stacks of paper on his desk. "Are there others?"

Static crackled over the line, then Owen's voice

came through loud and clear. "…one in New Mexico three days ago."

Daddy rubbed his forehead as if trying to stave off a headache. "How did we miss that?"

"Well, it's not like we have any sources in the free territories. But we probably would have missed it anyway. It was reported by the media as a typical dismemberment, as if there *is* such a thing. The police are keeping the cat angle quiet to weed out the nutball confessions."

Daddy walked around his desk and sank wearily into his chair, leaning forward with his elbows on the blotter. "The one in New Mexico was another girl?"

"Yeah. Just like this one. Hang on a second, Dad." More static, papers shuffling, and a muffled version of Dr. Carver's distinctive rumbling voice. Then Owen was back. "She was a sophomore at Eastern New Mexico University, in Portales, just across the Texas border. Raped, then mauled and partially… um…consumed. A groundskeeper found her in an alley."

I pulled my bare feet up onto the couch cushion, hugging my knees to my chest as I leaned back against the arm of the couch. *This can't be happening,* I thought. Two missing tabbies and two dead humans. All in the last three days. Daddy would never let me go now. Not that he would have anyway.

My father rubbed his chin in silence for a moment, staring down at his desk blotter. "I don't suppose there's any way you or Danny could get a look at her, is there?"

Over the phone Owen shuffled more papers. "There might have been, but she was buried this morning. I already checked."

"What about her clothes?"

"I'm sure they're in police custody." Owen paused while Dr. Carver said something I didn't catch. "But Dad, the chance of there being two different psycho strays operating at the same time with the same M.O. is practically nil. It's got to be the same son of a b—"

"I agree," Daddy interrupted, leaning back in his chair. "I was just hoping to be able to confirm my suspicions."

I glanced at Michael to find him staring at the rug between us, but I knew better than to think he'd zoned out. He'd heard every word Owen said, and was filing it away in his lawyer's brain for later use. If I knew Michael, he'd know everything there was to know about both murders by the end of the day, having used every professional resource at his disposal. And when those ran out, he'd surf the Net, riding the waves of information like a first-generation digital surfer, which is exactly what he was.

"So, what do you want me to do?" Owen drawled, his accent thickened by tension.

Daddy sat up, laying one forearm against the top of his desk. "Thank Danny and come home. And tell him to keep his eyes and ears open."

"What if the stray strikes again?"

I closed my eyes, silently praying he wouldn't. My heart ached for Abby and Sara, and for those two human girls, who'd probably never known what hit them. If they were lucky.

The desk chair creaked, and I looked up to find my father standing in front of his desk, with his back to me. "If he does, Danny probably won't have access to the victim. This stray would have to be an idiot to strike twice in the same state."

"Maybe he *is* an idiot," Owen said. "He's certainly crazy."

"Crazy, no doubt. But if he were stupid, we would have known about him before now." Daddy's voice was tight with anger. He was mad at himself; I could hear it in the way his words were clipped short. He was angry that he hadn't known about the stray sooner, and about the girl in New Mexico. "Come on home."

"There's a flight out at nine," Owen said, his words coming faster than usual. He must have recognized the anger, too. "I should be home by eleven."

"Fine." Daddy dropped the phone into its cradle and stared at it. I heard his heartbeat slow, then steady, and I knew he was counting silently in an attempt to rein in his temper. His shoulders rose and fell with each deep breath as he prepared to turn from one problem to face another: me.

"Faythe, this is not a good time for your theatrics," he said, tugging down his jacket sleeves.

He was right about that; my timing was awful. But there was nothing I could do about it now, short of backing down completely. And that wasn't an option. Not if I wanted him to ever treat me like an adult.

I set my feet on the floor and started to stand, but one glance at Michael froze me in place. He would follow the letter of Daddy's law until otherwise instructed. So I took a deep breath and launched my argument from the couch, substituting good posture for the erect stance I would have preferred.

"I'm not being theatrical," I said, doing my best to project a respectful tone into my voice. "I'm completely serious. I'm leaving."

My father finally turned to face me, and the gravity in his expression made my mouth go dry. "Stop arguing on autopilot and listen to what I'm really saying."

Nervous and curious in spite of my determination

to stand my ground, I nodded. Could he possibly be saying something other than the usual *no?*

My father eyed me somberly, as if to convey the weight of what he was about to say through expression alone. "Freedom from the Pride doesn't mean true freedom for you." I started to argue, but he cut me off. "What would happen if I let you strike out on your own in a free territory? Do you think the strays would respect your wishes? Would they leave you alone?" He paused, but I made no reply. I was too busy thinking.

"Whether you see it or not, you have choices here. I do care what you want. But the strays in Mississippi won't give your rights a second thought. They'll care what you're worth, and how having you would affect their rank among the others."

I frowned as if I didn't understand, but his point was frighteningly clear, and devastating to my argument. Alone in the free territory, I would be a living, breathing status symbol. A trophy for the biggest, fastest and strongest stray. Unless I was willing to fight every day of my life, I would have no life worth living. Not in the free territories, anyway.

But what about the south-central territory? I thought, a new plan rising from the ashes of its predecessor. Daddy had more land than he knew what to do with. I could live six hundred miles from the ranch and still be safe within the territorial boundaries.

"Fine." I nodded in concession to his point. "You're right. Leaving the territory isn't the greatest idea I've ever had. But it's a big territory, and I don't have to leave to gain a little privacy and independence. I'll go to Oklahoma. Or Kansas. I'd still be a member of the Pride—just living on my own. Like Michael." I glanced across the rug at my oldest brother, hoping for his support. I should have known better. He wouldn't meet my eyes, unwilling to take my side against our father.

Daddy shook his head slowly, but I could see him thinking…

"I'll do holidays on the ranch. And my birthday. And Father's Day." Did that sound too desperate? "I was at school for five years, and everything was fine. This would be just like that."

"The guys took shifts watching you for all five of those years," he said, frowning as if I'd missed something really obvious.

"Yeah, but that was a total waste of resources." My father's color deepened to an angry red, and I decided to rephrase. "I was fine. And I *will* be fine. Because I'm going." There. Decision made. And it wasn't even unreasonable—at least in my not-so-humble opinion.

But my father clearly disagreed. He watched me intently now, his expression unreadable. There was no frustration, no more anger, and no glint of determination. Definitely not good.

"Listen to me carefully," Daddy said, his words as slow and deliberate as each measured step he took toward me. "Because what I'm about to say isn't coming from a father to his daughter. It's coming from an Alpha to his subordinate Pride member." His voice was low and dangerous, almost a growl. I'd heard him take that tone with few other cats, all of whom had been repeat offenders, intruders being offered one last chance before he turned them over to Marc.

Surely that wasn't his plan for me. I wasn't breaking in; I was trying to break out.

He stared down at me, not quite three feet from where I sat. I'd never seen him this mad, and the worst part was knowing that there would be no wiggle room because his anger stemmed from concern for me. He wouldn't compromise my safety for anything. Even if the danger was only theoretical.

"I absolutely forbid you to leave the ranch…"

I opened my mouth to interrupt, but he held up a hand to cut me off.

"…but I acknowledge that I can't stop you if

you're determined to go. The choice is yours." He took a breath deep enough to strain the buttons of his dress shirt, and dread made my heart thud in my chest. "However, if you choose to leave now, I will send every tomcat at my disposal to bring you back. You'll be lucky to see daylight by your next birthday."

I gaped at him, wide-eyed, my pulse racing. I'd turned twenty-three less than a month before; he was threatening to lock me up for nearly a year. I didn't know whether to be angry or scared. Or pleased, because he was finally taking me seriously. My father had never threatened me before. Well, not as Alpha anyway.

"Do you understand what I'm saying, Faythe?"

"If I run, you'll send the guys to drag me back by my hair and toss me into the cage." I aimed for nonchalance in my expression, as if I were threatened by an Alpha every day. But my heart was skipping entire beats in an attempt to slow itself down, and I knew he could hear it.

He smiled his polite-company smile and returned to his armchair, smoothing his suit coat into place as he sat. "I prefer my manner of delivery to yours, but yes, that's what I mean. Do you still intend to go?"

Did I? It wouldn't do any good; he was right, I wasn't really willing to hurt my brothers. And they would catch me, eventually. Daddy would use every resource he had to track me down, and I suspected that if I pushed him that far, my stay in the cage might stretch out long past the year he'd threatened.

My eyes found Michael, looking for his take on our father's threats. He shrugged, apparently unsure whether or not to take Daddy seriously. But in my entire life, I couldn't remember my father making an empty threat. Not once.

I inched forward to the edge of the couch, hoping that would make me look confident and alert rather than like I might bolt at any minute. "I assume if I say yes, you'll lock me up."

He nodded, his hands clasped in his lap. But his thumbs were twitching. That meant something. It didn't mean he was bluffing; I couldn't get that lucky. But it might mean he wasn't as confident as he seemed to be in his ability to find me if I took off. I was a kid the last time I ran away, and I'd accumulated several more years of real-world experience since then. Or at least several years of college campus experience.

I held my breath, thinking. "What if I say no?"

"If I think you're sincere, I'll settle for twenty-four-hour supervision until you've proven yourself trustworthy."

If, I thought, finally onto something. *We're both*

speaking hypothetically... A smile blossomed on my face, slow and sweet. "Are you willing to negotiate?"

He arched one eyebrow, and I knew I'd said the magic word. My father loved to negotiate. He enjoyed the process of begrudging give-and-take the way most cats enjoyed the thrill of a good chase, and he considered himself very tough to bargain with. He was right. However, if I'd judged correctly, he would go easy on me because he'd view a request to negotiate as a sign that I was coming closer to accepting my place in the Pride. But that was his mistake, not mine.

"What did you have in mind?" My father leaned forward in his chair, eyes glinting in anticipation.

I fiddled with my watch, buying a little time to think. He would see through that, but it didn't matter. What mattered was that I was playing his favorite game. "I'll agree to defer my decision about leaving until Sara and Abby are found, if you'll forget about the round-the-clock supervision until we revisit the issue of me moving out at a later date. How's that sound?"

He smiled. "Nice try, but you'll have to be more specific than that."

My hope faltered, and I shifted on the sofa, leaning forward to mirror his pose. "Meaning what?"

"Name the later date."

"But I don't know when we'll find them. Soon, hopefully, but I'm not psychic, Daddy."

Michael chuckled, and I glanced away from Daddy long enough to glare at him.

"You don't have to be psychic," my father said. "You just have to be explicit. The key to negotiation lies in stipulating the details."

I barely resisted rolling my eyes. I'd heard that line at least a dozen times since my twelfth birthday, but I merely nodded, playing the part I'd signed on for.

"Let's set the date of your decision for the day after the last missing girl is found, in case Sara and Abby are found separately or someone else disappears between now and then. And if we find the girls before we catch the jungle stray, you have to put off your decision until he can be found and disposed of."

"Fine." I had no problem with that because I agreed with Marc's theory that the jungle cat was involved in the abductions. "So—for the record—if I agree to wait until the abductors and the trespasser are caught and disposed of, you'll forgo the twenty-four-hour babysitting?"

He sat back in his chair, considering, and for a moment I thought I'd won. Then he spoke and I realized what a fool I'd been to think he'd go easy on me. "Your agreement to put off your decision is good enough to keep you out of the cage, but the chaperone is nonnegotiable."

My jaw dropped, anger blazing through me. "Then you haven't conceded anything! You would have caged me even if I hadn't agreed to put off my decision."

"You're right." His voice took on an instructional quality, as if he were addressing a class full of students instead of one very angry daughter. "Another important principle of negotiation is knowing when you have the upper hand and when your opponent has it. And right now, I have the upper hand."

I shrugged. "So there's no reason for me to wait."

"How about this." He couldn't keep satisfaction from his face. He loved putting me through hell! "Round-the-clock supervision, with restroom privacy on a trial basis?"

"No way. That's bullshit," I cried, pounding on the arm of the couch. I hadn't even realized bathroom privacy was an issue, and I certainly wasn't going to use it as a bargaining chip. He had no right to, either.

Michael started to object to my tone, because whether he was acting as my father or my Alpha, no one got away with cussing at Greg Sanders. But

Daddy held his palm up for silence, cutting off Michael's protest without a word.

"No, that's compromise," he said to me. "If you were not willing to put off your decision, I'd offer you no privacy at all. I'm sure Jace would be happy to observe your shower to head off any attempts to crawl through the bathroom window."

I cringed. "Daddy, how could you say something like that?"

"I'm not your father. I'm your Alpha." His smile was gone; he was absolutely serious. And he wasn't going to give in on the watchdog issue. "Whether you believe it or not, even Jace has the ability to concentrate solely on the job at hand. I wouldn't employ him if he didn't." He shrugged, but the casual gesture looked alien on my suit-and-tie father. "However, if you'd rather forget your first attempt at negotiation, there's always the cage. Of course, the cage has no privacy at all… And no shower or proper toilet."

He had a point, and I knew I'd lost round one. But round two would come soon enough, assuming I hung around long enough to fight it.

I pouted, slumping against the back of the couch. "Fine. You win. But if you send Marc into my room at night, I swear he'll come out a eunuch."

Daddy nodded. "Fair enough. Marc stays on the

day shift." He glanced at Michael, amusement lifting the corners of his mouth. "Make the arrangements."

"No problem." And with that, Michael left to strip away another of my civil rights. You'd think his law school education might have at least made him hesitate. Whatever happened to the Bill of Rights? But apparently Baylor Law didn't teach complicated concepts like that. What was the world coming to?

Fourteen

Jace wound up with the first shift of Faythe-sitting, because Daddy wanted Marc to help greet the arriving Alphas and bring them up to speed. Ethan got the same assignment, along with Parker, once he'd returned from the airport with the Di Carlos. Every half hour or so the doorbell would ring as another Alpha and his small entourage arrived. After the third large man in a dark suit asked me how I was holding up, Jace and I retreated to my room with a plate piled high with food from my mother's buffet.

"So, what'd you do?" Jace asked me around a mouthful of ham and cheese on whole wheat. I lay sprawled across my bed on my stomach, the plate of food in front of me. He sat in my desk chair, which he'd pulled up to the bed so he could reach the food.

I licked a smear of pimento cheese from my finger and reached for another tiny sandwich. "What do you mean?"

"You know what I mean." He brushed crumbs from his shirt, and my eyes followed his hand, lingering on the lines of his chest, clearly visible through the thin white cotton. "What's with the babysitting detail? Is it because of Marc's leg, or did Ethan rat you out about the guy in the woods?"

"Why? You have something better to do?"

"Not a thing in the world." He sniffed the air in my direction. "But you do smell a little ripe. Maybe you should go run a bath."

I laughed, jiggling the bed and the plate of food. "Nice try, but I've been granted restroom clemency."

"It was worth a shot." He shrugged, popping a cube of sharp cheddar into his mouth. "So, was it Marc's leg, or the hunter?"

"Neither."

"What then? How could you possibly have had time to get into any more trouble between then and now?"

That was a very good question. I speared a chunk of honeydew on a toothpick topped with a strip of green cellophane, making him wait while I chewed extra well to prolong the suspense. Swallowing, I motioned for the Coke we were sharing. Jace grunted in impatience as he handed me the can from my nightstand. He chose another sandwich while I drank, and I waited until he took the first bite before finally answering. "I told Daddy I was leaving the Pride."

His eyes widened, and he made a wet, strangling sound, nearly choking on the bite in his mouth. I pounded his back, and he turned angry eyes on me. "That's not funny, Faythe."

I shrugged. "I said I'd stay within the territory. And don't worry, I didn't mention my winning our little—" Before I could finish the sentence, he flew out of his chair, launching himself at me before I had time to do anything more than drop my sandwich on the comforter. I landed flat on my back, the top of my head pressed against my headboard. Jace's right hand covered my mouth, and his knees straddled my stomach.

Damn. Pinned again. I was going to have to work on my reaction time.

"Are you trying to get me killed?" he demanded in an urgent whisper, brown hair flopping onto his forehead.

I shoved his hand away, grinning at how familiar our casual play felt. Along with Ethan, we'd been chasing and tackling each other since I was ten years old, and deemed sturdy enough to run around with the boys. I'd kind of missed being with people who wouldn't break if I played too hard.

"Daddy wouldn't kill you," I said, beaming up at him.

"Shit, I'm lucky Marc didn't. If you take my car, he'll tell your dad about our bet, and Greg will skin me alive and hang my hide in his office as a warning to all future enforcers not to mess with his daughter." I laughed, but he never even cracked a smile. "Promise me you won't go."

"I already promised Daddy I'd wait till we find Sara and Abby. Then we're going to 'revisit the issue.'"

He relaxed and sat up, moving back to straddle my thighs instead of my stomach. "How'd he get you to listen to reason?"

"It was either that, or have my mail permanently forwarded to the cage." I propped myself up on one elbow and gave him a shove with my free hand. Jace fell over sideways on the bed, rebounding into a sitting position almost instantly.

"Oh." He pouted for effect. "Surely a few hours with me is better than a night in the cage."

"Tough call." I grinned, watching him sulk. "But he wasn't talking about just one night. Seriously. We're talking long term. Months, at least." I sat up, noticing that Jace had knocked the food over when he'd tackled me.

He rounded up several stray grapes while I righted the plate and started picking up the sandwiches. His hand brushed mine as he dropped the fruit on the plate and a tiny spark of excitement charged up my arm, making my next breath sharp.

Jace paused, a glint in his eyes and a cube of cheese in his free hand. "Your dad was exaggerating. He had to be. He's never locked anyone up for more than a couple of weeks."

Of course, that was me, the last time I'd run away. Two weeks in a damp, dark basement, with nothing but an old can for a toilet and not so much as a magazine to distract me from my mounting rage.

"Nope, he was completely serious." I brushed crumbs from my comforter onto the floor. "So, I guess you're stuck with me."

"Well, if that's the case—" he flopped back onto the pillows, lacing his fingers behind his head as he winked at me suggestively "—we might as well make the most of the next few hours. After all, it's either me or the cage."

I laughed to disguise the tremor his heated look sent thrumming through me. "I doubt that's what Daddy had in mind."

"It could have been. What did he say, exactly?"

I tilted my head, pretending to think. "Well, he did say something about letting you watch me in the shower…" Jace's eyes widened comically in surprise, and I laughed for real. "He meant it as a threat."

"So, if you misbehave, I'm your punishment? What a fascinating punitive system."

"I'm glad you're amused." I lay down next to him, my hands folded over my stomach.

Jace propped himself up on one elbow, looking down at me through eyes just a shade lighter than my mother's cobalt wineglasses. A girl could get lost in those eyes—if she let herself.

It took every bit of self-control I possessed to pull my gaze from his. Suddenly, Daddy's threat wasn't so threatening anymore. It wasn't funny, either. How could I have thought of Jace as a brother for so long, then suddenly find him so exciting, so tempting in a forbidden-fruit kind of way?

Jace was starting to step over some pretty well-defined boundaries, and Daddy wouldn't be very forgiving of either of us if he found out. Not to mention what Marc might do. Yet even knowing the consequences, I wanted to look into his eyes again. I wanted to think about what might have happened the night before if Marc hadn't interfered. I wanted the possibility of a little excitement I didn't need anyone's permission to enjoy.

Jace stared down at me as if he knew what I was thinking, his finger tracing a lazy, coiling pattern on the comforter between us. "You know, if Marc hadn't stopped me, I'd have won our bet."

"I thought you didn't want to talk about the bet." With no thought for what I was doing, I reached up for his arm, my eyes focused on the well-defined curve of his biceps, where it lay half hidden by his sleeve. His pulse jumped as my fingers brushed his skin, and I realized what I was doing. Mortified, I tugged his sleeve down where a section of the hem was folded up, feigning concern for his appearance.

He grinned, clearly seeing through my lamentable act. "I didn't want to talk about you snatching my keys. But me winning our bet is just about my favorite conversational topic in the world right now."

"You didn't win," I reminded him, my hands clasped together tightly, each keeping the other out of trouble. I wanted to let them wander, to find out how soft his hair was and whether his chest could possibly be as firm as it looked. But that would be opening a door I just couldn't walk through. Though I might not put up much of a struggle if someone were to give me a shove.

Starting something with Jace would be like spitting in Marc's face. It would also be going against a direct order from my father, which could bring the full force of his wrath down on us both. But being alone with Jace made me feel daring and fearless, as if the consequences didn't matter. His touch made me light-headed; it made my pulse race, as only Marc's had ever done before. And that was awfully hard to resist. *What Daddy doesn't know won't hurt me,* I thought, still just toying with the idea.

"I would have won if he hadn't held me back," Jace said, his voice almost wistful.

"Ah, what might have been…"

His eyes brightened. "Exactly."

"I was kidding, Jace," I said, marveling over how very blue his eyes were. Had they always been that blue? Surely not.

"I wasn't." He stared down at me, his focus shifting back and forth between my eyes. I knew I should look away, but I couldn't do it. Before, Jace had always been safe, good for a little harmless flirting and ego-boosting, but nothing more. But last night something had changed. *He* had changed. And I'd been so sure I was the only one…

Jace tucked a strand of hair behind my ear, his hand lingering longer than necessary against my skin. He lowered his face toward me. His lips brushed mine softly as his hand moved to cup the base of my skull, tilting my mouth up to meet his. A shudder thrilled its way through my body, bound for points south of the equator. I closed my eyes, breathing in his scent, so familiar yet somehow all-new and exhilarating.

He kissed me again, gently, hesitantly, as if waiting for me to push him away. I should have. But I didn't. For some reason having more to do with lust than logic, I just didn't. I hadn't felt such a spark in years. Not since Marc. And I wanted that spark.

Jace took my failure to resist as consent, and he kissed me harder, deeper, his tongue parting my lips while his hand smoothed my hair across the pillow. Eyes still closed, my left hand found his lower back, where his spine curved beneath the hem of his shirt. My fingers clenched around the material, my arm drawing him closer. He moaned into my mouth.

My pulse quickened as his fingers trailed the length of my hair to my arm. He paused at the crook of my elbow before moving on to my waist. His touch danced across my skin, tickling my stomach as he traced the edge of my waistband toward the button just below my navel.

He reached the button and hesitated, pulling away from my lips. He left my mouth empty but still open, still waiting. I held my breath, afraid to move and break the spell. Then he kissed me again, his tongue plunging into my mouth as his hand tugged gently at the flap of denim surrounding the buttonhole.

The button gave way, and my eyes popped open.

He'd gone too far. Too fast. That touch wasn't playful; it was intimate, and a little too bold.

I had one hand on his chest, just starting to push him away, when my bedroom door flew open, smashing into the doorstop with a startling thud.

Marc was on us before either of us could sit up, before I'd even realized who had come in. He pulled Jace off me and heaved him across the room and into the wall, where the dent I'd made that morning was swallowed by the impression of Jace's back in the Sheetrock.

I scrambled to my knees, kneeling on the bed as I stared at them both in shock. "Marc, what—?"

He ignored me, focusing his rage on Jace, who sat hunched over on the floor where he'd fallen. Ethan appeared in the doorway and started toward Jace, but Marc slammed the door in his face. The doorknob turned, but Marc ripped it from Ethan's grasp, accidentally pulling him part of the way into the room.

"Get out," Marc growled, every muscle visibly tensed and trembling with fury.

Ethan gestured toward Jace. "He's hurt."

"Out." Marc thrust him into the hall, then shoved the door closed. Ethan didn't try again, but the shadow of his feet remained beneath the door. He wouldn't completely abandon his best friend.

"Marc…" I tried again, and this time he turned on me.

"Shut up, Faythe."

I cringed, though he hadn't shouted, because the look on his face was rage. Pure, jealous rage. I crawled to the edge of the bed, but he put up a hand to stop me. "Stay there."

I stayed, because though I'd never seen him that angry, I'd heard stories of what he'd done on my father's behalf to trespassing strays and wildcats. From his perspective, Jace was a trespasser. Jace had crossed into territory Marc still claimed for himself, triggering every violent instinct he possessed. And I didn't want to make it any worse.

Marc thumped to his knees on the floor, curling his fingers in a handful of Jace's soft brown waves. He tugged back until those beautiful blue eyes stared up at him, only half-focused. "What did I say I would do if I caught you alone with her again?"

"Marc, Daddy sent him." I stuffed my hands in my pockets so he wouldn't see them shaking.

"To watch you, not to molest you." He never took his eyes from Jace's semiconscious face.

"He wasn't—" I stopped, and Marc's head swiveled slowly in my direction, his eyes dark and dangerous. There was no good way to finish that sentence, so I took a deep breath and started over. "I'm a big girl, Marc. I can take care of myself."

"You wanted him to…touch you?"

Had I? I'd known I was making a mistake even as I made it. And that was my choice, wasn't it? "I… It's none of your business what I wanted," I snapped, anger flowing in to replace my rapidly fading confusion. "The point is that I can handle it myself. I don't need you to come bursting in here, throwing people into walls. I don't *want* you in here, Marc." I propped my hands on my hips in irritation, and the motion drew his eyes down to my waist, where, I now realized, my shorts were still unbuttoned.

My face flushed, and my fingers fumbled with the button, trying to shove it through the stupid hole. I finally got it, but it was too late. He'd already made his own interpretation, and giving him my version wouldn't be much better.

Pain surfaced through the haze of anger in Marc's eyes as they rose to meet mine, and I saw him quash it. I actually saw him turn off his pain, like a plumber twisting off the hot-water valve. He shifted his gaze back to Jace without acknowledging a word I'd said.

"Are you awake? Do you understand what I'm saying?" he asked. Jace nodded slowly, flinching in pain. "What matters to you is what *I* say, not what *she* says, and certainly not what she does. No matter what you think you feel for her, it isn't mutual. She's just using you to make her father mad, and to make me jealous. And she's doing a damn fine job."

My blood boiled, and my temper beat against the battered gates of my self-control, demanding to be let out. But I knew better. Trying to rationalize with Marc before he calmed down would be dangerous, for all involved.

On the floor, Marc released Jace's hair in favor of a tight grip on his chin, as if he were scolding a disobedient toddler. "I told you to leave the door open. I told you not to touch her. And I meant it. If you lay a hand on her again, you'll have more to worry about than her ripping out your heart. I'll save her the trouble and do it myself."

My mouth went dry, and my jaws ached from holding back angry words. I'd had enough. Damn his uncontrollable temper. I couldn't let him get away with threatening Jace's life. Especially since he meant it. Like my father, Marc never made idle threats. He'd learned from the master. Or, in this case, the Alpha.

I gripped the nearest bedpost, using it to steady myself as I stepped onto the floor. My right foot landed on the shirt Marc had left there earlier. Annoyed, I kicked it out of my way, hugging the post for balance. I suffered from nothing more than shock and deeply rooted anger, but that was enough to make me unsteady on my feet. Unfortunately even the most convincing discourse imaginable would be forgotten in an instant if I fell flat on my face.

I'd just taken a breath to start shouting when the door opened. Marc whirled around, prepared to shove Ethan more convincingly that time. He came face-to-face with my father instead.

My jaw snapped shut, my furious words forgotten with one look at the anger on my father's face. *Thank goodness I already buttoned my shorts,* I thought.

"What's the problem, Marc?" Daddy demanded, his tone outwardly civil but cold as Arctic snow. "And let me remind you that we have guests." As if to underline his point, the doorbell rang again.

"There's no problem. We've reached an understanding. Right, Jace?"

Jace nodded, and Marc pulled him to his feet, brushing dry flakes of plaster from his shoulders.

Daddy eyed the new Jace-size dent in my wall, then glanced at where I stood at the end of the bed. "Everything okay?" he asked. I looked at Jace, and he nodded at me, so I nodded at my father. "Good. Ethan, take him to the guesthouse."

Ethan stepped out from behind my father and

helped his best friend into the hall. Jace didn't look at me on the way out, but Ethan shot me an angry look, as if it had all been my fault.

That's right, everything's always Faythe's fault.

Daddy eyed me harshly, one fist still clenched around the doorknob. "Parker's on his way to the airport again, and since Ethan's tending Jace, that only leaves Marc to finish the shift as chaperone."

Great, he blamed me too. And apparently he'd decided to torture me as punishment for my part in the disturbance.

"No," I said, burying my nails in a bulbous section of the bedpost. "I'd rather spend the rest of the day in the cage."

"That can be arranged," Daddy said, his expression completely indecipherable. "In fact, it's easier than sparing one of my men to watch you." He wasn't bluffing.

Wonderful. Marc it was.

Fifteen

As soon as the door closed behind my father, I snatched Marc's shirt from the floor and threw it at him, wadded into a ball. He caught it, probably due to instinct rather than intent. While he watched me carefully, apparently expecting me to throw a fit, I grabbed a change of clothes and stomped into the bathroom, slamming the door in his face. Daddy had granted me bathroom clemency, and I was damn well going to use it. I ran a deep, hot bath and soaked until it got cold. Then I let the water out and drew more to wash in.

At first Marc tried to talk to me. He paced back and forth in my bedroom, stopping occasionally to listen, or maybe to think of some new approach to get me out of the bathroom, short of pounding his way in and dragging me, dripping, from the tub.

"I'm sorry, Faythe," he said, much closer to the door than I'd expected.

I tried to ignore him, wishing desperately that I'd grabbed my headphones before locking myself in.

"I didn't plan this. I just wanted to talk to you."

You should have knocked, I thought, clenching my jaws shut to keep the words from leaking out. He'd take even the most hostile reply on my part as encouragement to keep trying.

"I couldn't help myself. When I saw him on top of you like that, touching you, it was all I could do to keep from smashing his head in."

Unfortunately, I knew he wasn't exaggerating. His possessive instinct really ran that deep, but I was no longer willing to accept that as an excuse. Yeah, we were cats, and thus subject to the bizarre behavioral impulses that came with having fur and claws. But we were people too, and Marc seemed to have forgotten that. It was a good thing my father had never sent him to spy on me at school. One night of watching me and Andrew would have been more than Marc could take.

"I like Jace," he insisted, still pacing. "You know I do. He just doesn't know when to quit sometimes."

Neither do you, I thought.

"I know, you probably think I don't either, but I do."

My fist slammed into the water, splashing raspberry-scented suds all over the floor. *I hate it when he does that.*

"I know when to quit, Faythe. I quit when my heart tells me there's no chance of success. But it's not telling me that. Not yet. Not about you."

I let my face slip into the water, as much to escape Marc's tenderhearted babble as to rinse my hair, and I only came up when I had to either surface for a breath or drown.

"…can ignore me for as long as you want. For the rest of the day, or for the rest of the month. For five more years if that's what you need. But when you finally realize I'm right, I'll still be here waiting."

He stopped talking, but he wasn't gone. I heard him plop down in front of the bathroom door, waiting, just like he'd said he would. *Damn, that man is stubborn,* I thought, not quite sure whether I should be flattered or annoyed by his persistence.

Finally tired of hiding out in my own bathroom, I stepped out of the tub onto the lavender bath mat, curling my toes in the soft, shaggy fibers. I snatched my robe from the hook on the back of the door and snuggled into it. Egyptian cotton. Mmm. At least my mother had gotten one thing right.

In my bedroom, Marc cleared his throat, reminding me he was still there. As if I could possibly have forgotten. Though, admittedly, I'd tried.

Using my foot, I flipped down the little chrome lever to open the drain. The bathwater swirled out of sight, leaving only the artificial scent of raspberries and my fervent wish that Calgon really had taken me away. *False advertising. Figures.*

I could hear Marc breathing, and somehow that was worse than listening to him talk. I needed noise. Something loud enough to block his heartbeat from my ears, so that—for a little while at least—I could forget he was there.

Tying the sash of my robe around my waist, I searched the bathroom for something loud. The toilet? No. I'd feel pretty ridiculous after the third consecutive flush. The shower? No. If I spent any more time in water, I'd come out looking like a shar-pei. My eyes settled on the tail of a cord sticking out of a closed vanity drawer. My blow-dryer. Perfect.

I brushed my hair while I dried it, until no single strand remained damp. When I turned the dryer off nearly twenty minutes later, I expected to hear Marc talking again, or at least breathing. But I didn't.

On bare feet, I crept to the door and pressed my ear against it. I heard nothing. Well, nothing from Marc. A woman was crying somewhere near the front of the house. My guess would be Donna Di Carlo or my aunt Melissa. Men spoke to each other in hushed, frantic tones all over the house, but I was almost positive Marc's voice was not among them.

Where had he gone? Surely he wouldn't have left me alone, against Daddy's orders.

Curious, I hung up my robe and dressed in a hurry, then had to stop and turn my shirt around because I'd put it on backward. I opened the door and scanned my bedroom. Marc was gone. Something was wrong. What now?

Dread flooded my body, settling into my feet like lead and weighing them down. I could barely lift them, and I didn't really want to. I didn't want to know what was wrong, or who else had gone missing. There were only five tabbies left to choose from, unless the kidnapper had changed his pattern and gone after one of the dams, the Alphas' wives.

We were all in trouble if he had.

There wasn't an Alpha in the world who wouldn't shred anything and anyone standing between him and his wife. Marc's attachment to me paled in comparison with what most Alphas felt for their wives, which was probably why Daddy hadn't punished him for what he'd done to Jace; Daddy understood. There was nothing my father wouldn't do for my mother. Nothing at all.

I crossed my bedroom slowly, reluctantly, and was reaching for the doorknob when it began to turn on its own. The door swung open. I stepped back, expecting to see Marc. It was Michael, looking just as surprised to see me as I was to see him.

"Marc said you locked yourself in the bathroom."

I stared up at him, trying with no luck to read his expression. "I'm out now."

"I see that. Can I come in?"

"Why? What's wrong?"

"Sit down," he said, coming in without permission. I stepped back to make room for him, but remained standing. He closed the door, and my heart began to pound.

Crossing my arms over my chest, I took another step back, rubbing my elbows to have something to do with my hands. "Did Daddy send you?"

Sympathy leaked into his eyes. "You know he did."

I nodded. Marc wouldn't have left without my father's permission and a really good reason. Something was wrong, and it had to do with the whispers coming from the living room and the woman crying in the kitchen. "What happened?"

"Are you going to sit?"

"No. Just tell me." I was already tired of begging for answers. Why was everyone always beating around the proverbial bush, as if I were too delicate a flower to withstand whatever had gone wrong this time?

Michael leaned against the door and took off his glasses. He exhaled softly as he inspected the lenses of his useless spectacles. "Vic just called. They found Sara."

They found her? That was good news, so why wouldn't he put down the damn glasses and look at me?

A chill raced through me, leaving my hands cold. I crossed the room to my dresser and grabbed a bottle of lotion. My hands shook as I squeezed a dollop onto my palm. I used the back of my wrist to flip the lid closed and tried to set the bottle down gently, but it fell over on its side. "Where?" I concentrated on smearing the lotion all over my arms, working it in especially well on my elbows.

Michael settled his glasses onto his nose. "At home. The bastards propped her up against a tree in her own backyard, like a life-size doll."

My eyes darted to his face as I tried to make sense out of what he'd said. *Propped her up?* I could think of several reasons Sara might need to be propped up, but there was only one reason to bring her home, and it wasn't because she'd said "pretty please."

Michael's lips were still moving, but I couldn't hear him. I glanced down at my arms, rubbing at the lotion in quick, spastic motions.

"Are you listening to me, Faythe?" he asked,

concern narrowing his eyes. He took three steps away from the door, then hesitated.

"No, I'm not." I reached across my dresser for more lotion and knocked over an unopened bottle of perfume my mother had given me for Christmas three years earlier. The glass didn't break, which was fortunate, because I knew without ever having smelled it that the scent would give me a migraine. Nearly everything my mother picked out for me gave me a migraine. Or maybe they were tension headaches.

"You okay?"

I glanced at Michael, almost surprised to realize he was still there. "No. Are you?"

He shook his head. "I guess no one's okay right now."

Squeezing my eyes shut against tears, I turned the lotion over my palm and squeezed, but nothing came out. I shook it and squeezed again with the same result. Irritated, I turned the bottle right side up and glanced at the lid. *Damn. Forgot to open it.* "Do her parents know?"

"Dad told them in private." Michael shuffled his feet on the carpet, head bent to watch them. "Mom's helping with Donna. They had to sedate her."

"What about Kyle?" I set the lotion back on my dresser, still unopened. I was moisturized enough.

"Not yet. His flight lands in about half an hour, and Dad doesn't want him to know until he gets here."

That was probably wise. Kyle would need privacy to voice his grief, and an airport was hardly private.

"How…?" I closed my eyes, and tried again. "What did they do to her?"

"No, Faythe," Michael said, and I opened my eyes to see him frowning firmly. "You don't need to hear the specifics. It won't help."

"She was my friend, and I need to know."

He shook his head, slowly, and not unsympathetically. But he didn't speak.

"Please, Michael." That worked. Or maybe he just finally understood that her death wouldn't really sink in until I heard it out loud.

"I don't have many details," he said, shoving his hands into the pockets of yet another dark suit.

"Just tell me what you know."

He nodded, shuffling back to lean against the wall by the door, as if he needed support. "They beat the shit out of her. Hit her in the head with something hard. The whole back of her skull was smashed in."

My fists clenched around air, and his face blurred as tears distorted my vision. "You said 'bastards.' Plural. How do they know there was more than one?"

Michael dropped his eyes and felt around for the doorknob, as if he'd rather leave than say anything more.

"Please, Michael. I need to know."

Frown lines appeared around his mouth. "Vic said he could smell them on her. Three of them. All over her, Faythe. One was a stray, but the only scent he recognized was Sean's."

Sean. I'd been right, for once. At least in part. But being right didn't feel good. It felt like shit.

"Her clothes," I whispered, fingering the hem of my own green halter top. "Vic smelled them on her clothes, right?"

He shook his head slowly, and this time his hand found the doorknob. "They didn't find any clothes."

I couldn't catch my breath. Air was there, but it wouldn't fill my lungs. I opened my mouth, and that solved the problem. I'd forgotten to breathe.

They'd raped her and beaten in the back of her skull. Then they'd taken her home for her brothers to find. It was just like the human girls, only worse. They'd gone through special efforts for Sara because she was one of them. One of us. She was one of ours, and they'd killed her. Then put her on display.

Nausea gripped my stomach with an iron fist. My knees buckled. The room lurched, walls flying past my eyes. As I fell, Michael lunged for me. He got one arm beneath my shoulders before I hit the ground and gently eased me the rest of the way to the floor.

My vision grayed, and I fought to remain conscious. Somehow I won. I was on the floor, but not by choice, and all I could see was my ceiling. Michael was right; I should have sat down.

"Is she okay?" Marc asked from somewhere outside my field of vision. I hadn't even heard him come in.

"Stay with her," Michael said, and his arms were gone. My door latch clicked softly and his footsteps faded as Marc's face appeared over mine, eyebrows furrowed in concern.

"Can you sit up?"

I nodded and shoved away the hand he offered, pushing myself up to lean against the dresser. I hadn't passed out, but I might as well have. Falling on the floor still made me look the part of the delicate woman they were always trying to protect. *Why don't you just buy a corset and a parasol while you're at it, Faythe?*

"You heard about Sara?" I asked, rubbing the sore spot on the back of my head.

"Yeah. Your dad told me." He swiveled to join me against the dresser, scooting several inches away to avoid the handle poking into his back. "We'll get them," he said. "I promise you we'll get Abby back." His jaw tensed, the muscles clenching and releasing rhythmically.

I trailed my finger along the pattern in the carpet, avoiding looking at him. "We may not have to. It looks like they'll bring her home in a couple of days."

"Stop it, Faythe," he snapped. Then his voice softened. "We'll find her, and she'll be fine." He seemed to need me to believe it, so I nodded. But I didn't believe him. I didn't believe in anything at all at that moment, except my own need for revenge, convulsing through me like an emotional seizure.

"What are we going to do, Marc?"

"Greg wants you to stay in your room until things calm down a little."

"That's not what I mean." I didn't know how to explain it, and for the first time I viewed my lack of enforcer experience as a true drawback. I didn't want to know what to do with my hands, or how to keep my mind occupied. I wanted to know what we were going to *do*. How were we going to find the monsters who killed Sara? And how were we going to make sure they didn't kill Abby, too? I wanted practical information, a plan of action. I wanted him to tell me how I could make those sons of bitches *pay* for what they'd done. I wanted them to pay with their lives, but not before someone had a chance to slice them each open and—

My face throbbed, the sudden pain breaking into my thoughts. Something sharp pricked my lip, and I tasted blood.

Marc stiffened beside me, inhaling deeply. "Are you bleeding?"

I touched my mouth with one finger. It came away bloody. "I think I bit my lip," I said, but the words didn't come out right. I ran my tongue carefully over my upper teeth, gasping to feel sharp, not quite unfamiliar points. "What the hell?" My hands hovered around my mouth, shaking, as I tried to figure out what to do with them.

Marc sat up on his knees and took my chin in one hand, turning me to face him. I opened my mouth obligingly, in a grotesque imitation of a smile. His eyes widened, and he touched the point of one tooth gently.

"Holy shit, Faythe. Your teeth Shifted. Just your teeth. No, wait." He took my head in both hands and turned it toward the light. I winced, slamming my eyelids shut against the piercing glare, but he'd already seen what he wanted. "Your eyes Shifted, too."

"That's impossible." My mouth butchered the words. "My teeth feel different, but my vision hasn't changed. I still see like a human." I could barely understand what I'd said, so I expected Marc to look confused, but he didn't. He just gestured toward the mirror.

"See for yourself."

I stood in front of the dresser, staring at my face in the mirror. My mouth looked strange. My jaw was elongated, but only slightly. It might not even have been noticeable if not for the full-size canines growing down from my upper jaw and up from my lower one. I couldn't even close my mouth.

The effect was bizarre, and less than attractive. And pretty damn scary. I shivered, frightened by my own appearance.

I glanced at Marc in the mirror, bracing for the disgust I was sure I'd see on his face, but it wasn't there. He looked fascinated. He leaned forward to see the changes up close. Again. "How the hell did you do that?"

"Don't know." *Donno*.

"Look at your eyes."

I leaned toward the mirror until my nose almost touched the glass. He was right. They were different. But as with my jaw, the Shift was incomplete. The shape of my actual eyeballs hadn't changed, but my pupils and irises had. Rather than the normal round shape of a human's pupils, mine were vertically oriented ovals, with pointed edges at the top and bottom, instead of gentle curves. They were a cat's pupils, and even as I watched, pulling back slightly from the mirror, they narrowed to slits, constricting the flow of light into my eyes.

But my pupils weren't the most amazing part. My irises were extraordinary. I'd always thought the color remained the same in either form, but I'd been wrong. I'd only seen my cat eyes two or three times, since a cat had few reasons to look at its own reflection. As a cat, I hadn't been able to see the tiny yellow specks, or the subtle color variances in every shade of green. And I had certainly never noticed the dizzying pattern of striations echoing the shape of my iris.

Yet for all that my eyes had changed, brightening the room almost unbearably, my vision stayed the same. I still saw the full spectrum of colors visible to the human eye, and objects were clear even at a distance. The odd combination of human and cat characteristics was disorienting, and brought to my mind images of the Egyptian goddess Bast, though I didn't really resemble her with my human ears and nose. I had an urge to laugh at the absurdity of my own appearance.

Marc didn't find it the least bit funny. "Here. Try this." He flipped the wall switch, and the light went out. It wasn't a very good test of my night vision because the sun was still up, and light filtered into the room through the cracks in my blinds. But it was enough. In the pale evening shadows, I saw like a cat, in muted hues of blue and green, and a dozen shades of black, white and brown.

"Cat vision," I said, and again he understood me.

"How did you do that?" he asked again.

I shrugged, looking around my room in awe. "I was thinking about what I'd like to do to Sean and his accomplices, then my face ached and I tasted blood."

"I've never heard of a partial Shift."

"Me neither." *Eee-er*. Though surely I wasn't the first to have such an experience. I made a mental note to ask around about it once everything was back to normal. Assuming that ever happened.

"Can you Shift them back?" Marc asked, still eyeing me in amazed curiosity.

I shrugged again and closed my eyes in concentration. After a moment, it worked. My face ached again, in my jaw and behind my eyes, like a sinus headache. I ran my tongue over my teeth. They were back to normal.

My reflection confirmed it. I looked human again. Completely.

"Your father's not going to believe this."

I cringed, trying to imagine surviving two inter-
rogations in one day. And what if I couldn't perform
on command? I'd look like a fool. Or worse, like a
spoiled child trying to soak up all the attention on a
day of mourning.

"I don't want to tell him. Not right now," I said.
"He has enough to deal with as it is." And it just
seemed wise for me to stay safely below his radar
until his temper cooled a bit. Or until I had a chance
to swipe his key to the cage and have a copy made.

Marc opened his mouth to argue, but I held up my
hand to shush him, turning toward my bedroom
window. Tires crunched over gravel, and I recognized the low rumble of a van's engine. "Parker's
back with Kyle."

Sixteen

Two car doors slammed, and more gravel crunched as Parker and Kyle approached the house. Marc and I slipped into the living room in time to see my father usher a bewildered Kyle through the foyer and into his office. For once, I was thankful for the extra-thick concrete walls. I could imagine Kyle's reaction well enough without having to hear it.

A plaintive stillness descended in the house around us as Sara's death began to sink in. Only her mother's disconsolate sobs marred the uneasy silence.

The Alphas appeared composed and sedate in their conservative suits, glancing at each other with grave, knowing expressions. But their calm was like the visible portion of an apparently tranquil sea, hiding a churning, agitated current beneath its glass-smooth surface.

They had come together to combine forces and expand the search for our missing tabbies. Now they had my description and Sean's scent as a solid starting place, and Sara's murder to fuel their fury. When they found the captors—and find them they would—the Alphas would strike with the full power of the council, making an example out of Sean and his accomplices, the memory of which would echo forever in werecat lore.

As stunned as I was by Sara's murder, dark anticipation thrilled through me at the prospect of a large-scale hunt, even though I knew better than to get my hopes up. My father would never let me help.

Umberto Di Carlo left for the airport shortly after Kyle arrived, without having said a word to anyone that I heard. He was going home to arrange his daughter's burial. Donna wanted to go with him, but she was in no shape to travel. I never found out what they used to sedate her, but half an hour after her husband left, she sat in the kitchen staring at my mother with unfocused eyes and a gaping mouth. Daddy promised to send her home the next day, under escort, but no one volunteered for the job. He chose Michael, who accepted the assignment with his usual stoic dignity.

The rest of the evening passed in a blur of front-
door chimes and hushed voices, with all the quiet
dread of a wake, because that's essentially what it
was. A bitter, angry wake. The Alphas sipped
Daddy's brandy in small groups in the office and the
living room, whispering to each other about the
tragedy of a young life wasted. Sara's mother and
my aunt Melissa sobbed at the kitchen table, while
my mother and two other dams kept their teacups
full. And little Nikki Davidson, only eight years old,
sat in one corner of the living room for hours, her
face blank with shock. I was pretty sure she'd overheard more of the details than she should have, but
I had no idea what to do about it. So, like everyone
else, I did nothing.

People shot me nervous glances every few
minutes, but no one approached me. They were all
thinking what I was trying hard not to admit to
myself: that if tabbies were being targeted, I could
be next. But I wasn't worried. They'd have to get
through a houseful of Alphas first, and that just
wasn't going to happen.

When the whispers and stares grew old, I settled
into an overstuffed armchair near the living-room
window, turning my back to the crowd as I watched
the sun set. I curled my knees up to my chest and
wrapped my arms around them, slumping my shoul-

ders to look unapproachable, in case anyone got brave. It worked, and everyone left me alone. In fact, after a while, they seemed to forget I was even there, just like they'd forgotten about Nikki. Except for Marc. He was still on Faythe-sitting duty, and he kept one eye on me at all times. But at least he was courteous enough to do it from across the room.

I'd been watching moths gather around the front-porch lights for a solid half hour when a couple of the northern Alphas wandered near my chair, taking no notice of me at all. They still sipped from short thick glasses, but my nose told me they'd switched over to whiskey at some point.

At first I paid no attention to their exchange, bored to death with the political maneuvering that persisted even under such grave circumstances. But my ears perked up when I heard their conversation shift to Sara's funeral arrangements and their own plans to attend.

Sara would have to be buried in private, on her own property, because her death couldn't be reported to the police. There would be no autopsy and no investigation. Her human friends and neighbors would be told she'd gone abroad for some time to herself before settling into married life. Then, in about a week, her parents would announce that she'd died in an accident in Europe. They would erect a memorial and hold a public service for her in a local cemetery.

Similar arrangements were necessary anytime a Pride cat met a violent end, but because Sara was one of very few tabbies, her death was a devastating blow to everyone, especially her immediate family, who couldn't publicly mourn her, or even acknowledge her death until the memorial service. Worst of all, their grieving process would be forever shadowed by the horrific circumstances of their daughter's murder. It was a terrible way to deal with such a loss, but like so much else, it was completely beyond their control.

Still listening to the Alphas' discussion as I stared out into the dark, I wondered if my father would let me out of the house long enough to attend Sara's funeral. Probably not.

Soon, the conversation moved on to a topic I had yet to consider: the future of the southeast territory. Had Sara lived, she would one day have taken over her father's Pride and its territory with Kyle at her side. But with her death, all that had changed. Instead, Kyle would live the rest of his life like most tomcats: single, with no wife and no children. And because the southeast territory now had no heir to bear the next generation, its future existence was tentative at best. Once Sara's father died, if they'd found no tabby to replace Sara—as heartless as that seemed in the midst of grief—his territory would most likely be divided up among his closest neighbors, some of it, through necessity, becoming free territory.

Having filled my brain with more disturbing questions than I'd ever thought possible, the northern Alphas left for my father's office to refill their glasses. While they were gone, the last Alpha arrived, and Daddy escorted the entire council into his office. They didn't come out until after midnight, not to request a tray of sandwiches or drinks, not even for a bathroom break.

Not long after my father closed his office door, my mother knelt by my chair, her eyes still swollen and rimmed in red. She said she was about to clear away the buffet and asked me to fix a plate of food for Nikki Davidson while she got Donna settled into a spare bed. I had no idea what eight-year-olds ate, but arguing with my mother would have been an exercise in futility, so I headed for the kitchen, crossing my fingers that Nikki liked port-wine cheese balls and salmon croquettes.

On my way to the kitchen, Ethan cornered me in the empty dining room, backing me into an alcove created by my mother's huge china cabinet and the wall perpendicular to it. He planted one palm on the wall and the other on the cabinet, blocking my escape.

I briefly considered knocking him on his ass, but rejected the idea because I knew that if I caused any more trouble while the council was convened, I could pretty much kiss daylight goodbye for a very long time.

Ethan glared at me in silence for almost a minute, as if trying to guilt me into making a confession. When it became clear that I would do no such thing, he heaved an irritated sigh and spoke. "Jace wanted me to tell you he's okay. His back is bruised, and he has a bump on his head, but nothing serious." His face made it clear that he hadn't volunteered for the mission.

I twisted a strand of hair around one finger, avoiding his eyes. "Good."

He rolled his shoulders, clearly uncomfortable in the button-down shirt he'd put on in concession to our important company. "Were you even worried about him?"

"Of course I was." The ends of the strand went into my mouth, and I chewed automatically. I *was* worried about Jace. I just hadn't known how to make the situation any better.

Ethan growled and pulled my hair away from my face, giving it a brutal tug for good measure. "Jace thinks he loves you," he whispered, glancing over his shoulder to make sure no one overheard.

Suddenly I found my bare feet fascinating. Big toe, like a thumb on my foot. *That one would be opposable, if I were an ape,* I thought, wiggling it for good measure. Middle toe, longer than the first one. And those tiny little ones on the end, which weren't terribly well articulated, in spite of theoretically functioning joints.

Ethan snapped his fingers beneath my nose. "Faythe, did you hear me?"

"Yeah, I heard you." I made myself meet his eyes. Whatever I might have been, I wasn't a coward. But not from lack of trying.

"I'm not going to ask you how you feel about him, because I'm pretty sure I already know the answer. But I will say this. Let him down easy, and do it soon, before this gets out of hand. You've already screwed him up emotionally by leading him on."

I bristled; if I'd had fur, it would have stood on end. "I didn't lead him on," I snapped, standing straighter. I was glad to finally have something I could legitimately argue about.

"The hell you didn't." His eyes blazed. "He told me you let him kiss you, and I heard what you didn't say to Marc."

I blinked, turning one ear toward him as if to improve my hearing. "What I *didn't* say to Marc?" Okay, now I was confused. The list of things *I hadn't* said was endless, no matter how much Marc claimed I talked.

"He asked if you wanted Jace to touch you, and you didn't say no. If you'd said no, Jace would have known the truth, but since you didn't, he thinks he has a chance with you. But if he takes one more shot, Marc will kill him. He won't be able to stop himself. And it will be *your* fault."

I exhaled, frustrated and angry. "You can't blame me for something I *didn't* say, and you certainly can't hold me responsible for anything Marc does. If you have a problem with his behavior, take it up with him." I glanced away, fingering a swirl in the wood grain of the china cabinet. "Besides, I didn't *let* Jace kiss me." Ethan started to object, but I cut him off. "Well, maybe I did for a minute, but I was about to push him away when Marc came in." That sounded weak, even to me, and Ethan didn't buy it for a second.

"Frankly, Faythe, I'm a little creeped out by having to think about what my sister does in private. But apparently you're not thinking about it enough. These aren't house cats you're playing around with. They aren't college boys, either. If you don't tell

them both the truth, someone's going to get hurt.
And it won't be you."

A spark of irritation flared in my gut, only slightly
smothered by encroaching guilt. "First of all, I'm not
playing around with anyone." I glanced away from
his face, hesitant to admit the rest. "And I'm not
sure I know what the truth is."

"Well, figure it out. Fast." With that, he stomped
off to the living room, where I could hear Jace and
Parker trying awkwardly to comfort Kyle.

I was relieved that Jace was okay. And I really had
been worried about him. But I had no idea how I
could have prevented Marc's temper tantrum. Okay,
maybe I could've pushed Jace away a little sooner,
but honestly, I was getting pretty tired of being held
responsible for Marc's lack of control. What concern
was it of his what I did with Jace? Absolutely none.

But he'd made it his business, and that was the
bottom line. I was starting to understand that in the
real world nothing else mattered.

Around nine, my mother put Nikki to bed in my
room and said I could either make a pallet on my own
floor or sleep on the couch. I told her I'd stay in the
guesthouse with the guys, and Ethan promised to
keep an eye on me, since Marc's Faythe-sitting shift
had ended. My mother just nodded. I don't think

she'd heard about my threats to abandon the Pride. I hadn't seen or heard her talk to Daddy since breakfast.

An hour later, Mom ran out of chores to keep her mind off the tragedy at hand. She'd dusted the entire house, cleaned up the buffet and stored the leftovers, and made enough tea and coffee to keep the bathrooms occupied for the rest of the year. Since courtesy forbade her to vacuum around our guests' feet, she settled for trying to drive me out of my mind with inane questions. It was her second-favorite hobby, and one she'd perfected ages ago.

I knew the moment she settled next to me on the couch, knitting bag in hand, that it was time for me to retire for the evening. I just didn't know how best to pull off my escape.

"What did your father want with you this afternoon?" she asked, tucking a strand of hair behind my ear.

Swatting her hand away, I shot desperate looks at Ethan and Parker, where they sat across the room, still huddled around Kyle, who clutched a nearly empty bottle of whiskey. I couldn't bring myself to look at Jace. Not until I knew what to say to him.

"Faythe?" my mother said, and I turned back to look at her. "What did your father want?" I tried to relax my fists as I watched her run one hand over her smooth gray hair, turning the edges under. It made me want to shake my head like a wet dog, until I looked as different from her as was humanly possible, considering that I'd inherited her nose and cheekbones.

I wanted to lie. Damn, I wanted to lie, because one of my biggest goals in life was to avoid discussing men with my mother. But eventually she'd find out the truth. "He wanted to talk about my boyfriend."

"Your boyfriend?"

"His name is Andrew." I stared hard at Ethan as I answered through gritted teeth, but he only grinned and waved. He thought I deserved it.

My mother reached into her bag, pushing around balls of colored yarn and knitting needles with both hands. "What year is this boy in?"

Keep it short and simple, I thought. That was what Michael told all his clients before they took the stand. "He's not a boy, Mom. He's a grad student. In the math department. He wants to teach."

"Children?" She glanced at me with one hand over her heart, clearly aghast.

So much for simple, I thought, mentally cringing. "No, college."

"Oh. Good." She smiled in polite relief, digging again in her bag. "I was afraid he might like children."

That was my mother's secret code for "I'm glad you aren't thinking of marrying this man, because you know you can't give him any babies, and it would be wrong to condemn a teacher to a life without children." Nothing was ever simple with my mother, which was strange, because she seemed never to think about anything complicated.

"You know," she continued, pulling a small bundle of pale blue yarn from the bag. "By the time I was your age, I already had two boys and was pregnant with Owen."

I closed my eyes so she couldn't see how far they'd rolled back into my head. "I know, Mom. You and I are different."

She made an odd, cooing sound and I reopened my eyes to see her carefully spreading out the small bundle. It took on a vague, curved shape, curling over one knee.

"We're not as different as you think, dear."

Yeah, right. My mother was a regular rebel without a cause. "Sure, Mom. I'm your carbon copy."

"There's no need for sarcasm, Faythe."

I huffed in disdain, and the sound came out clipped and harsh. "If you really believe that, then we're nothing alike."

She sighed, taking up a long, metallic blue needle

in each hand. "I intend to have a serious conversation with you someday."

"I can barely contain my excitement." I watched as she began to knit-one and purl-two, or whatever it was that made the separate threads of yarn hold together. The shape of that little blue bundle looked so familiar…

"You know, I wasn't born a wife and mother." She took both needles in one hand for a moment, glancing at me as she smoothed out the length of yarn trailing from one. "I was your age once."

"And by your own admission, you already had a husband and two and a half kids."

My mother frowned, lowering her knitting to her lap. With disapproval clearly visible in the frown lines around her mouth, she really did look like me. Or like I might look after another quarter of a century, if my life didn't drastically improve. "Really, Faythe. Half a child? Is that any way to refer to your brother?"

"I just meant that you hadn't had him yet."

"I know what you meant," she snapped, knitting furiously. I stared at the yarn in growing horror. I knew what she was making. A bootie. A tiny, pale blue baby bootie. My mother was the Denis Rodman of subtlety. A master craftsman in the art of creative manipulation. Without saying a word, she'd reminded me once again that my life was off track by her standards and shown me what I should have been thinking about. "Really, you place too little value on life. Particularly on your own."

"What are you talking about?" Determined to ignore the bootie unless she mentioned it, I met her gaze, hoping to drive her away with a little confrontational eye contact. "I value my life very highly."

"Then why waste it?"

Ouch! I shot an irritated glance at Ethan, but he was pretending not to see me. I knew he was pretending because he couldn't quite stop grinning, even when Michael elbowed him in the ribs. They were supposed to be comforting the grieving fiancé.

"I'm not wasting my life, Mom. I'm doing exactly what I want to do."

"With your nose in a book all day?"

My hands curled into fists in my lap. "I *like* books."

"You hide behind your books, like you used to hide behind my legs." Her needles clicked together rapidly, a sound I'd identified early in life as the most annoying noise in the world.

"I never hid behind you, and I am *not* hiding behind my books."

Her hands paused, and she smiled softly, as if remembering something sweet and long gone. "You hid behind me every time we had company until you were five years old."

I let my head fall onto the back of the couch, staring at the ceiling. "I don't remember that."

"There are a lot of things you don't remember," she said, her fingers flying once again.

"Such as?"

"Such as when I sat on the council with your father."

I lifted my head, narrowing my eyes at her in suspicion. "You sat on the council?"

She beamed, clearly pleased to have caught my attention. "Yes, I did. I was the only woman."

"Why?" I plucked a ball of yarn from her lap, watching it spin slowly in my palm as her repetitive motions gradually unwound it. It was soft and fuzzy, tickling my hand with an almost unbearably gentle sensation.

"Why was I on the council?" she asked, and I nodded. "Because their decisions were important to me, and I wanted to have some input."

"Did Daddy make you quit?"

My mother laughed. She actually threw her head back and laughed, drawing stares from across the room as she shattered the surface of a tense, grieving silence with a sound of genuine amusement. "Your father has never *made* me do anything," she whispered, glancing around discreetly to make sure no one was bothered by her outburst. "But he did try to convince me to stay on the council."

"He wanted you to stay?" I couldn't keep disbelief from my voice. She was turning my entire world inside out, with no idea of the impact of her words. I could almost believe the sun would rise tomorrow to light a purple sky and shine down on bright pink grass.

"Is that so hard to believe? He thought the Alphas needed to be tempered by a less aggressive influence. Together, they're pretty easily riled, you know."

"I know." That was true for men in general, in my opinion. "Why weren't there any other dams on the council?"

"Well, I can't speak for the other women, but none of them seemed particularly interested in discussing dry politics and border negotiations."

That was understandable. "So, why did you quit?"

"I had more important work to do."

"You mean raising us?" I asked, my tone dipping once again into my endless supply of disdain. *Why would a woman who'd served on the council want to give up such an important position to change diapers and pack bagged lunches?*

"You, mostly." Her hands went still again as her eyes stared off into the past with a look so wistful it made me ache for her. "The boys tended to take care of each other, but you were too much for anyone else to handle."

I poked at the ball of yarn, avoiding her eyes. "I wasn't that bad."

She smiled. "You broke Ethan's arm."

"It was self-defense. He wouldn't let go of my foot."

"He was helping you tie your shoe."

I shrugged. I remembered it differently. He'd held my foot down with his hands around my ankle, so I kicked him in the chest with my free foot. He fell onto his backside. When he stood, face flaming in anger, I swept his legs out from under him with the foot wearing the untied sneaker—my childish attempt at poetic justice. Ethan threw one arm back, trying to catch himself, and we both heard his wrist snap. Everyone in the house heard him howl. He was eight, and I was six.

"What about the time you super-glued Ryan's—" She stopped, glancing down at her lap. After a moment, her fingers flew into action, needles clicking with an all-new speed and intensity. She'd been about to ask about the time I'd super-glued Ryan's hands to the handlebars of his bike. It was a clear-cut case of justifiable retaliation, but she would no more listen to my excuses than she would finish the story herself.

My mother hadn't mentioned her second son's name in ten years. She could deal with his decision to leave the Pride, but only if she didn't have to think about it. Or talk about it. Ryan was my mother's kryptonite, her only weakness, at least that I knew of. He was the prodigal son who'd never returned. And his name was off-limits, even to my father.

Ethan crossed the room quickly, but I couldn't tell whether he was coming to my rescue or hers. Either way, he knew we'd had enough. "Hey, Mom," he said, plopping down on her other side. "Do we have any more of those cookies you made yesterday?"

Her fingers never paused. "Ethan, there's no possible way you could still be hungry after three trips to the buffet. And no, you finished all the cookies this morning. After breakfast and before your midmorning snack."

He grinned, holding up one end of the bootie for my inspection. I flipped him off behind my mother's head, but he only grinned harder, still watching my face as he spoke to her. "I don't suppose you feel like making some more, do you?"

She sighed and her hands settled into her lap. I saw the beginning of a frown on her profile just before she turned to face him. "It's late, Ethan. Go make yourself a sandwich if you're still hungry."

From my left, Parker tapped me on the shoulder and jerked his head toward the hall. I nodded, sliding carefully off the sofa as Ethan tried to convince our mother that he had no idea how to assemble a decent club sandwich.

There are several advantages to being a cat that carry over to a lesser degree in human form, but stealth is the best by far. By the time my mother realized I was gone, I was racing across the backyard, with Jace and Parker on my heels.

Seventeen

"Wait." I slowed to an abrupt stop, breathing heavily as I curled my toes in the cool, soft grass halfway between the main house and the guesthouse. Parker and Jace ran several steps behind me, their hair blown back by the persistent evening breeze.

Parker sidestepped me seconds before his momentum would have knocked us both to the ground. "What?" he asked, smoothing salt-and-pepper hair with one hand.

"Aren't you guys supposed to stay with Kyle?"

One corner of Parker's mouth curled up in amusement. "He's fine. We left him with Michael."

"He'll pass out soon anyway," Jace said, moonlight glinting blue-white in his eyes as he came to a stop on my other side. I'd been afraid of what I'd see on his face, but he wore his usual carefree grin, as if nothing had happened. "We've been giving him whiskey as fast as he'd drink it. The man's a lightweight."

"He's grieving, Jace," Ethan said, slinking out of the thick shadows behind us. "And by the way, Faythe, you owe me." His eyes were hard, his anger about far more than having to come between me and our mother. He was still mad about my involvement with Jace.

"Bill me," I snapped, wishing he'd mind his own business. Jace wasn't mad, so why should he be?

"You're lucky I haven't taken it out of your hide." He wasn't smiling, and his voice was almost a growl.

I stepped away from the others, giving myself room to maneuver. "You're welcome to try." I could still take him down, and now that he was grown, he'd fall even harder.

Ethan grinned, but not because he was happy. If he'd had real canines, he would have been flashing them at me. "Don't tempt me."

"Okay, boys and girls, that's enough for now." Parker put one heavy arm around my shoulders, and the other around Ethan's, steering us toward the guesthouse at the edge of the tree line. Ethan and I would both be staying there, me on the couch and him on a pallet on the floor, because he'd given his bed to Michael for the night. My mother had fixed up Owen's bed for Kyle.

Ethan shrugged Parker's arm off. "I need a drink," he muttered, taking off ahead of us at a fast walk.

"Me, too." Jace jogged past me to catch up with Ethan, sparing only a short glance in my direction. Long shadows trailed behind them as they approached the light on the guesthouse porch.

"Yeah, I could use a drink," I said. "Or two, or three."

"Well, we can certainly oblige." Parker squeezed my shoulder, and I glanced up at him gratefully. "I think a little binge drinking may be in order tonight. There's no better way to deal with tension and grief."

I took issue with his concept of therapy, but I kept my mouth shut because I couldn't think of any better way to cope, especially considering the outcome of my hunt that morning. Besides, Parker was the world's all-time best drinking buddy. He'd had lots of practice.

Ahead of us, Jace and Ethan jogged up the porch steps and through the front door, clearly determined to claim a couple of bottles before Parker got near the kitchen island, which doubled as a fully stocked bar. The guys did quite a bit of drinking on their nights off, which wasn't as bad as it sounded. It's really hard to get a cat drunk, possibly because of our accelerated metabolism, which also makes it difficult to sustain a buzz.

Out of habit, I paused with my hand on the old iron porch rail, looking up at the second floor. The light was on in Marc's room; he was still up. I'd never been able to pass the guesthouse without looking up at his window. Not once. It was an addiction. A pointless, self-destructive addiction. But really, is there any other kind?

Parker, true gentleman that he was, opened the front door for me, then followed me into the living room. The guesthouse was small but much warmer and more comfortable than the main house. And though the occupants sometimes changed—as older enforcers moved on, and younger ones came to replace them—the ambience stayed the same. The guys kept the fridge stocked with soda, squirt cheese, and frozen burritos, food my mother never served, and to my knowledge had never tasted. Ever since we were old enough to walk, my brothers and I had been welcome to make ourselves at home anytime we needed a junk-food fix.

A couple of years ago, the guys went in together on an obscenely large wide-screen television, which they kept tuned to sitcom reruns, action movies or ESPN. There were always empty glasses on every flat surface and discarded clothing on the floor. It was like going away to summer camp every time I walked through the door—until Marc and I broke up. I hadn't been in the guesthouse since, in almost five years.

But one glance at the living room told me nothing had changed. The floors were still scarred hardwood, because the guys couldn't keep carpet in decent shape. The walls were dingy white and almost completely bare, because they didn't know what to hang up. Cheap miniblinds covered the windows, and the only plates in the cabinet were made of paper. Video-game controllers and DVD boxes littered the living-room floor. And the entire place smelled like sweat and old pizza, scents I associated with some of the best times of my life.

I couldn't help but smile.

Parker waved a hand at the couch against one wall. "Sit down. I'll get you a drink."

"You guys could use some new furniture," I said, brushing off a crumb-crusted cushion before I sat. The couch was upholstered in 1980s brown-and-yellow plaid, the cushions flattened to half their original thickness. When I sat, I sank deep enough to place my navel several inches lower than my knees.

"Nah," Jace said from behind the makeshift bar, a bottle of tequila in one hand and a shot glass in the other. "It would take us years to break in anything new."

I laughed. "That would sure be a shame."

"What's your pleasure?" Parker asked, lining up a series of bottles on the faded Formica countertop. If Marc or Jace had asked the same question, I might have raised an eyebrow at the choice of words, but not with Parker. His only vice was alcohol, and even under the influence he was the most polite man I knew. And the gentlest, other than Owen.

Before I could reply, wood groaned behind me, and my words died on my lips. But someone else answered for me. "Margarita on the rocks, heavy on the salt."

I whirled around and felt my hair swing out in an arc behind me. Marc stood at the bottom of the stairs, wearing only a snug pair of jeans with both knees worn through. Light from the bare bulb in the stairwell played on muscles I'd watched him develop years ago. He had one hand in his pocket and the other wrapped around the neck of an empty beer bottle.

Sensitive parts of me tightened as my eyes lingered on the lines of his chest, drawn to the four long, parallel scars that had brought him into my life. It was all I could do to keep from squirming on the couch. I hated that just seeing him like that could affect me so strongly, and I hated it even worse that he knew it. And he wasn't the only one. Everyone in the room heard my raspy intake of breath, and they'd have to be blind to miss the flush scalding my cheeks as I took in Marc's scent from across the room. At the edge of my vision, Jace downed his first shot, following it with a slice of the lime he'd just cut. Then he snatched the shot Ethan had poured for himself and tossed it back too, ignoring my brother's grumbling protest. I saw it, but it barely registered. I couldn't drag my focus from Marc.

"How did you know that?" I whispered, knowing he could hear me. I'd been barely eighteen when we broke up, and too young to drink. So there was no way he could know my drink of choice. At least, there was no way he *should* have known.

"Vic told me a couple of years ago." His face was completely blank, impossible to read. "He watched you at Hudson's on your twenty-first birthday."

My blush deepened. If Vic had witnessed my birthday binge, he'd know I hadn't left the bar alone. And Marc would know, too. I'd been an idiot to think my life at school and my life on the ranch were unconnected. They were hopelessly intertwined around me, like two different vines fighting to strangle the same poor tree, and only my desperation for privacy had kept me from seeing it.

Marc looked away first, and my eyes followed him into the kitchen. He took a juice glass out of the dish drainer and half filled it with whiskey, then finished off the glass with Coke from a can. Without even a glance in my direction, he sat at the island on a bar stool, his back to me.

"Sorry, Faythe," Parker said, waving a clear plastic carton with less than a single swig of bright green liquid at the bottom. "We're out of margarita mix. What's your second choice?"

"I don't know." I'd only had a couple of drinks since that night at Hudson's. I'd never been much of a drinker, in part because I didn't know how to achieve a buzz without looking like a lush in front of my friends. But the guys did, Parker in particular.

Parker was the oldest of six boys, each no more than eighteen months apart. As teenagers, the Pierce brothers were infamous for putting their mother through hell. On one notorious occasion, Mrs. Pierce came home to find all six of her boys, the youngest of whom was then fourteen, passed out drunk in what remained of her formal living room. Her husband was at the Lazy S at the time, attending a yearly council meeting. He took the call from his wife in my father's office, surrounded by his fellow Alphas. And me, of course, though at the time I had no idea why Daddy kept including me.

As luck would have it, Mr. Pierce accidentally pushed the speakerphone button at exactly the wrong moment, and the entire room heard his wife turn over responsibility for all six boys to him. In one long, near-hysterical sentence, she said that grooming Caroline, their ten-year-old daughter, was all she could handle at the moment, and he could do what he wanted with his sons, so long as he kept them away from her.

Mr. Pierce's first act as de facto warden was to get rid of the three boys who had already come of age. He negotiated right then with the leaders of three other territories, making arrangements for his sons to serve as enforcers, to teach them discipline and responsibility. Parker had been at the ranch ever since, for the better part of ten years.

"The trick is to drink it quickly, then start on another one," Parker said, crossing the room to hand me a tall glass filled with a dubious-looking brown liquid.

I held the glass up to the light, looking for a justifiable reason to hand it back. Maybe spots on the glass, or a hair floating on the surface? No such luck. To be polite, I'd have to try it. "What is this?"

"Long Island Iced Tea."

Oh. I could handle tea.

But, if I'd watched him mix my drink instead of

watching Marc's tanned shoulders tense and relax, I would have known that the only thing a Long Island Iced Tea had in common with its namesake was color. I took a drink and made a face but managed to swallow it. For a moment, I considered asking Parker for a plain soda instead, but then my eyes settled on Vic's empty recliner, and I remembered why I was there in the first place instead of asleep in my own bed. Sara. Raped and murdered. And put on display.

I took another sip, and then another after that, trying to drown out my thoughts and wipe the gory images from my mind. But no matter where I looked, I saw her body as Michael had described it. Every time I closed my eyes, even just to blink, Sara's eyes stared back at me, brilliant blue and framed by lashes that had never needed mascara. So I kept drinking, desperate to forget the way she died, to hold back tears I still hadn't shed. I drank to numb an ache so acute that my heart throbbed painfully with each beat, and my head pulsed with a near-paralyzing pressure, like it might burst and end my misery once and for all.

And finally, after thirty minutes and three Long Island Iced Teas, my liquid anesthesia began to take effect, though the taste failed to grow on me.

Across the room, Marc had settled into a faded

and lumpy armchair. In one hand he gripped the bottle of Jack Daniel's, and in the other he clenched its cap, as if he were afraid of what his hands might do if he left them unoccupied. My bet was that he would ruin more drywall, and maybe break a couple of his own fingers in the process. He didn't deal well with anger or grief, both of which showed clearly in the lines of his face.

Marc had abandoned his glass along with the Coke and was drinking whisky straight from the bottle, openly watching me between gulps. I'd never seen him drink like that, and the binge worried me until after my second refill. By then, I didn't care. He was just as upset as I was, and we both seriously needed to relax.

At some point, I switched over to screwdrivers. I'd tried straight vodka but just couldn't swallow it. When I spit the first mouthful all over the floor, Parker sent Ethan to the main house for a carton of orange juice. The juice made all the difference.

Jace stuck to tequila and lime slices, and for a while I watched him, waiting to see the familiar grin he usually wore. But he never smiled, only opening his mouth to take another drink. If he was drinking to forget about Sara, he was doing a very poor job of it; I'd never seen him look sadder. He tried to match Marc gulp for gulp but couldn't do it. He passed out slumped over the bar, with the bottle still clenched in his right hand.

I giggled, thinking it served Jace right for calling Kyle a lightweight. Then I laughed at myself for giggling, and that was when I realized I was drunk. There was no other logical explanation for why I might find that funny. But at least I was a happy drunk. Marc was just plain moody.

Eventually, Parker and Ethan carried Jace up to his room to sleep off the tequila, but by then, very little of what I saw was actually sinking in. And even less of what I heard was.

Alone in the living room with Marc, I became uncomfortably aware of his eyes on me. Intentionally ignoring him, I concentrated on what I could hear upstairs. Parker and Ethan were talking, but my concentration was shot, so I only picked up a phrase here and there.

"…if we don't get her back?" Ethan asked. Metal springs groaned as they lowered Jace onto his bed.

"We will," Parker said, his voice followed by two thunks, which I assumed to be Jace's shoes hitting the floor. "And they'll all pay…"

A door closed somewhere overhead. "…we're too late?"

"…another drink?" That was Parker. Definitely Parker.

"...on't want another drink. I want to pound the shit out of someone."

"...have an idea..."

I glanced away from the stairs when Parker's feet came into view. He started to say something else to Ethan, then noticed that my glass was empty and veered in my direction instead. He refilled my drink—again—and by the time I had to use the restroom, I could no longer remember where it was. Or how to walk.

Ethan grudgingly helped me to the bathroom door but said I was on my own from there. I made it, but barely. In front of the toilet, as I did the universally recognized "I have to pee" shuffle, I cursed Levi Strauss for his insanely complicated system of buttons and corresponding holes. What was wrong with a simple drawstring?

When I got back to the living room, Ethan and Parker, who seemed least affected by the liberal flow of alcohol, were taking out their anger vicariously through a video boxing game on the huge television, their digital counterparts pixilated and nearly life-size. And very bloody.

Averting my eyes from the simulated death match, I saw that Marc had taken my seat on the couch. I stopped in the middle of the room, trying to make the floor quit rolling while I waited for him to move. By the time I realized he wasn't going to, I was past the point of caring where I sat.

"I won't bite," he said, staring up at me through half-closed eyes. "This time."

I sighed and rolled my eyes, which turned out to be a bad idea. When the room stopped pitching like the deck of a ship at sea, I relented. "Fine, scoot over."

"There's plenty of room." He patted the six inches of threadbare cushion between him and the arm of the couch.

"Scoot, before I throw up on you." That did it.

Marc moved several inches to his right, and I dropped onto the vacated cushion. My empty glass sat on the floor by my foot, and I thought about asking Parker for a refill but decided that if I was too drunk to get it myself, I was too drunk for another. That turned out to be a really good decision. It was the only smart thing I'd done all day. If only I'd done it a little earlier.

My left arm rested on the arm of the couch, my short fingernails scratching back and forth across the rough plaid pattern. The rhythm of my nails skimming over the raised threads echoed through my head like the beat of a hopelessly unimaginative drummer. For some reason, I found the sound fascinating.

"I can hear your heartbeat," Marc said, dragging me from my drunken rhythmic epiphany.

I glanced at my lap and realized our legs were touching from knee to hip. My shorts ended at midthigh, and I could feel the heat of his skin against mine through the layer of denim covering his leg. It felt so good, so familiar, even after all those years apart.

"I can hear yours, too." I turned slowly to look at him, and my eyes were only a few inches from his. A few completely insignificant inches. His breath was warm on my cheeks and on my lips. He didn't look drunk anymore. Maybe he wasn't. Just because I'd done a fine job of retaining my buzz didn't mean he had.

"You are so beautiful," he whispered directly into my ear. His chin rested on my shoulder, bare except for the thin strap of green cotton holding my shirt on.

"I am?" I could barely speak. My pulse raced in my throat, seeming to say more than my mouth ever had. I blinked, trying to hold my head still as vertigo claimed my attention, surely the result of his declaration rather than of alcohol. Or maybe my head *was* still, and the room was spinning.

He spoke slowly, as if to make sure I understood, and each word sent a tantalizingly intimate puff of breath against my ear. "Yes, you are. Loud, stubborn, and infuriating at times, but almost too beautiful to look at."

I heard what he was saying, and some part of my brain even processed it. But at the time, his meaning seemed much less important than the sound of his voice, a deep rumble rolling through me, triggering responses in all the right places, the way the rippling surge of an earthquake will sometimes set off burglar alarms.

"And you came back," he said, chin stubble scratching my shoulder.

"I came back." Something was wrong with that. Damn it, something was wrong with that statement, but for my life I couldn't remember what. And in that moment, I just didn't care.

"I need to feel something real. I need you, Faythe," he said, his lips brushing my cheek as his fingers tangled themselves around mine, clinging desperately. I heard the pain in his voice, the raw need for so much more than I had to give, and my chest tightened.

I'd never been needed. Not by anyone, much less by someone whose entire purpose in life was to be strong for everyone else, and I liked the feeling of power that gave me, the feeling of strength. He was asking for my help, and—so help me—I wanted to give it to him. I wanted to make everything okay, and let him do the same for me. I didn't just want it. I *needed* it. I needed something familiar, something warm and strong to help me forget and make me feel safe. I needed Marc. And all I had to do was admit it.

"I need you, too." It was true when I said it, and even drunk I wondered why I hadn't realized it earlier. Oh, the miracle of alcohol! Everything that had seemed so terribly, hopelessly complicated when I was sober was suddenly so simple. I needed him and the memory of what we'd been, the memory of something safe, and substantial, and good. Something I understood, when life as I knew it was falling apart at my feet. I understood Marc; he wouldn't fall apart. For me, he'd hold it together. The least I could do was return the favor.

He kissed me, and I didn't just let him, I kissed him back. We fed from each other with an urgency born of starvation, of desperation. I couldn't touch enough of him, couldn't reach deep enough to soothe myself, to bury my pain in memories of pleasure. But I could try.

I hid my face in his neck, drowning in his scent. He smelled like masculinity personified, like musk and unscented soap and something else, something powerful, and dangerous, and exciting. I breathed him in, and the thrilling combination of danger and absolute security tingled through me, igniting every nerve ending in my body. I felt like a kid holding a lit firecracker, wondering if he could handle the charge, and whether or not he'd get burned.

My hands found his chest, and his found my hair. He pulled my head back and kissed the length of my throat, hesitating just a moment over my pulse, flicking his tongue against my skin as if the thin flesh covering my jugular vein tasted just a little sweeter than all the rest.

Ohhh, and it did. It must have, because his did too.

"We're trying to concentrate here," Ethan grumbled from the floor, momentarily breaking the spell. I pulled away from Marc long enough to glance at my brother. He looked disappointed for a moment, but then he nodded at me as if something had been decided.

Had something been decided?

Before I could think it through, Ethan turned back to the video game, his thumbs executing a complicated series of movements on the controller even as he spoke. "Get a room."

A room. That was a great idea. My room was occupied, but Marc's was empty, and it was right upstairs. We kissed all the way up the steps, and only his grip on the banister and around my waist kept us moving forward instead of tumbling to the hardwood floor.

We paused on the landing at the top of the stairs, where he pinned my hips to the wall with his body while he pulled my shirt off, tossing it to the floor.

His motions were hurried, frantic, and I understood the reason. If we hesitated, we'd have to think, and neither of us wanted to think. We wanted to feel, to lose ourselves in something all-consuming, something powerful enough to block out reality, and the pain and fear it would inevitably bring. And together we were explosive.

Before, that had been part of the problem, but now it was the solution. It was the fireworks-in-the-sky, forget-your-own-name, can't-feel-your-toes solution to all my problems. At least for the moment.

We stumbled past the bedroom Vic usually shared with Jace, and I barely registered the sound of slow, sleep-regulated breathing. By contrast, Marc's breath was hot and fast, almost a pant. His room was at the front of the house, the last one we came to, and he was impatient by then. He picked me up, and I wrapped my legs around his waist, rounding my spine so I could reach his ear with my tongue. He moaned as he carried me into his room, barely pausing to kick the door shut before setting me gently on the floor.

The hardwood was cool against my bare feet; it acted as an anchor, tethering my body to the ground as my head floated far above my shoulders. I closed my eyes, concentrating on the feel of his hands running all over me, ridding me of the encumbrance of my shorts, the restriction of my bra. Dropping to his knees, Marc wrapped his arms around my waist, resting his head on my stomach as he clung to me, trembling silently.

I gasped to feel him lift my breast, bringing as much as he could into his mouth. He pulled gently on my nipple, his tongue hot against my skin, his mouth demanding. I moaned, burying my hands in his hair, my head thrown back and my eyes closed.

His hands trailed down from my waist, easing my panties over my hips. The thin cloth hit the floor seconds before he picked me up and tossed me onto the bed. I had a single moment to think as I heard his zipper go down and the soft brush of denim against skin as his jeans followed suit.

In that moment, everything threatened to cave in. Without Marc there to reinforce them, my defensive walls were crumbling, succumbing to the pressure of outrage and fear.

But then his face appeared over mine, and his weight dropped onto me, heavy, and warm, and so very real. He propped himself on his elbows and I stared up into his eyes. Yellow specks sparkled in the deep brown of his irises, glistening through a layer of unshed tears.

"I'm scared," I whispered, wrapping my legs around him.

"Me, too."

I felt how hard his heart beat and knew it was the truth.

He moved against me, then inside me.

I exhaled, letting go of more anguish than I'd known I held. I closed my eyes, and my own tears spilled over, running down my cheeks to dampen my hair and his sheets.

Then he said my name, and suddenly there was no room for pain, no room for fear. Marc took up all the room there was, in my head, in my heart, and inside me. He filled me, not just with himself, but with memories of what we'd been, of what I'd given up.

My fingers skimmed the lines of his arms, up over his shoulders, then down his back. When I got to his hips, I added pressure, urging him on as I rose to meet him. Marc matched my pace, apparently eager to spend his pent-up energy without breaking anything. He couldn't hurt me. Even better, considering my recent delve into all things human and fragile, I couldn't hurt him.

When I finally remembered to breathe again, our combined scents overwhelmed me. I was suffocating on the very aroma of hunger and need—an exhilarating blend of his, mine, and ours—and I never wanted another breath of fresh air. The smell of sex itself was almost enough to bring me, screaming, to the edge.

Already panting, I put a hand on Marc's chest, begging him with my eyes to wait. I wasn't ready. Not yet. I needed much, much more.

He smiled, a trace of satisfaction glinting in his still-damp eyes. He altered our rhythm, watching my face as he slowed, moving deeper with each stroke. Marc remembered what I liked even better than I did.

Each time our bodies met, sparks tingled through me, racing across my nerve endings in violent jolts of pleasure bordering on pain. My fingers curled at his hips. My nails sliced through his skin.

Hissing, he arched his back, but his smile never faltered.

The sharp tang of blood filled my nostrils, adding one final layer to the bouquet of scents forming the foundation of my lust. I held him tight, smearing wet streaks across his spine. I arced into him, desperate for one more touch, one last powerful thrust that would bring us both peace, however temporary.

Marc knew what I needed. He tangled one hand in my hair and pulled my head back, opening my mouth. He thrust into me, hard. His lips covered mine, swallowing my scream of release and claiming it for himself.

He pounded against me over and over, fighting for control. My nails carved fresh gouges into his shoulders, and that was all he could take. He shuddered against me, moaning into my mouth. And finally he collapsed on top of me, his cheek against mine, his lips brushing my ear.

"I love you, Faythe," he whispered, still inside me. And then, so quiet I could barely hear him, he said, "Don't leave me."

Eighteen

Holding my breath, I tried for the third time to roll out of Marc's grasp without waking him. No luck. Every time I moved, his breathing quickened and his eyelids fluttered, as if he'd wake up any moment. Even asleep, he'd tried to make sure I couldn't get away; he had one leg draped over mine and one arm around my waist.

I groaned, and clamped one hand over my mouth as Marc shifted in his sleep. His leg slipped off me, but the weight of his arm across my middle was still very real. Biting my lip in concentration, I took Marc's wrist gently between my thumb and forefinger. I lifted his arm off my stomach, barely stifling a sigh of relief as the pressure on my bladder eased. When his next breath came, deep and relaxed, I lowered his arm to the bed between us as he exhaled. Finally free, I made myself wait through two more torturously slow breaths before easing silently off the mattress and onto the floor.

The moment my feet hit the ground, my eyes flew to the clock. Green segmented numbers stared at me in the dark: 4:34 a.m. That was weird. The color, not the time. My alarm clock numbers were red, which always made me feel anxious and hurried, like I was late for something every time I woke up. The green numbers were calm and soothing, assuring me that I still had a couple of hours left until dawn, yet I tottered on the thin, sharp edge of panic.

According to the clock, I'd gotten maybe three and a half hours of sleep after Marc and I collapsed onto his pillows, mercifully too exhausted to think. But now, standing naked in the middle of his bedroom, I could do nothing else.

Now look what you've done, Faythe, I thought, staring down at Marc's sleep-relaxed face. *You're not going to be happy until you've screwed up not only your life but everyone else's too.*

But that wasn't quite true. I wouldn't be happy then, either.

I needed to think. And I needed to pee. My bladder was quite insistent on that last part and had, in fact, woken me up to take care of business. But since I wouldn't be coming back after my trip to the bathroom—to gain any kind of perspective, I needed to distance myself from the problem—I'd have to get dressed. Unfortunately, my clothes were nowhere in sight.

Squeezing my eyes shut, I made myself concentrate on the order of last night's events. Each flash of memory felt like someone ramming a fist through my chest to squeeze my still-beating heart. And if it hurt me, I could only imagine what it would do to Jace. Or to Andrew. Shit, what about Andrew?

What the hell was I thinking?

I hadn't been thinking *anything;* that was abundantly clear. It had also been the whole point. I'd given my brain the night off, abandoning my body to the mercy of hormones and alcohol. And grief. The truth was that I'd needed comfort, and so had Marc, and we'd found it in each other. As wonderful as that had been, the unbelievable freedom of letting go, of giving myself completely to someone willing to do the same, morning would bring to light the inevitable consequences of what I'd done. But I wasn't ready to face them. Not just yet.

So where the hell were my clothes? I peeked carefully beneath the edge of the sheet draped across one of Marc's legs and twisted around the other. *Aha.*

Found my shorts. One article of clothing down, and only three more to go.

I found my bra dangling from the closet doorknob and my panties peeking out from under the bed. Dressed but for my shirt, I searched the room frantically with my eyes but saw no sign of the green halter top I'd put on after my marathon bathing session the day before.

Marc grunted in his sleep and rolled over onto his side. His hand landed in the warm hollow my hip had occupied moments earlier, and a fresh surge of panic flooded my body. I grabbed the first piece of cloth I found and pulled it over my head. It was the old, black Aerosmith T-shirt Marc had worn the day before. It still smelled like him.

The shirt was huge on me, effectively hiding my shorts, but it would have to do, because I had to use the restroom. Immediately.

I eased open the door, crossing my fingers against squeaky hinges, and slipped into the upstairs hall. The hall was more like a big rectangle, with the stairs rising up from the center and one door on each of the four walls. Three of the doors led to bedrooms and the fourth was the bathroom. That was the one I needed.

And there, on the floor between the landing and the bathroom door, lay my shirt, a crumpled pile of green cotton triggering the memory of how it got there. Images and sensations roared over me as I remembered Marc pressing me against the wall while he pulled the shirt over my head. The memory was still powerful enough to send tremors down the length of my body. My stomach clenched in dread and confusion. *What the hell am I going to do about Marc?*

The sound of running water came from the bathroom, and I froze, three steps from my shirt. Someone else was up.

The door opened, and I tensed. Jace stepped out. I stopped breathing. Completely.

At first, he didn't notice me. The hallway was dark, and—like me—he'd probably thought everyone else was asleep. He smiled when he saw my face, but his expression wilted as his gaze traveled over my tousled hair and down the front of Marc's shirt, to my apparently bare legs.

"Jace…" I began, desperate to explain, but no words came to follow his name.

He knelt to pick up my halter top. "You lost something," he said, and the cold quality of his voice made it clear that he didn't just mean the shirt. He threw it at me.

My shirt landed on my head, covering most of my face. I couldn't bring myself to pull it down until I heard his bedroom door close.

Faythe, you coward. My shirt hanging limp from one fist, I glanced at Jace's door, then at Marc's room. I'd made a mistake. It was understandable, and a good one, as far as mistakes go, but nothing had changed. At least not for the better. I wasn't home by choice, and I couldn't stay to be with Marc any more than I could stay to be with Jace. One round of consolation sex wasn't enough to change that, no matter how well it had worked. Or how good it had been.

My bladder pleaded with me to go into the bathroom, but I couldn't do it. I had to get out before Marc woke up and wanted to talk. Or do anything else. I dropped my shirt on the floor and took the stairs two at a time.

Ethan's obnoxious snoring greeted me on the bottom step. He lay sprawled on the couch, one arm dangling over the side. *Great.* There was nowhere for me to sleep. It didn't matter, though, because I couldn't have stayed in the guesthouse anyway. But I had to go somewhere.

My mind grasped at possibilities while my eyes roamed the room, and I knew what to do when I saw what lay unattended on the counter, amid a jumble of empty bottles, lime rinds, and sticky glasses: Jace's keys. I hesitated for a moment, my fingers hovering over the Kentucky Wildcats key chain.

Then I grabbed it and ran for the door. The keys were mine. I'd earned them.

I had a brief moment of doubt in the driver's seat of the new Pathfinder when it occurred to me that Jace would never forgive me for taking his car, in spite of our bet, because I'd promised both him and Daddy that I would wait. But he'd never forgive me for sleeping with Marc either, so what did it really matter? Besides, I wasn't running away. I just needed to drive around and think. I'd be back before anyone woke up, and with any luck, they'd never know I'd left at all.

As quietly as possible, I pulled past the house, relieved when the headlights shone on Owen's truck, parked in his usual space. He'd made it home safely.

At the end of the driveway, I rolled down the window to push the button on the automatic gate opener. But then I hesitated again. Beyond the gate, a narrow paved road separated our property from a small patch of forest. Several miles down, the road intersected a highway, and from there, I could go anywhere I wanted. Anywhere at all.

I looked in the rearview mirror, watching the main house as I contemplated what to do. I'd taken that road before. Twice. Both times had been in the middle of the night, in a stolen car. Both times I'd been running away. Both times I'd been caught. But

I couldn't run this time, even just to think. I'd spent every moment since my homecoming trying to convince my family that I'd changed, that I was older and wiser. Sitting at the end of the driveway, freedom within sight, I realized that I couldn't blame them for not believing me. If I wanted them to take me seriously, I'd have to prove I'd changed.

Leaving would only prove that I hadn't.

Quickly, before my nerve failed me, I slammed the car into Reverse and stepped on the gas with my bare foot, backing carefully toward the main house. I was through running. I would face the consequences of my actions like the adult I'd claimed to be.

But as the front gate grew smaller in the windshield, my resolve began to falter. I was still determined to confront my fears—just not yet. I still needed to think. I couldn't face Marc again without knowing what I was going to say to him. Not to mention Jace.

Halfway down the driveway, I noticed the ruts Owen's truck had carved through the grass on repeated trips to the barn. I stopped the Pathfinder, staring at the outbuilding in the middle of the eastern field. *The barn.* I hadn't been in the barn in ages. We'd played there as children, all five of us. Six, if Jace was visiting. We didn't have animals, but we always had plenty of hay until Daddy sold it as winter feed. So during the summer, we'd play in the barn, using the bales as forts, castles, wrestling mats, tables and anything else our fertile imaginations could envision.

Eventually, the others outgrew our hay bale playground, but I never did. In a houseful of boys, I'd needed someplace quiet to think and to read. Even years later, the smell of fresh hay brought to mind hours spent in the company of Jane Austen, Charles Dickens and Louisa May Alcott. The barn had served as my refuge once, and it would do so again.

Using the side-view mirror for guidance, I backed past Owen's ruts and shifted out of reverse, then turned onto the dirt path, already imagining the smell of hay. I pulled to a stop twenty feet in front of the barn, leaning over the steering wheel to stare out the windshield for a moment in silence. Nothing had changed. It was as if time stood still on the ranch, like we lived in some kind of weird warp zone of nostalgia.

I opened the car door and got out, leaving the keys in the ignition and the headlights on. I wouldn't be able to see much of anything, otherwise, unless I wanted to Shift—which I did not. Serious thinking was best done in human form, with no feline instincts to get in the way.

My hand was on the knob of the small corner door, about to pull it open, when my bladder gave me my final warning. If I didn't find a restroom soon, or at least a clump of brush, I was going to embarrass myself and ruin a perfectly good pair of shorts.

Desperate for relief, I searched the dark for somewhere appropriate to relieve myself. Several yards away stood an apple tree, short but healthy and beautifully formed. It wasn't my first choice but I no longer had the luxury of being picky. I headed for the tree in an all-out sprint, and almost fell twice as my feet slipped in the cool morning dew.

The thin tree trunk didn't provide much cover, but with no one else around, I was only hiding from my own humiliation.

With the pressure on my bladder relieved, I took my time sauntering back toward the Pathfinder, mentally composing an apology to Marc. Goodness knows I'd done plenty of that in the past. Especially that infamous summer five years earlier.

Two years before that, when I was sixteen and becoming seriously interested in boys from school, my mother and father had begun to push me toward Marc. They pushed, and I resisted, and they pushed some more. Eventually, they pushed too hard, and I actually fell—right into his bed. And wouldn't you know it, as soon as they got what they wanted, they reversed course, telling us to slow down, that we had our whole lives to get to know each other *that* well.

From then on, they'd tried to keep us chaperoned, at least until I was old enough to get married, the summer I turned eighteen. But by then, as I watched my classmates apply to college and choose their future careers, I'd realized what I would be giving up for Marc: my entire life. So, the night before our wedding, I'd snuck out of the house with my savings and taken Ethan's then-new convertible for a two-week journey of self-discovery, hunting when I was hungry, and sleeping whenever and wherever the opportunity arose.

They'd found me, of course, and because I'd still loved him, the apology I owed Marc was the single hardest thing I'd ever had to compose. But this new one came in a close second.

I was less than a foot from the double barn doors when the headlights flickered to my left. Concerned for Jace's battery, I turned away from the barn, squinting into the bright light as I veered toward the Pathfinder.

Metal creaked in front of me, and the lights sank, then bobbed, blinding me all over again. Startled, I jumped, my hand moving automatically to shield my eyes. They focused reluctantly. I froze, my mouth suddenly dry.

A man leaned against Jace's grille, his features indistinct in the wedge of darkness between the two cone-shaped beams of light. Had Jace heard me start his car? With my eyes crippled by the headlights, my nose came to the rescue. One whiff of the dew-scented, early-morning air told me exactly who I'd let sneak up on me.

Sean.

Cold sweat broke out behind my knees as I sidestepped to my right, out of the blinding glare. As my eyes adjusted to the dark, I made out his face, confirming the identity his scent had already given me. Sean had a rather prominent nose and short, light brown hair, crowning a slender build that almost made him look frail. But he was a tomcat, and no cat was frail. Sean could probably throw your average muscle-bound creep through the wall and into the next room, and the creep wouldn't realize his mistake until he was already airborne.

I realized my mistake. I just didn't know how to fix it. Unless...

My mind raced as an ambitious idea took shape. I glanced around without moving my head, searching discreetly for any sign of his accomplices. If Sean was alone, I was certain I could take him down by myself. Surely then my father would realize I didn't need to be protected—or confined. I saw nothing out of the ordinary. Except for Sean.

"I don't suppose you're here to turn yourself in?" I said, keeping him in sight as I backed slowly toward the front wall of the barn. My voice sounded obscenely loud to me in the predawn hush.

If Sean was worried about anyone hearing me, he gave no sign. Nor did he smile. He just shook his head slowly, firmly. "I'm sorry, Faythe," he said finally, confirming my suspicion. He had come for me. And from the look in his eyes, I could almost believe he actually *was* sorry. So why risk coming into Alpha territory—onto my father's private property, no less? He had to know he didn't stand a chance.

"The guys are on their way," I said, glancing around again as I wiped my sweaty hands on the tail of Marc's shirt.

Sean shook his head again, a small smile playing on his thin lips. "No they aren't. Greg would never let you out alone in the middle of the night." His eyes flicked to my feet. "And barefoot, at that. They don't even know you're gone yet."

Damn. He'd called my bluff.

I took another shuffle-step back, my feet sliding across the gritty dirt. "You were watching the ranch," I said, realizing I was right even as I spoke. "Where from?" Each minute I could keep him talking would increase the chances of Marc waking to find me gone.

Sean tossed his head toward the road without ever taking his eyes from me. Smart. "The woods across from your front gate."

I blinked at him, my face blank with confusion. He was lying. He had to be. How could a houseful of Alphas not have known the enemy was at the gate—literally? "How long?" I clenched my hands into fists, preparing to fight as adrenaline flooded my veins, bringing with it a sense of panicked determination.

He grinned, clearly proud of himself for evading the entire council. "Less than an hour."

Oh. That's how. He'd arrived after the other Alphas left for their hotel and we'd all gone to bed, some of us sleeping off massive amounts of alcohol. I guess patrolling our own property hadn't been such a bad idea after all.

My heart thumped painfully as self-doubt chipped at my confidence, wearing away my plan until there was nothing left of it but a foolish impulse. *Would anyone hear me scream?* I wondered, wishing I could see the main house from my position. Anyone awake would hear me easily, but I wasn't sure about those sleeping soundly, as everyone surely was.

Sean shifted against the grille, settling one red sneaker on the front bumper. He propped both elbows on the hood behind him, and my eyes checked automatically for dents in Jace's new car. "This was supposed to be reconnaissance, strictly look-and-listen. But then you pulled up to the gate, right in plain sight, and he couldn't resist taking a shot at the grand prize." Sean shook his head as if he were disappointed in me. "You could have at least made him work for it."

"Him?" I asked, already dreading the answer. And too late, I realized what he was doing. Sean was the diversion. He was keeping my attention focused on him, and away from what really mattered.

The answer to my question came from behind me, the barest whisper of a hard sole on packed dirt. "*Buenos días.*"

My heart lurched, and the first flood of true fear washed through me, tingling and scalding at the same time. He was so close his breath stirred my hair, but he hadn't been there a second ago. I would have sworn to it.

And the scent was wrong. Close, but wrong. This was definitely a jungle stray, but *not* the one I'd fought the other night.

Pain pricked my bare thigh, and my breath caught in my throat. The tranquilizer burned as it invaded my system. A hand clamped over my mouth, cutting off my scream before it even began. Terror unfurled in my stomach and I battled nausea, determined not to choke on my own vomit.

I half turned and caught a glimpse of strong Hispanic features similar to Marc's, except for the savage gleam in the stranger's eyes. Then he swung me back around, his other arm encircling my waist, pressing my back into his chest. All I could see then was the hood of Jace's Pathfinder, where Sean no longer leaned.

Giving in to panic, I clawed at the hand over my mouth, confused when my nails wouldn't sink into his flesh. With my next breath I smelled rubber and understood: he wore long, thick gloves. He'd come prepared. And in that moment, I realized how desperate my plight had become; I'd put myself at the mercy of my greatest fear. Just when I thought I'd reached the pinnacle of bad judgment, I'd surprised myself again.

Eyes wide with terror, I glimpsed movement ahead and to my left: a car door swinging open. My captor lifted me off the ground, carrying me ahead of him as I struggled. I kicked at his legs, still clawing at the gloves. But before he'd even reached the car, the tranquilizer began to take effect. My arms grew heavy and dropped to my sides. My legs hung limp. I could do nothing to stop him from stuffing me into Jace's car.

At the driver's side of the Pathfinder, he let go of my mouth to buckle my now limp form into the seat, using the shoulder harness to hold me upright. Sean sat behind the wheel with the car already in gear. *Why on earth had I left the keys in the ignition?*

Adrenaline raced through me, trying to propel my limbs into action. But nothing happened. I was terrified by my helplessness, my complete inability to command my own body. My head lolling to one side, I stared through tears and graying vision at my abductor as he slid onto the seat next to me. "You're the stray," I whispered, mildly surprised by the calm but mushy quality of my own voice. "The jungle cat." As he nodded, my eyes closed and refused to open, leaving me in the dark, terrified of the hand caressing my face and the voice in my ear.

"Buenas noches, mi amor," he whispered, his breath warm against my cheek. It was the last thing I heard before losing the battle for consciousness.

Sometime later—though *how* much later, I couldn't have said—I woke up enough to recognize the jostle and sounds of highway travel, and to realize that the sun had come up. I lay on my side, on the floor of a windowless commercial van. My hands were tied behind my back, but I didn't have the strength yet to test my bonds. My right arm was completely numb and impossible to move, which I hoped was a temporary state caused by lying on it for too long. But before I could test that theory, I passed out again.

The next time I woke, the light was brighter through the front windshield, and I still lay on my side in the van. But it wasn't moving. Two men were arguing in Spanish at the front of the vehicle. Sean and the stray.

I tried to wiggle the fingers of my right hand, concerned because it was still numb. My fingers worked, but the movement shot an unbearable wave of pinpricks up the length of my arm. And apparently that one small movement caught someone's attention.

"Ella está despierta," the stray said. Vinyl creaked behind my head, and the van rocked. He knelt by my side and took my chin in his hand, tilting my head up so that I had to either look at him or close my eyes. I closed my eyes.

"You will look at me eventually." His accent was spicy, the auditory equivalent of a good, hot salsa. Under other circumstances, I might have found it pleasant, but in my current predicament, pleasure was a foreign concept.

Heart pounding, I pressed my eyes shut tighter, on the theory that passive resistance was my best shot at survival.

He slid one hand beneath my shorts and stroked my inner thigh.

I jerked my chin from his grip and scooted backward, skinning my arm on the carpet. Undeterred, his hand followed me, triggering the memory of Marc's hand in the same place only hours earlier. Marc's touch had made me cry out, made me writhe in anticipation as I lifted my hips to meet him.

The jungle cat's hand sent nausea rolling through me, as much from the contrast as from terror and revulsion. My passive-resistance theory melted away like snow in July. I opened my eyes to glare at him. Fury lent me courage. "Fuck you," I growled, but it may not have been my best choice of words.

"Soon, *mi gatita*," he said, his breath hot and wet on my cheek.

I knew enough Spanish to translate that much. He'd called me his little kitty.

Tossing my hair from my face, I tried to look as threatening as I hoped I sounded. "Get your filthy hand off me before I bite it off." My neck ached from holding my head up, but I wasn't willing to take my eyes off the stray. At all.

Smiling, he squeezed my thigh hard enough to make my eyes water, but I refused to cry out. Laughter met my ears. I *hate* being laughed at.

Closing my eyes briefly, I said a silent prayer for speed and force. Then I sucked in a deep breath and kicked out with my left leg. I arced high, aiming for his face.

The stray caught my ankle in midair. He twisted my leg down and around, using the leverage to flip me onto my stomach. With one hand, he pinned my ankles together, holding my feet in the air above my hamstrings.

I thrashed, trying to free my feet. It did no good.

Behind me now, the stray leaned against my legs, pressing the fronts of my thighs into the rough carpet from knee to hip. Straining to look over my shoulder, I saw him pull a coil of nylon cord from his pocket.

"I enjoy a challenge, *gatita*." The cord scratched my skin as he looped it around my ankles tight enough to bite into my flesh. I still fought to free my legs, but he pinned me with his body weight. "And from what I've heard, you promise to be the best one yet. *Maravilloso*."

I could guess at that one, too. He was pleased. *Great.*

"You underestimated the dosage, Miguel," Sean said from somewhere behind my head. The van swayed again as he stood. "We're only halfway there."

Miguel glanced up, knotting the cord as he spoke. "Fill another syringe."

I heard Velcro rip open and the distinctive clink of glass on glass. Panic clutched at me with fingers of ice, sending chills throughout my body.

"Here," Sean said, and Miguel knelt at my side to accept the syringe. "What if that's too much?" Sean's concern sounded real.

I craned my head to look in the direction of his voice, hoping to make eye contact, but all I could see was a familiar red sneaker near the edge of my field of vision.

"Then she will sleep through the best part." Miguel thumped the side of the syringe, studying the dosage.

The lump in my throat felt as big as a peach pit, but I spoke around it, staring at the needle. "If you sedate me again, I swear the first thing I'll do when I wake up is kick your ass all the way back to the Rio Grande." My threat might have been more impressive if I wasn't speaking with one cheek pressed into the filthy commercial carpet of a rented van.

Miguel chuckled. "First of all, *mi amor,* my ass, as you say, is Brazilian, not Mexican. But *mi amigo,* here, does not understand Portuguese, so we are limited to Spanish and English for our conversations." He smiled, a grotesque travesty of joy, and the sight triggered my gag reflex. I swallowed convulsively to keep from vomiting, but the worst was yet to come. "And second of all, this tiny prick—" he waved the needle in front of my face "—is the least of your worries, assuming you wake up to feel the next one." His laugh left little doubt about his meaning.

Terror tightened my stomach. Pain shot through my limbs as I fought my bindings. I tried to stop, knowing I would hurt myself long before the nylon cord broke, but I couldn't. Struggling had become an involuntary response.

Miguel waved the needle in front of my face again, apparently just to watch me thrash. I banged my knee against something hard. Pain shot up my leg, settling in for the long haul behind my kneecap. Angry and hurting, I shouted a series of foul curses, any one of which would have made my mother wince.

Miguel only smiled.

"Please don't make me gag such a beautiful mouth." He ran one finger across my bottom lip. I strained forward to bite him but my teeth chomped into air. His finger was gone, leaving only the lingering scent of his touch, and my rage and frustration.

He tapped the syringe one last time, drawing it back out of my sight. Something cold and sharp brushed my upper leg, and I tried to squirm away.

He wrapped his hand around my thigh to hold it still, his fingers skirting dangerously close to my no-fly zone.

Okay, bravado hadn't worked, but I wasn't above begging. "Please, Miguel." I let a little fear leak into my voice, which wasn't hard, under the circumstances. "Please don't. I'll be quiet. I swear."

He smiled, stroking my hair as if I were a house cat in need of attention.

I ground my teeth together against more foul language, knowing it wouldn't help.

"You also swore to kick my ass back to the border, *mi amor*. I'm afraid I can't put much trust in your words."

"No, you can." I blinked up at him, terrified of what might happen while I was unconscious. "I won't move a muscle. I swear."

"Now, what fun would that be?" He stabbed the needle into my thigh. Again. And again his face was the last thing I saw.

Nineteen

I lay still in near darkness, unwilling to move until my eyes had a chance to adjust. As a cat, I would have had no problem seeing, but my human eyes make much less efficient use of the available light.

Wait a minute…

I closed my eyes in concentration, willing them to Shift, as they'd done in my bedroom the afternoon before. For more than a minute I waited, lying on my stomach, trying to force the change in my face. Nothing happened. When I opened my eyes, I saw only vaguely defined shadows against a background of murky gray.

It was that damn tranquilizer. It had to be. I added an inability to Shift to my growing list of reasons not to ever let anyone sedate me again.

My hands and feet were unbound, and my watch was gone. When my eyes had adjusted to the gloom, I sat up. My fingers tingled, and my wrists and ankles felt raw when I rubbed them, my flesh still indented from the nylon cord. I hadn't been free for very long.

Suddenly panicked by the memory of Miguel's lecherous leer, I ran my hands over Marc's Aerosmith T-shirt and my denim shorts, looking for rips. There were none. A quick check for cuts and bruises revealed only a fresh bruise on my knee and the two needle marks I remembered receiving—one on each thigh. I sucked in hot, humid air and sighed, relieved to find no unaccounted-for marks or aches.

Satisfied with my physical condition, all things considered, I turned my attention to the bare twin mattress beneath me. It was thin and cheap but felt new and smelled clean. *How thoughtful. A new mattress, just for me.*

"Faythe?"

I spun in the direction of my cousin's voice, but the tranquilizer had left me dizzy, and I almost fell flat on the mattress. "Abby?" I squinted in the dark. "Where are you?"

"Over here. In the cage across from you."

Cage? She was in a cage?

My eyes were starting to focus, and I made out a

double row of metal bars, one several feet beyond the other. I was in a cage, too, in a basement, if I had my guess. We had to be underground or in some kind of concrete-reinforced room for outside sound to be muffled so effectively. I could hear nothing but my heartbeat and Abby's. The near silence was eerie. Just like the basement at home.

Great. I've traded one prison for another.

Standing for a better view, I gripped the bars for balance as vertigo threatened to topple me again. Yes, it was a basement, lit only by muted daylight filtered through two grimy, horizontal windows near the low ceiling. The floor was concrete, cooler than the warm, humid air, and rough against my bare feet.

"Are you okay?" I asked, squinting again as I looked her over for obvious injuries. Her clothes appeared undamaged, a T-shirt bearing her high-school mascot and a pair of tight jogging shorts. A deep bruise marred one side of her face, a purple stripe stretching from below her eye to the edge of her chin. Her huge brown eyes were ringed with dark circles, which made them look haunted. Fortunately, other than the bruise and the bags beneath her eyes, she looked unharmed.

Abby's hair had grown since I'd seen her last; it now fell halfway down her back in a bright red curtain of perfect corkscrew ringlets. But nothing else about her had changed. She was still tiny—just over five feet tall—and thin, with almost no curves to speak of. At seventeen years old, she could pass for twelve.

Though my brain knew she was almost grown, my eyes saw a child locked behind bars in a dark basement, bruised and scared. But she wasn't alone anymore.

"I've been better, how 'bout you?" Abby asked from her own cell, maybe five feet away.

"Fine, as far as I can tell. How long have I been out?" I turned in a slow circle, glancing around at what little I could see of my new surroundings. There wasn't much to look at.

"I don't know. They brought you down about an hour ago. Maybe a little less. I didn't believe they'd actually caught you until I saw your face. I was so sure they were lying."

I didn't know whether to thank her for what I assumed was a compliment, or explain how—idiot that I was—I'd swum right into their net. So, I changed the subject. "What do they want?" I sank onto the floor to sit with my legs crossed.

She shrugged. "I was hoping you could tell me. Didn't they send a ransom note, or a list of demands, or something?"

"Nope." I shook my head. "No contact at all. Not so much as a phone call to take credit."

Her disappointment tugged at my heart, but I didn't know how to make it any better. So I changed the subject—again. "Any idea where we are?"

Abby shook her head. "I don't know anything. I'm not even sure how long I've been here. What's today?"

"Wednesday."

Her eyes widened. "Only Wednesday? Really?"

I nodded, intimately familiar with the way time sometimes seemed to stand still. "Assuming I wasn't unconscious for more than a day."

"You couldn't have been," she said, staring past me, obviously deep in thought. "They got me Monday night, but it was morning when I woke up here. And they didn't leave to go after you until…" Her eyes met mine in question. "This is Wednesday?"

"Yeah."

"Last night, sometime shortly after dark."

A timeline began to take shape in my head. They'd gotten Abby roughly thirty-six hours earlier. "Wait a minute." I glanced at her, daring a tiny smile. "You've only been here a day and a half."

"So what?"

"So, they got me around five this morning, and if they were here with you at dusk the night before, we can't be more than six or eight hours away from the ranch."

She rolled her eyes, unimpressed with my Nancy Drew routine. "Yeah, but that could be anywhere."

"Not really." I stood to pace the length of my cell, thinking aloud. "They'd be stupid to keep us in any of the territories. We're in one of the free zones. We have to be." Pausing in mid-pace, I closed my eyes to study the U.S. map I'd committed to memory back in junior high, overlaying it with the territorial boundaries I knew by heart.

Impressed with myself, I opened my eyes and smiled at Abby. "Mississippi is the only one they could have gotten to in less than eight hours."

Huh. I guess my teacher was right after all; geography *had* come in handy in the real world. But I had yet to use an augmented matrix outside of class.

"How far is Mississippi from the Lazy S?" Abby asked, her eyes tracking my movement as I resumed pacing.

"You can drive to Jackson in about six and a half hours. How long did it take you to get here?"

She shrugged. "I have no idea. I was in and out of consciousness. But it felt like a long time."

I frowned as if that told me something important. It didn't, but I saw no reason to shoot holes in my own credibility. "I bet we're in Mississippi."

Abby was quiet for a moment, processing the new information. "Okay, so how does that help?"

Good question. It took me nearly a full minute to come up with an answer. "Knowing we're in Mississippi means it won't take the cavalry long to get here. The council's meeting at the ranch now." Not great, but it was the best I could do. And figuring something out, however small, made me feel useful.

"The whole council?" Abby asked, excited now. "My dad?"

"Yeah, and your mom too." I used Marc's shirt to wipe sweat from my face. My heart throbbed painfully as his scent triggered a jarring flashback of the night before.

"Faythe?" Abby stared at me, concern weighing down the corners of her mouth. "You were talking about the council…" she prompted.

I blinked, clearing my head as well as my vision. "Yeah. Daddy called a meeting yesterday."

She stood, following me from behind her own bars as I resumed pacing across the front of my cage. "Do they have a plan?"

"I don't know. I wasn't in on the meeting." I just couldn't tell her that I was getting drunk and laid while the Alphas were trying to figure out how to get her back.

We paced in silence, and I used my stride to measure the size of my cage. Fourteen steps across the front, placing my feet heel-to-toe. By my guess, the cell was about ten feet long.

In her cage across from mine, Abby lowered herself to sit yoga-style on the floor, watching me with huge, sad eyes.

"Abby?"

"Yeah?"

I wanted to ask her about Sara but was at a complete loss for a tactful way to broach the subject. I'd been waiting for her to bring it up, and could only think of two possible reasons to explain why she hadn't. The first, and most preferable, was that she didn't know. Sara could have died before they took Abby. In fact, Sara's death might even have been *why* they took Abby. A new toy to replace the broken one.

The second possibility was much more disturbing. What if Abby hadn't mentioned Sara because she knew exactly what had happened and wasn't ready to talk about it yet? What if she'd seen what they did to Sara?

"Faythe?" Abby said, pushing a sweat-damp curl from her forehead.

"Sorry. I zoned out again." I decided not to ask her about Sara. She'd tell me what she knew when the time was right. For her, not for me.

Abby drew her knees up to her chest and wrapped

her arms around them. "Yeah, well, zoning out may come in handy later." Her eyes drifted down to a spot on the floor between our cages, making it impossible for me to interpret her expression.

Oh, no, I thought, sitting across from her as she sniffled and refused to look at me. Because she was alive and apparently unharmed, I'd assumed they hadn't touched her. At least not yet. But I was wrong.

Before I could work up the courage to ask her what had happened, wood creaked overhead, and her focus swung up to the ceiling. Mine followed automatically. It was the first sound I'd heard from outside the basement since regaining consciousness. I knew what it meant, but Abby said it for me.

"Someone's coming," she whispered, hugging herself in a gesture so automatic I was sure it was unconscious. She scooted away from me on her backside, putting as much room as possible between herself and the door to her cage. "Pretend you're still out, and he'll leave you alone for now," she said, her eyes wide and shiny with unshed tears.

"What do you mean?" I rose to grip the bars, dread twisting my stomach into knots.

"Shh," she hissed. "Lie down. And don't move, no matter what. I'll be okay."

Something squealed overhead: an old doorknob turning.

There was no time to consider the wisdom of taking orders from a seventeen-year-old. There was no time to do anything but comply.

Slick with nervous sweat, my hands slid down the bars. I dropped onto the mattress just as light flooded the basement from an open door at the top of a wooden staircase.

For one precious moment, the whole room was illuminated, but from my position, I saw only cinderblock walls and a third, unoccupied cell. As I watched with one eye slit open, a pair of boots appeared on the top step. They were unfamiliar, as was the voice accompanying them.

"Good evening, Abby-cat." He closed the door, and the light winked out, blinding me again until my eyes had another chance to adjust.

Abby didn't answer. I couldn't see her without moving, but I heard her shoes slide across the concrete as she continued toward the back of her cage, now on her feet.

The boots clomped down the stairs, marching into view beneath a pair of faded jeans and a plain white T-shirt. The man wearing them had wavy blond hair and a build sturdy enough to strain the material of his shirt. He was a tomcat, and definitely not a stray, based on his smell. But try as I might, I couldn't identify his birth Pride.

He sneered, twisting his mouth into a frightening approximation of a smile as he stepped down onto the concrete. "Aren't you going to say hi, Abby-cat?"

"Fuck off, Eric."

I almost laughed out loud. I'd never heard my baby cousin cuss before, but she did it well. I was proud.

"Now, that wasn't very nice." Eric pulled his shirt off, dropping it on the floor just outside her cage, and my heart ached as I stared at it. "We'll have to work on your manners."

He dug into his front right pocket and came up with a key, which he used to open the padlock holding her cage door closed. I couldn't see him anymore, but the squeal of metal on metal assaulted my ears as he opened the door.

Abby's heart rate increased, and I knew that as a cat, I would have smelled her panic.

Eric's heart sped up too, but in anticipation, rather than fear. "Are you going to behave yourself?" he asked.

She huffed at him. "Are you?"

He laughed, and a chill traveled up my back, making my imaginary fur stand on end. "Never, Abby-cat."

"Quit calling me that."

Metal clanged as he swung the cage door shut, but I didn't hear him lock it. "What would you prefer?"

"I'd prefer that you take a few deep breaths underwater." Abby sounded scared, which I'd expected, but she also sounded weary, as if her big talk was merely to cover up how tired and hopeless she really felt. Lying there listening, I knew her rebellion wouldn't go beyond words. She might have fought in the beginning, but now she was too worn down.

Eric's boots clomped twice. Rubber slapped the concrete as Abby dodged him, presumably running for the cage door. She'd only taken three steps when I heard a scream, followed by a dull thunk and her moan of pain. Then there was nothing but twin racing heartbeats and his deep breathing.

I turned my head for a better look, but Eric was too preoccupied to notice my movement. He was using a handful of Abby's bright red curls to press her face against the bars.

That's how she got the bruise, I thought, fury scorching a path from my heart down to my toenails.

Eric's free hand slipped beneath her shirt. Abby whimpered once, then her jaws tensed as she gritted her teeth. "That's better," he said in a falsely soothing voice. "See, it's not so bad." He ran his hand down her stomach and beneath the elastic waist of her jogging shorts. Abby stiffened and closed her eyes. A tear ran down her cheek.

Son of a bitch! I couldn't just lie there and watch, no matter what she'd said. I sat up, fists clenched in my lap. "Get your hands off her," I whispered, fighting to sound calm and in control, neither of which I actually felt.

Eric's head swung in my direction, but he recovered from his surprise quickly. "Hello, tabby," he said, visibly tightening his grip on my cousin's hair.

"No, Faythe," Abby moaned, but I ignored her. As long as my heart was beating, I couldn't sit there and watch someone hurt her without trying to help.

I used the bars to pull myself up, shooting Eric my best pick-on-someone-your-own-size look. "Let her go. Now."

"And if I don't?" He grinned, jerking her head back.

Abby gasped, and another tear rolled down her bruised cheek.

I growled, showing Eric my human teeth. "I'll rip your throat out."

"That'll be kind of hard from all the way over there."

"So come closer and give me a fair shot."

Faced with a personal challenge, Eric couldn't turn me down without looking like a coward. I'd already concluded—based on his looks—that his ego might get in the way of his common sense. I was right. Yes, I was judging a book by its cover, but Eric was a picture book at best, with no large words to distract from the pretty illustrations. Besides, some stereotypes have their basis in truth, and my bet was that I was looking at one very dumb jock.

Elastic snapped as he pulled his hand from Abby's shorts. Still sneering at me, he tossed her across the cell by her hair. She hit the far wall of bars, but this time her raised arms absorbed the impact. By the time she sank onto her mattress, rubbing her new bruises, he had already swung her cage door shut.

Abby looked from him to me through wide eyes, shaking her head at me in silent warning. We both ignored her.

Eric clicked the lock closed, already leering at me with a slimy smile. "I was hoping you'd wake up soon," he said, pocketing the key.

"You're in luck." I tried to control my galloping pulse, knowing he could hear it. At least, he could if he bothered to listen for it. "Why don't you come see how far you can get with a real woman? Or do you only have eyes for little girls?" In spite of my bravado, my chest tightened as he ran his eyes over me, lingering in all the usual places. His appraisal showed a pathetic lack of imagination.

"Aren't you the eager one?" he said, still a good three feet from my cage. "Don't worry, your turn's coming. Not with me, though. Miguel wants you all to himself."

I pressed myself against the bars, trying to tempt him closer. I only needed one good shot... "You scared?"

"Not of you, tabby." He licked his lips in appreciation of the view, and I swallowed to keep from gagging. "But I have a healthy respect for Miguel. Those jungle cats don't like anyone else's shit in their litter box."

Litter box? I thought. *No wonder the guy has to play snatch-and-grab to get some attention.*

Flattered as I was by the description of me as someone's toilet, I managed to keep my reply on topic. "Sounds to me like you're a scaredy-cat."

Eric's eyes hardened as he came a step closer. "Talk to me tomorrow, and we'll see who's scared." He scowled down at me, clearly trying to intimidate me with his height and bulk. Apparently he'd had some success with that tactic in the past, because he seemed unable to understand why it didn't work on me.

I met his eyes without blinking, letting him see how undaunted I was. I saw no reason to fear a man who preyed on children. Men like Eric chose victims who didn't fight back; he'd want nothing to do with me when there weren't bars between us. Unfortunately, that meant he probably wouldn't come close enough for me to snatch his key, either.

"Stay away from my cousin," I demanded, hoping to piss him off by ordering him around, like an Alpha to his subordinate Pride member.

Still well out of reach, he gave me a taunting smile, and I was reminded of people who go to the zoo to tease the lions from behind a thick pane of safety glass. "Sorry, but that little tabby's mine," Eric said. "Bought and paid for."

Bought and paid for? A chill shivered through me at his phrasing, and I glanced at Abby for clarification. "What's he talking about?" I asked, but she shook her head. She didn't know.

"You'll figure it out," Eric said. "I heard you're a smart one. College girl, right? You're a long way from campus now. Long way from home, too." He started to turn away, and I saw my chance for escape slipping through my fingers.

Desperate now, I clucked my tongue, shaking my head in mock sympathy. "Just not Alpha material, are you, Eric?" I said, daring him to prove me wrong.

He pivoted slowly and wrapped his hands around the bars of my cage, on either side of my own. Staring down at me, he growled deep in his throat.

Unimpressed, I let contempt shine in my eyes. I'd heard better. Hell, I'd *done* better. "Come on in and prove you're a real man. Or can't you get it up for an adult?"

Eric snarled, his face aflame with rage. Before I could react, he thrust one hand into the cage and grabbed the back of my head, slamming the left side of my face into the bars. Pain exploded in my cheekbone, radiating in all directions. Soon I'd have a bruise to match Abby's.

Wincing, I pushed against the bars with both hands, trying to pull my face away from the cool steel. It did no good; Eric was as strong as he looked.

Great job, Faythe, I thought. *You've got him right where you want him, now.*

"What's wrong?" I asked, my words muffled from having my jaw pressed into the bars. "Did I strike a nerve?"

His fist clenched, pulling several of my hairs out by the root. "You just remember who roughed you up first when Miguel has you nailed to the floor."

"Remember this." My right hand shot out, and I raked my nails down the length of his face, echoing the shape of Abby's bruise. Though short, my nails were sharp and hard, even in human form, and I gouged four long ruts into his cheek. He howled and let go of my head.

Pleased, I stepped back out of his reach as he clapped a hand to his ruined cheek. It came away bloody.

"You stupid bitch!" he yelled, turning to snatch his shirt from the ground. He pressed the wad of white cotton to his face to absorb the blood. And there was plenty of it, for such shallow wounds.

Maybe they'll scar, I thought, barely resisting the urge to clap my hands and jump up and down with glee. Instead, I made a show of slowly licking his blood from my fingertips, one at a time. "Mmm. Tastes like fear to me."

Eyes wide, Eric spun and ran for the steps, tripping and fumbling his way to the top. Voices and light flooded the basement as he shoved the door open, but they stopped abruptly as he stepped across the threshold. An instant later, the new silence was replaced by derisive ribbing. I couldn't help but gloat.

"The kid too much for you?" Miguel asked between fits of barbed laughter.

"*Your* bitch-kitty did this," Eric said, fury rolling from his voice like smoke from a fire.

"Faythe's awake?" a new voice asked, and my smile died on my face. I scrambled to the far corner of my cage, desperately pressing my still-throbbing cheek into the bars. But no matter how I turned, I couldn't see into the room at the top of the stairs.

"I told you not to touch her," Miguel said, his accent thick with anger. "You got what you deserved. Close the door." Someone pushed the basement door shut, cutting off the light and the voices. But I'd heard enough.

I sank to my knees, numb with shock and betrayal. I'd recognized the new voice. I hadn't heard it in ten years, but I'd know my brother's voice anywhere. It was Ryan.

Twenty

"You shouldn't have done that," Abby said, her voice trembling on the last word.

I wanted to look at her, but I couldn't drag my focus from the landing at the top of the steps. I drew in a breath slowly, concentrating on each inhale and exhale until I was sure I could speak coherently. "Shouldn't have done what?" Still kneeling on bare concrete, I turned to face her, not surprised to find her standing at the front of her cage, her eyes wide with alarm.

"Scratched him. You shouldn't have scratched him."

"Why not?" I asked, though at the moment I didn't really care about the answer. I only cared about getting the hell out of that cage so I could rip

Ryan's throat out. Or maybe just his tongue, so he would live to face my father and the rest of the council.

"You embarrassed him, and pissed him off."

Using the bars to pull myself up, I crossed my cell to the wall nearest her cage. "That was kind of the point, although knocking him out and taking his key was what I actually had in mind." I smiled and shrugged, pretending I wasn't completely devastated by my failure. "Besides, apparently Miguel won't let him touch me."

Even as I spoke, my cheek throbbed, reminding me that Eric had, in fact, touched me. But I'd touched him back.

Abby sat down facing me, her knees brushing the bars. "Miguel's bad enough by himself," she said. "And anyway, Eric will just take it out on me next time."

Next time. Great. We'd simply have to make sure there *wasn't* a next time.

I sat to mirror her position, and nothing separated us but two rows of bars and five feet of bare concrete. It may as well have been the Grand Canyon.

"Are you okay?" I asked, eyeing her cheek. A new stripe was forming less than an inch from the old one, as if her first bruise had developed a shadow. I touched my cheek gingerly, knowing I would bear an identical mark. But at least nothing was broken. I'd live, which was more than I could say for Eric, if I ever got another shot at him.

"No." She frowned, watching me feel my face. "Are you?"

"So far, so good, actually." I grinned. "That was kind of fun."

Abby gave me a hesitant smile, the corners of her mouth curving up toward freckled cheeks. "I bet it was."

"He really did taste like fear. Yummy." I licked my lips in jest.

She laughed, but then her face sobered quickly. "I'm sorry they caught you, but I'm so glad you're here." She rubbed her arms as if to warm them, but it was far from cold in the basement. There was no air-conditioning, and I was already sticky with sweat.

"Thanks," I said, for lack of a better response.

"I don't suppose you have a plan?"

"Yeah, don't let them touch me."

Abby snorted. "Brilliant. Why didn't I think of that?"

"Ahhh. Wisdom comes with age, my child." I gave a small head bow, my hands templed beneath my chin. But the moment of levity faded as I thought of Sara and wondered whether either of us would live long enough to accrue any true wisdom.

"How many of them are there?" I asked, glancing away to keep her from reading my expression.

"Just four that I know of."

Four. I counted them in my head. *Miguel, Sean, and Eric, and…* "Was that Ryan?"

She nodded solemnly.

"He hasn't…?" Unable to finish the question, I stared at the concrete, studying a long crack a couple of feet from my cage door. I couldn't ask her if my brother—her own cousin—had raped her.

"No," she said, and I exhaled in relief. Abby stared at her shoe, scraping dirt from the sole with one jagged pink fingernail. "Just Miguel and Eric. Ryan only brings the food."

Thank goodness. It wasn't exactly good news, yet still better than the alternative. I was certain Ryan hadn't touched Sara either, because if he'd made physical contact, Vic would have smelled his scent on her. Or maybe Vic had, and Michael had lied to me. *No,* I thought. *Michael wouldn't lie.* And Ryan wouldn't rape. So what the hell was he doing here?

With Ryan, there was no telling. He'd always been different from most other toms. He had the strength and speed of a cat but never developed the instinct to properly use them. And until his eighteenth birthday, he never seemed to mind his own mediocrity.

A couple of months after Ryan came of age, Michael quit his job as an enforcer to attend law school full-time. Ryan wanted his job. Unfortunately, with the best interests of the Pride in mind, my father couldn't give it to him; Ryan just didn't have what it took. Daddy hired Marc instead, though he wouldn't turn eighteen for another month. Ryan left the Pride that night, in spite of the only screaming, crying fit I'd ever seen my mother throw.

I pushed damp, stringy hair back from my face, trying to push back my memories at the same time. Thinking about my family would only make me homesick, a cruel irony, considering I'd nearly fled the ranch on my own only hours earlier.

"What about the other jungle cat? The second stray?"

My cousin's brow crinkled in confusion. "I've only seen one stray. Miguel."

Hmm. Was it possible that the two crime sprees, both committed by foreign strays, were unconnected? Surely not.

"How did they catch you?" Abby asked, smashing tiny clumps of dirt into powder with her thumb.

"I got stupid," I admitted, my face warm with embarrassment.

She looked up expectantly, but a faint creak overhead saved me from having to elaborate. We both turned toward the sound, just as the door opened. This time, along with light, I caught the aroma of beef and onions. I tensed, expecting to see Miguel's black work boots on the steps, but saw a worn-out pair of tennis shoes instead. That, combined with the scent of food, told me who was coming.

Time for a little family reunion.

My pulse raced in anticipation as Ryan slunk down the stairs. A hundred questions chased each other in my head, and I bit my lip to keep from shouting them all at once. I wanted answers, and he was going to give them to me. One way or another. Starting with what the *hell* had happened to him.

My brother's formerly bright brown eyes were dull, his sandy hair lank and lifeless. He looked taller than I remembered, and it took me a moment to understand the optical illusion at work. He wasn't taller; he was thinner, as if he hadn't been getting enough to eat. But for a cat, hunger should never be a problem. Even if he was too broke to buy food, he could always hunt. So why did he look like he belonged in a commercial alongside Sally Struthers?

Ryan carried two fast-food bags in one hand and two plastic bottles of springwater in the other. My stomach growled, fighting with my anger for top priority as I realized I hadn't had any breakfast. I wanted answers, but I *needed* food.

He dropped one bag and bottle on the floor next to my cage and marched right past me, without a word of acknowledgment. But I watched him closely, and his gait was anything but relaxed. He knew he'd have to face me eventually.

At Abby's cage, he slipped the bag between two bars, holding it out to her, but she backed away from him, all the way into the far corner. Ryan's narrow shoulders slumped. "Come on, Abby, be reasonable," he said, clearly exasperated. "Take the burger."

Burgers. How original.

Abby shook her head, curls bouncing around her face. "I told you, I'm on a hunger strike."

He sighed, lowering his arm. "You'll only feel worse when you're too weak to move."

"What do you care?"

"He's right, Abby," I said. "Take the food. You need energy to fight."

"That's not what I meant." Ryan turned to glare at me, brows furrowed. "It'll only be worse if she fights them." His gaze flicked to the empty cage next to mine, then back to me quickly.

"How much worse could it get?" I gripped the door of my cage, my hands white with tension. "She's already been kidnapped, caged and raped."

Ryan winced at my last word, dropping his eyes to the concrete. American tabbies were protected and often spoiled by the men in their lives. Hitting a woman was grounds for expulsion from the Pride. Even if she deserved it. Even if she threw the first punch. Even if she begged for it. And though I'd never heard of a tabby being raped before, I was pretty sure such a crime would justify a death sentence.

Ryan must have thought so too. He was clearly troubled by what had happened to Abby. But not enough to stop it. "She's alive, isn't she?"

"No thanks to you," I spat, pleased to see him wince again. He was suffering major guilt. *Good.* I could work with guilt.

"I haven't touched her."

"You haven't let her go, either."

He wagged his finger at me, as I'd seen our mother do a thousand times, and the familiar gesture made me ache with homesickness. I couldn't remember the last time I'd wanted to go home, but I would have willingly locked myself in my father's cage at that moment. I'd have even let my mother nag me. Or knit me a sweater.

"I'll deal with you in a minute," Ryan said, jerking me out of my private pity party. "After I convince her to eat."

I exhaled in a huff. "Abby, take the bag so Ryan can 'deal' with me."

Abby glanced up sharply, surprised by my harsh tone. But then she took several steps forward and snatched the bag and water bottle from him. Pouting, she carried them back to her corner, where she dropped them on the mattress, unopened. It was better than nothing. And frankly, I was kind of tickled to have someone take orders from me without argument.

"Thank you, Abby," Ryan said, sounding genuinely relieved.

She flipped him off, and that time I did laugh. I couldn't help it.

Grumbling something unintelligible, Ryan nudged my paper sack with his foot, shoving it between two of my bars without meeting my eyes. He left the bottle where it sat, within reach, should I want it.

"Do I have to threaten a hunger strike to get you to talk to me?" I asked. "Or don't you care if I starve myself."

"He cares," Abby said, arms crossed over a nearly flat chest. "Miguel will kill him if anything happens to either of us."

I raised my eyebrows, thrilled with that little tidbit of information. "So, you're our keeper? How does one find a job like that? Answer an ad in the classi-fieds? 'Wanted—werecat with a small brain and even smaller heart.' Do you get benefits? Dental, maybe? 'Cause you're going to need it when I break off every tooth in your mouth."

Ryan frowned, looking more ashamed than frightened. "I was in the wrong place at the wrong time. That's it."

"A victim of circumstance, huh? And since misery loves company, you decided to hand your sister and cousin over to be murdered by a group of feline serial killers?"

"He's not going to kill you, Faythe," Ryan said, rolling his eyes at my melodrama as he shoved his hands into the pockets of a tattered pair of jeans. "You're too valuable."

I bit my tongue to keep from asking whether he'd promised Sara the same thing.

Ryan glanced away again, too chicken to meet my eyes as he continued, "He won't even hurt you if you'll just shut your mouth and cooperate."

Furious, I gripped the bars, squeezing until my hands throbbed. *"Cooperate?"* I hissed through clenched teeth. "You must be fucking joking, Ryan. You do *know* what he wants, don't you?"

"Better than you do." He stared at his feet, scuffing the toe of his sneaker on the crack in the floor.

My heart clawed its way up my throat. "What's that supposed to mean?" Trying to get closer to my brother, I shuffled sideways, moving my hands arm over arm from one bar to the next.

"Nothing." Ryan shook his head, and I was reminded of a child shaking an Etch A Sketch to clear it. When he finally met my eyes, his own were blank, as if he'd done exactly that. "Look, I'm only trying to help. Don't make things any harder than they have to be, okay? This isn't the time to make trouble."

Funny, I couldn't think of a *better* time to make trouble.

"How could you do this?" I demanded, trying to rattle the bars. They wouldn't budge, and that only made me angrier. "How could you sell me out?" I didn't have words strong enough to tell him how pissed off I was. How betrayed I felt. But if he'd come just an inch or two closer, I could sure as hell show him.

"I had nothing to do with it." He stared at me boldly for the first time. "I never even mentioned you, but when Miguel found out about Dad, he put it together."

"Who told him about Daddy?" I did my best to look curious rather than enraged as I lowered myself to the floor, hoping to appear less threatening off my feet.

Ryan shrugged, and his shirt drooped at his throat, exposing too-well-defined collarbones. "My guess would be Eric," he said, sitting on the ground across from me. "But it could have been anyone. There isn't a cat in the country, stray, wild or Pride, who doesn't know that Greg Sanders is head of the territorial council."

"Did you at least try to stop them?"

"You can't stop Miguel," he said, frowning at me as if I should have known better.

"Shit, Ryan, you didn't even try?" I slammed my fist into the ground and regretted it almost instantly. The rough surface of the concrete skinned the outside edge of my hand, leaving it raw and slowly oozing blood. Wonderful.

"What was I supposed to do, suggest an alternate choice? Would you really have wanted me to trade you in for someone else, maybe even younger than Abby?"

Of course not. I let silence answer for me, but my anger at him didn't fade. Ignoring him, I dug through my fast-food bag for a napkin, and used it to dab at my raw skin.

"Besides, I thought they'd never get another shot at you once you went home."

My head snapped up, my hand forgotten. *"Another* shot?" He knew about the stray on campus?

"Yeah, Miguel had someone watching you at school, waiting for an opportunity that never came."

Never came? He didn't know I'd been attacked? Apparently they weren't the best-organized criminal cartel. Or maybe Miguel hadn't been sharing information with his toadies.

Ryan shrugged, as if none of that mattered. "And if you'd stayed put, like you were supposed to, they never would have gotten a second chance." He smirked, accusation clear in the curve of his mouth. "But you couldn't, could you? Dad puts you under house arrest and round-the-clock supervision, so you sneak out just to prove you're still up to the challenge."

Enraged, I jumped to my feet, and he mirrored me from the other side of the bars, automatically taking a defensive stance. "So it's *my* fault I'm sitting in a cage in some filthy basement in Mississippi?" I growled, throwing the blood-smeared napkin at him because I had nothing else to throw. But then I froze, staring at him as the growl faded from my throat. *Wait. What was that he'd said?*

Ryan caught the napkin in his palm and crushed it, his fist hanging in the air like an unspoken threat. He came a step closer, eyes narrowing in suspicion. "How'd you know we're in Mississippi?"

"How did you know about the house arrest and babysitting?" I countered.

He dropped the napkin, and it rolled to rest against one of the bars. "You first."

"Deductive reasoning. It's a perk sometimes available to those of us on the top rung of the evolutionary ladder." *And you just confirmed it,* I added silently.

He cleared his throat, glancing away. "Deductive reasoning for me, too."

I rolled my eyes. "Bullshit, Ryan. You couldn't deduce your own name if it wasn't written in your underwear." I lunged at him, smashing my chest into the bars. My fingers grazed the front of his shirt, and he backpedaled quickly out of reach. "Who have you been talking to?" I demanded, stepping back from the bars to glare at him.

"No one," he insisted, but I'd already figured it out. Of the enforcers, only Marc was privy to privileged information about the council's plans, and he would never talk to Ryan. But there was one other person who had a history of involvement with the council and in whom my father confided…

"How long have you been in contact with Mom?"

Ryan flushed, and at first I thought he'd refuse to answer. Then he hung his head in defeat, a gesture left over from childhood. "Almost eight years."

"So you're still Mommy's boy." I couldn't resist a satisfied grin. For years I'd dreamed of being just like Ryan, gutsy and independent. And he'd been faking it the whole time. Mom had been secretly helping him out. No wonder she wouldn't talk about him. She was afraid of incriminating herself.

Furthermore, my brother's admission brought up a disturbing new question: Had Mom known what Ryan was doing? There was only one possible answer. No. She hadn't had a clue. Mom was no doubt doing what she thought best for the whole family, trying to convince her second-born to come home. Unfortunately for us all, it hadn't worked.

Ryan glowered at me. "She sends me money. And she talks, mostly about you and the golden boy."

I blinked in surprise, caught off guard by the depth of his anger and resentment, still thriving after all these years. "You're doing this because of Marc?"

"Marc." Ryan laughed bitterly and for a moment I thought he'd barked at me. "This has nothing to do with Marc. It doesn't even have anything to do with me. I didn't do this to you." He leaned forward, over-pronouncing each word to make sure I got the picture. *"I'm not in charge."*

I stared at him, absorbing the truth of his statement. Ryan, powerless? That was easy enough to believe. "Then help us," I said, challenging him to take a stand for once. "Open the doors and let us out."

He flinched, his expression bitter. "I don't have a key. Miguel won't give me one."

Damn. "Okay then, tell Mom where we are. Please, Ryan."

Behind him, Abby gripped the bars of her cage with tiny, white-knuckled fingers, waiting for his answer just as desperately as I was.

He shook his head. "Dad would put a price on my head. You know he would. Even Mom couldn't stop him."

"What do you think Miguel's going to do when I tell him you've been talking to your mommy?"

Ryan just looked at me, but something in his expression was off, something about the tight line of his mouth…

"He knows, doesn't he?" I said, my inner light-bulb blinking to life. "You son of a bitch, you've been using Mom to spy on the council. And she was only trying to help you, trying to get you to come home." I rammed the bars again, bruising my shoulder, and Ryan took another step back, farther out of my reach.

"She's the only reason I'm alive," he said, his voice calm, resigned. His shoulders slumped as his eyes traveled up to meet mine. "A couple of weeks ago, I ran into Miguel outside a bar in New Mexico. He was about to kill me when I told him I had connections in the south-central territory and a source on the council. I told him they'd miss me and hunt him down.

"He didn't care about that—wasn't the least bit worried about being caught. But he wanted information. He wanted to know what the council was doing, what strays they were watching and who they had patrolling each territory." Ryan stuffed his hands in his pockets and shrugged apologetically. "I had no choice, Faythe. And I didn't hand you over to him. You did that yourself."

He backed toward the stairs slowly as I blinked at him, trying to come up with something to say to convince him to help us. Nothing came to mind. He was right; no matter what he did now, he was dead. "Now, if you'll excuse me, I have to go call Mom. I'm sure she's had a rough morning, and will need someone to talk to."

"Don't do it, Ryan," I said, dismayed by the desperation in my voice. "Don't spy for them." But I knew it was useless; he'd already made his alliance. He was more scared of our father than of Miguel. And so help me, I couldn't really blame him for that.

"It's all I'm good for, Faythe," he said. Without another word, he jogged up the steps and into what I assumed was the kitchen, slamming the door shut on the dark, and on us.

Twenty-One

Alone with Abby again, I dropped onto my mattress and unwrapped my burger, determined not to dwell on Ryan's betrayal. I had no doubt he'd get what he deserved in the end, whether from my father or from Miguel. Or from me.

My burger was tasteless, in spite of the tantalizing aroma of grilled onions, but I ate it anyway. "You should eat that," I said to Abby between bites.

"I'm not hungry." She lay on her stomach on her mattress, her chin resting on one arm. Her other hand hung over the concrete at the end of the mattress, tracing a swirling pattern in the dirt she'd scraped from the bottom of her shoes.

I drank from my water bottle, still watching her. "Yes, you are. Eat. You can't fight them off if you don't."

"You can't fight them off anyway."

"The hell I can't." I tore into the burger again, pretending it was Miguel's throat.

"You don't understand," she said, staring at me with haunted eyes. "If they can't make you cooperate, make you play their game, you're no use to them, and they'll kill you."

Like Sara, I thought, finishing her sentence in my head. As badly as I wanted to know what had happened, I wouldn't ask. I had to wait for her to bring it up on her own. So I said the only thing I could think of to comfort her. "Ryan said we were too valuable."

"I don't care what he said. Miguel will kill you if you push him too far."

I plucked a fry from its cardboard carton, miming a sword fight with an imaginary foe. "I'd like to see him try," I said, lunging to slit my invisible opponent's throat. Abby didn't even crack a grin. *Tough room.*

"If you die, I'll be alone with them again." Her voice cracked on the last word, and tears formed in her eyes.

Damn. Stuffing the fry in my mouth, I watched her expression grow from fear to terror as I chewed. "He won't kill me," I said. "I won't give him a chance. And he won't touch me, either."

Abby sat up, brushing moisture from her cheeks

with dust-streaked palms. "Faythe, you can't fight him. You don't know what he did to Sara."

My heart pounding, I froze, waiting for her to continue. But she didn't. She wasn't ready to tell me yet. I took another swig of water, trying to wash down the lump in my throat along with the last bite of hamburger. "Yes, I do."

Abby's eyes widened, her mouth forming a silent circle. "How do you know?"

I hesitated, but she looked desperate for information, and I knew the feeling. "They took her home and propped her against a tree in her own backyard. Vic found her."

Blood drained from her face, and even in the dim light, I saw her bottom lip tremble. "Wasn't killing her enough? Why did he have to humiliate her like that? Her poor family… Why would anyone *do* that?"

"Because he's sadistic." I dropped my carton of fries back into the bag, my appetite gone. "He had to know a stunt like that would make the council even more determined to find him. And punish him. But he doesn't care. He thinks he's invincible."

Careful of my skinned right hand, I rolled down the top of the fast-food sack and tossed it into the far corner of my cage. "So what do you think they really want?" I asked, gently touching my injured skin with one finger. The bleeding had stopped, but the edge of my palm was still an angry shade of red.

"What do you mean?"

"This can't be it." I waved my battered hand around the basement. "If this was their grand scheme, they wouldn't need Ryan because they wouldn't care what the council was doing. They'd have their fun with us, then kill us, like Miguel did with those human girls."

Abby's hand clenched around the hamburger she'd been staring at. "What human girls?"

I exhaled slowly, trying to decide how much to tell her. "Dr. Carver's office received the body of a girl raped and killed by a cat. A jungle stray. Owen went to investigate and came across another murder fitting the same pattern. It happened three days earlier in New Mexico." *Where Ryan had said he'd met Miguel.*

"I knew it," she moaned, squeezing her burger until juice from the beef ran down her arm. "They're going to kill us."

"No, that's just my point. They're not. Not intentionally, anyway," I amended, thinking of Sara. "If Miguel was looking for disposable playthings, he'd have picked a couple of human girls. But he didn't. He went through a lot of trouble to snatch us. Ryan said we were too valuable to kill, but too valuable for what? Or to whom?"

Abby frowned, confused. "But Miguel killed Sara."

"I know." I sighed, trying not to get impatient with her just when she was starting to open up. "Maybe he lost his temper."

She nodded vigorously. "Which is exactly why I said not to fight him."

"If we don't fight, we won't get out."

"And if we do fight, we might not get out alive."

It was my turn to frown. "Your logic sucks, Abby."

"So does yours."

I laughed, and it felt so good, I did it again. After a moment of hesitation, Abby joined me, and her smile was radiant, almost bright enough to make up for the tiny, grimy windows.

Feeling a little better, more from laughter than from the meal, I walked to the center of my cell with my hands on my hips, studying the enclosure carefully. The cinder block basement wall served as one side of the enclosure, and the remaining sides were made of a series of one-inch aluminum bars, welded to a square frame of the same material. The frames were attached to the floor with huge metal screws and secured with bolts more than an inch in diameter. The metal was welded together at the corners and bolted directly into the cinder blocks at the back. Overhead, a nearly identical frame was covered with a sheet of steel mesh, and either bolted or welded to all three aluminum sides and the cinder block wall.

"What are you doing?" Abby asked around a mouthful of hamburger.

"Checking for weaknesses." I pulled on each individual bar, making my way around the cage until I'd tried them all. It was a long shot, but I had to try. Not one bar budged, which wasn't surprising.

Next, I tried every bolt I could reach. None of them moved. I stuck my arms through the bars on the front wall and pulled on the lock, wedging my feet against the frame for support. I'm pretty strong, but the damn thing didn't even creak. It was made of aluminum, too. *Great.*

As a last resort, I looked up, studying the steel mesh. The basement had a low ceiling—only about seven feet from the floor—and the top of my cage was maybe six inches below that. I could reach it easily, but tugging on the mesh would do me more damage than good. It was made of a single sheet of steel, punched through with row upon row of vaguely diamond-shaped holes. And each edge of each hole was sharp. Very sharp, from what I could see. Any attempt to grab the mesh would shred my hands, seriously hampering any other escape effort I might come up with.

Having exhausted all of my options, I sat down on the mattress and took another swig from my water bottle. "So, what happens when I need to pee?"

Abby wadded up her empty burger wrapper and dropped it into the paper bag. "Do you?"

"Yeah. Not horribly yet, but yeah."

"There's a coffee can back there by the wall. See?"

Following her pointed finger, I saw an empty plastic Folgers canister just outside the bars at the back of my cell. "That's what I was afraid of." Wiping sweat from my face with my sleeve, I trudged to the back corner of the cage and pulled the canister through. I had to hold it by the bottom because it was too wide to go through with my fingers wrapped around the sides.

Abby smiled sympathetically. "It takes some getting used to but they come empty it pretty often. They don't like to smell it when they're down here."

"I don't blame them." I stared into the container in distaste. "I'll just hold it."

"Why? They aren't going to let you out to use the restroom. Besides, Ryan said you were in a cage for nearly two weeks, once. What did you use then?"

"Something similar to this, actually." I tilted the can toward my nose and sniffed. It was clean and still smelled like coffee. *I could really use some coffee,* I thought, uncomfortably aware that the smell of my makeshift toilet was making my mouth water. Yuck.

"They can't keep us in here forever," I said, tossing the can into the corner with my other trash. "They have to know we'll escape eventually."

"Why would we?" She ripped the top edge from a tiny paper packet of salt and upended it over her fries. "You didn't escape the cage at the ranch."

I smiled ruefully, lounging on my mattress with my bottle of water. "Only because no one gave me a chance. But unless I'm wrong, Miguel is going to want to join me in here eventually—"

"You can pretty much count on it."

"—and he'll have to either bring the key with him or leave the door unlocked." I paused, picturing his face covered in blood. "Every time he opens that door, he'll be giving me a chance to escape. He must know it's only a matter of time."

Abby plucked one fry from her carton. "He's probably counting on keeping you too busy to snatch the key."

"Then I'll just have to make sure he can't."

"What if he brings another tranquilizer?"

I thought aloud, watching her eat. "I don't think he wants me sedated. He had ample opportunity to do whatever he wanted with me while I was unconscious, but he didn't. I think he wants me alert and scared." *Sick bastard,* I added in my head.

"What if you're wrong?"

"Last time he had the element of surprise. He's lost that now, and I'll be watching for a needle. If he brings one, I won't give him a chance to use it."

"Yeah. Good luck with that," she said, her skepticism obvious as she munched on a limp fry.

"Thanks."

Overhead, the loose floorboard groaned again and my head swiveled toward the stairs before I could stop it. *Wow,* I thought, *I've only been here for a few hours, and already I'm acting like one of Pavlov's dogs.* Only my conditioned response was not salivation, but fear.

"It's Miguel," Abby whispered, a thin tremor in her voice.

"How do you know?"

The soft *whoosh-whoosh* of her pulse sped up as she dropped her fries back into the paper bag. "Trust me. It's him."

Wonderful.

"Carpe diem," I mumbled, scrambling to my feet as I tried to recall the Latin translation for "Seize the cat by the balls." Marc had taught it to me years ago. Too many years ago, apparently. "Any advice?"

Abby scooted backward on her rear. "Think about something else."

"Like ripping his throat out?"

She stared at me in astonishment, then a grim smile spread slowly over her face. "That might work."

I had my doubts, but the image of blood pouring from Miguel's neck was pretty damn appealing.

The creak of the door opening interrupted my fantasy with an unhealthy dose of reality. A sudden flood of light from the staircase made me instantly alert. I forgot my need for the restroom. My hand clenched around the plastic bottle. Water spilled over my fingers and onto the mattress. Fresh sweat broke out behind my knees and on my forehead. My muscles tensed. My chest tightened.

The woman in me watched the steps in dread, but the caged cat was eager, because everyone who entered the basement represented my shot at freedom. Even if I had to fight for it. And I was ready to fight.

I screwed the lid on my water bottle and let it fall to the mattress as I stepped onto the concrete, struggling to control my pounding heart.

Black work boots appeared on the top step. Abby glanced up.

"Buenos días, chicas," Miguel said. His words sounded beautiful and exotic, in startling contrast to his apparent intentions.

But I didn't give a damn about his intentions. I had plans of my own.

Twenty-Two

Miguel clomped down the stairs, his steps heavy and pronounced. I held my breath, hoping to hear him stumble in the dark and fall to his death. Unfortunately that only seems to happen in the movies. He took the stairs slowly, and I was sure he did it intentionally, to prolong my dread. But if that was the case, the joke was on him, because I had lots of practice waiting anxiously. Inspiring fearful anticipation was Daddy's specialty. My father was the master at making you wait until you were willing to punish yourself just to get it over with.

And waiting on Miguel had a benefit for me that he'd probably never considered. By the time he hit the last step, my eyes had readjusted to the gloom, and I could see him pretty well.

He stopped at the foot of the stairs, facing Abby. "How are you this evening, Ms. Wade?" Each word was crisp and carefully spoken, his pronunciation seasoned with the distinctive rhythm of his native Portuguese.

Abby glanced at me with wide, scared eyes and backed up until she hit the cinder blocks at the back of the cage, her palms flat against the wall, as if she'd like to pass through it.

"Don't worry, *niña,*" Miguel said. "I'll be visiting our new guest today." He turned his back on her, and Abby slid down the wall to sit with her arms wrapped around her knees. She watched through eyes narrowed to slits as Miguel sauntered slowly toward me, stopping two feet from the door to my cage. "How do you like your accommodations, Ms. Sanders?"

"My accommodations?" Ignoring my rolling stomach, I glanced around the basement, pretending to consider the question. "I assume you were going for stark simplicity with the metal-and-concrete decor, but it just doesn't work for me. It's too 'third-world detention center' for my taste. As are the restroom facilities. And room service here sucks. I can't think straight in the morning without a healthy dose of caffeine, and I have yet to see a single cup of coffee. But the worst is the food. Tell Ryan to get off his ass and make me something decent. Maybe some chicken, with a little rosemary? He'll know the recipe I mean."

Miguel smiled, clearly amused. "Anything else I can do for you?"

I scratched my head, just behind my left ear. "Um, let me think. Yeah, there is one more thing. Fuck off."

Chuckling, he pulled a small silver key from his front pocket. "As delightful as that sounds, I was thinking of something a little more…collaborative."

Collaborative? How very civil, as if he wanted to cochair a committee with me.

"I get the impression you don't play very well with others, but if you'd like a set of scars to match Eric's, by all means, come on in." I backed into the center of the cell, feet spread for balance, arms open wide to welcome him into my *accommodations*—at his own risk.

Miguel paused to take in my defensive stance, one hand cupping the padlock. He looked relaxed and confident, dark eyes blazing not with fear but with anticipation. And just in case I had any doubts regarding his intention, the bulge in his pants spoke quite clearly.

Shoving aside fear and self-doubt, I met his eyes, aiming for absolute confidence in both my stance and my voice. "My father taught me to disarm my opponent at all costs—regardless of his choice of weapon," I said, glancing pointedly at his groin.

"Are you threatening me?"

"Damn right. Lay one hand on me and you'll never stand to pee again."

His eyes darkened, and his laugh sounded forced. "You're very funny, *gatita*."

"I'm glad you think so. I've always considered my sense of humor to be largely underappreciated, so it's nice to finally meet a fan."

Miguel laughed again, more genuinely this time, and unlocked my cage with a needlessly harsh twist of the key. The lock popped open with a sharp click and fell into his cupped palm.

Okay, time to get serious. I let my smile fade slowly and lowered my pitch, as no human woman could have. "I'm not joking this time. If I see it, it's mine, and you won't get it back at the end of the school year." I growled, deep and long, savoring the feel of the vibrations in my throat, as if the sound alone could save me. It wasn't quite a cat's growl but it was damn close. And it was his last warning.

Miguel dismissed my threat with an easy smile, and my stomach clenched. *Oh, yeah, Faythe. You have Puss shaking in his boots, all right.*

I kept my eye on the key until he shoved it deep into the right front pocket of his jeans. The key was my goal, and everything would be all right once I had it. At least in theory.

Miguel opened the door and stepped inside, then closed it and reached through the bars to replace the lock. Behind him, Abby scooted into her favorite corner and buried her head in her arms. She couldn't help hearing, but she didn't have to watch. Seeing her like that made me want to kill him before he'd even laid a hand on me.

"Esto no tiene que ser difícil, mi amor." He leaned against the door, waiting patiently while I puzzled my way through the translation. How courteous.

As I searched my brain for remnants from my high-school Spanish class, I stole a moment to try to force my face into a partial Shift. I stretched. I strained. I twisted my mouth into a horrible grimace. Nothing happened.

Miguel chuckled, apparently assuming my problem was linguistic in nature. It wasn't. By the time I realized my face wasn't going to Shift on command, I had the translation. He'd said something like, "This doesn't have to be difficult." But his eager grin said he was lying; he wanted me to resist.

He was about to get his wish.

Still watching him in my peripheral vision, I glanced around my cage, desperate for something to use as a weapon. There was nothing but the plastic coffee canister and the mattress. *Shit.*

Miguel's heart raced, and eagerness shined in his eyes. He was practically humming with anticipation. Instinct told me to back away from him, but I fought the urge because once I reached the wall, I'd have nowhere left to go. Better to keep my options open.

"Esto va ser una diversión."

I was still trying to translate the new phrase when he pounced, driving me back by my shoulders. He pinned me easily to the only solid wall of the cage, in spite of my attempt to avoid being trapped.

Grunting, I threw my knee up hard, aiming for his groin. Miguel stepped back, deftly avoiding the blow. Seizing my left arm, he yanked me forward. In a single, frighteningly fast movement, he spun me around, twisting my arm behind my back.

I sucked in a short breath, and Miguel pulled up on my elbow. Pain exploded in my shoulder. He shoved me face-first into the concrete blocks. I turned my head just in time to avoid a broken nose. I got a skinned cheek instead.

Aiming blind, I kicked backward and caught his shin with my heel. Miguel cursed in Portuguese and jerked up on my left arm. Fresh pain ripped through my shoulder, burning deep within the joint. I screamed. Miguel writhed against me, obviously aroused by my agony.

Not again, I thought. *He won't hear me scream again.*

"Do you like it rough, *gatita?*" he whispered, his sultry accent at odds with the repugnant nature of his question.

In reply, I shoved my right elbow into his ribs as hard as I could.

Miguel bellowed in pain and surprise. Clearly irritated now, he pulled my right arm straight up and pinned my wrist to the cinderblock, pressing my body against the wall with his own.

"Let me go now, and we'll call it a tie," I said, panting with my cheek still pressed into the concrete. I thought it was a pretty generous offer, but Miguel only chuckled.

He made a show of sniffing my neck and behind my ear.

I closed my eyes, my skin crawling with revulsion.

"You reek of stray, *mi amor,*" he said, nosing aside a sweat-damp strand of my hair. "All over. Your Mexican lover, maybe?"

My eyes flew open, and I gasped.

He laughed. "Yes, I know all about your boyfriend. The golden boy, Ryan calls him. I was pleased to find a purebred princess willing to spread her legs for a scratch-fevered tom."

Clearly, this was not the time to mention that Marc was no longer my boyfriend, and that his scent on me was just a drunken mistake. Since Miguel thought otherwise, I decided not to disappoint him.

"He'll kill you for this," I said between quick, near-panicked breaths as his knee slid between my thighs, forcing my legs farther apart. "If I don't do it first."

Despite my threat, I was truly scared. I'd known Miguel would be strong, but he was faster than I'd expected. Too fast. I didn't think he'd kill me—not on purpose, anyway—but there were things I feared worse than my own death.

"You can do better than this, then?" he asked, sliding his knee toward my crotch.

I breathed deeply, determined not to give him the satisfaction of making me squirm. "Even if I can't, you don't stand a chance. It'll take both of your hands to keep me from killing you, which leaves you no way to get your pants down. Or mine. So why don't you give up now and save us both the trouble?"

His breath oozed across my bare neck, and I cringed to feel it, hot and damp. "This is no trouble, *bella*. This is only foreplay."

I clamped my lips shut on a groan. *Great. A*

psycho. That figures. No dumb jocks for Faythe. I got the crazy bastard who gets off on causing pain.

Suddenly Miguel's hands were gone, along with his knee. My left arm dropped to my side, and fresh pain shot through my shoulder, radiating down my arm.

Behind me, Miguel shuffled backward three steps. Convinced it was a trick, I didn't move. He took two more steps, and I turned slowly to face him, cradling my injured arm.

His eyes shone. "Come on, *bella.* Come get me. If you win, you get the key. If I win, I get you. However I want."

Now, why did that sound so familiar?

It was almost exactly the same bet that had gotten me into this mess in the first place. But this time I wasn't even tempted. "You'll have to kill me first," I said, focusing on his eyes, letting the anticipation glinting in them fuel my anger.

"And you me. *Te atrevo darme.*"

Wonderful, a death match on my first day behind bars. Some girls have all the luck.

Rolling my head on my shoulders, I took inventory of my various aches and pains as I stretched my neck. My right cheek stung, and my knee was still bruised from my ride in the van. And my left arm was no use at all, possibly for a very long time.

Fortunately, my right arm still worked, and there were always my feet, assuming I could keep from breaking any toes. And as a last resort, I could scratch and bite.

Too bad I hadn't been able to pull off the partial Shift. I could really have used a few more inches of teeth.

Eyeing Miguel warily, I struck my fighting pose, both fists raised with my knees bent and my feet apart, just like Daddy had taught me. Well, sort of like Daddy taught me. This time my left fist was low and stiff, held against my side for stability.

Miguel watched me in amusement, an ugly grin warping his mouth. I was entertaining him, giving him a laugh. And that pissed me off.

I lunged forward, hugging my wounded arm to my stomach. My right wrist rotated as it flew, smashing head-on into that revolting grin. I don't think he even saw me move.

Miguel stumbled backward into the bars, slapping one hand to his mouth to cover a split lip and two broken teeth. Blood leaked from between his fingers to drip on the floor. He gaped at me, eyes wide in shock and anger. Apparently he wasn't expecting me to throw any actual punches, which wasn't surprising. Most tabbies had no reason to learn to fight; they had fathers, boyfriends and enforcers to protect them. But my father thought I should be capable of my own defense, and I'd never been happier in my life to admit that he was right.

I shook my hand, surprised by how much it hurt. I'd punched Ethan countless times and never injured myself. Of course, I'd never really tried to hurt him. But I meant to hurt Miguel.

Watching him warily between two fingers, I inspected the damage to my hand. Three of my knuckles were cut and smeared with blood. I flicked my tongue across them, tasting. Some of it was mine, but most of it was his. I'd drawn first blood. *Yeah me.*

Unfortunately, the surprised phase passed pretty quickly, for both of us. "You crazy bitch!" Miguel spat, spraying pink saliva across the concrete.

I frowned. *Why am I a bitch every time I draw blood?*

He wiped his stained hand on his jeans. Starting forward, his hands were curled into fists. He looked like a deranged boxer, eyes blazing with fury and barely focused. I'd finally fazed him, and anger was getting in the way of his concentration. It was about time something went my way.

I dodged him to the right, jumping onto the mattress. "What's wrong?" I asked, lunging to the left in time to evade another blow. "I thought this was your idea of foreplay."

"He meant he likes to hit girls," Abby said. From the corner of my eye, I saw her standing at the front of her cage, brown eyes wide and eager.

Miguel glanced back at her, fist raised. "You shut up, *niña*," he shouted, shaking his fist at Abby. He must have been pretty shaken to take his eyes off an opponent. Or maybe he still didn't consider me a serious threat. *How insulting*. "I'll deal with you when I'm finished with—ugh!" I cut off his threat with a kick to the groin.

It wasn't a great kick. For a great kick, I'd have needed a pair of shoes with hard toes. But I've been assured by several of the men in my life that just about any kick to the crotch is pretty effective.

Miguel bent over, clutching himself as he turned half away from me. Rotating my hips, I whipped my right leg around again, kicking him in the face. I was careful to use the inside of my foot to protect my bare toes. The awkward angle blunted my force, but it worked. He fell over backward with what I hoped was a broken nose. I couldn't tell, because his hands were cupping the injury. But my foot was pretty sore, and slick with enough blood to threaten my balance.

I wiped the bottom of my foot on the edge of the mattress, briefly considering the victory dance Ethan taught me the year he played peewee football. But then Miguel groaned, and I dove for the key instead. I sat on his right leg with my knee pressing into his injured groin, forcing my fingers into his pocket. It was too tight. I couldn't reach the key.

Determined, I pushed my hand in farther. The tip of my middle finger brushed something hard and smooth. The key. I wiggled my fingers, but only pushed it in deeper. I shifted forward for a better angle. And then I made my critical mistake: I took my eyes off his face.

Miguel let go of his swollen nose. His left hand shot past my head. He grabbed a fistful of my hair, twisting it around his palm. Using his grip on my hair for leverage, he pulled me down, pinning me to his chest. He yanked my head back, wrenching my neck to expose my throat.

I tried to swat his hand away, but my left arm wouldn't move, and my right hand was still stuck in his pocket. With his free hand on my hip, he pushed me to the left and rolled on top of me. My injured shoulder hit the ground and I screamed. We wound up on the mattress, with me on the bottom.

Miguel leered down at me. He gave my hair one more vicious tug, then let go. Several strands came away with his hand, stuck to the drying blood. Smiling, and dripping more blood on my face and shirt, he plucked my hand from his pocket and pulled my arms over my head. Tears standing in my eyes, I bit my lip to keep from screaming again as he jerked on my injured arm. He pinned my wrists to the mattress with one hand. "I'll take the top, if you don't mind, *gatita.*"

I swallowed back a sob, speaking through teeth gritted against the agony in my shoulder and the panic in my chest. "I do mind. Get the hell off me."

He sat up, straddling my hips, and pulled my hands forward. My fingers dangled in the air above my stomach, my wrists trapped in his left hand. I struggled to free my hands. He drew his right arm back and slammed his fist into my cheek.

Pain erupted in my face. Lights floated in front of my eyes. I opened and closed my jaw to make sure it wasn't broken. My face was still intact, but it sure didn't feel like it.

Miguel forced my wrists back onto the mattress, and by then I had little resistance left to offer. At least physically. Verbally, I could have sparred all night, but apparently he no longer appreciated my wit. "I've had just about enough of your mouth," he said, dribbling a trail of blood from my chin down to the center of my shirt as he repositioned himself over me.

"Really?" I tried to ignore the throbbing in my face. "I'd have thought you'd be more bothered by my fists."

"Don't flatter yourself, tabbycat." He shoved my shirt up over my stomach, smearing me with blood. "Compared to *mi padre,* you hit like a toddler."

"Not bad for a girl, though, huh?" I said, still trying to free my hands, despite the pain in my shoulder.

He glared down at me, nostrils flaring in anger. "I'm done playing, bitch. You're risking your life every time you open your mouth."

A smart woman would have shut up. Did I? Hell no. Intelligence is overrated anyway. "Oh, come on. Wouldn't you rather go upstairs and lick your wounds? Maybe make an ice pack for your crotch?" I was trying to get him mad enough to make his concentration slip again. He wasn't falling for that twice.

"I'd rather make you pay for my nose." He unbuttoned my shorts with one hooked finger. Definitely a scary skill.

I swallowed thickly as my pulse thundered in my ears, begging me to take the easy way out for once and keep my mouth shut. But there was no easy way. It was either rape or death, and I couldn't live with rape. "Don't forget your teeth," I said as he jerked down on my zipper.

Miguel's eyes narrowed and he sat straighter, running his tongue over newly jagged front teeth. His face turned purple with rage. He hadn't even noticed them. Maybe I should have left well enough alone.

He punched me again, on the same side of my face, and that time I didn't even see it coming. "That's for my teeth."

My head rocked to the side. Tears formed instantly, running over when I blinked. My vision darkened and for several seconds I felt nothing. But then sight and pain came roaring back as I won the battle for consciousness. My face was alive with pain, and my body begged for relief. But I couldn't oblige. To stay awake, I let the pain take over and block out everything else—even fear.

"Okay, that's not funny anymore," I growled, hiding my bruised cheek against my arm in case he took another shot. The left side of my face felt hot and swollen, throbbing with an agony all its own, yet somehow in harmony with my shoulder.

"Let's see if you think this is funny." He tugged on one leg of my shorts, which slipped halfway down my hip, dragging the waistband of my panties along for the ride.

No, in fact, I did *not* think that was funny. And it was even less funny when he pulled down the other side.

Panicked, I kicked and bucked, trying to toss him off my legs. Miguel hung on tight. He seemed to enjoy the ride, in fact, which made my stomach churn. Luckily, he hit a snag when my shorts were at midthigh. He couldn't get them any lower while he sat on my legs, but he couldn't get up without letting go of my hands. Or so I thought.

He leaned forward, his weight threatening to crush my wrists, and got to first one knee, then the other, straddling my lower thighs. He reached down for my shorts, and I brought both knees up into his crotch.

I didn't have the leverage to put much power behind my thrust, but I didn't need much after that last kick. He let go of my wrists to clutch his groin again, and I saw my chance. I shoved him in the chest with both feet. He fell over backward on the floor. His head smacked the concrete with a promising thud. I mentally crossed my fingers as I sat up, hoping he was unconscious.

No such luck. Miguel was one tough son of a bitch. But he was hurt. He was bleeding from his nose and his mouth, and had taken two strikes to the crotch. Surely he'd had enough.

I scrambled onto my feet and pulled my shorts back into place, buttoning them with one eye on Miguel. If he got me down again, I wanted him to have to work just as hard the second time around. In fact, at that point, I would have voluntarily donned a chastity belt.

Miguel lay motionless on the ground, still breathing. I pulled my foot back to kick him in the groin one last time, to make sure his favorite weapon would be out of commission for a while. But as soon as my foot left the ground, he swept the other one out from under me.

I landed on my ass on the edge of the mattress then fell over onto my back. My teeth snapped together hard enough to jar my brain. My left arm swung away from my waist before I could stop it, and the pain that had subsided to a persistent ache began screaming all over again.

One minute I was up, seriously reconsidering Ethan's victory dance, and the next I was flat on my back, relearning how to breathe. And waiting for Miguel's weight to drop onto me again.

But it didn't. He'd finally had enough, at least for the moment.

Metal scraped metal, and I heard the lock click open. He was leaving, which meant he'd have to open the door. Exhausted but desperate, I rolled over my uninjured arm and jumped to my feet. Miguel had the door open. I ran for it, holding my left arm against my side. I came at him as fast as I could, but his fist was there to meet me. He punched me in the stomach, absorbing my forward momentum and knocking the breath from my lungs. I doubled over and fell backward onto the ground, curled around the agony in my abdomen.

As I lay on the floor, gasping and unable to move, the lock clicked shut, and I knew I'd missed my chance. I cried. I couldn't help it. I screamed in rage and frustration, sobs shaking my body with enough force to knock my head against the concrete.

I didn't watch him leave, though I knew he was limping from the syncopated rhythm of his feet on the stairs. I couldn't look at Abby. I couldn't even open my eyes. Shrieking at the pain in my shoulder, I crawled onto my mattress and cried until sleep came to my rescue.

Twenty-Three

As the sun set on my first day behind bars, I sat on my mattress in the rapidly fading daylight, evaluating the various injuries vying for my attention. My left shoulder screamed in protest as I stretched, and my face felt raw enough to qualify for examination by the Food and Drug Administration. My stomach, now rainbow-hued, was too tender to touch, as was my right foot. I tried to run a hand through my hair, but my fingers got stuck in Miguel's dried blood a couple of inches from my scalp.

Lovely. And me without my shampoo.

After a careful inventory of the rest of my body, I pronounced myself fortunate that nothing was broken. I was pretty sure Miguel hadn't been so lucky.

Digging through the remains of my lunch, I found an unused paper napkin, which I dampened with the last of my water. I couldn't do much about my hair without a good hot shower, but at least I could mop up the rest of the mess. Well, most of it, anyway.

The back of my right hand was swollen and crusted with dried blood, so I began there, wiping at my knuckles with short, measured strokes intended to spare my shoulder from unnecessary movement. After several minutes of slow work, I uncovered the source of my own minor blood loss. Miguel's teeth had gashed my fist in three places, but the cuts were small and already scabbed over. More good luck.

With my hand reasonably clean, I started on my face and neck, avoiding my left cheek entirely. Without the benefit of a mirror, I had to explore my skin with my fingers, searching for each drop of blood Miguel had dripped on me. I scrubbed until the napkin fell apart in my hand, then scratched the rest off with my fingernails.

As clean as I could get without a shower, I glanced into Abby's cage, where my cousin lay asleep on her mattress. Watching her, I realized she was right; if I was no use to Miguel, he had no reason to keep me alive. Once he'd healed, he would kill me. I had no doubt about it. I wouldn't go out without a fight, but there wasn't much I could do against two men at once, and I was pretty sure he'd bring Eric along next time, even if just to hold me down or sedate me. Miguel wasn't stupid. He was just psychotic.

With the big threat stewing in the back of my mind, my thoughts to turned to a more immediate problem: I had to use the restroom. Soon. Disgusted but desperate, I picked up the discarded coffee can and glanced inside. *You've survived worse,* I told myself, but it didn't help. Peeing in a can was just another in a series of dehumanizing humiliations to be endured, like being snatched, sedated, tied up, groped, knocked around and groped some more.

Not my best day, overall. In fact, house arrest didn't seem so terrible anymore. Hell, the state penitentiary was starting to look good.

I'd almost talked myself into using the coffee canister when the basement door opened—this time without warning. The rest of me froze as my head swiveled toward the steps. The plastic jug shook in my grip. I wasn't ready to take another beating in defense of my honor. Not yet.

Thankfully, the aroma of fried chicken gave Ryan away almost immediately. My tension eased and my stomach growled. There was no rosemary, but even KFC was better than another burger.

"If I ask nicely, will you turn on the light?" I

asked, trying my best to sound friendly as I dropped the coffee container on the ground.

Ryan paused on the third step. "Let me hear the magic words."

"Pretty please." Abby beat me to it. I smiled, glancing at where she now sat cross-legged on her mattress. But instead of returning my smile, she gaped at me in horror. I blinked at her in confusion for a moment, but then I remembered my face clashing with the wall. And with Miguel's fist. Twice.

Good thing I wasn't vain. Much.

Ryan flipped the switch, and Abby gasped, still staring at my face. Evidently the light was unflattering. Even without a mirror, I understood her alarm. In the weak overhead glow, I saw the swollen edge of my cheek at the bottom of my vision, like a purple half moon on the horizon. "It looks worse than it feels," I said, wondering if that was even possible.

"Good, because you look like shit." Ryan stared at me from the bottom step, again holding two fast-food bags.

"You should see the other guy."

"I have. Miguel's furious. He's been stomping around for two hours, cussing in Portuguese and making everyone else miserable."

At least there's an upside. I smiled at the thought of Miguel's mutilated face.

"You should have listened to me, Faythe," Ryan said, coming to a stop in front of my cage. He dropped the food on the ground and reached through the bars to turn my face toward the light, inspecting my injuries with his brow furrowed in concern. "He's talking about replacing you."

My pulse jumped. "Does that mean I get to go home?" *Please, please, please let that mean I get to go home.* But I knew better.

"Hardly." He tilted my face to the right. "He and Sean are going after another girl first thing in the morning. If you aren't a little easier to deal with when they get back...well, he won't really need you then."

I stepped back, jerking my chin from his grasp. If he was really concerned about me, he'd do something to help instead of lecturing me on acquiescence. "Just say it, Ryan," I snapped, angry over much more than my brother's inability to say exactly what he meant. "Just say he'll kill me."

He bent over to pick up the bags, too much of a coward to meet my eyes. "Yeah. He might. I don't think he'd do it on purpose, but you have this way of bringing out the worst in people..." Ryan shrugged, leaving the rest to my too-fertile imagination.

My throat felt thick as I swallowed, ignoring his

insult in favor of his actual point. Death marks the end of pain and humiliation, but captivity only marks the beginning of it.

Ryan shoved a paper bag through the bars of my cage, but I stood in front of him with my arms crossed beneath my breasts, refusing to accept it. "Take the food, Faythe." He shook my dinner as if it were a box of Nine Lives, but I just stared at him. "Fine." He opened his fist and let the bag drop to the ground.

I didn't even glance at it, choosing to glare at him instead. Ryan rolled his eyes at me and marched toward Abby's cell. He slid her bag into the cage, seeming first surprised then pleased when she took it with no resistance. "Now, see? Abby's being cooperative, so why can't you?"

"I have to go to the bathroom."

"So, go." He waved his hand at the empty coffee can.

"You're not listening." I didn't bother to screen irritation from my voice. "I want to go *to* the bathroom."

He shrugged. "I couldn't help you even if I wanted to. I don't have a key."

Oh, shit. I'd forgotten. "That's right. Miguel doesn't trust you."

"Look, pee if you need to, and I'll empty the can

for you. That's the best I can do, and pissing me off isn't going to change anything. Unless I decided to let your can sit for a while."

Okay, he had me there. The situation wasn't going to improve, so I might as well get it over with. Glowering, I bent to snatch the canister from the floor. "Turn around."

"Happy to." He turned with his back to the bars, and I glanced at Abby. She sat facing the back wall of her cage, chewing something crunchy. Ryan huffed impatiently. "You've done this before, so hurry up."

"Yeah, well, the indignity of peeing in a can wasn't something I thought I'd ever have to repeat."

"Just get it over with," he snapped.

I did, and briefly considered making them both plug their ears. But that would have only emphasized my embarrassment. I used another napkin from the burger bag to wipe, and dropped it into the can too. A girl has her standards, even behind bars.

Carrying the container to Ryan was an exercise in degradation. "I'm going to write to my senator," I said, trying to cover my humiliation with sarcasm. "These prison conditions are appalling." I slid the coffee can through the bars to Ryan, and he took it with both hands.

"Your senator. That's good. While you're at it, tell him my salary is below the minimum wage, and my hours are inhumane." He carried the can through a doorway beneath the stairs, which presumably hid a small bathroom. I heard the toilet flush and smelled vanilla-scented soap as Ryan washed his hands. When he returned, he sat on the floor across from the empty cage, facing both me and Abby.

"I don't suppose you have any hand sanitizer?" I said, holding my palms up for inspection.

"Nope. Sorry." He shrugged.

"There's a wet wipe in your bag," Abby said, now facing me with a half-eaten chicken breast in one hand.

"Thanks." I rummaged through the bag until I found it, careful not to touch the food. Ripping open the little foil package, I cleaned my hands as well as I could, even wiping off the last flecks of Miguel's blood. Then I dove into my meal. Two fried-chicken breasts, potatoes and gravy, a half ear of corn, and a biscuit. No butter, no salt. "It's not as good as Mom's but hardly reason to complain," I said around a mouthful of chicken. They'd even given us silverware. Well, plasticware.

"Glad you're pleased." Ryan dug a bottle of water from each of two long pockets on the sides of his baggy khakis. He handed one to me and tossed the other into Abby's cage and onto her mattress.

I opened my bottle and swallowed half of the contents in one long drink.

Above my head and to my right, the doorknob squealed as it turned. I screwed the cap on my bottle, my eyes glued to the stairs. My heart fluttered as I wondered which of our abductors I'd be facing this time. I glanced at Ryan, hoping for some clue as to what was about to happen, but he just shrugged and stood up, stuffing his hands into his pockets.

Red canvas sneakers appeared on the top step. It was Sean. I started to relax, remembering the genuine sound of regret in his voice on the ranch, and the fact that he hadn't touched Abby. But then I remembered that his scent had been all over Sara, and I tensed again, my hands curling into fists at my sides.

"Hey, Sean," Ryan said, and I saw tension fade from his face. He wasn't afraid of Sean, which meant I probably shouldn't be either.

Sean stopped, leaning down from the fifth step for a better view of the basement. "Ryan." He exhaled deeply. "You scared the shit out of me. I thought you were Eric for a minute."

"Nah, it's just me. Whatcha need?"

"Nothing. I just came to say hi to Faythe." He jogged the rest of the way down the steps and turned his eyes to me. "Hi, Faythe."

"Hi." I set my food aside and stood, looking from him to Ryan in amazement. The relaxed quality of their greetings gave me chills.

"Come on down," Ryan said.

Sean shrugged. His gaze darted to the cage on my right as he passed it. His jaw tensed and moisture gleamed in his eyes.

Oh, shit. I thought. *That was Sara's cage.* How could I not have realized that?

"How are you, Faythe?" he asked, tearing his eyes from the empty cage to meet mine.

I propped my hands on my hips. "How do I look?"

"Like hell."

"Yep." I nodded. "That about sums it up."

"I'm really sorry about all this," he said, stuffing his hands in his pockets to duplicate Ryan's pose. "I never meant for any of this to happen."

That made two of us. "What did you mean to happen?" I asked, curiosity getting the better of me. I thought I understood Sean's motive for snatching Sara. But killing her...?

"Nothing. I just wanted to talk to Sara. I didn't know they had any of this planned." His voice sounded strange. Kind of hollow.

"What *did* you know?" I asked as Ryan shook his head frantically at me from behind Sean. I ignored him. "Why did you let them take her?"

"I..." He paused, meeting my eyes for just a second before bowing his head and glancing away again. "Damn, this is going to sound bad, Faythe, but I bought her."

I blinked, staring at him without even a spark of comprehension. He bought her. Eric had said he bought Abby, but what the hell did that mean? How do you buy a person?

"You *bought* Sara?" I asked, still trying to understand. "Who did you buy her from? How much did she cost?"

"Nothing." His face was disturbingly composed, yet he sounded offended, as if I should have been ashamed for asking the question. That was wrong in *so* many ways. "I didn't pay money. Hell, I didn't *have* any money. I promised my labor, just like Eric did for Abby." He glanced at her briefly over his shoulder. "I have to work for him for two years, or until he agrees that my debt is paid, whichever comes first."

For a moment, no one spoke, as Abby and I tried to absorb what he'd said. Then she screeched, outrage reddening her face. "You paid for Sara by helping kidnap *us?*"

Sean dropped his eyes, finally showing a little shame, but it was much too late to garner any sympathy. "I told you it would sound bad."

Abby nodded hysterically, curls flying. "It sounds fucking terrible."

"She's right, Sean." I struggled to keep my voice

calm and even. Behind him, Ryan rubbed his forehead, mouthing some kind of warning at me.

"I know." Sean ran one hand through his lank brown hair. He looked as if he'd just been scolded for drinking from the milk carton. "I know how bad it sounds, but I never meant for any of this to happen. I only wanted to talk to her alone, so she could listen to me without her parents whispering in her ear. It just—" he glanced down "—it didn't go like I planned."

I shuddered as a frightening realization rolled through me. "You had her kidnapped so you could *propose* to her?" I couldn't keep disbelief from my voice.

Ryan threw his hands into the air in exasperation, glaring at me.

Sean cringed. "That sounds bad, too, huh?"

"Yeah." I nodded, so stunned my skin was tingling. "Really bad."

Sean stepped toward my cage, his eyes wide and intense, pleading with me to understand what he'd done. "She only chose Kyle because her parents liked him better. But Sara liked me. I know she did. And Miguel said he could get me some time alone with her. For a price."

"So you promised him your services. For two years."

"Yes." He nodded enthusiastically, as if pleased that I finally understood. "I would have promised him anything. But I didn't know who he was, or how he expected me to pay my debt. And I had no idea he was going to lock Sara up."

I made myself let go of the bars, trying to appear calm, as if I didn't want to rip out his throat. "When you found out, why didn't you let her go?"

He shrugged, but his eyes held too much pain to pull off such an offhand gesture. "I wanted to, but Miguel said her Pride was already looking for her, and that if we let her go, she'd turn us in. Her father would have had me killed. You know he would have." He glanced at me for confirmation, but I didn't know what to say. He was right.

"So you let them kill her instead," Abby said. It wasn't a question.

"I…" He glanced at me, then at her, already backing toward the stairs. "I'm sorry. I shouldn't have come down here. I can't expect you to under-stand."

"Sean, wait," I said, following him as far as my bars would let me. But he didn't wait. He turned and ran up the stairs, slamming the door as he left.

"I tried to warn you," Ryan said, shaking his head at me as if it were my fault.

"Is that what you were doing?" I sat at the base

of the bars, pulling the fast-food bag back into my lap. "I thought maybe you were trying to fly."

"Cute." He leaned back against the staircase, thin arms crossed over his chest. "Sean isn't doing so hot today."

"So I noticed. What happened?"

He frowned. "I'm not sure. It may have been going after you. Or maybe knowing they're gonna take—" he caught his slipup just in time "—another tabby. The whole thing's snowballing, and he knows there's no way out. He's acting like he might let go of that last shred of sanity any minute."

"Serves him right," Abby said. We both turned to look at her. She held a biscuit clenched in one hand, crumbling between her tiny fingers.

"Yeah, well, I think he'd agree with you," Ryan said.

"If he feels so guilty, why'd he let them kill her?" I asked.

"He didn't *let* them. He just wasn't here to stop it. And I'm not sure he could have, anyway."

"Michael said Sean's scent was all over her," I said, my food untouched on my lap.

Ryan sighed and sat down, apparently resigning himself to a long explanation. "That was from before. When Eric and Miguel went after Abby—" he glanced at her, but she wouldn't meet his eyes

"—they left me and Sean here with Sara. Sean spent the whole time down here with her, trying to work his Don Juan magic. He left the door open, and I heard part of it from the kitchen.

"He told her how much he loved her and begged her to marry him instead of Kyle. She said all the right things, agreeing to everything he asked and telling him she loved him. According to him, they even 'made love,' but I suspect she was just too scared to say no. Afterward, I heard her crying, begging him to let her go home. Sean completely freaked out, accusing her of lying to him. He came upstairs blubbering and said Miguel was right, that they couldn't let her go. He slammed the front door on his way out, and I remember thinking he was gone for good, and we were down to three out of five."

My head snapped up in surprise. "Five? Who's the fifth?" But I was pretty sure I already knew, that I'd already met him. And broken his nose.

"Luiz. The cat Miguel sent after you. He left before I got here, so I never met him, but Eric said he's another jungle stray." Ryan met my eyes. "I heard Miguel talking to him on the phone, but I don't speak Portuguese, so, you know..." He shrugged both thin shoulders.

I gaped at my brother, stunned by how casually he'd prattled off the news of another murderer on the loose, as if such things happened every day. Maybe they did.

Ryan shook his head as if to clear it. "Anyway, when they got back with Abby, Miguel hit the roof. He said if I couldn't find Sean by sunrise, they'd go after Hailey to teach him a lesson."

I gasped in horror. Sean's little sister was about Abby's size, but she was only thirteen years old.

"I looked in every bar in town, but by the time I found him and dragged him back, Sara was dead."

Silence fell over us like a heavy quilt, but instead of warming me, it gave me chills.

"They thought I was unconscious," Abby whispered. Her words seeped beneath the blanket of silence like a cold draft.

I turned slowly toward her, hoping I'd misunderstood. She'd abandoned her food for the comfort of her favorite corner of the mattress. Tears stood in her eyes. She hugged herself, rocking back and forth as she spoke. "I saw what they did to her." Her words sounded choked, as if she was trying and failing to hold them in.

My breath caught in my throat, and I coughed to expel it. I'd had a feeling she'd witnessed Sara's death, but hearing her say it was different.

"I'm so sorry, Ab," Ryan said, and I couldn't help but believe him.

Tears slid silently down Abby's face and she turned her back on us both, curling into the fetal position on the mattress. Even in human form she moved with a cat's grace and flexibility; her posture was as expressive as most people's eyes. I knew by the tension in her arms and the curve of her spine that she was reliving Sara's final moments.

"Miguel came down first," Abby said, her account punctuated by sniffles. "Sara screamed and cried. She tried to throw him off, but he was too strong. He ripped her clothes off in pieces. She wouldn't shut up, so he choked her 'til she passed out. She was still unconscious when Eric came down for his turn, but she woke up at the end, screaming. Afterward, she curled up in a corner, trying to cover herself with scraps from her shirt.

"I tried to talk to her but she wouldn't answer. She just cried for her mom. Then Miguel came down again. As soon as she saw him, she tried to scream, but she'd lost her voice. She clawed at the floor when he pulled her out of the corner. She—" Abby sobbed again, and I wanted to tell her to stop, that she didn't have to say any more. But she seemed to need to get it out of her system. "Sara kept slamming her head into the concrete like she was trying to knock herself out, but he didn't care. He just let her. When he was done, he picked her up—set her on her feet like a mannequin. She couldn't talk anymore by then. She looked like she could barely even move. But then he touched her face. Her ran one finger down her cheek, and she lunged at him. She bit his finger, and he howled. He jerked his hand away, and she just stared at him, blood dripping down her chin.

"Miguel lost it then. He screamed at her in Spanish, or something like that. He hit her in the face with the back of his hand—*hard*—and she went flying across the cage. Her head hit one of the bars over the mattress, and there was this awful crunching sound. Her arms just hung there for a second, then she slid to the floor. There was so much blood…"

Ryan looked sick, and I knew exactly how he felt. "Abby…" I didn't know what to say to her. I didn't want to hear any more, but I couldn't bring myself to say it.

"I couldn't cry for her," Abby said, her words so choked with sobs that I could barely understand them. "I was afraid he'd come for me if he knew I was awake."

For several minutes, we sat motionless, listening to Abby cry. I wanted to comfort her but I couldn't. There was nothing I could say to save her from her memories. I didn't even know how to fight off my own.

All I could do was change the subject. I was good at that.

When Abby's sobs faded into quiet hiccups, I glanced at Ryan to find him staring at the ground. "Did you call Mom?" I said, dreading the answer even as I asked the question. But it was better than thinking about Sara.

Ryan cleared his throat, claiming a stoic expression with obvious difficulty. "Yeah, a couple of hours ago," Ryan said. "She's pretty upset."

"Ah, the light at the end of the tunnel." I pulled the lid from my container of mashed potatoes and dug in with my spork. I'd lost my appetite after listening to Abby's account, but needed something to do with my hands.

"You should lay off her," he scolded. "She cried in my ear for twenty minutes because she felt guilty about the last conversation you two had."

"Well, she should." I gulped water from my bottle. "My personal life is none of her business." But Mom crying over me took me by surprise. I'd known she would be upset, like everyone else, because without me there would be no next generation of the south-central Pride. But if she felt guilty for nagging me about Andrew, she must actually miss me. Not the future dam, but me, all my faults included.

And, in truth, she wasn't the only one who had been thinking about our last conversation. I'd had plenty of time to mull over what she'd said about being on the council and about my father never making her do anything. All my life, I'd assumed my mother was trapped in her life, and just didn't realize it because she didn't know there were any other appropriate options for a woman. But she'd turned my theory on its ear. She'd had power and turned it down, content to make her mark behind the scenes. I'd always thought my mother was weak because she had no obvious strength. But she wasn't weak, she was just humble. And I'd been stupid and unfair.

Great, now I felt guilty for pigeonholing her as a 1950s model she-bitch. Guilt is a vicious cycle, an emotional slippery slope. I don't recommend it.

"I tell you what, Ryan," I said, my voice unusually soft with regret. "If I ever see her again, I'll apologize."

Confusion knit his brows together, as if it had really never occurred to him that I might not see our mother again, in spite of his own warnings that Miguel might kill me. Sometimes I suspected Ryan was merely visiting the real world, on vacation from his permanent residence in la-la land.

Before I could decide how to respond to his delusion, he changed tracks completely. "Aren't you going to ask me about Marc?"

I tensed involuntarily, and my spork snapped in half. *Smooth, Faythe.* I dropped the now-useless plastic handle into the bag. "Why would I?"

Ryan grinned, clearly enjoying my discomfort. "Mom said you two had a reunion of sorts the night before you ran off."

I stuck the functional end of my spork into the half-empty container of potatoes, setting them both aside so I could focus all of my energy on burning a hole through Ryan's forehead with my stare. "First of all, I didn't run away. I just went down to the barn to clear my head and try to gain a new perspective." I smiled, pleased with myself for having put a hell of a good spin on a phenomenally stupid mistake. *Damn, I should write speeches for the president.*

Ryan sneered. "A new perspective on why you slept with Marc after ignoring him for five years?"

"No, smart-ass." I picked the potatoes back up, stirring them aimlessly as I spoke. "I just needed some fresh air. And the thing with Marc was a mistake. I drank too much. That's it." I took a bite of mashed potatoes, satisfied that my point had been made, and that I'd told the truth. Or at least one version of it.

"Yeah, that's what Jace said."

I nearly choked on my self-congratulatory mouthful, and had to wash it down with another swig of water while pounding on my own chest. "Jace said I drank too much?" I asked when I could speak.

"He said that you sleeping with Marc was a mistake." Ryan shot me an evil grin. "You know, I always liked that kid. It's too bad about what happened to him."

My hands went cold, and I dropped the potatoes to wipe sweat from my palms onto my shorts. "Please tell me Marc didn't kill him." My voice came out in a tiny, scared whisper.

"Nope," Ryan said, still grinning. "Came damn near, though. Mom said it took all three of the other guys to drag your sweetie off Jace. Only a direct order from Dad kept the peace."

Damn it, Marc!

It was all my fault. Not for sleeping with Marc, but for taking Jace's car. Marc knew about the bet, and knew I had a claim on Jace's keys. But he didn't know that I hadn't run. He probably thought I'd driven off on my own, right into the open arms of my waiting abductors. And that Jace had given me the means.

"How bad is it?" I asked, dreading the answer.

Ryan ticked the injuries off on his fingers, and with each one, my guilt increased, weighing me down almost literally. "Broken nose, two black eyes, cracked jaw, three broken ribs, and four broken toes, all on one foot. Concussion, and possible internal bleeding in his abdomen. It's bad enough that he'd be in the hospital, if he were human."

I groaned, picturing Jace lying in the guest bedroom, encased in a body cast and hooked up to an IV. He couldn't go to the hospital for the same reason Sara's death couldn't be reported to the police: medical evidence.

Dr. Carver explained to me once that our blood is different from human blood. Apparently the difference is obvious enough to be noticed by any competent lab tech, which means that under no circumstances can we allow ourselves to be examined by a human doctor. To avoid meddling from schools and local governments, several Prides claim religious beliefs which forbid medical treatment. Fortunately for us, Dr. Carver makes himself available during emergencies for members of the south-central Pride.

Because of the risk of exposure, Jace's recovery would proceed without a hospital staff catering to his every need. But thanks to Dr. Carver, his bones would heal straight and he would have medication for pain. Of course, like alcohol, tranquilizers, and even food, painkillers didn't last long because of our high metabolism.

Still, it could have been worse. Marc could have killed him.

"I can't believe this," I whispered, shaking my head in denial.

"Really?" Ryan arched his eyebrows. "I wasn't all that surprised. Marc's always been a brute. What else can you expect from a stray?"

My temper flared, and I knew I should bite my tongue. But I didn't. "Are you a stray, Ryan?" I demanded, forcing myself to stay seated. "Because Marc has a hell of a lot more courage than you've shown lately. A damn sight more honor too. He would get us out of here if he had to chew the bars open with his own teeth, so tell me again how little you can expect from strays!" I was shouting by the time I finished. I couldn't help it. I'd had enough of his jealousy and sniveling cowardice.

Ryan didn't answer. He just glared at me.

I chewed on a bland bite of chicken, waiting for my brother to stomp out of the basement, but he didn't, for no reason I could have named. I'd certainly pissed him off, but apparently the murdering bastards upstairs were even worse company. Go figure.

He stared at the floor with his elbows on his knees. Abby glanced at him, then back at me, her face swollen from crying and her posture stiff. When

Ryan looked calm again, I decided to try a new method of pumping him for information—the direct approach. He was clueless enough that it just might work.

"So, who did Eric and Miguel go after?" I asked, trying to sound casual. There were only two more tabbies within a reasonable driving distance of Mississippi: one in Missouri, the other in Kentucky. Even the smallest hint might help me eliminate one.

Ryan frowned. "Don't start. You know I can't tell you." He picked at a crack in the concrete, and I visualized it widening, to swallow him whole.

"Why not?" I grabbed the white paper bag, digging through it for the second chicken breast. "It's not like I can tell anyone else," I said, but he only shook his head. "Fine, don't tell me who she is. Just tell me who she's for. Is she for you?" I carefully peeled the skin from my chicken, trying to look as if I didn't really care about his answer. But I did.

"Hell no, she's not for me!" Ryan shouted.

"Who, then? Luiz?" I asked, going for breezy. But the carefree tone fit my question about as well as Marc's shirt fit me. I watched Ryan from the corner of my eye as I dropped the grease-coated skin into the bag. Yes, in cat form I ate raw flesh and organ meat, but as a human, I couldn't put something as disgusting as deep-fried, bump-covered chicken skin in my mouth, no matter how hungry I was. Every girl has her limits, and forcible sex and poultry skin both crossed mine.

"She's for Miguel, if you don't shape up," Ryan snapped, staring at my food as he spoke. *Like that was supposed to motivate me!* "Other than that, I don't know."

His refusal to make eye contact confirmed my suspicion that there was something he wasn't telling me. Something I needed to know.

I dropped the chicken breast back into the bag, almost untouched. "Come on, Ryan, if you don't want to tell me, just say so. But don't lie."

He bristled. "I'm not lying. I don't know. Miguel won't tell me."

"Why not?" My stomach clenched, unhappy not with the food I'd sent its way, but with the gut feeling raising the hairs on the back of my neck. I was about to get bad news. I'd known Ryan long enough to recognize his body language. He knew something terrible and he was about to say it.

"I think he won't tell me because he's planning to kill me."

Careful not to use my injured left arm, I stood and stepped up to the bars. "I thought you were useful," I said, glancing at Abby. She was watching my brother through red-rimmed eyes, as if her life depended on his answer. Maybe it did. Maybe mine did, too.

Ryan stood up in front of me, his shoulders slumped in resignation. "Once he's out of the council's reach, he won't need me, and I'm sure I won't live an hour past that point." He ran a hand through sandy hair and met my eyes. "See, you're not the only one with problems."

Biting my lip, I declined to point out that he could always run. He could leave while Miguel was gone, and be out of the country before they even realized he'd left the house.

I didn't say it because I was afraid he'd take my suggestion if he thought it was possible. I was afraid he'd leave us, and as furious as I was at him, he was better company than Miguel. And Eric. And Sean, if I wanted to be honest. Sean sounded like he might crack up at any moment, and the only thing more dangerous than an angry cat was a crazy one.

"Why would he be out of the council's reach, Ryan?" My voice was low and dangerous. I heard it but I couldn't help it.

His face filled with scorn, and I blinked. That was new. "Oh, come on, Faythe. Did you really think he was going to keep you here forever? You're smart. Surely you knew this was only temporary." In fact, I had, but I bit my tongue and stared at him, hoping for more information. "He has a buyer, Faythe. Some Amazon Alpha who wants a mate and is willing to pay big."

My hands fell into my lap, ice cold, while my brain raced fast enough to give me an instant headache. *Oh, shit. Shit, shit, shit.* It was my worst nightmare. Literally. And in that moment I realized something important: I knew more about Miguel's plans than Ryan did.

My brother was right about one thing: he really had been forced into working for Miguel, at least according to his own skewed perspective. Ryan didn't have the mind of a criminal. A lazy, naive coward, yes. But not a criminal. That bad-guy handicap had kept him from seeing the truth about Miguel's scheme.

Miguel didn't just have one buyer waiting in South America. Catching us was too much trouble for anything on that small a scale. He had to have at least two buyers, and maybe three or four. He'd used Sean to go after Sara, not because he wanted Sara in particular, but because Sean did, and Miguel needed help. But he never planned to let Sean keep her. Sara had been bought and paid for before Miguel ever crossed the U.S. border. So had Abby, and the third girl. And so had I.

If I was right, Miguel would use Ryan, Eric and

Sean to get us to Brazil. Then he would kill them, probably with the aid of the buyers and their loyal tomcats, assuming they had any. And I was inclined to assume they did, because they would have to be pretty powerful to convince Miguel to kidnap several American tabbies. Either that, or Miguel was stupid. And I already knew he wasn't stupid.

So, what did it say about me that I understood the way Miguel's mind worked? Nothing I wanted to think about, not that I could keep from it. The obvious possibility was that I shared some kind of depraved thought process with him. But more frightening for me was the probability that Marc and my father had been right: without even realizing it, I had been trained to lead the Pride. Somehow I'd developed the ability to think like the enemy, a definite advantage for any leader to have. The only problem? I didn't want to be a leader. I just wanted to be a survivor.

But both of those roles were out of the question, if I couldn't get out of this damn cage.

In one corner of the basement, water dripped from a leaky pipe, dropping into a growing puddle on the ground. The drips seemed to count the seconds of anxious silence as they passed, urging me to say something. To find out the rest of what I needed to know.

"When is he leaving, Ryan?" I asked, trying not to frighten him with the strength of my stare and the intensity of my voice. I gripped the bars so tight I could almost hear them groan, although realistically my fingers would snap long before solid metal bars would. I stared at Ryan, trying to slow my pulse and keep panic out of my eyes. Of course, he chose that moment to clam up completely. But who could blame him?

"When?" I shouted, and he jumped, eyes wide. I hadn't meant to scream at him, but I couldn't help it. If I could have reached him in that moment, I'd have squeezed his throat until his eyes popped out of his head, for being such an idiot.

He glanced at the stairs, obviously listening for footsteps. "They're leaving in the morning, and plan to make the grab sometime after dark. They'll be back the next morning, and we're all leaving that night."

I did the math in my head. Two days. I had approximately forty-eight hours to get us out of there, or make contact with the council. But how? I needed Miguel to take another shot at me. I needed to get him to open my cage, or at least come near me with the key. But according to Ryan, he wouldn't come back downstairs until he had the new girl. I couldn't afford to wait that long.

"You can stop him, Ryan," I said, dipping my head to catch his eyes. I tried to project confidence in my voice, rather than desperation. "Call Mom. You can stop him and save your own life." I already knew he didn't give a damn about mine.

"No." He shook his head like a toddler denying he'd made the puddle on the floor. "He'll kill me."

I wasn't sure whether he was talking about Miguel or Daddy, since either could have been true, so I went with what I hoped was a safe answer. "No, he won't. I won't let him. Just call Mom and tell her you saw something, or smelled something. Tell her you think we're here, and have her send someone to check it out. That's all it would take, and you'd be a hero." Another positive spin. I was on a roll!

Ryan shook his head again, as if denying the existence of voices in his head. Or maybe his conscience. He shuffled backward toward the stairs. "I'm sorry, Faythe. I can't do it. Miguel said they'd go after Mom if I help you."

Mom? They'd take Mom just to get back at Ryan? Boy, they knew where his loyalties lay. But surely it was an empty threat. Going after Sean's sister was horrible, but it made sense. Snatching Mom didn't. What would they want with a tabby who was past childbearing age?

"Ryan, they won't take Mom. They're not going

to waste that much time and energy on revenge. Besides, they'd never be able to get near her."

Ryan bumped into the hand rail and glanced around as if surprised to see the stairs behind him. "They got you," he said, backing onto the first step. "Do you really want me to take that chance on Mom?"

How the hell was I supposed to answer that? I knew deep down that they'd never get close enough to snatch her, but Ryan had thought the same about me, and we all knew how that theory had panned out.

He read my answer on my face, and turned his back on both me and Abby, taking the steps two at a time.

Frantic now, I appealed to his sense of self-preservation. "So you're just going to let Miguel kill you, and leave your corpse for the jungle cats to snack on?"

He stiffened, and his hand shook on the doorknob. Without turning, Ryan squared his shoulders, then opened the door and stepped into the kitchen, leaving us alone again.

He'll change his mind, I thought. *He has to.*

The door closed with a final-sounding click, and I dropped onto the edge of the mattress, glancing in disinterest at the remains of my meal. I looked over at Abby, barely registering the raw terror on her face.

But I did notice that I could still see her pretty well. Overhead, a single seventy-five-watt bulb illuminated our basement cells with depressing clarity, in spite of the darkness outside.

At least this time he left the light on, I thought. Sometimes, you thank God for the small things, especially when they're all you have.

Twenty-Four

After Ryan left, I hit a new low, lying on my back on the mattress because that was the only comfortable position I could find. My stomach was threatening to return my latest meal, largely unused. I was sticky with sweat and I ached all over.

Two days. I had two days to break out of a welded aluminum cage before Miguel sold me as a combination sex toy/baby factory to a Brazilian jungle cat. And the only member of my family who knew about it was helping my captors instead of me. It was enough to make me wonder what kind of monster I'd been in my previous life. Really, it had to be karma. There was no other explanation for my horrible luck.

But if I was dispirited, Abby was truly despondent. She lay on the edge of her mattress, staring at nothing, her sweat-damp curls spread out behind her. She'd been like that ever since Ryan left, taking any hope of a rescue with him.

I felt as if I should comfort her, but I had no idea what to say. I wanted to believe my brother would change his mind. I was desperate to believe it. Surely even he wouldn't be stupid enough to hand over his life to Miguel without a fight. Or maybe he would. Ryan had never been much of a fighter.

After I'd indulged in at least an hour of bitter self-pity, brought on by fantasies of grape Popsicles and air-conditioning, Abby's gentle snoring interrupted my reverie. I envied her the oblivion of sleep, but found it impossible to achieve for myself. I was too busy thinking. About everything. I thought about Marc, and about Jace. I thought about how worried and angry my father must be. I thought about my mother, wondering if she'd decided to reclaim her seat on the council now that their decisions once again directly affected her life and the future of her Pride. And I thought about Eric and Miguel, wondering which of my friends' lives they were about to ruin.

Eventually, I fell asleep, with visions of Miguel's mutilated face dancing in my head like Tchaikovsky's sugarplum fairies. But even after such sweet dreams, I woke to the same dismal basement

I'd first seen nearly twenty-four hours earlier. Outside, the first rays of sunlight struggled to penetrate the filthy windows, but their efforts were as futile as my own quest for a key. If not for the overhead bulb, I'd have woken up to daylight too weak and murky to do anything more than outline vague shapes in the dark.

Thank goodness for that lightbulb, I thought, determined to start off the new day with a dose of optimism. *Without it, I'd have to Shift just to be able to see.*

Wait, maybe that wasn't such a bad idea. Surely the sedative had cleared from my system.

Excited now, I sat up and turned to face Abby, who was just waking. "Hey, Ab, you want to hear my brilliant new plan?" It wouldn't get us out of our cages, but it just might throw a wrench in Miguel's plans. If he couldn't get close to us, he couldn't sedate us. And they'd have to be crazy to try to load two fully conscious, pissed-off tabbies into the back of a van.

Abby rubbed sleep from her eyes and pushed herself into a sitting position. "I guess."

"Shift."

"Shift?" Her forehead wrinkled in confusion.

"Yeah." I smiled. "Shift."

"That's it?"

"Yup. That's it. Brilliant in its simplicity, if I do say so myself. I can't believe I didn't think of it before." I thought she'd laugh, or at least crack a smile. But instead, she burst into tears.

I came as close to her as my cage would allow, wishing more than anything that I could give her a hug. "If we have claws and canines, I don't think they'll try anything. There's no way Miguel can take my cat form in his human form. And if he Shifts first, he can't get into the cage. If he's stupid enough to come in as a human, then try to Shift, I'll have plenty of time to take him out before he finishes."

Abby sobbed harder and threw herself facedown onto the mattress.

I frowned. "Okay, maybe it's not exactly a *brilliant* plan, but it's no reason to cry."

She sat up, curls clinging to one damp, splotchy cheek. "I can't do it."

"Sure you can."

"No, I can't. I woke up in the middle of the night and couldn't go back to sleep, so I tried to Shift, just to have something to do. But I couldn't do it. I'm too upset, or tired, or something." She glanced away in embarrassment. "It's happened a couple of times before. I get nervous, or upset, and I can't Shift."

Well, shit. She couldn't Shift and I couldn't snatch a key. Together we'd ruled out both of my escape plans. I closed my eyes, desperately searching my brain for a third brilliant idea. I came up blank. So much for the third time being charmed. So…back to plan number two. She'd just have to work through her problem.

"Don't worry about it, Abby. All you need to do is calm down and concentrate. Can you do that for me?"

She nodded, but her face showed no conviction. Her forehead was lined in fear, her expression pure despair. She hadn't smiled since recounting Sara's murder, and I saw in her tear-damp eyes that she expected to die the same way.

I took a deep breath, trying to relax in hopes that if I did, she would too. "Clear your mind completely, and try to think about nothing but the process of Shifting."

"Okay." After a moment's hesitation and a nervous glance at the stairs, she took off her clothes, carefully folding them on one corner of her mattress. On hands and knees, she glanced up at me, tension warping her features into a mask of fear and dread.

I sighed. This wouldn't work unless she could loosen up. "How 'bout if I do it with you?"

"Thanks." She nodded gratefully, obviously trying to relax.

"No problem." I stripped and tossed my clothes

aside, trying not to let pity show in my expression. The last thing she needed was a reason to be embarrassed, as well as tired, hungry, and scared. And probably dehydrated. I know my mouth was dry. "You ready?" I asked, lowering myself carefully onto all fours. My left shoulder screamed in protest, refusing to bear any of my weight. I winced, shifting to support myself with my right arm.

Abby nodded, but I wasn't convinced. She still looked pretty nervous.

"Okay, now I want you to start at your toes and work your way up, relaxing each body part as you come to it. Okay?"

She nodded again.

"Relax your toes, then your ankles, and so on. Do your feet feel relaxed?"

"I think so."

Shit. If she wasn't sure, they weren't relaxed.

I smiled, trying to encourage her. "Now move onto your legs. Relax your calves and thighs." I spoke slowly, keeping my voice even and smooth. "Can you feel your muscles loosening up?"

"Yes," she said, but her posture betrayed the lie. I considered stopping, since the exercise obviously wasn't helping her, but I was afraid that admitting failure would upset her even more.

"When your whole body is relaxed, start to visualize your Shift. Instead of dreading the pain, welcome it because it's—" I couldn't speak anymore. My Shift had begun. My routine was so ingrained, so automatic, that my body did what it was told, even though my brain hadn't meant for it to. I could have stopped it, but that would hurt worse than just letting it happen. So I did my best to let go and let my body take over for a while.

Unfortunately, that was easier said than done. I'd never Shifted with a serious injury and had no idea how badly it would hurt. The first stages were agony like I'd never experienced. My body was literally tearing itself apart, ligament by ligament and joint by joint. That was one thing for my healthy joints and ligaments, but something else entirely for my wounded shoulder. It was on fire, my injury inflamed by the physical changes forced on it.

The pain eased as the last stages of my Shift came and went, the various parts of my body settling into place. By the time it was over, my shoulder throbbed with the dull pain of an old injury.

I stretched, testing my new configuration of muscles and bones. To my amazement, my shoulder felt much better. It was far from healed, but I could now bear my own weight. Marc had mentioned something similar happening to him once, but I hadn't thought about it much since. His theory was that since muscles and bones change during a Shift, they began to heal automatically as they were reattached in new positions.

Cool, I thought pleased by my discovery. *I should have Shifted earlier.*

Now dressed, Abby watched me, her expression a mixture of envy and awe. "You make that look so easy, like it doesn't even hurt."

I huffed air through my nose, knowing she would understand. It hurt plenty, no matter how it looked.

Flexing my muzzle, I arched my whiskers forward, then back to lie flat against my face. Then I extended my forepaws as far out as they would go, my rump in the air. After my stretch, I glanced around at my surroundings, seeing the basement for the first time on four paws.

I usually loved the first few minutes in cat form, because every sight and smell I knew by heart as a human felt so novel, so new and different to my cat's senses. But this time my feline body felt awkward and out of place in the basement, where nothing stirred and nothing grew. No rodents scurried across my field of vision. No twigs or rocks poked at my paws, and no burrs caught in the soft fur over my belly. There was no breeze, not even the artificial cool of an air conditioner. And though I could hear sounds of civilization coming from the house above me, compared to Daddy's woodland preserve, my underground prison was eerily quiet, and *wrong,* as only a man-made habitat could be.

Experienced as a cat, the basement was a concrete-lined pit, fouled by everything human. It was an assault on my senses. The floor was harsh against my paws, like walking on rough-grit sandpaper. From overhead came the sound of canned laughter; someone was up, watching TV. The bars surrounding me stank of metal, and the personal scent of everyone who had recently touched them. But the predominant smell was blood.

It was Sara's, and it came from the empty cell to my right. No amount of scrubbing could disguise the scent of blood from a cat, and what frightened me most was knowing that the majority of what was spilled had been disposed of along with the mattress. What I smelled was only a fraction of what Sara had lost, along with her life.

There were other smells, of course, like the disturbing combination of Marc and Miguel. I smelled them both, no matter which way I turned, because their personal scents were *on* me, and wouldn't completely fade until my next shower.

Abby smelled like baby powder—scented deodorant, surely several days old now, and something young and feminine, and all her own. But pervading her scent was the distinctive, sour odor of fear.

Miguel had said he liked the smell of fear, which told me more than I ever needed to know about him.

Cats stalk and hunt for several reasons, including practice, leisure and as an excuse to socialize. But we only kill for food or in self-defense. The smell of fear does nothing to improve our appetites, nor is it an aphrodisiac.

Miguel's fear fetish belonged to his human half, not his feline half. It was something he had in common with countless prison inmates all over the world, but not a single zoo cat. He was a human monster, whom some clumsy idiot had armed with lethal teeth and claws.

I'd love to get my hands on the cat responsible for Miguel's first Shift, I thought. But knowing Miguel, that cat was probably rotting in peace—or in pieces—somewhere in the middle of the jungle.

In addition to blood and fear, I identified the residual smell of my own urine in the coffee container. As a cat, the smell didn't offend me in the least. It was a natural part of my own biology, unlike the metallic smell of the bars and the lingering odor of spilled oil.

But the only smell I was interested in at the moment came from the white paper bag in the corner. The remains of my dinner from the night before. It wouldn't be enough, but it was better than nothing. I clamped the bottom of the bag between my teeth and shook my head, scattering trash along with the remaining chicken breast and the scraps of the first. As a cat, I wasn't bothered by the skin, though I wasn't particularly fond of the extra-crisp batter. In less time than it had taken me to Shift, the breast was gone, skin and all. I might have crunched through a couple of small bones, too.

After my meal, I sat on my haunches, cleaning my face and paws. I wasn't full but was finished nonetheless.

"Want some more?" Abby asked, dangling her second chicken breast from her thumb and forefinger. I should have shaken my head. It wasn't right to take her dinner just because she hadn't been able to Shift. But because I had, I needed food. And she didn't seem to want it.

I blinked at her and cocked my head to the side. *Are you sure?*

"Yeah, go ahead." She tossed the chicken breast through her bars, underhand. It landed a foot and a half from my cage. I padded to the front wall of my cell and lay on my stomach, my front right paw extended between two of the bars. *Almost there.* Unsheathing my claws, I lunged at the breast, turning my head to the side and slamming my ear into the bars as I sank my claws into the meat. It hurt, but it worked. I pulled my meal along the floor and into the cage, then tore into it. It didn't last any longer than the first one had.

I purred, staring straight at Abby.

"You're welcome," she said.

Metal springs groaned overhead, and wood creaked. Someone had just gotten out of bed. Based on the pasty color of Ryan's skin and the dark circles under his eyes, I was willing to bet he hadn't been to bed in a couple of days. And if he was telling the truth, Miguel and Sean were probably already on the road. That only left one possibility. Eric.

In her cell, Abby lay staring at the ceiling, oblivious to the activity on the ground level. She'd known Miguel from the sound of his footsteps earlier, but this time she hadn't heard a thing. On two legs, our hearing was much better than a human's, but it was nothing compared to that of a cat. As a cat, I could hear frequencies well beyond the upper range of a human, or even a dog.

I growled softly and Abby looked up. "What's wrong?"

I pointed my muzzle at the ceiling.

"You hear something?" she asked, and I nodded. "Is someone coming?"

Rotating my ear flaps, I located the direction of

the sound and listened carefully. I heard heavy footsteps, then running water. Eric was taking a shower.

With no way to tell her anything more specific, I settled for shaking my head.

"Thank goodness," she breathed, eyeing the ceiling warily. I disagreed. We couldn't get out without a key, and hours spent wishing for one had done us no good. We needed Eric to come unlock one of the cages. Preferably mine.

The shower ran for several minutes as I listened, occasionally rotating my ears to make sure Ryan was still watching TV. Or that the set was on, at least. I hadn't heard him enter or leave the living room, but that was all I had to go on regarding his position in the house.

The water stopped, and Eric stepped out of the shower. If he took the time to dry off, I couldn't tell; seconds later he was in another room, searching for clean clothes, based on the sound of wood scraping wood as he opened and closed dresser drawers.

Okay, time for action. I sat up straight and flattened my ears to my head, preparing to give a good roar. It was the only thing I could think of to lure him downstairs, and though I still hadn't figured out how to get him to unlock my cage, I'd decided to take things one step at a time. Beginning with the roar. It had to be loud enough for Eric to hear, but not loud enough to alarm the neighbors. Volume was always a judgment call because of the possibility of being heard by humans.

But as it turned out, I didn't have to make any noise at all. The footsteps turned toward what I assumed was the kitchen and I closed my mouth, listening. Eric paused, possibly at the fridge, then continued toward the basement door. Apparently he liked a little recreation first thing in the morning. Lucky us.

Staring at the steps, I growled to warn Abby. She glanced at me, then followed my gaze, her eyes round and her posture tense.

The door opened, and she leapt to her feet. Fast. I was glad to see she still had a little energy left, since I'd eaten half of her dinner. And since I wasn't sure I could keep him away from her a second time.

"Good morning, girls," Eric called from the top step. "You did know it was morning, didn't you?" Neither of us replied, and he paused to turn off the light then jogged down the stairs.

I didn't care. I could see in the dark far better than he could. But Abby was breathing so hard and fast I worried she'd pass out.

Eric stopped short at the foot of the steps, staring at me as a drop of water fell from the end of a still-wet strand of hair onto his collar. In less than a second, his face cycled through fear and surprise before finally settling into an amused grin. The first two expressions were closer to how he actually felt, and no display of perfect white teeth could convince me otherwise, even if his canines had been bigger than mine. Which they weren't. Not by a long shot.

He smelled fresh and clean, like Zest soap, cheap shampoo and mint-flavored toothpaste. That pissed me off. The fur on my head stood up in stiff clumps, matted by dried sweat and blood, though I hadn't had fur when I accumulated either substance. I hadn't brushed my teeth in roughly thirty-six hours, and I'd never needed a shower worse in my life. In a word, I felt gross. On the upside, surely gross was rape-repellent. But even if it wasn't, claws sure as hell were.

I paced across the front of my cage, slinking around each time I met the opposite wall, pausing every now and then to growl at him. Eric's eyes followed me. He was obviously searching for something clever to say and coming up empty. Big surprise.

"Fur suits you, Faythe," he said finally.

Claws suit me better, I thought, eyeing four long, scabbed-over scratches running from the corner of his left eye to the peak of his chin. I licked my muzzle, pleased with my handiwork.

Eric lurched forward, as if he'd found a hidden stash of courage and wanted to use it all in one careless spending spree. But he stayed well back from my bars. Digging in his front right pocket, he came out with a small silver key, holding it up for my inspection. "As inviting as your cell looks, all littered with napkins and chicken bones, I think I'll pay a visit to your little cousin this morning. She's more my type."

Cowards always like them young, small and helpless, I thought, wishing I could voice the insult. But all I could do was watch.

For every step Eric took toward her, Abby took one back, until she hit the wall. She shook her head slowly, tiny fists clenched at her sides, eyes wide with terror. She glanced at me and I growled, not at her, but at Eric. He stopped two feet from her cage, turning to look at me. "What's wrong, kitty? You jealous? That's too bad, since you didn't give me a very warm welcome last time." He touched the angry slashes on his cheek, and I could swear he knew I was smiling.

I huffed at him through my nose, inches from my front wall of bars.

"Yeah, I saw what you did to Miguel," he said. "Pretty proud of yourself, aren't you? I guess you've figured out by now that he's given up on you. Gonna trade you in for a newer model."

I'd hoped he would drop the name of the girl they'd gone after, or at least give me a hint, but he did neither. It did me no good to know she was younger than I was. I was the oldest unmarried tabby in the country. Knowing they would be back by morning told me more than Eric had.

"I said he could probably still wear you down, but he's lazy at heart. He'd rather have a girl who doesn't make too much work for him. Me, on the other hand, I like a bit of kick to my *queso,* if you know what I mean."

I knew what he meant, and I knew it was a lie. If he really liked a challenge, he'd be headed toward my cage instead of Abby's. But like I'd said, he just wasn't Alpha material. Apparently Miguel wasn't either.

Eric cupped the lock to Abby's cage in his hand. I growled again, and again he glanced at me. "Sure, you can watch."

You chickenshit son of a bitch! Of course, since I was a cat, it came out as a roar, and a damn good one at that.

"What?" Eric asked, his exasperated tone con- trived. He was up to something. "Don't watch if you don't want to. Lie there with your paws over your ears, for all the good it does. But as long as you have claws and a tail, there's no way you can stop me."

What? My ears perked up—literally. Was he saying that if I Shifted back I *could* stop him? I cocked my head to the side. *What do you mean?*

"Did you think I was heartless?" he asked, clearly uninterested in an honest answer. "I know you're a good big cousin and would like to spare Abby any more pain. And I'm willing to do my part. But not unless you Shift back."

I tilted my head to the other side. *Go on.*

"A simple trade. You, for her. But I'm not into bestiality, for obvious reasons. Those claws look pretty sharp."

Yawning, I showed him my teeth were sharp, too.

"Yeah, and those canines could do some real damage. They'll have to go if you want to make a deal with me."

There has to be some way to negotiate without using words, I thought. I wasn't willing to Shift back until I knew exactly what he had in mind, other than the obvious. After my Shift, I'd be naked and vulnerable, which was no big deal when surrounded by my own Pride members. But with Eric as my only company, it was nothing less than suicidal.

"I tell you what," he said, tapping his watch pointedly. "I'll give you one minute to decide. You Shift back and agree to play nice, and I'll leave Abby alone. For now. Or, you can sit with your tail curled around your haunches and listen to how well your cousin likes it. She's a screamer, you know."

Abby refused to look at me. She was clearly terrified, now sitting in her favorite corner with her knees pulled up to her chest. But she wouldn't ask me to do it. She wouldn't wish what she'd been through on anyone else. She was just a kid and already so strong—but she shouldn't have to be.

"Thirty seconds," Eric said, barely hiding a smile as he bounced the key in his palm.

What the hell is he up to? Miguel had said Eric couldn't touch me. Could that have changed? Or was Eric taking advantage of the boss's absence? Maybe Miguel gave Eric a chance to try to break me, before giving up on me entirely. That certainly sounded like something Miguel would do, and for him it was a win-win situation. He could send Eric in to wear me down so I'd be too tired to resist when he got back. Even if Eric lost, I'd be exhausted from having fought him off. Plus, if Eric got hurt, Miguel's injuries wouldn't be so humiliating by comparison.

But then the scariest possibility of all snaked its way into my brain. What if this was my fault and had nothing to do with Miguel? What if challenging Eric's masculinity and embarrassing him in front of the others had made him want to prove himself?

Shit. With a mouth like mine, who needs mortal enemies?

"Seven, six, five…" Eric counted, eyeing his watch.

I growled at him one last time. *I'll kill you if I get the chance.* If he understood, I saw no sign. He smiled in ignorance, convinced he'd won. For once, he was right. I couldn't sit there and listen while he raped my cousin. Again.

"Do we have a deal?"

Just for a moment, I hesitated, my heart pounding as I looked at Abby. She still wouldn't meet my eyes, so I nodded. It wouldn't be as bad for me as it was for her. Hopefully.

Eric smiled, and my stomach churned. "Good. You're a wonderful cousin. Now Shift back." He glanced at Abby over his shoulder. "I hope you appreciate what your cousin's doing for you," he said.

That was all she could take. "Don't do it, Faythe," she whispered. "You don't have to do this."

But I did have to. I'd already given my word, in a manner of speaking. Anyway, he'd have to open the door to get in, which was what I'd wanted in the first place. And when opportunity knocks…

Eric came closer to my cage, still standing well out of my reach. "Get on with it, before I change my mind."

I wanted privacy for my Shift but knew he wouldn't oblige me, even if I had a way to ask. So I Shifted on the rough concrete floor while he watched, ogling each phase as it came.

At the end of the first phase, Eric came close enough to wrap his hands around the bars. He knew he was safe. If I could have lunged for him, I would have, but I could no more pounce during a Shift than I could sprout butterfly wings and fly away.

I considered reversing the process, hoping he wouldn't realize what I'd done until it was too late. In the end, I didn't do it because I knew it wouldn't work. And because once I'd tried and failed to kill him, he'd go after Abby, just to punish me. My best shot would come once he'd locked himself in with me.

Still panting from my Shift, I knelt on the floor, naked and shivering. I was too exhausted to maintain my own body temperature, even in the middle of the summer, because I'd Shifted twice with no water and too little food. And because I hadn't had a decent night's sleep in days.

Eric allowed me no time to recover. He wouldn't give me another chance to attack him. Not intentionally, anyway.

He had the lock off and the door opened before I'd even made it to my feet. He wasn't as fast as

Miguel, but I was tired and weak. My body wouldn't take much more stress and deprivation without serious consequences. Like passing out. I desperately didn't want to pass out with Eric in my cage. Unlike Miguel, he didn't want me to fight back. I wasn't even sure he'd wait for me to wake up.

He closed the door, and I jumped when he snapped the lock into place.

So much for bowling him over in a rush for the exit. Instead, I struggled to remain standing. My vision darkened and my head swam. I held my arms out at my sides, trying to maintain my balance.

"You okay?" he asked, clearly pleased, rather than concerned by how weak I'd become.

"I'm fine." I wiped cold sweat from my face with both hands, then realized I had nothing to wipe it on. "Let's get this over with."

His eyes roamed my body, and I cringed, crossing my arms over my breasts. Yes, I knew his eyes were the least of my worries, but the invasion still angered me. And anger was good. It helped clear my head and forced me to focus. As weak as I was, I would only get one shot at him. If I missed, his first retaliatory punch was likely to knock me out. So I would have to choose my moment very carefully.

"Okay, ground rules…" he began.

"There are ground rules?" I laughed. I couldn't

help it. Imagine how fortunate I felt to have gotten a rapist who had ground rules. But all the rules turned out to be for me. *Figures*.

"If you hit, or scratch, or pull any of that kicking shit like you did with Miguel, I'm out of here. I'll leave you in here to pound dents in the bars, and Abby and I can have another go at it. Can't we, Abby-cat?"

I glanced at her, but she had her back to us both. And if I wasn't mistaken, her fingers were in her ears. Either way, she didn't respond, so Eric turned back to me.

"Do you understand?" he asked, and I nodded, because there was nothing else could I do. My moment hadn't come yet. "So we have a deal?"

Another nod. But then neither of us moved. He didn't seem to know what to do next, as if my compliance had confused him, and I wasn't about to volunteer my understanding of the process. Several awkward seconds passed. Awkward for him, anyway. I was just tired and pissed off. Finally, he put on a resolute face and pulled me forward by my left elbow.

I jerked my arm free on instinct, pleased and surprised to realize that the pain in my shoulder wasn't that bad. Shifting back had done even more to help heal my injury.

Eric shot me a warning glance and a growl. I focused on Abby's curls, and the next time he took my arm, I let him. He kissed me, and I just stood there. I could taste his toothpaste and smell his shampoo. My veins pumped scalding fury throughout my body, but I didn't know what to do. I didn't have the strength to hit him hard enough to hurt him, and if I tried and failed, whatever he did to Abby would be my fault. I'd have to take him out with a single strike. Anything less than a death blow wouldn't be good enough.

If I could just figure out how to Shift my teeth…

I closed my eyes in concentration, doing my best to ignore Eric's hand cupping my ass as I tried again to make my face Shift. *Come on, damn it, change.* Nothing happened.

Eric was oblivious to my efforts and to my mounting frustration. He shoved his tongue into my mouth, deep enough to make me gag. The intrusion shattered the vestiges of my concentration like an ax through a thin sheet of ice. I barely resisted the urge to bite his tongue off. I could have done it, even with blunt human teeth, but I didn't, because it wouldn't have killed him. Not fast enough, anyway. It would damn well have pissed him off, though.

He walked me backward, his mouth still sucking at mine, until I was trapped between his body and the bars. His hands roamed, squeezing and prodding. His tongue trailed down my neck. I closed my eyes, again trying to force a Shift. His teeth pinched my earlobe, not hard enough to break the skin, but hard enough to leave indentations. He was marking me. I *hate* being marked.

But the worst by far was the hard lump in his jeans. It throbbed against my stomach through the denim, a warning of worse things to come.

Eric unzipped his pants, and that tiny whisper of a sound thundered through me like the roar of jet engine. My eyes flew open. He pushed his jeans down without ever taking his mouth from my neck.

This was going too far. If my moment didn't come soon, it would be too late.

Angry and beyond mortified, I stared at the back of Abby's head, trying to keep in mind the reason I was submitting without a fight. It didn't help. Pain, I could take. I understood pain and knew how to deal with it. But I didn't understand this. This was absolute degradation, with no purpose but to humiliate me and break my will. And it pissed me off.

My hands curled into fists at my sides. My nails bit into my palms. I was losing control, in spite of my determination to do whatever it took to keep Abby safe. I needed to concentrate, or I was going to make things worse for both of us.

A familiar jolt of pain shot through my jaw. My heart jumped, and I stiffened. I ground my teeth together against the pain, but my lips curved into a smile. It was happening. The partial Shift. I was going to have my moment after all, so long as he didn't notice until it was finished.

"Relax," Eric whispered into my neck. "You're tensing up."

You have no idea, I thought, privately tickled to have finally found the key to the partial Shift. Flaming anger and intense concentration. Good to know.

Eric pushed his briefs down with one hand. His fingers slid up my bare thigh. I clenched my fists again, drawing more blood from my palms. It took everything I had to keep from shoving him away and ruining my best shot yet at taking him out.

The pain was worse than it had been the first time; this Shift was more complete. The throbbing in my face grew to a screaming, blinding agony. I had to unclench my jaws, had to open my mouth. But I was grateful for the pain. It demanded attention. It kept my mind off Eric's hands and mouth.

I felt several tiny cracks, as the bones of my face Shifted, and —from my perspective at least—gunfire couldn't have been any louder. Another crack ripped its way through my jaw, and Abby stiffened where she sat. She started to turn toward us, then seemed to think better of looking and buried her face in her arms.

Oh, shit. What if Eric heard that? He was much closer to the source than Abby was.

And he must have heard it, because he started to glance up. I did the only thing I could think of to distract him. I shoved my chest forward. He purred and his mouth traveled down to engulf my nipple. I cringed, but he mistook my shudder for one of pleasure.

Boy, are you delusional, I thought, taking short, shallow breaths as the pain in my face reached its apex. Why are guys always so willing to believe in the power of their own sexual magnetism, even when all evidence points to there being none? I think some men are born with big egos, to make up for the lack of certain necessary equipment. Like a brain.

The aching subsided, and I ran my tongue over my teeth. I gasped, feeling full-length canines and an entire mouthful of pointed teeth, both top and bottom. Eric moaned around my nipple, mistaking my gasp just as he had my cringe. I resisted the urge to smack him. I didn't need to hit him anymore. I knew just what to do with him.

Eric tucked one hand beneath my left knee. He lifted my leg, curling it around his waist as he pressed himself against me.

Now, I thought. My moment had finally come.

I growled in warning. Eric froze, my nipple still in his mouth. My leg slid back to the ground. He rose slowly. Our eyes met. I have no idea what mine looked like, but his would have comfortably seated several little green men apiece.

I took a millisecond to enjoy his shock and fear. Then I lunged for his throat.

Twenty-Five

Blood never tasted sweeter to me than Eric's did at that moment, pouring into my mouth from his neck on its way down from his brain. Or maybe that was the taste of carnal justice. Whatever it was, it was wonderful.

Eric tried to scream but could only manage a bubbly gurgle. He floundered for several seconds, his arms waving wildly, bumping against my sides and hips ineffectively. Though I'd broken the skin, actually puncturing his jugular vein, I hadn't ripped his throat out. That would have been an almost instant death, and he didn't deserve my mercy. Instead, I crushed his windpipe with my jaws, slowly suffocating him as he bled.

During my first partial Shift two very long days

earlier, my mouth wouldn't have opened that wide. Luckily, this transformation was much more complete. I couldn't see myself, but my best guess was that I had a hairless muzzle and cat's nose, protruding from an otherwise human face. It couldn't have been a pretty picture, combined with my already battered cheek. Fortunately, being pretty mattered even less to me then than it ever had. I was interested in efficiency, and my new monstrosity of a face was very efficient.

Eric spasmed one final time, and by then I was supporting his weight with my arms around his rib cage. When I was sure he was dead, I opened my mouth. His head flopped backward, bobbing for a moment under its own inertia. His limp weight was grotesque and faintly nauseating.

Heaving him up, I tossed him onto the mattress at my feet. I stared at him, listening to the sound of my own breathing. Shock hadn't set in yet, but I was thinking clearly enough to know that it might at any second. I'd never killed anyone before. Deer, yes. Rabbits, yes. And once, a cow that somehow wandered onto my father's property and into the trees. But I'd never taken the life of anything with the ability to reason, however poorly that ability was used, and I was not naive enough to think I would suffer no consequences from it.

Short, gasping breaths caught my attention. I squinted at Eric's chest, waiting to see it rise. It didn't. I looked up gradually in the direction of the sounds. Abby stared at me through eyes wide with fright. When my eyes met hers, she gave a startled yip and jumped back from the bars, turning her head slowly from side to side, in denial of what she saw.

"Abby." But I couldn't enunciate with my cat's jaws, so it came out as a short string of vowels, inarticulate nonsense that had little in common with her name. *Ah, yes, now I remember the downside.* Cat's jaws isolated me from the more verbally gifted of Earth's inhabitants.

Running my hands hesitantly over my face, I began to share her horror. I was grateful for my new ability, since it had saved me from what would surely have been the most humiliating, demeaning experience of my life. Even so, I had no desire to ever see my in-between face for myself.

I turned my back on Abby and concentrated, forcing my face to Shift back. The pain was worse without the rest of my body to sympathize with agony of its own, but it went quickly. When it was over, I verified the results with my hands and my tongue. Everything felt right. Sticky with blood but otherwise normal.

Turning, I wiped blood from my mouth with my

arm, which really wasn't much of an improvement. "Abby, it's me."

She squinted at me in the dark and sighed in relief, as if she thought the shadows had been playing tricks on her eyes before. "Are you okay?" she asked, wrapping her hands around the bars again. It's amazing how fast that becomes habitual.

"Yeah. Messy, but okay." I glanced at my pile of clothing, then down at the blood drenching my chest. I'd have to clean up before I could get dressed.

"Eric?" Abby asked.

"Dead."

She burst into tears for the second time in less than an hour, but these were tears of relief and I was glad to see them.

"Give me just a minute, and I'll have you out of there," I said. She nodded, and moved down to the door to wait.

I sat on the mattress by Eric's corpse, doing my best to ignore the blood staining his shirt and my own bare flesh. I stuck my hand in his right pocket and came out with a key. But only one. Mine.

My key clasped in my left fist, I dove into his left pocket, searching frantically. I turned it inside out in my haste to find the other key, but the pocket was empty. No loose change, no lint, and definitely no key.

"There's only one," I whispered.

"Maybe it works on both locks," Abby said, her voice shrill with desperation.

I thought back but couldn't rule it out. The first time, Eric had unlocked her cage but not mine. Miguel had unlocked mine but not hers. Sean and Ryan claimed not to have keys. And this time Eric had only opened my cage, so maybe she was right.

Key in hand, I stuck my arms through the bars and opened the lock. I pulled it loose from the latch and clenched it in my fist. Holding my breath, I pushed the door open. Then I stepped across the threshold.

I felt like something should have happened, like an alarm blaring or fresh air blowing my sweaty, sticky hair back from my face. Or maybe theme music playing from some cheesy prison-escape movie. But nothing happened. What a letdown.

Abby's eyes were glued to the key as I pulled it from my lock. I tried it on hers, but it wouldn't even go all the way in. The light in her eyes died, replaced by a look of confusion. "I don't understand," she said. "Where's the other key? He had to have it if he came down here for me."

I understood all too well. "He didn't come for you. Not this time." Eric had set me up, and I'd fallen for it completely. Outsmarted by a Neanderthal. *Faythe, you idiot!* I wanted to smack my own forehead but settled for staring at my feet instead. Until the blood trailing down my torso caught my attention, and I had to close my eyes.

"What?" she asked. "What happened?"

"He used you to get to me. He didn't bring your key because he wasn't after you this time. He only acted like he was so I'd try to protect you and he could offer me his little trade." Eric was a moron. A truly substandard intellect. So what did it say about me, that I'd fallen for his performance? Not as much as his death at my hands said about him.

Back in my cage, I glared at his body. I would have kicked him in the head, if I wasn't completely creeped out by touching a corpse, even one I'd created. So, I walked around him on my way to examine my clothes. I'd blocked most of the splatter with my own body, so my shirt and shorts were pretty clean, other than the thin, dry trail of Miguel's blood. Best of all, the shirt still smelled like Marc.

Careful not to let it touch my soiled skin, I held the material up to my nose, inhaling deeply. Marc's smell made my heart pound and my blood rush, not all of it to my head. For the first time, I realized that there was a chance, a teeny speck of a possibility— microscopic, really—that sleeping with him might not have been a complete mistake. Because while a mistake might be fun, might even be worth repeating a couple of times, people don't have physiological responses to a reminder of said mistake thirty-two hours later. That just didn't happen. Did it?

I rolled my clothes up and carried them to the bathroom under the stairs. "What are you doing?" Abby asked, still clutching her bars.

"Cleaning up. Then I'm going to get dressed and go find your key. Or a hammer. If I go up there without cleaning off the blood, Ryan will smell me the minute I open the door."

"What are you going to do about him?"

Grinning, I shrugged. "I could take him as a kid, and I'm a lot stronger now."

She smiled hesitantly, clearly skeptical. I nodded toward Eric, as a reminder, then closed myself into the restroom beneath the stairs.

The bathroom was nothing but a toilet and a low sink, crammed into a space too small to hold two people. A damp hand towel sat on the back of the toilet, and it looked clean. I put down the toilet lid and set my bundle of clothes on it, then turned on the faucet.

I ran as little water as possible, afraid Ryan might hear it and know something was wrong. But I was determined to wash away all of the blood, in spite of the risk. There was no mirror, so I did the best I could without one. I lathered my hands with the vanilla-scented soap and scrubbed my face over and over, until my hands came away clean. My body was easier, because I could see the blood.

When I was finished, and smelled overwhelmingly of vanilla, I blotted myself dry with the hand towel and got dressed. Abby was staring at me when I opened the door. I could almost taste her anxiety.

"What's wrong?" I asked, glancing around for the source of her concern. Eric still lay dead in my open cell, which was good, because I don't do walking corpses. There was no one else in the basement.

"Don't leave me," she begged. "Please."

I reached through the bars to hug her. "I wouldn't leave you here for anything in the world, Abby. I'm just going to find the other key, and a phone, so I can call my dad. I'll be right back."

She clutched me, clasping her hands at my back. "Promise?"

"I swear."

"Okay." She let me go, and I stroked her hair, pushing it back from her face.

"Give me a few minutes, and I'll have you out of there."

She nodded, and I headed for the stairs. I took them two at a time, with a cat's easy gait and stealth. I was still tired and hungry, but adrenaline kept me going. It was even better than caffeine.

On the top step, I flipped the light switch up and glanced at Abby one last time. She gave me a hesitant smile and a thumbs-up. I turned the knob, my heart pounding so hard in my ears that I couldn't tell whether or not the hinges squealed as I pushed the door open. I paused, waiting for Ryan's footsteps, but they didn't come.

My palm damp on the doorknob, I stepped onto faded linoleum and eased the door shut behind me. Beneath my feet, a flowering-vine pattern crept across the floor and under a cluttered pressboard table before disappearing beneath a wall of kitchen cabinets. Above the sink, directly across from the basement door, was a window, its thin lace drapes open to expose an eerily perfect residential street, complete with sidewalks, yard gnomes, and mailboxes in cute shapes like birdhouses and barns.

I crept silently around the table, leaning over a stack of dirty dishes to stare out the window. As I watched, enthralled by an ordinary scene of suburban serenity, a car drove by, bobbing for a moment as it went over a yellow speed bump before passing the driveway out front. The *empty* driveway.

My pulse jumped. The van was gone. Sean and Miguel had already left.

Staring out the window, I looked freedom in the face, but my eyes were drawn back to the basement door. I'd promised Abby I wouldn't leave her, and I never broke my promises. But even without a promise I could no more have left her than I could have let Eric hurt her.

To my left was an arched doorway, leading into what had once been a formal dining room. It was empty now, and beyond it lay a small, tiled foyer and the front door. To my right stood an identical arch, leading into the living room. The couch faced away from me and the television was on, tuned to a morning-news talk show. Ryan was nowhere in sight.

I scanned the table, searching for the key among sticky dishes and abandoned food. It wasn't there, but I did find a cell phone, fully charged and receiving a strong signal. *Mine, now,* I thought, slipping it into the front pocket of my shorts as I turned toward the living room.

The phone rang when I was inches from the doorway. A digital, polyphonic version of "Bad Boys." Someone had a really cheesy sense of humor. I slapped my hand over the phone in my pocket, then dug for it desperately. I got it on the second ring and jammed my thumb down on the End Call button. Nothing happened. *Shit, wrong phone.*

In the living room, less than five feet away, Ryan moaned and sat up on the couch with his back to me.

He rubbed his face with one hand while his other searched blindly on an end table for the ringing phone. I slid back from the door frame in case he turned around. And I listened, frozen in place.

The song stopped. "Hello?" Ryan asked, still half-asleep. Then, sharper, "Why the hell didn't you write it down the first time? Or at least wait 'til you got closer to call for directions. I could have slept for several more hours."

He paused, and I held my breath. It had to be Sean, because he wouldn't talk to Miguel like that. Or Mom. And I was fairly certain no one else would call Ryan.

"Okay, okay. But find a fucking pen this time." Another pause. "You ready? Okay, the town is called Oak Hill. It's eighty-five miles southwest of Saint Louis. You'll be on I–55 until…"

I quit listening; I'd heard all I needed. They were going after Carissa, but they wouldn't be there for hours, so there was still time.

A minute later, Ryan hung up the phone with a curse and a grunt. *Classy.* He fell back on the arm of the couch and was snoring in seconds.

In a rush of relief, I released the breath I'd been holding for nearly two minutes. It was about time something went my way.

I tiptoed, literally, back to the basement door and

eased it open long enough to slip through, then closed it soundlessly.

"Faythe?" Abby whispered.

"Yeah, it's me. Just a sec." From the top step, I checked the reception on the cell phone. Two bars. Still watching the screen, I took the steps one at a time. On the fourth step, I lost one bar, and by the sixth, I had no reception at all. I ran the rest of the way to the basement floor and straight to Abby's cage.

"Did you find the key?" she asked, her face eager, eyes bright.

"Not yet, but I found this." I held up the phone. "I think it's Eric's."

She smiled. "Great. Call the council."

"I can't. It doesn't get any reception down here, and Ryan's still upstairs."

Abby glared at me, accusation frosting her eyes. "So what?"

"He hasn't exactly been helpful so far, has he? He may change his tune now that I'm out, but what if he doesn't? What if he calls Miguel, and they get back before I can get you out?"

Panic spread across her face. "We can't let him do that."

"Exactly. But I can't just kill him."

She nodded, as if she understood. "Because he's your brother."

"There's that." Although I wasn't exactly feeling the familial bond right then. "But also, we need him to cooperate."

She frowned. "Why?"

"If Sean and Miguel call, and no one answers the phone, they'll know something's wrong. Either they'll turn around and come back, possibly before I've found the key, or they'll run. If they run, we may never catch them. Don't you want them to pay for what they've done to you? And to Sara?"

She didn't hesitate. "Hell, yeah. I want them to suffer like they made her suffer. And me." The expression on her china-doll face was fierce enough to startle me. "So, what's the plan?"

I grinned, relieved by her enthusiasm. I'd been afraid I'd have to talk her into it. "I say we let the punishment fit the crime." I nodded toward my cage, still standing open.

Abby's forehead wrinkled in distaste. "You're gonna put him in there with Eric?"

I shrugged. "I'd rather put him in the empty cage, but the bait's already waiting in mine, and I'm *not* moving the body." I wrapped my hands around hers on the bars and squeezed gently. "If you can wait until I lock up Ryan, I can get us both out of here. And…" I paused for emphasis. "I know who Miguel's after."

"Who?"

"Carissa Taylor."

She flinched, and I was sure I knew what she was thinking. It was creepy to know that Carissa was going about her life, shopping with friends and talking on the phone, with no idea that in a few hours she might be locked up, awaiting her new existence as the personal property of some sadistic Alpha in the middle of the rain forest, thousands of miles from home.

I couldn't let that happen.

"Can we stop him?" Abby asked, doubt drawing her frown into a grimace.

"The council can. But if we hurry, I think I know how they can catch him, too. Are you okay with waiting?"

She stared at me, looking for some kind of reassurance, but I had nothing left to offer her. She sighed. "Yeah. But hurry."

"I'll try." Bending, I plucked my lock from the floor and stuffed it into my pocket, next to the key and the cell phone. "Hey, Abby, I need you to do one more thing," I said, backing toward the bathroom beneath the stairs.

"What?"

"Scream."

"Scream?" Her mouth turned up in a hesitant smile.

"Yeah. Scream as loud as you can. When Ryan comes in and asks you what's wrong, point at Eric. I'll take care of the rest. Okay?"

She nodded. "Say when."

I stepped into the bathroom and pulled the door most of the way closed, leaving a crack just wide enough for me to see through with one eye. "Now."

Abby screamed. Boy, did she scream. It was every cliché in the book: bloodcurdling, glass-shattering, and eardrum-bursting. It was a high-pitched wave of sound that resonated in my bladder and probably startled dogs all over the neighborhood. It was perfect. She'd found the ideal outlet for her pent-up fright and pain.

Footsteps pounded on the floor overhead before she'd even closed her mouth. Ryan threw the door open and rushed down the steps, nearly tripping over his own feet in his haste to investigate. "Abby, what the hell?" he demanded, just out of my sight.

She pointed at my cage with her trembling right hand. The other was pressed to her mouth in very real horror.

Ryan came into view slowly, taking in my open cage and the body on the mattress. "Oh, fuck."

Go look, I thought, mentally urging him forward.

"Oh, shit." He turned to Abby, his face scared and pale. "Where's Faythe?"

No, I thought. *Go look at Eric. Go.* But he didn't go.

"Abby, where the hell is Faythe?" he asked again, approaching her cage with heavy, threatening steps. I was almost impressed.

She backed up and shook her head, her hand falling to hang limp at her side. She wasn't enjoying her performance at all, probably because art was imitating her real life. Her initial glee had fled at the first sign of my brother's temper, which worried me on behalf of her recovery.

"Answer me!" Ryan shouted, slamming his fists on the bars. "They'll go after my mom, now tell me where the hell she is!"

Abby jumped when he yelled. "Gone," she whispered, real tears standing in her eyes. "She left me here."

"No," Ryan whispered, his denial simple and desperate.

"I think he's still breathing." She pointed at the body on the mattress.

Good girl, I thought, pleased that she still had the presence of mind to redirect Ryan's focus.

He glanced back at Eric, and my hand tightened around the lock. "Oh, great. What am I supposed to do, call a doctor?" He threw his hands in the air, as if a mortally injured accomplice was a huge inconvenience to his busy schedule of television watching.

Ryan stomped toward the open cage, dragging his feet in dread. The moment he crossed the threshold, I ran for it.

He knelt beside the body, his back to me. His hands hovered over Eric's shredded neck, trying to decide where best to check for a pulse. My bare feet were silent on the concrete. He didn't know I was there until I slammed the door shut.

Ryan leapt to his feet, whirling around. Furious, he lunged for the door. I slammed the latch closed. He hit the bars with his shoulder. He shoved, the muscles in his neck bulging under the strain. The door opened half an inch, then an inch more. He had the advantage in both size and strength. I couldn't hold him in for long.

I readied the lock in my right hand. Ryan pushed again. I let the door open a few more inches. Grunting, I braced my right foot against his chest and shoved with every spark of energy left in my body.

Ryan stumbled backward. He tripped over Eric to land on the soiled mattress. Scrambling back, he stared in horror at the corpse in front of him. I swung the lock up and through the metal loop on the door. It snapped closed with a decisive-sounding click.

Ryan scurried around Eric and lunged at the bars, but I backed out of his reach. "You little bitch," he spat. "You did this on purpose."

"You bet your ass."

"Think you're so smart…" He pulled his cell phone from his pocket, holding it up for me to see.

Squinting at the display, I was dismayed to see that unlike Eric's Nokia, Ryan's Sony Ericsson got a decent signal in the basement. Three bars. Great. I couldn't let him keep the phone.

"You're bluffing," I said, still squinting as if I couldn't focus on the tiny screen. "You can't get a signal down here."

Doubt flickered across his face, and he glanced at the phone. "Three bars," he said, grinning smugly.

"The only bars I see are made of metal."

"Get your eyes checked." He thrust his hand from the cage, holding the phone out for my inspection. I sprang forward, plucking it from his fist before he had a chance to react.

My brother swore under his breath, and I smirked. "*That* is why you couldn't make it on your own, Ryan. You either ignore your instinct, or you have none. That's why Daddy couldn't make you an enforcer, and why he's going to put you out of your misery." I paused to give him a moment to think over his predicament. "However, if you say the magic words, I might be willing to speak to him on your behalf. For a price."

His eyes narrowed. "What do you want?"

"Cooperation. Help. A chance to redeem yourself, as you should have done earlier."

He hesitated, clearly weighing his options. I knew from the resignation on his face that he'd come to the same conclusion I had. "Can you guarantee my life?"

"I can try," I said. He nodded, and I beamed in triumph. "Excuse me for a moment, please, Ryan. I have to make a call." After a moment of indecision, I pulled Eric's phone from my pocket and replaced it with Ryan's. Bubbling over with smug satisfaction, I hugged Abby one more time, then skipped toward the stairs.

My brother's scream of rage and defeat followed me all the way into the kitchen.

Twenty-Six

I dialed my father's personal line on my way up the stairs, and punched the SEND button from the kitchen. As the phone rang, I rummaged through the fridge. My mouth was full of someone's leftover burrito when Michael answered the phone.

"Hello?"

"Hey, Michael, it's me," I said around a mouthful of cold beef and beans. "Let me talk to Daddy." Why the hell was he answering our father's phone, anyway? I took another bite and popped open a can of soda, deciding I didn't care who I talked to, so long as someone came to pick me up. Soon.

"Faythe? Where the hell are you?" His voice dimmed, and I knew he was talking to someone else. "Go get Dad. Now." I heard a door close, and

Michael was back. "Are you okay? What happened? Did they let you go?"

"One question at a time." I took a long swig of soda and felt my body welcome the caffeine like a soldier home from war. "First of all, we're fine. A little banged up and pretty hungry, but basically okay. One of our captors turned out to be brain dead, and I took advantage."

"Where are you?" Michael asked, relief obvious in his voice. A pen scratched paper as he began taking notes.

"Somewhere in Mississippi. Hang on a minute, and I'll get you the address." I shoved the last of the burrito into my mouth and chewed all the way through the empty dining room and out the front door. From the porch, I glanced up and down the block for a street sign while Michael relayed what I'd said to someone else on his end of the connection.

"Who's we?" he asked me.

"Me and Abby. She's locked up downstairs, but I'm about to break her out."

"Is she...okay?"

"I think she will be. She couldn't fight them off, but that may have saved her life. Dr. Carver will probably say she needs therapy, but if you ask me, she could use a good punching bag."

There was silence over the line for a moment, as if Michael didn't quite know how to respond. Then, finally, "What about you? Did they—" He stopped and started over. "Are you…?"

"I'm fine. Really."

Michael exhaled in relief and a second later I heard him shuffling papers over the line. "Good. You got that address yet?"

"Working on it." The house was on the middle of the block, and though I could see a street sign on each corner, I couldn't quite make out what either of them said. I didn't want to leave Abby alone to go look, nor did I want to waste time jogging down to the corner.

The house number was nailed to the front-porch support, in shiny brass numbers, 104. I was at 104 something-or-other street, somewhere in Mississippi. I'd almost decided to go ask a neighbor, but was still working out an explanation for my injuries and the fact that I didn't know where I was, when I noticed the mailbox. It was one of those old wrought-iron things, attached to the wall of the house right next to the door. And it was full. Miguel must not have checked the mail all week.

The first envelope I grabbed was addressed to Occupant, at 104 Douglas Circle, Crystal Springs, Mississippi. I read the address to Michael, and he read it back to me as he wrote it down, spelling the name of the town to make sure he'd gotten it right.

I shoved the envelope back into the mailbox and went inside, locking the door behind me. A single dead bolt wouldn't do much good if Miguel got back before we left, but it might at least give me some warning.

"Listen, Michael, I need to talk to Daddy. Now."

"He's coming. He was meeting with the council." Something scratched against the mouthpiece on his end of the connection. He'd covered it up. "Wait, Faythe, here he comes. Dad, she wants to talk to you. She's with Abby, and they're both fine."

Another pause as the phone changed hands. Then I heard my father's voice. "Faythe? Is it really you?"

"Yeah, Daddy, it's me." Nerves tightened my chest as I spoke, and I resolved, once the excitement was over, to have a normal, calm conversation with my father. Just one, to see what it would feel like without the usual emotional charge.

He exhaled in relief, and I couldn't help but smile. It was good to be missed. "Are you really okay?" Daddy asked, and I heard the tension in his voice. He expected the worst.

"I'm fine. Michael has the address." I stopped by the fridge again and snagged an unopened package of cold cuts. Ripping open the bag, I stuffed four slices into my mouth, barely pausing to chew them before I swallowed, washing them down with more soda.

"I know. He's already on the other line, sending the closest search party your way. We had five guys in Louisiana. They can be there in an hour and a half, barring catastrophe." There was the barest of pauses as he inhaled, clearly steeling himself to hear the details. "Tell me what happened."

I rubbed my forehead, trying to decide how to begin. "I wasn't running away," I said, leaning against the kitchen counter for support. "I want you to know that. I just went out to the barn to think."

"We can talk about that later. It doesn't matter now." A chair creaked, and I knew he'd sat down behind his desk. "Are you in any immediate danger?"

"I don't think so." I closed my eyes, wrestling with indecision. I'd have to tell him everything eventually, but so much of it would be awkward over the phone. Taking a deep breath, I plunged ahead with the necessary information. "I bit through one guy's throat and locked another in the basement." I paused, waiting for his reaction, but none came. His exhale was long and smooth, and very controlled. He had something to say but was saving it for a better time. So I continued, "I haven't seen the stray I fought on campus, and the other two were already gone when I broke out, and they shouldn't be back until tomorrow."

"Good," he said, and I knew he had his emotions in check. Having established that the immediate threat was over, he turned his attention to the next course of action. "I want you to take Abby and go to the nearest public building. A store, a gas station, anything you can find, so long as there are plenty of people around in case—"

"We can't leave yet, Daddy," I said, interrupting him. "I'm still looking for the key to Abby's cage, or for something strong enough to knock the lock off. And I'm not in any shape to be seen in public."

"Why? Are you hurt?" His voice was tight with anger, for once not directed at me.

"Just bruised," I said, comforted when he exhaled in relief. "But I'm barefoot, and I'm sure my face looks like hell."

"Are you sure you're safe until the guys get there?"

"As safe as I'd be anywhere else," I said, despite the voice of dissension in my head screaming for me to run away as fast as I could. "There's no one left here to be scared of."

"Who are they?"

"You know about Sean, and there was another

named Eric, but he's dead now. Luiz is the cat I fought on campus, but no one's seen him in a couple of days. R—" I stopped in midsyllable, for a last second rephrase. "Miguel might have killed him, but I don't think we can be sure of that yet. Miguel's the jungle cat they smelled on Sara. He's in charge."

"The jungle cat. I'll be damned," he said, and I choked on a mouthful of soda. I'd never heard my father cuss before. "What about the fifth?"

I hesitated, thinking of my mother. Finding out about Ryan would kill her. "Are you alone?"

"I can be. Why?"

"Just make sure no one can hear you, and I'll tell you the rest."

He cleared the room while I finished off the lunch meat and drained the can of soda. Out of habit, I threw my trash away and rinsed my hands at the sink. Then I went in search of the key to Abby's cage.

"Okay, it's just me now," Daddy said as I scanned the living room, picking through junk piled on end tables made of used fruit crates. "I take it you know the cat in question?"

I put one hand over my eyes, as if that would shield me from his reaction. "It's Ryan."

Silence, as he considered what I'd said. "Ryan." Anyone who didn't know my father might have assumed that he was calm because his voice was steady. I knew better. Daddy's temper was like lava, slow-moving but unyielding, and hot enough to incinerate anything in its path.

"Yeah…Ryan." I tossed threadbare couch cushions to the floor. "But before you decide what to do with him, you should know a few things." I shoved my hands between the seat of the couch and the back, feeling for the key.

"What things?"

The living room had produced no keys, but on the right, a hallway led to four more doors.

"He didn't want to be involved at all," I said. "He only cooperated with Miguel to save his own life, and Mom's. They told him they'd go after Mom, and he believed them." I opened the first door on the left and inhaled deeply. From the scent alone, I knew I'd found Sean's room. I didn't stop to look; he didn't have keys.

"That's no excuse," my father said, his voice as smooth and hard as polished stone. "They could never have gotten to your mother. Ryan should have—"

"I know. I've already been over all that with him." I opened the second door and inhaled again. Bingo. It reeked of Miguel, and his room was a wreck. It would take forever to search.

"I'm not saying he shouldn't be punished," I said, picking through empty candy wrappers and loose change on the dresser. "I was tempted to rip his tongue out myself. I'm just saying that none of this was his idea, and he didn't go along voluntarily."

A strange grating sound met my ears through the phone as I squatted to search a small trash can beside the dresser, in case the key had fallen in. At first, I didn't know what I was hearing, but then I understood: Daddy was grinding his teeth. "Go on," he said, his voice barely audible.

Frustrated, I shoved the can aside. It didn't matter how little Ryan had participated and why, because being involved at all was bad enough. Even if my father was willing to spare Ryan's life—and it wasn't looking good—at least two other Prides would demand my brother's blood. Unless I could give them a good enough reason not to…

"He's still in contact with Miguel and Sean," I blurted, then rushed on before I lost my nerve. "Daddy, we can use him, if the council is willing to let him live."

"Use him for what?" he barked over the line.

A fur coat, I thought, but held my tongue. Daddy certainly didn't need any suggestions on what to do with traitors. His imagination was far more capable than mine in that respect. "To catch them."

"What did you have in mind?"

I fell on my rear on the filthy carpet, stunned by his response. I hadn't expected my father to care what I thought, and here he was asking for my opinion. Encouraged, I took a breath and jumped into the deep end of the pool. My father's end. "Sean and Miguel are checking in with him by phone. If they call and he doesn't answer, they'll know something's up, and they'll run. And we may never catch them. But if we can get him to answer like nothing's happened, they'll keep going, and we can be there waiting for them."

Daddy's chair squeaked as he sat up suddenly. "You know where they're going?"

"Yeah. They want one more girl." Which reminded me that I still hadn't told him what they wanted us *for*. There would be time to explain that later. Or maybe I should let Ryan have the honor…

One by one, I opened Miguel's drawers, tossing clothes to the floor. Luckily, two of the four drawers were empty, another indication of how temporary their living arrangements were meant to be.

"Who are they after?" Daddy asked.

I hesitated, leaning against the empty dresser.

"Faythe?" His voice was hard and dark, if it was possible for a sound to be dark. "Tell me where they're going. Now." It was his business tone, the one

no one ever challenged—until now. I couldn't let
Miguel get away. Not after what he'd done to Sara
and Abby. Not after what he'd tried to do to me. I'd
go after them on my own if I had to, but I stood a
much better chance with my father's help. And I
knew how to get it.

"Are you willing to deal with Ryan?" My pulse
pounded as I waited for his answer.

A pause, then, "Are you trying to negotiate with
me?"

I crossed my fingers and swam in a little deeper,
hoping I'd learned something since the last time I
bargained with my father. "Yes."

"Why? I want to catch them too."

"I have a plan. And I want to lead the hunt." I held
my breath, preparing to have my request denied. I
wasn't disappointed.

"No, Faythe." Now he sounded weary. "It's too
dangerous, and you don't have the experience."

Pushing away from the dresser, I took a firm
stance, even though he wasn't there to see it. "I had
the experience to fight off Miguel and save my own
life. I had the experience to kill Eric and break out
of my cell. I had the experience to lure Ryan downstairs and lock him up." My father tried to interrupt
but I cut him off, desperate to have my say. "I
deserve a shot at Miguel, Daddy, and I'll do

whatever it takes to convince you. I'll work with a partner and however many of the guys you want to send with me. Just give me a chance."

My father sighed. "If we're negotiating, I need to know what you're bringing to the table. Tell me who they're after and outline your plan. Quickly."

"Promise not to decide anything until you've heard me out," I said, kneeling by the nightstand to rifle through X-rated magazines and packs of chewing gum.

"Fine."

"They're going after Carissa, but they're driving, and it'll take them all day to get there." I dumped the contents of the night-table drawer onto the bed, and went through it with one finger. More loose change, more candy and gum wrappers, a Spanish-language audiocassette, and a coil of nylon cord. *Hmm, where have I seen* that *before?*

"When did they leave?"

"Sometime this morning. Ryan could tell you exactly, if you're willing to deal with him." I plucked a small bottle of Tylenol from the junk on the bed and popped open the lid. My shoulder and cheek throbbed dully, but it was nothing a couple of gel tabs couldn't fix.

A pause, a thump, and the rustle of pages turning. Daddy had opened his trusty atlas. "Crystal Springs,

Mississippi, to Oak Hill, Missouri. That's at least a nine-hour drive. What do you have in mind?"

With the phone wedged against my shoulder, I shook two pills onto my palm and blinked. They weren't Tylenol. And they certainly weren't over-the-counter. Evidently Miguel had discovered something stronger than alcohol to help him escape the demanding life of a modern-day pillager.

Taking a deep breath, I dumped the pills back into the bottle and closed the lid, then dropped the container on the bed. "If you just move Carissa somewhere safe, you'll never see Miguel. He'll have a plan. He'll sit outside and wait for her to come out alone. If she doesn't, he'll move on, and you'll never even know for sure that he was there. He's smart, Daddy."

"You're stalling, Faythe. Get on with it."

Another deep breath. "Carissa's about my height, maybe an inch or two shorter, but Miguel won't know that. And her hair's dark enough to look black at night. Mine's a little longer, but he won't know that either."

"No. Absolutely not." The desk chair groaned, and I knew he was on his feet. "I'm not going to give him another chance at you."

"Just hear me out." I spoke over his next objection. "The guys will be right there. The best and the fastest. Marc, Parker, Ethan, if he wants. And anyone else you can get there in time. You know the Di Carlo brothers will want a shot at the man who killed Sara. And goodness knows, Uncle Rick will want justice for Abby."

My father sighed as if I was testing his patience. "He'd only need one whiff of you to know he's being set up."

Okay, so far so good. He'd only said no once. I could work with one no. "He might," I admitted. "But I'll wear Carissa's clothes and perfume. By the time he gets close enough to recognize my scent beneath hers, the guys will already be closing in on him."

"No. It's too much of a risk."

Damn. A second no. I sank onto the unmade bed, gathering my resolve. It was time to play my trump card. I'd really hoped I wouldn't have to use it, but my anger raged just thinking about what Miguel had done, what he was still trying to do. I would do anything to stop him. To punish him.

Unfortunately, the key to negotiating with my father was to hide my desperation. Easier said than done.

"You've been trying to make me take an active role in the Pride since I was a kid. Is that still what you want?" I took out my nerves and frustration on Miguel's pillow, ripping open an end seam as I waited for my father to take the bait. Feathers fell from the breach, floating to the floor to tickle my bare feet.

"I'd like nothing better," he said, his voice cautiously optimistic.

"Good. I'm ready to compromise."

Daddy laughed, and under the circumstances it sounded pretty strange. His chair groaned again as he sat back down, comfortable enough with the turn of the conversation to relax physically. "Let me get this straight. If I let you set the trap, you'll quit school and train to take over the Pride?"

"Well, that's where the compromise part comes in." A smile snuck up on me and I realized with more than a little alarm that—just like my father—I enjoyed negotiation. *Damn. I hate it when my parents are right.* "If you let me set the trap, my way, I'll agree to take next year off from school and work for you, on a trial basis."

"Not good enough," he said without a second of hesitation, and I knew I was no longer talking to my father. The Alpha had arrived. "Five years. It will take at least that long to train you, and I gave you five years for school."

"No way." I shook my head, though he couldn't see it. "That's too long, especially if I don't like it. Two years, max."

Static crackled in my ear as he turned on the

speakerphone. I could almost see him thinking, eyes closed, hands crossed over his stomach as he leaned back in his chair. "Three years. And you give Marc another chance."

Indignant, I huffed air through my nose. "Nice try, but my private life is *not* part of the deal. I'll give you two and a half years, and Marc can partner me on the hunt. Take it or leave it." A tingle zinged through me. I'd always wanted to say that to my father.

"You'll stay within sight at all times?"

"Of course. Is that a yes?" I held my breath, waiting for his answer.

"Is that your final offer?"

"Yeah, and you're damn lucky to get it."

He chuckled, apparently amused by my attempt to hardball him. "Done." He paused, and I heard what sounded like a pen tapping against the top of his desk. "That's assuming I can get Umberto and Rick to go along, since this involves their Prides, too. And the Taylors. But I think I can convince them."

Yes! A successful negotiation with my father was almost as good as another chance to kick Miguel's ass. Both at once? Better than Christmas. I stood in front of the mirror doing Ethan's victory dance, pointed fingers and all.

"Faythe?"

I glanced back at Eric's phone, lying on Miguel's

bed where I'd dropped it when the urge to dance struck. Flushing from embarrassment, I grabbed it and held it back up to my ear. "Yeah. I'm here. Sorry, I dropped the phone." I knelt on the floor and looked under the bed but found nothing more than a frighteningly thick accumulation of dust.

"I'll have Michael make the arrangements." More papers shuffled. "The guys should be there to get you in just over an hour. You'll all be flying out of Jackson Municipal Airport on the first available flight. I'll make the reservations. Do you need anything else from me?"

I hesitated, going over the plan in my head. "Yeah. I need one of Carissa's brothers to stay behind and help, so everything looks normal. Or maybe one of the enforcers. Can you swing that?"

"I'm sure I can."

"Great. Thanks, Daddy." I left Miguel's room and tried the next door. It was a bathroom, which I passed over in favor of the last remaining room. It had to be Eric's, and my nose confirmed my guess.

"What about Abby?" I asked, tossing clothes from Eric's dresser. We couldn't bring her, even if she wanted to go. She'd been through so much already, and should never have to see Miguel again.

"One of the guys can drop the rest of you at the airport, then drive her back to the ranch. Her parents are pretty anxious to see her."

I poked through Eric's desk drawer, pushing aside pencils, stamps, paper clips, and several unlabeled CDs. "You can tell them it's mutual. She's something else. Very strong."

"I'll tell them you said so." Coming from a cat, there was no bigger compliment than being told you are strong, whether physically or mentally. Speed and strength are our most valued assets.

"Daddy?" I paused in front of the bedside table, searching it with my eyes only, because the entire surface was coated in a sticky, sweet-smelling, brownish film. My best guess was that Eric had spilled soda and hadn't bothered to clean it up. The key was not in the sticky scattering of junk.

"Yes?"

I paused, rethinking what I was about to say. But I'd made too much progress toward conquering my fears to back down now. "Can I talk to Marc?"

"He's not here."

"Oh." I swallowed thickly, trying to hide my simultaneous relief and disappointment. The last thing I needed was Daddy reading anything into my request. I'd never hear the end of it.

"You'll see him in an hour." Daddy let his meaning hang in the air for me to do with as I would. He was learning.

"Oh. Okay." Marc was with the nearest search

party, on his way to Mississippi. My pulse raced, and I was glad my father couldn't hear my heartbeat over the phone. At least, I didn't think he could.

"I need to talk to Ryan now," he said, gently drawing me out of my thoughts.

"Sure, just a sec." I grabbed a pair of jeans lying over the back of Eric's desk chair. Abby's key was in the right front pocket, and I took the time for another abbreviated victory dance with it clenched in my fist. Then I ran all the way down the hall, through the living room and kitchen, and shoved open the basement door with the phone in one hand and the key in the other.

"Abby, I found it," I shouted the minute my foot hit the first step. I stopped on the fourth tread, checking my signal to make sure I hadn't lost the connection with my father. So far, so good. As I knelt to set Eric's phone on the step, the first notes of "Bad Boys" rang out from my pocket.

Damn. Standing with Eric's Nokia pressed to my ear once again, I shoved the key into one pocket, then fished Ryan's phone from the other. The area code was unfamiliar; it couldn't be my mother. I only knew of one other possibility.

Ryan confirmed it for me. "That's Miguel's dedicated ring."

Twenty-Seven

"**D**addy, Miguel's calling Ryan." I spoke into one phone with the other held at arm's length, as if it might explode.

"Tell him if he plays along, I'll let him live," my father said. "That's all I'm willing to promise at this point."

I stared at my brother. "He says—"

Ryan cut me off with an impatient wave of his hand. "I heard him, but I need more than that. I want out of the cage."

"No." I didn't bother to ask my father because I knew he'd agree with me. "Daddy made his offer. Your life for your cooperation. But if your hesitation blows our chance at catching them, even if Daddy spares your life, Miguel won't. And I'll leave you locked up for him to find."

"Bad Boys" played on, and Miguel was seconds away from being diverted to voice mail.

"You'd leave me here to die?" Ryan's face made it clear he didn't believe me.

"Assuming I don't decide to kill you myself."

His eyes grew smug, his leer cocky. "You wouldn't kill me."

I glanced pointedly at Eric's body, and he followed my gaze. "Would you have let Miguel sell me to the highest bidder?"

Ryan crossed his arms over his chest, considering, and his phone kept ringing. His pose was relaxed, as if he thought he had the upper hand, but a bead of sweat rolled slowly down his forehead. I'd scared him. Without unsheathing a claw, I'd scared my brother worse than my father had managed to do in twenty-eight years. That made me wonder what else I was capable of.

"Take it or leave it," I said. "Now."

"Fine. But you have to tell Dad I was coerced."

"I already have." I set Eric's phone down on the fourth step to keep it from disconnecting, then raced down the stairs to hand the other one to Ryan.

"What do you want me to do?" His voice shook as his thumb hovered over the Yes button.

"Answer the phone and act normal. If he suspects anything, the deal's off. Same thing goes if you try to keep the phone afterward," I said in a last-minute burst of good sense.

Ryan leaned his forehead against the bars and answered his phone. "Hello?" Hopefully Miguel would hear grogginess in his voice where I heard defeat.

From the other end of the line came the response. It was Sean, using Miguel's phone. I repressed an urge to jump for joy over my luck as I tiptoed back up the stairs. It was about time the tables turned.

"I was on the pot." Ryan rolled his eyes while Sean yelled something about missing his exit. "No, you did it right. Just keep going north until you see the sign for…"

When I was sure there would be no problem, I tuned him out and whispered goodbye to my father, promising to call him if anything changed. To Abby, I motioned that I would let her out as soon as Ryan hung up the phone. She nodded, but I knew she was getting impatient, and I didn't blame her. But I couldn't take the chance that Sean or Miguel might overhear me opening the cage.

"I swear Sean is an idiot," Ryan said, tucking the phone into his pocket. "His sense of direction is so poor I can't understand how he found his way out of his mother's womb."

"That's a lovely picture, Ryan, thanks." I bounced

down the steps and let Abby out of her cage. She nearly bowled me over with the enthusiasm of her hug.

"Let's get out of here," she said, glancing at her empty cage in disgust and undisguised fear.

"Sure." I nodded toward the stairs. "There's plenty to eat in the fridge, if you can stand to look at the mess in the kitchen. Why don't you go have some breakfast."

She stared at me like I'd suggested she step back into the cage, for old time's sake. "Faythe, I can't stay here. We're out. Let's go."

"Marc and the guys will be here in less than an hour. We have to wait for them."

"Great. A family reunion," Ryan groaned, still leaning against the front wall of his cage. "It can't get much better than this." He hadn't moved since I'd snapped the lock into place, and as far as I knew, he'd only glanced at Eric once.

"You're right." I held out my hand for his phone. "You've got it pretty good. Unless I decide to kick your ass while you're locked up and defenseless."

Ryan laughed as he fished the phone from his pocket. It was not the reaction I'd expected. "If you're implying that you've ever been defenseless, in any sense of the word, you are sorely mistaken. I think Eric, here, is ample evidence of that."

I glared at him, considering a retort. But in the end

I kept my mouth shut because he was right. I wasn't defenseless. In fact, I was glad to have the fact acknowledged, even if only by him. Grinning, I turned back to Abby.

She was gone.

"I'm sorry, Faythe," she said from halfway up the stairs. "I can't stay. It's too…horrible."

I caught up with her in the kitchen, grabbing her arm to stop her. "Sit down for a minute, Abby." I pushed a kitchen chair toward her and she stared at it as if it might swallow her whole.

"I'd rather stand."

"Fine. I understand. But I can't let you leave by yourself. Daddy has a team on the way, and one of the guys will drive you to the ranch. Your parents are there waiting for you, Abby. Don't make them worry any more than they already are by running off on your own."

How had I gone from being a habitual runner to counseling my cousin to stay put?

She hesitated, begging me with huge, haunted brown eyes not to make her stay. I felt for her but I stood firm. She couldn't go without an escort. Since I'd agreed to work for my father, she was officially under my protection, and if anything happened to her on my watch, there would be hell to pay for all involved. Especially me.

I was two seconds from threatening to lock her back up when she gave in with an exaggerated sigh. "Fine, I'll stay. But I could use a shower."

Thank goodness. I *really* hadn't wanted to physically detain her after all she'd been through already. "Through the living room and down the hall. Second door on the right. I can't vouch for how clean it is."

"So long as there's soap and hot water, I don't care." She turned on her heel, still clearly irritated with me. The shower started a minute later, and soon afterward, sobs joined the rhythm of the running water, with a halting, hiccuping beat of their own. I wished there was somewhere I could go to give her privacy. She had the right to grieve for her innocence alone, but I wasn't willing to go back into the basement.

Ten minutes later, Abby joined me in the kitchen. She was wearing the same clothes but she smelled like soap and her hair was clean, hanging halfway down her back in damp curls.

"Feel any better?" I asked, kicking out the chair opposite me at the table.

"No." She wrapped her hands around the curved chair back. "Just cleaner. And hungry."

"Help yourself." I nodded toward the refrigerator.

She chose three frozen breakfast burritos, stuffing them all in the microwave at once. We sat in silence until the timer buzzed, then I watched her chew as I tried to think of something to say. We'd been through a lot together in the last couple of days, but somehow discussing any of it seemed wrong, like a child's reluctance to talk about a bad dream for fear of it coming true. Only, our nightmares already had.

Abby stared out the kitchen window as she ate, her expression one of desperate longing. I knew how she felt, like as long as we were still in that house, we weren't really free. Like Miguel might return at any minute and lock us back up. Like we were stupid for staying when we were free to escape. Every instinct I had, both cat and human, told me to grab her hand and run as far and as fast as I could. But I didn't, because I'd told Daddy we would wait for the enforcers, and it's never a good idea to break your word to an Alpha. The only guy I knew who'd done that walked with a permanent limp and wore false teeth. Including his canines.

Outside, an engine growled as a vehicle approached the house. My head snapped up. I stared out the window but couldn't see it yet. My breath caught in my throat as I waited for the car to pass. But it didn't. It pulled into the driveway.

Twin rectangles of light flashed on the wall, sunlight reflecting off chrome to shine through the window in the front door.

Abby froze, her last bite halfway to her mouth. Her hand shook in terror.

I wanted to look out the window but couldn't chance exposing myself. I glanced at the clock. Marc was fast, but not that fast. It couldn't be him. Not yet.

Abby dropped her food on the table. She didn't even pause when she missed the plate. She stood quickly. Her chair fell over, clattering on the linoleum. She backed slowly toward the living room. Her eyes never left the front door.

My heart pounded. Adrenaline surged through my veins as my body prepared to fight. I wouldn't let him put his hands on me again. I wouldn't go back in the cage. Not as long as I was breathing. After that, it wouldn't matter.

Outside, one car door opened, followed by another. Heavy footsteps thumped up the porch steps. The front door flew open, splintering the rectangles of light into shards of shadow.

Marc called my name.

Relief washed through me like an Arctic wave, extinguishing flames of rage that had flared up especially for Miguel. My arms hung limp at my sides, my fingers tingling. I was numb with shock, frozen in place.

"Faythe?" Marc called again.

"We're in here." Abby flew past me into the

dining room and threw herself at Marc, hanging from his neck like a Velcro-pawed monkey. He tried to pry her off, but she clung to him, sobbing as if she'd discovered a fresh reserve of tears. Marc glanced at me over her head and motioned for help, but I just watched them. I couldn't move.

Someone peeled Abby's arms from Marc's neck, but I didn't see who, because I couldn't tear my eyes away from his. When he was free—Abby now clinging to someone else—he stared at me from across the room.

What? I thought. *What is he waiting for?* Then I understood. He thought I'd left him. He thought I'd run out on him again without a word of warning, as I'd done five years earlier. And I had. Only this time I'd meant to come back, even if only to explain.

I smiled hesitantly, and he smiled back, his eyes shiny with tears. I didn't so much see him move as feel the air displaced in his wake. The next moment, I was in his arms, my feet dangling several inches from the floor while he squeezed me hard enough to crack my spine.

He lowered me slowly, watching my eyes as I slid down the front of his body. He was searching for rejection, or even doubt. If he'd seen any, he might have actually given up. He might have finally believed I didn't love him. It was the opportunity I'd been waiting for. Only I was no longer sure I wanted it.

The one thing I was sure of was that I wanted to lay my head on his chest and listen to his heartbeat. So I did. He wrapped his arms around me, and for a long moment neither of us moved.

"How the hell did you get here so fast?" I asked, my battered cheek pressed into his shirt.

"He nearly blew up Dad's van, that's how," Ethan said. I glanced up to see his usual goofy grin, and eyes a shade greener than I remembered. He was happy to see me. It was mutual. "He drove a hundred miles an hour almost all the way from Louisiana."

I laughed, not a bit surprised.

Marc tilted my face toward his, claiming my attention for himself. He hesitated, waiting for my permission, and I knew what he wanted. I nodded, and he kissed me gently, as if afraid he might hurt me. But when he pulled away, his face was etched with pain, as if I'd hurt him instead.

Marc lifted a strand of my hair, smelling it. Storm clouds rolled across his eyes, dark with the promise of danger to come. His fist clenched around the strand, and I saw the conflict raging within him. He released my hair one finger at a time, very slowly, fighting with each movement to maintain control.

"What did they do to you?" he whispered, low

Rachel Vincent

enough that no one else could hear. Low enough that I wasn't sure whether I'd actually heard him, or read his lips.

"Nothing," I said as comprehension drenched me, cold and clear. He thought I'd let them have me, that I'd sacrificed my body for my life. He didn't understand that I would rather have died than give in to them.

In an instant, a single agonizing instant, panic consumed me. It rolled over and around me like the incoming tide, threatening to wash me out into a sea of misery. The sudden irrational fear that he might not want me now left me numb with shock and sick with dread. After all these years of him chasing and me running, he would finally give me up because he couldn't stand what he thought had happened.

And in that moment I realized I didn't want him to give up on me. I might not have been ready to give in to him completely, but neither was I ready for him to stop trying.

"Out," Marc growled at the others, his eyes still holding mine captive.

Ethan stuttered an objection, unwilling to leave me alone with Marc without my permission.

"Out, now," Marc ordered again, and I nodded at Ethan. Parker ushered everyone onto the sun-bathed back porch, then closed the door with one last questioning glance at us.

I watched Marc, bracing myself for the worst. I expected more anger or disgust, but I saw neither. He wasn't mad. Not at me, anyway. He was hurt, and trying to hide it, even from himself.

"I can taste him on you." He leaned over and sniffed me, my face and my neck. He would have gone farther down but I stopped him, pulling him back up to eye level. "I can smell them. Two of them. I'll kill them, Faythe. Just tell me what they did, and I'll kill them."

I stiffened and backed away from him. "You'll have to stand in line." His eyes widened in surprise as I continued, "They learned a lesson, Marc. That's what they did. The one you taste is Eric. He's downstairs with Ryan, and by my estimate, he stopped breathing over an hour ago. Right around the time I bit through his throat.

"And this one…" I touched the side of my neck, where Miguel had left his distinctive jungle scent. "This one is Miguel, and this is his." I pulled out the front of my shirt, stiff with dried blood. Well, the shirt was actually Marc's, but it wasn't the time to gripe over technicalities. "I'm not done with him yet. But when I am, he'll bear a striking resemblance to the corpse downstairs. At least from the neck up." I paused, amused by his astonished expression. "Any more questions?"

"Actually, yeah. Several." I laughed, but he just frowned at me. "What's so funny?"

"Nothing." I stepped back into his embrace. "I'm just glad you're here."

He tilted my face up. "Are you really okay?"

"Better than ever, actually. Kicking ass is surprisingly therapeutic."

"I've been saying that for years but nobody listens."

"Welcome to my world," I said, and he laughed. "I guess we'd better let them in."

"In a minute." He kissed me again, and I let him, fighting the urge to cling to him like Abby had. It would have felt so good to let him hold me, to cry while he stroked my hair. But that wouldn't have been a very good way to start my first assignment. Especially since I was supposed to be in charge.

So instead, I settled for one more kiss, then pushed him away gently. "Go get the guys. Please."

Marc opened the back door, and Abby came in, followed by my very first team of enforcers. I took note of each as he passed, taking mental inventory of the bodies under my command.

The man who'd rescued Marc from Abby turned out to be her oldest brother, Lucas Wade. He was built a little like a linebacker and a lot like a Mack truck, with shoulders wide enough that he had to enter most rooms sideways. People generally took one look at Lucas and walked the other way, especially if they ran across him at night. In cat form, he was the largest tom I'd ever personally met, weighing in at more than three hundred pounds and measuring over seven feet long, including his tail. While his human form was shorter—just under six and a half feet—Lucas was big enough to make me wonder if Miguel had known about Abby's brother when he grabbed her. If so, I'd have to seriously rethink describing Miguel as smart.

From the doorway, I glanced around the room, counting my blessings. Along with Marc and Lucas, Daddy had sent Ethan, Owen, and Parker. Except for Jace, all my favorite guys were present and accounted for.

After a quick round of hugs and greetings, I noticed several of the guys watching me closely, as if they wanted to ask me something but weren't quite sure how to start. "What's up, boys?" I asked, snagging a fresh can of Coke from the fridge.

Ethan answered, after a quick glance around at his fellow enforcers. "It's not that we're doubting your skills or anything, Faythe, but we gotta know. Dad said you bit through some guy's neck…" He paused for confirmation, and I nodded, thoroughly enjoying the look of admiration I got in return.

"How the hell did you get him to come near you in cat form?"

I grinned, and took a swig from the can. They still didn't know about the partial shift. "That's a long story. When this is all over, remind me that I have something interesting to show you guys."

Parker frowned, but the glimmer of curiosity in Ethan's eyes only grew. I laughed and Ethan leaned back against a cabinet, waiting for someone to start talking. Owen cleared his throat, and I looked up to find everyone staring at me. *Oh yeah,* I thought, blushing. *I'm supposed to do the talking.*

Six pairs of eyes followed me as I stepped forward to begin my very first briefing. "I assume Daddy told you about my idea," I said, speaking to the room in general.

Marc's eyes sparkled in amusement. "Well, he did mention something about you suffering delusions of competence and responsibility. His theory is that you took a pretty good hit on the head."

I smiled at him gratefully, instantly at ease. "Ha-ha. You just don't like the idea of me as your boss."

"The way I heard it, we're partners." He leaned against the kitchen sink, crossing his arms over his chest in a familiar, cocky stance. He'd been standing just like that the first time he asked me out.

"Well, if you want to get technical…"

"I want to get out of here," he quipped.

"Me, too." I really wanted to hold his hand. "How soon do we need to be at the airport?"

"Our flight leaves at two-thirty," Parker said. "It will take us at least half an hour to get to the airport, and we need to be an hour early to get through security."

"Security. Shit." I sank into a chair, already mourning the failure of my first assignment.

"What's wrong?" Abby asked.

"I can't fly. I don't have any ID. Damn it!" I kicked an empty chair with my bare foot. It flew across the room and slammed into the wall, leaving a dent the size of a child's fist. I might have been impressed with myself, if not for my throbbing big toe.

Marc knelt in front of me, his hands on my knees. "Tell me you love me." His grin was irritatingly smug and cryptic.

I watched him through narrowed eyes, not bothering to hide suspicion. "Why?"

"Because it's true."

"You'll have to do better than that."

He pouted for show. "I've already come to your rescue. What could be better than that?"

"The way I remember it, *I* came to my rescue. I don't see your bite marks on the dead guy in the basement."

Ethan snickered, and Marc glared at him. I grabbed his chin and turned him back to face me. "If you have a point, make it."

"Fine. But you'll say it one of these days, and there just might be a witness around to keep you from denying it later."

"Don't hold your breath," I said it with a smile, but Marc still looked hurt. He reached into his back left pocket and pulled out my wallet. I took it with wide eyes. "Why do you have my wallet?"

Pain flashed in front of his eyes for an instant, then it was gone, and I knew that whatever he said would be only half the truth. "Because your father taught me years ago to prepare for every possible complication. Like an unexpected flight."

That was exactly the kind of advanced planning I was going to have to master to enjoy any success at my new job. "Thank you." I closed my eyes, trying to remember what I'd been saying.

"We need to leave around one this afternoon," Parker said, bringing me back on track.

"One p.m. Right." I glanced at the clock over the sink. "So that gives us just under three hours to get this place cleaned up. Let's get going." But they already were. And, really, I shouldn't have been surprised. Even if I was technically in charge, they all knew what needed to be done a lot better than I did.

Owen knelt in front of the sink, searching for cleaning supplies. He came up with a roll of large black trash bags and nothing else. "Not so much as a Brillo pad. Someone will have to go shopping."

"Fine." I glanced down at my ruined clothes. "Parker, you go. Take Abby with you," I added as an afterthought, hoping something as normal as a shopping trip might make her feel a little better. "There's probably a drugstore nearby, or a Wal-Mart, if we're lucky. Get what you need to clean, and get some fresh clothes for me and Abby. And tooth-brushes, too," I said, thinking of Eric's tongue in my mouth. Marc wouldn't mention it again, but I knew it bothered him. It bothered me, too.

"You want me to buy clothes?" Parker wrinkled his forehead in uncertainty.

"Unless you think I could make it through airport security drenched in blood."

"I guess not," he grumbled, glancing down at my shirt. "But, uh, what kind of clothes? And what size?"

"Come on, Parker, I know what to get." Rolling her eyes, Abby grabbed his arm and tugged him out the front door and down the steps.

As my father's van backed down the driveway, Ethan grabbed several trash bags and trailed the rest of the guys into the basement. "Time to shear the black sheep of the family," he muttered, his usual smile grim and brittle. "What do you wanna bet momma's boy's less than happy to see us?"

"Go easy on him," I said. "We're not done with him yet."

Ethan shrugged, noncommittal, and I started to follow him, but Marc pulled me aside. "Faythe, why don't you let us handle the cleanup?"

"You? Clean?" I feigned shock, one hand over my heart. "Have you *seen* where you live?"

He laughed. "Just because I don't dust compulsively doesn't mean I don't know how to deal with a corpse. This isn't my first dead rogue, you know."

I did know, but knowing something isn't always the same as understanding it. I'd always known that being an enforcer sometimes meant getting your hands dirty, but I'd never thought about what that meant for Marc and the guys. Now I was seeing firsthand what all was involved in dealing with a rogue.

A rogue was any cat guilty of breaking Pride law, be he wild, stray, or Pride. Those terms denoted social status, but said nothing about the cats they labeled. There were honorable strays, like Marc. And there were criminals among the natural-born cats, like Eric. Miguel, Luiz, Eric and Sean were rogues because they'd kidnapped, raped, and killed. Ryan was a rogue too, strictly speaking, because he'd helped.

By necessity, rogues were dealt with quickly, in a manner harsh enough to discourage potential copycats. In our territory, and in some of the free zones, Marc was the one who dealt with rogues, though rarely alone.

Unless the offense was serious, like murder or Shifting in front of a human, Daddy usually settled for a warning: a deforming scar or handicap. But no one got more than one warning. If a rogue was stupid enough to mess up twice, Marc would take him out of the game. If he was lucky, it would be a snapped neck. However, if the crime was especially brutal, Marc might make an example of the doomed cat. That usually took a while. And it was usually messy.

"Yeah, I guess you probably know what you're doing," I conceded.

"Yeah, we do." His smile faded into a serious look I didn't quite care for. "Besides, you shouldn't have to mess with this after what you've been through." Marc stopped talking abruptly, but I knew he wasn't done. He glanced down at the blood on my chest. "And you should probably take a shower. I guess I can forget about getting my shirt back, huh?"

"Sorry."

He shrugged, handing me a trash bag from the

pile on the table. "It was old anyway. Put your clothes in here when you take them off, and we'll get rid of them with everything else."

"Thanks." I took the bag and turned toward the living room. Then, on second thought, I spun back to face him. "Hey, Marc?"

"Yeah?"

"Don't forget Daddy made a deal with Ryan." He nodded, but I wasn't convinced. "That means you can't touch him. Promise me."

"I swear on all nine of my lives."

I laughed. No, we don't really have nine lives. That would be cool, though. Especially in Miguel's case. If he had nine lives, we could each take a turn killing him. Oh, well. We'd just have to settle for doing it right the first time.

Twenty-Eight

Parker and Abby weren't back with the clothes yet when I got out of the shower, so I wrapped myself in a big white towel secured with a safety pin I found in the bathroom. I stared at my reflection in the mirror, my hair twisted up in a second towel. I'd avoided looking at myself so far, but finally had to admit that I was being a coward. After all, I'd earned my battle scars, and I might as well know what they looked like.

It wasn't pretty. Beneath the towel, a carnation bloomed on the left side of my stomach, dark purple, with pink, knuckle-shaped petals. It was too tender to touch, as were the ribs on that side of my body. My left shoulder throbbed dully along with my pulse, and a chain of bruises adorned my wrist like a bracelet, the latest in fine jewelry for battered women.

But the worst by far was my face. In fact, if my recent Shift had helped heal my cheek as well as my shoulder, I couldn't imagine how bad I must have looked before. Now the entire left side of my face was swollen and bruised, an ugly bluish-purple, darkest on my cheekbone. *Damn Miguel.*

My eyes watered, and I squeezed them shut, trying to deny the tears an outlet, as if they didn't really exist if I could keep them from falling. Being manhandled by Miguel hadn't made me cry. Hearing that Marc had nearly beaten Jace to death hadn't made me cry. Killing Eric hadn't made me cry. But staring into the mirror at the love child of Smurfette and Rocky Balboa was more than enough to bring me to tears.

"I've been trying to figure out how to make you cry for more than twenty years," Ethan said. I opened my eyes and met his in the mirror. He stood behind me, a half-full garbage bag in one hand.

"All you had to do was aim for my face."

"Makes sense, but Mom would have killed me." He dropped the bag and turned me around by my shoulders. I put my head on his shoulder and let him hold me while I cried. I felt like an idiot, crying over a few bruises, but I couldn't help it.

"How many times have you seen me with a black eye or a broken nose?" Ethan asked, stroking my hair.

Several times, but that was one area where women's lib dared not tread. A mutilated face was always different for a woman than for a man, no matter how highly she valued her equality and asserted her independence. "Besides," he said, "compared to Jace, you look great."

I groaned. How could I not have asked about Jace? "How's he doing?" I pulled away from Ethan, wiping my face on a mostly clean bath rag.

"He's fine. It's nothing a few months in traction won't fix."

"Traction? Shit." I frowned up at him. "No one said anything about traction."

Ethan smiled grimly, dropping a grimy razor from the countertop into the bag. "It was a joke, Faythe. His arms and legs are fine. And by some miracle, he didn't lose any teeth."

That was the best news I'd heard yet, because while a dentist could replace a broken or missing human tooth, the artificial parts would have to come out before Shifting. There was nothing that could be done about broken teeth in cat form. At least, not for a cat that wasn't supposed to exist.

"I feel terrible. I shouldn't have taken his keys."

Ethan shrugged. "I told him I'd hold you down

once he's back on his feet, so he can get in a good swing or two."

"Just not my face. Please." I ran my fingers through damp hair, arranging and rearranging it, looking for a way to cover the left side of my face without compromising my vision. No luck. I could either satisfy my vanity or preserve my depth perception, but I couldn't do both at once.

"Okay, you've primped enough. Now go bug someone else," Ethan said, shooing me out the door. "I have to clean the bathroom."

"That should be interesting," I quipped. "Maybe I should stay and watch."

"Maybe you should stay and help."

Cupping one hand behind my ear, I grinned, pretending to listen. "I think I hear Marc calling."

Ethan grunted and opened his trash bag, and I left him to his work.

I'd had serious doubts about the guys' ability to clean, in spite of Marc's reassurance, but never in my life had I been happier to be wrong. I'd spent less than half an hour in the bathroom, but when I came out, there wasn't a soda can or pizza crust in sight. The floors and furniture were still dusty, downright filthy in places, since there wasn't so much as a bottle of Windex in the entire house. Still, the transformation was unbelievable.

Eight large black trash bags sat piled against one wall of the dining room, each bulging with irregular shapes and closed with a white wire tie. Against the opposite wall, three more bags stood, half-full and still open.

"Those are for the burn pile," Marc said from behind me, nodding at the row of open bags. "The rest we'll drop into the nearest public Dumpster."

"What's in the open ones?"

"Anything that could expose us or identify them. Eric's ID, his bloody clothes and shoes, all his personal possessions."

Nausea stirred the contents of my stomach. "Please tell me you didn't put him in a bag, too."

Marc chuckled. "You've seen too many movies."

"You've buried too many bodies."

"I won't argue with that." He put one arm around my shoulders and squeezed. "Eric's still in the basement. We don't have time to deal with that kind of cleanup. We're just playing Merry Maids." He paused, glancing at me out of the corner of his eye. "Haven't you seen *Pulp Fiction*?"

I smiled. That was one of my favorite movies, and he knew it. "Let me guess, the Wolf is coming to tidy up my mess?"

"More like the Pink Panther. Your dad's sending Michael over tonight with another crew to deal with the big stuff. The body, the mattresses, dismantling and disposing of the cages." Marc ticked off the details on his fingers like he might name items on a grocery list. A bag of sugar, a loaf of bread, a gallon of milk, the corpse in the basement...

He grinned. "Rule number one for closing the site of an incident—never dispose of a body in broad daylight."

"I'll try to remember that," I said. "What about the furniture?"

"They'll burn all the mattresses, including the ones up here, and leave the rest of the furniture, what little there is. The landlord can do whatever he wants with it."

"So, you guys are almost done?"

"Just about. But we're still waiting on Parker and..." Listening, he turned toward the kitchen window, which I noticed they'd covered with a rough square of cardboard. "They're back."

"Good. I need some clothes."

"Really? I heard terry cloth was in this year." He grinned, hooking a finger beneath the top edge of my towel. I slapped his hand away, trying to maintain a stern face. It didn't work. "Come on, you look good in Egyptian cotton."

"I look better out of it," I teased.

His mouth dropped open, and his moan followed

me through the dining room and into the entryway, where I peeked out through the glass in the front door. Abby tripped going up the front steps, smiling at something Parker had said, and I opened the door in time to catch her before she flattened the bulging Wal-Mart bags dangling from each hand.

"Thanks." She brushed past me into the house, seemingly almost…normal. I glanced at Parker, one eyebrow raised.

He shrugged. "She just needed to get out."

"I guess so." But I credited her improvement to the houseful of familiar cats, rather than the fresh air. Smiling, I took the bag he offered. Clothes. Finally.

Abby followed me to the bathroom, where Ethan was still busy. She dropped a bag of cleaning supplies on the counter and I led her to Sean's room to change, on the assumption that his scent would bother her less than either Eric's or Miguel's.

My cousin had decent taste. Either that, or she knew me better than I'd realized. For me, she'd picked out a pair of low-rise jeans and a dark red tank, with wide shoulder straps. Black hair looks good against red, so I was pretty happy. Until I looked in the mirror. I should have known better than to look in the damn mirror.

Abby smiled sympathetically at me in the glass, and I immediately felt guilty for my self-pity, when she'd been through so much worse. "Here," she said, handing me a shoe box. "We had to guess your size, but I thought you'd like the style."

I lifted the lid to find a pair of white Reeboks with red-and-black accents. "You guessed well." They were only half a size too big. "Thanks. It'll be good to wear shoes again."

"No problem."

We laced up our new shoes together. Hers had pink-and-purple accents.

In the hall, whistling accompanied a set of heavy footsteps. "If you're all dressed, make yourselves useful," Lucas said, leaning against the door frame. "Catch." He tossed a can of dust spray to Abby and a bottle of no-wax floor cleaner at me. I say *at* me because Abby caught hers with the ease of nine years as a softball catcher, but mine slipped right through my congenital butterfingers and burst open on the floor.

Lucas laughed. "Well, that's one way to do it. There's a mop in the kitchen, by the fridge."

Abby and I got to work, and half an hour later Marc officially declared the house clean. "They'd even get their security deposit back, if not for the dent Faythe put in the wall," he said.

"Like you're one to throw stones," I retorted.

Parker and Owen stuffed the trash bags into the

back of Daddy's twelve-passenger van, while Ethan gathered up the cleaning supplies and made a last-minute check to be sure we hadn't over-looked anything.

While everyone else piled into the van out front, Marc and I stood in the basement, watching Lucas prepare the prisoner for transfer. Ryan's perpetual frown deepened as he stared at the transport re-straints: solid steel wrist and ankle cuffs, each attached with little slack to a waist chain of the same material. The restraint system was one of a pair kept in the back of the van, for emergencies. I'd never seen them used before; we rarely had the opportu-nity to bring anyone back alive. Ryan didn't seem particularly grateful to be the first.

"Put both hands through the bars, wrists together," Lucas ordered.

Rubber soles shuffled on concrete as Ryan stepped forward to comply. He looked both scared and irritated, but was wisely exercising his right to remain silent. So far, at least. Handcuffs closed around my brother's wrists with a metallic click-slide–catch. More clattering followed as Lucas opened the cage and cuffed his prisoner's ankles together.

"A cat's body can sustain a lot of damage without actually dying," Lucas said, his voice as deep as the rumble of the earth itself. "You just think about that before you so much as scratch yourself without permission."

Ryan gulped and nodded, still mute.

Marc had chosen Lucas as the transport guard for two reasons, both of them obvious. As the biggest cat any of us had ever met, Lucas stood the best chance of intimidating Ryan into submission without having to lift a finger. And since every finger lifted against Ryan endangered our chances of catching Miguel, we needed him to remain conscious and cooperative.

But mostly, Marc chose Lucas because as Abby's brother, he had more reason than anyone else present to want Ryan dead. And Ryan knew it. It was Marc's way of scaring the living shit out of my brother. It was also the only revenge any of us would have until Ryan had worn out his usefulness.

Twenty-Nine

Owen drove us to Jackson International Airport, parking in a nearly empty pay-by-the-hour lot rather than in the crowded loading zone. We couldn't risk a passerby noticing the thin and obviously exhausted man chained hand and foot inside a van registered to my father. Unless the officer called to investigate happened to believe we were into traveling orgies and bondage, we'd spend the rest of the night in jail, trying to come up with a suitable explanation before Daddy arrived to bail us out.

Yeah, better to avoid humans altogether.

Marc, Parker, Ethan, and I stood in the parking lot, while Lucas repositioned Ryan in the second row, where Abby could reach him from the front passenger seat. She had his cell phone, and would hold it up to his mouth if Miguel called.

Lucas gave Ryan one final warning, involving how little room his shredded corpse would take up in a garbage bag if he so much as sneezed on Abby before they got to the ranch. Then he slammed the sliding door shut on Ryan's protests that he wasn't *violent,* for crying out loud. By then, we'd all heard enough of his sniveling about being forced into working for Miguel, and no one was happier than I was to be separated from his nasal whine by a sliding sheet of steel and tinted glass.

Lucas said goodbye to his sister and warned Owen not to get pulled over. Then he slapped the hood of the van like the flank of a horse. Owen pulled out of the parking lot, his brake lights flashing at us, and Abby waved goodbye with her head hanging out the front window. Lucas waved back until Owen turned a corner and the van drove out of sight.

We stood in line at the ticket counter to show our IDs to an overcaffeinated clerk tapping away at a keyboard we couldn't see. Our tickets were already reserved and paid for. Daddy had bought them over the phone as soon as he knew for sure who would be driving back with Abby and Ryan.

Unfortunately, there were no direct flights from

At my side, Marc stiffened, watching the guard watch Lucas. I glanced at Marc as discreetly as I could. He looked relaxed, his free hand stuffed casually in the pockets of his jeans, feet spread a comfortable distance apart—but I knew better. I could hear his heart thump and knew he was already planning the best course of action, should the guard decide to make trouble.

By some miracle, none of us had set off the metal detector, but no one looked shocked when the suspicious guard chose Lucas to be searched by hand. Physical searches were supposedly conducted at random, but even I couldn't blame the guard for choosing him. If he wasn't my cousin, Lucas was someone I'd keep my eye on too.

He submitted to the search without complaint, demonstrating a level of patience that might have surprised anyone who didn't know him. It surprised none of us. Yes, he was big and scary, his nose having healed crooked the last time it was broken. Yes, he could have snapped the guard's neck between his thumb and forefinger. And yes, he'd be ready and willing to shred Miguel on sight. But while Lucas could handle any trouble that came his way, he never went looking for any. That would have been dishonorable, and far beneath him.

When the guard found no reason to detain Lucas,

he let us go. I felt tension roll off Marc like fog in front of a breeze. He smiled and squeezed my hand as we went to find our gate, and if I hadn't known better, I might have thought he was humming. But that must have been my imagination, because Marc didn't hum. He grumbled, and snapped, and sometimes cursed in Spanish when he was really pissed off. But he definitely didn't hum.

On each leg of our trip, I dozed fitfully, trying to make up for my nightmare-riddled sleep the night before. Unfortunately, I never got more than ninety consecutive minutes of rest, thanks to turbulence, frighteningly perky flight attendants, and the persistent demands of my bladder. Of course, that last part was my own fault, because I drank a twenty-four-ounce Coke in Jackson, and a sixteen-ounce coffee in Cincinnati. Yet in spite of all the caffeine, I felt more like a zombie than a shapeshifter when I got off the plane in Missouri.

When we landed in Saint Louis, the gate was packed. Row upon row of occupied, molded-plastic chairs greeted us, along with the conversational buzz of evening commuters: an army of corporate automatons, armed with cell phones and laptops, hell-bent on taking over the world one boardroom meeting at a time.

According to the itinerary Michael had given us,

car-rental booth and a line of people chatting and snacking on vending-machine candy. He took my hand, squeezing it as we walked. I glanced at him, but he was watching the people in the rental line. He growled, too low for anyone other than us to hear.

No one said anything or made any overt move-ments, but suddenly everything felt different. The guys' feet made no noise on the floor. Their bodies seemed to slink forward with each graceful step. They were moving more like cats than like people, and I followed their example out of habit.

The difference was nothing any human would have noticed consciously, but it definitely spooked them. People walked out of their way to avoid us, creating an open path in a fairly crowded lobby. They snuck furtive glances at us, gasping openly when they saw my battered face, yet no one dared approach to offer me assistance or sympathy. Thank goodness.

We stopped at the end of the line, with Marc and Parker in the lead. Several wide sets of eyes peeked back at us in short, nervous glances. Most of them needed only one look at our group to decide they'd rather buy a souvenir or have a drink before renting a car. Their excuses for leaving the line were a defense mechanism allowing them to retain a sliver of self-respect, rather than acknowledge their own fear. Humans were never willing to believe what their instincts had to say about the nature of the beasts they'd just faced. And that was fine with us.

I smiled to myself as a man in a generic black business suit stepped out of line in front of us to shuffle toward the restroom. After less than two minutes, the only customer left was the one currently being served. Behind the counter the harried employee wore a white plastic tag reading Please be patient, I'm in training.

Great. Enforcers out for blood are no good at being patient. Alternately curious and apathetic, yes. But not patient.

Marc tapped Parker on the shoulder. "Get something with dual climate control."

"And satellite radio." That was Ethan, who thought life without music wasn't worth living. He'd left his MP3 player at home for Jace, who was bedridden and apparently bored.

Parker grunted. "I'll do my best." From the look on his face, I doubted he even knew what satellite radio was.

When the employee-in-training brought out the third copy of an insurance form, dropping the botched second attempt in the trash, I ground my teeth, barely stifling a request to speak with his manager. Logically, I knew that my problem was nerves, not the nitwit behind the counter. But knowing that didn't help.

Coffee. I needed coffee. I couldn't get my thoughts together without a little more caffeine in my system. Luckily, the line at Seattle's Best moved faster than the one at Hertz, and I was passing out steaming insulated cups from two cardboard trays by the time Parker took possession of a set of car keys.

He'd rented a standard seven-passenger minivan, with leather seats and two sliding doors. It had dual climate control but no satellite radio. Ethan got over his disappointment pretty quickly when Marc threatened to find a creative new storage compartment for his headphones.

I was worried that the van would be too small, but Lucas reminded me that we didn't plan to bring back Sean or Miguel. At least not enough of them to need an extra seat. So a seven-passenger van should do nicely.

Parker drove, because he was the most reliable driver. Marc was the fastest, but he'd lost his driving privileges on the way to Mississippi. Which was fine with me. Having ridden with him countless times, I'd say my odds of surviving another attack from Miguel were better than my odds of surviving a fifty-mile drive with Marc, especially considering the cloud of nervous energy surrounding him like a cocoon.

We'd been on the road less than fifteen minutes when Marc's right leg began jumping uncontrollably. I glanced at him and he smiled, but his knee kept bouncing. I put my hand on his thigh, and his smile changed. It, like his eyes, grew deeper, somehow hotter.

Marc had misunderstood the purpose of my touch, but hey, it worked. His leg stopped bouncing; he'd found a new outlet for his energy. His nostrils flared as he breathed in my scent, and the yellow specks in his eyes seemed to sparkle. It was a look I hadn't seen in a while, and it was so intense it almost scared me.

He leaned into me, and his mouth found mine before I'd fully realized what he had in mind. I couldn't have resisted even if I'd wanted to. But I didn't want to. No matter what else was going on or how mad I was at him, it was always the same. Once he got that look in his eyes, resistance wasn't an option. It wasn't even a concept. Which was why I'd stayed so far away from him for so long. If I hadn't, it would have been impossible for me to sustain our breakup. My body responded to him without bothering to consult my brain.

"Would you two please cut that out?" Ethan snapped, elbowing me in the ribs. He sat on my right, with his fingers in his ears.

Marc pulled away from me long enough to growl at Ethan, but then his tongue was in my mouth before I could chime in with my own two cents. He'd finally figured out how to shut me up. I'd have to congratulate him—as soon as I regained the ability to speak.

"Seriously, guys," Parker said. If it had been anyone else, Marc would have snarled again, but he took Parker seriously. Marc let me go, and I glanced at the rearview mirror to find Parker staring back at me.

My face flushed and I laughed. But my smile froze in place as the first muffled notes of the Nokia ring tone met my ears. From my pocket. Eric's phone was ringing in my pocket, and I had no idea whether or not to answer it.

I dug the phone out and stared at it as if it would tell me what to do. But it didn't. Phones aren't very helpful in that respect. The number on the display was unfamiliar. "Does anyone know Ryan's cell phone number?" I asked.

Ethan stared at me as if I'd just spoken in tongues. "Okay," he said, glancing around the van. "Raise your hand if you knew Ryan had a cell-phone before this morning." No hands went up.

"Okay, point taken. No one knows. You could have just said that," I snapped. "Someone call Daddy." No one moved. "Now!"

Six hands dug in pockets for cell phones. Marc

won. He had Daddy programmed in under "boss." I should have guessed. "Greg, it's Marc." He paused, listening, and Eric's phone stopped ringing. Damn. "Do you have Ryan's cell-phone number? Someone just called Eric's phone, and we don't know who it was." Another pause. "Oh. Already?"

I couldn't hear Daddy over the highway noise, and not knowing was driving me crazy. See? No patience.

"Okay, here she is." Marc handed me the phone, his hand over the mouthpiece. "It was Ryan. He's at the ranch. Your dad wants to talk to you."

I took the phone. "Hi, Daddy."

"Ryan just got a call from Miguel." His tone was all business.

"What did he say?"

"He was just checking in. They're about two hours from Oak Hill, but coming from the opposite direction, so you shouldn't run into them on the highway."

I nodded, even though he couldn't see me. "Good. We'll beat them there by over an hour. Have you spoken to the Taylors yet?"

"Yes. Everything's set. Carissa and her mother left with four of their enforcers this afternoon. Brian will be there to let you in. He's happy for the opportunity to stay and help." Brian was one of Carissa's brothers. Her father was at the ranch with the other Alphas.

"Okay. That sounds good."

"Faythe?"

"Yes, Daddy?"

"Be careful."

My heart beat a little harder, and I swallowed. "I will. I promise."

"Good. Put Marc on the phone so I can threaten to flay him alive if anything happens to you."

I laughed. "I'm in charge, Daddy, remember? You should be threatening me."

"I've already done enough of that to last a lifetime. Just be careful."

"You already said that."

"I know." He sighed, and I pictured the lines on his face deepening as he frowned down at his desk. "It warrants saying twice."

I smiled, feeling strangely warm and fuzzy, considering my destination. "Don't worry."

"You always were one to ask for the impossible."

"Yeah, and to make it happen too. So stop worrying."

"I'll do my best." He paused. "Listen, Ryan says Miguel gave him a message for you. Do you want to hear it?"

My stomach clenched around airport lasagna, threatening to expel it. "I don't know. Do I?"

"I haven't heard the message, but Ryan says it isn't pretty."

Great. But what the hell. Words couldn't really hurt me, and maybe if he pissed me off, I'd fight better. "Yeah, put him on."

"Here he is."

I heard scratching sounds as the phone changed hands, then Ryan spoke into my ear. "Hey, I told Dad you wouldn't want to hear this, so don't shoot the messenger, okay?"

"What do you think I'm going to do, reach through the phone and snap your neck? I think you're pretty safe, at least until I get home."

Marc laughed and mimed snapping someone's neck. I didn't think it was very funny, but apparently I was in the minority.

"Thanks," Ryan said. "That's very comforting."

"Just spit it out. What did he say?"

"That you're going to pay for his face. This next part's a direct quote. He said he's gonna 'beat you until you beg for mercy, then fuck you until you bleed.'"

My mouth went dry. Fear clutched my lungs, making it hard to draw a deep breath. And for a moment I thought the low rumbling sound was my stomach preparing to heave. Then I realized it was Marc growling, his expression so fierce I couldn't stand to meet his eyes.

But before I could say anything, a loud whack

sounded in my ear. Ryan howled in pain. The phone clattered to the floor of Daddy's office, and I held mine out at arm's length to save my hearing. My father's voice came back on the line. "I'm sorry, Faythe. He should have known better than to pass on a message like that."

I clutched Marc's hand and tried to steady my voice. It almost worked. "He did warn me."

"He's used up all my patience and he should have known better," Daddy said. "Maybe now he'll think before he opens his mouth next time."

My heart sank as I realized how often those words could have been applied to me.

My father took a deep breath, exhaling into the receiver. "I'm going to let you go now so you can focus. Just remember to stay within sight of the guys and keep your eyes and ears open. You know what you're doing, so don't start second-guessing yourself. You'll be fine."

"Thanks, Daddy."

It wasn't until after we'd both hung up that I realized I should have told him I loved him. That's me, always a second too late when it mattered. But that habit was about to change, because a second too late with Miguel would mean my death. Or worse.

Thirty

It was nearly eight o'clock by the time we drove into Oak Hill. The setting sun cast rosy streaks across the sky and long shadows on the ground, warning us all that night was near, and that with it would come Miguel. And one way or another, this entire ordeal would be over.

We had no trouble finding Carissa's house, though none of us had been there in years. Nearly two miles after we passed the last residential neighborhood, Parker turned right off Highway 19 onto a private dirt road simply labeled Route 12.

The Taylors and their enforcers were the only residents of Route 12. Oak Hill was a very small town, and they lived on the northern edge of it, on a heavily wooded six-hundred-acre estate, which had been in their family for generations. Half a century earlier, when everyone else in the area was selling off large chunks of real estate for a quick profit, the Taylors had steadfastly clung to their property. Now they owned one of the largest acreages in the area. Like us, they treasured their space and their privacy, and there was plenty of both in the abundant Missouri woodlands, especially in their own private forest.

Several minutes after we turned, the Taylor house appeared on the right side of the road, at the top of a small crest half a mile from the highway. Behind it, the forest spread out as far as I could see, primarily a mix of oak trees—white, black, scarlet, and northern red—and other large tree species like black gum, maple, ash, elm, walnut and red cedar.

Against the lush, green backdrop, the house stood tall and proud, like the family it had housed for more than a century. It was a redbrick Greek Revival, with narrow white pillars, a wide, flat facing, and the trademark front gable. The house was set two hundred feet back from the road on a broad green lawn with a flower-lined brick walkway. It was beautiful, in both its strong straight lines and its wooded isolation.

The garage door opened as we turned into the driveway, revealing an empty space next to a high-end older-model sedan, painted beige, but probably called Autumn Harvest, or something equally pretentious. Parker pulled into the garage and turned off the engine. The door closed behind us.

"Okay, that's a little creepy," Ethan said, staring out the rear windshield.

"It's just Brian," I assured him. "Daddy said he'd be here to let us in." Sure enough, the door leading into the house opened, flooding the garage with light from a small utility room. One of Carissa's brothers stepped out. He was in his early twenties, too young to have accompanied his father to the ranch on council business, but old enough and experienced enough to help us catch Miguel, even if our plan fell apart.

"Hey, Brian." Parker got out and shook his hand while the rest of us climbed over each other in a tangled heap, each trying to be first out of the crowded van. I landed on my rear on the concrete, not a very dignified position for someone claiming to be in charge. Marc pulled me up by my hands and pressed me against the side of the van, a suggestive smile teasing the corners of his mouth.

"Give it a rest." Lucas grabbed Marc's belt loop as he passed, hauling him backward like a kid towing a wagon. Marc grinned at me and winked, but then his face was all business. By the time he turned to face Brian, he'd abandoned his smile in favor of a serious expression that managed to convey both competence and danger at once. I would have been happy to pull off either one.

After a quick round of masculine back thumping, I stepped forward and Brian held out his hand. "How are you, Faythe?" he asked, as if we were on a first-name basis. He probably thought we were. Because the ratio of tabbies to toms was so low, all the guys thought they knew us well, even the ones we'd only met once or twice. Especially me.

I'd made quite a reputation for myself by choosing college instead of marriage to Marc, and there were several toms who considered it their personal responsibility to tame the infamous shrew. Marc didn't look favorably upon attempts to "tame" me. Neither did I, as one memorable tom from the northeast found out. He was okay, though. Dr. Carver was able to straighten out his fingers with minimal complications. Besides, it was only his left hand. He didn't have much use for that one anyway, from what I understand.

But Brian Taylor didn't seem like the daring type to me. He wasn't cocky or brash. In fact, the opposite seemed true. He was polite, apparently genuinely concerned about me.

"I'm fine, thanks." I took his hand and made eye contact. "How's Carissa?"

"Okay. She's a little freaked out by all this, though," he said, and I nodded. That was understandable. "She said to tell you thanks for the warning. And good luck."

"Thanks, but I don't expect much trouble." I let go of his hand. "We have them outnumbered by four to one. Those are pretty good odds."

"I guess so. Come on in and let me show you around." Brian led us through the utility room and into a large, clean kitchen, dominated by stainless-steel appliances and a roomy island rising from a sea of white tile. Beyond the kitchen was the dining room, flowing into a sunken living area carpeted in spotless white cut Berber.

The interior of the house was as modern and comfortable as the outside was stately and beautiful. The floor plan was open and welcoming, the ideal place for a party—or a massacre. But I couldn't help imagining how bad a pool of blood would look against that immaculate white tile. Or soaking into the carpet. We'd have to make sure and kill Sean and Miguel outside, to save the Taylors a huge cleaning bill and a lengthy explanation to the authorities a cleaning service would no doubt call.

Fortunately, we were too far from large-scale civilization to have to worry about human witnesses. Or noise.

"These are for you." Brian said, laying his hand on a neatly folded pile of clothing on the dining-room table. "Your dad mentioned that you needed some of Carissa's clothes. She slept in these last night, so they still smell like her. Will that work, or should I look for something else?"

I held the nightshirt up to my face. It smelled like Carissa: young and healthy, with a hint of floral perfume and a moisturizing facial cream. "It's perfect," I said, laying the shirt back on the pile.

"Good. There's plenty to eat in the fridge, so help yourselves to whatever you want." That particular courtesy was in case we needed to Shift, which was a good possibility. I'd never met a cat yet whose re-frigerator wasn't well stocked. All the time. And judging from the Taylors' extra-wide, side by side, stainless-steel monstrosity, there would be plenty to choose from. "Do you need anything else?"

"Nope, this ought to do it," Marc said.

Brian nodded, and to his credit, he only looked mildly tense, which meant he was holding up better than I was. I was starting to get really nervous.

"Why don't you guys get something to eat and fill Brian in on the plan while I transform myself into Carissa."

"No problem," Lucas called, already neck deep in the fridge.

I used the first-floor bathroom to shower, trying to wash off as much of my own scent as possible. While I was at it, I used Carissa's soap, face wash, and shampoo. Clean, young-smelling, and dry, except for my damp hair, I changed into Carissa's pajamas. The shirt was a pink halter top, held on with spaghetti straps tied at the shoulders. It was a little tight through the bust—warping the petals of a large silk-screen daisy—but it would work. The pants matched the shirt: pink, with hundreds of tiny white flowers identical to the one stretched across my chest. The top ended just above my belly button and the pants rode low on my hips, even with the drawstring cinched, so a wide strip of my stomach showed in between.

Marc whistled when I emerged from the bathroom. "Why don't you sleep in things like that?"

I gave him a secretive smile. "Maybe I do."

"You don't. You haven't changed that much. You don't even own anything pink." Okay, he was right. My grudge against the color pink stemmed from my mother's fondness for it. However, I did like the soft, loose fit of the pants. Maybe if they came in red…

But that was a thought for another time.

The guys were gathered at the large kitchen island, each part of the way through one variation or another of a ham-and-cheese sandwich. "'Ere you go, Aythe." Ethan said around a mouthful of ham and Swiss on rye. He swallowed and held up a plate loaded with two sandwiches and a mound of store-bought potato salad. "Eat fast. We don't have much time left."

"Thanks." I took a bite. Several thin slices of ham, provolone, dill pickles, tomato, and real mayonnaise, on whole-wheat bread. My all-time favorite sandwich. "I can't believe you remembered this." I took another bite.

"I didn't," Ethan said. "Marc made it."

Marc. Of course. He never forgot anything, which wasn't as great as it sounded. "Thanks, Marc." I scooped up a bite of the potato salad. It wasn't as good as homemade, but not bad.

"You can thank me later. For now, just eat."

By the time I'd finished my first sandwich, the guys had cleaned up everything except my dishes. When I picked up my second sandwich, Ethan grabbed my plate, rinsed it, and loaded it into the dishwasher. Mom was going to be pissed to find out she had a whole army of Mr. Cleans who rarely lifted a paw at home. And they would pay for my silence. Boy, would they pay.

At eight-forty, as the last glimmers of daylight faded from the sky, we went over the plan one final time. The easiest way to tempt Miguel into going after "Carissa" would be to put her out in the open alone. That's how he'd grabbed the first three tabbies, though with me, he'd just gotten lucky. As badly as I hated to admit it, if I'd followed my father's orders, they never would have had a shot at me.

But now, thanks to Ryan, Miguel knew for certain that all the Prides were on alert. He'd know the tabbies were surrounded by brothers and enforcers, and were under orders not to go out alone. None of the other tabbies would ignore a direct order from her father, and even if Miguel didn't know that for sure, Sean would.

Sending "Carissa" on a long walk by herself would be too obvious; Sean and Miguel would know they were being set up. They'd run, and we'd probably never catch them. So how could we make her available without tipping them off about the trap? Where could we send her with few—maybe even just one—bodyguard, without raising their suspicions?

The layout of the Taylors' land had provided the solution: we'd send her to the cabin. It made perfect sense.

Unlike my father's men, the enforcers of the midwest territory didn't live in their Alpha's backyard. They had a house to themselves in a clearing about a quarter of a mile behind the main house. The cabin, as they called it, was essentially a three-bedroom bungalow, renovated and wired for electricity sometime in the seventies. It was completely surrounded by woods, except for the well-worn foot trail from the main building.

And the best part was that neither house was visible from the other.

Inside information from Sean and Ryan had worked against us from the beginning, but that was about to change. Sean knew about the cabin, and I was counting on the fact that he'd explain the layout of the Taylor property to Miguel.

If Carissa's childhood was anything like mine, she'd spent much of her youth wandering back and forth between her home and the cabin, eagerly welcomed in both. In fact, now that she was nearly grown, she probably spent a good deal of time there, just to be able to relax around someone other than her parents.

So a short trek on her own property would be harmless. Even understandable, considering how cooped up she must feel, having spent the past two days under the close observation of everyone around her.

But just in case a solitary forest walk looked suspicious, we had Brian. He was there to accompany "Carissa," to keep up the appearance of a strong defensive presence. If we'd used one of the other guys, Sean would know immediately that something was off. But Brian belonged on the Taylor estate, and would be a perfectly believable escort for his sister.

The plan was for my men to hide up in the trees along the trail, some in human form, some in cat form, so we'd be prepared to handle the kidnappers in either shape. There were two reasons for the elevated hiding places. First, they could see much farther in the air than they could on the ground. Second, their scents would be harder for Miguel and Sean to catch from overhead.

Marc would take a tree well back from the path, on the side of the property farthest from the highway, because his was the only scent Miguel would recognize. Sean would recognize all the others, but he'd probably assume the Taylors had called in some extra backup to help protect their daughter. Unless he smelled Marc. Every Pride cat in the country knew Marc would never take another assignment until he'd found me. So we had to keep him—and his scent—as far away from the path as was practical.

After several minutes of discussion, we'd decided that Anthony, Ethan, and Marc would Shift into cat form, and Parker, Vic, and Lucas would stay in human form. Brian and I would wait in the main house until we heard from one of the guys in human form that Miguel and/or Sean had shown up.

How would we hear from them? Well, Parker, Vic and Lucas had each programmed Eric's number into their cell phones, which were all on silent mode. As soon as any of them saw either of the rogues, he would call me and let the phone ring once then hang up. That would be our signal to leave the house.

Really, I don't know how people ever got anything done in the days before the Internet and cell phones.

Brian had already unscrewed the lightbulb from the back porch, so it would be nearly impossible for Sean and Miguel to get a clear look at my face. Even if one or both of them had Shifted, the dark would aid me rather than them. Cats see very well in the dark but they don't see very far; their best vision is in the midrange, not too close but not too far away. So no matter which form they took, they couldn't get close enough for a good look at me—or a good whiff—without alerting at least one of the guys.

Once we got the call, Brian and I would make some noise as we unlocked the back door. This was to give my men warning that we were coming, and to focus the bad guys' attention on us rather than on any activity going on over their heads.

Then, my "big brother" and I would cross the backyard and take off down the foot trail, laughing and joking on our way to the cabin. That would be the hard part—acting like nothing was wrong as I walked along, waiting for Miguel to pounce on me. Again.

If neither cat showed himself by the time we got halfway to the cabin, Brian and I would sweeten the bait a bit. We'd have to get big brother out of the picture, even if just for a few minutes. We'd strike up a playful game of tag, or decide to race each other to the bungalow porch. That would be a little tricky because Miguel was more than familiar with my voice—thanks to my own big mouth—so I'd have to be careful not to speak much. Or very loudly.

Either way, the idea was for Brian to run ahead to the cabin—which we'd leave unlit, so they'd know it was empty—leaving me alone on the path for a few minutes. I'd amble along, again waiting to be pounced on.

If they still didn't take the bait, I'd enter the cabin and watch TV with Brian, waiting for Sean and Miguel to attack. There were two of them, and we were hoping that if they thought I had only one escort, they'd think the odds of a victory were in their corner.

We were assuming Sean and Miguel would try

something similar to the way they'd nabbed me two days earlier: catch me off guard and try to sedate me. Only this time I knew what was coming and would be prepared to evade the needle.

As soon as the first bad guy showed himself, Lucas, Vic and Parker would drop from the trees above. Together, they would hold him immobile for questioning. We still needed to know exactly what had happened to Luiz, and who the South American buyers were, among other things.

Then, once we had our answers, the guys had my permission to pound him to death with as much gusto as they liked.

Lucas and Vic had made a deal. Vic would take charge if Sean showed up alone, since he was the reason Sara had been targeted. But if Miguel attacked me by himself, Lucas would have free rein. He was confident that he could take the jungle cat all on his own, but if there was any doubt about that when the time came, the other two had my permission to jump in.

Marc, Ethan and Anthony would take off in cat form in search of whichever one hadn't shown up.

If both rogues were stupid enough to show themselves at once, everyone would get in on the action. Oh, happy day.

As Marc recited his part in the plan, the importance of what we were about to do hit me with the force of a heavyweight's right hook. This was our shot. Our *only* shot. The whole thing was my idea, but I couldn't summon even a spark of pride for having thought up the plan we'd agreed on. I was terrified.

What if it didn't work? Or worse, what if someone got hurt? It would be my fault. If anything went wrong, I would be to blame because I was in charge, at least nominally. This was exactly the kind of responsibility I'd gone to school to avoid, yet there I was, buried in it up to my neck. But at least it was a figurative burial. I'd be pretty satisfied if I could end the night without requiring a literal one.

Ethan elbowed me in the ribs, and I glanced up to see that the powwow was over. It was go time.

We left the van in the garage on the assumption that Miguel would never see it unless he broke in, in which case we hoped to have him breathing through his neck before he had a chance to sniff around. At eight forty-five, Anthony, Ethan and Marc put their clothes in the van, along with mine, and went into the woods to Shift and find good hiding places.

Parker, Vic and Lucas double-checked their phones, then went to pick out trees they could climb easily on two legs. I watched them through the window in the back door until they disappeared down the path. The only one whose hiding spot was visible from the main house was Parker.

When the guys were in position, I sat on the tiled kitchen floor, my back against the dishwasher and Eric's phone in my lap. Brian paced in front of the dining-room table. He was too wound up to sit. Just watching him made me nervous.

For the first fifteen minutes, I was fine. Almost excited. My body was a treasury of bruises, in all shapes, sizes and colors, and I was eager to share the wealth with Miguel. But as the minutes stretched into a half hour, my palms grew damp and Carissa's pants started to cling to my legs. I tried to relax, aware that every drop of sweat soaking into the borrowed clothes made me smell less like Carissa and more like myself.

Every minute or so, I glanced at the digital clock on the cell-phone display. I was sure each time I looked that another quarter of an hour must have passed, but it never did. The clock was wrong. It had to be.

"Hey, Brian, what time do you have?" I whispered. I'm not sure why I whispered, except that it felt wrong to make noise in the dark. Irreverent, almost, like screaming in church. I'd turned on several lights upstairs and a lamp in the front of the living room so Miguel would think someone was home. But with only a single lamp lit, across the room and around a corner, the kitchen was a lair of shadows, hiding my worst fears among the dark, irregular shapes.

"Nine thirty-five," Brian said. He'd whispered, too.

I glanced at the phone again. Damn. It was right.

My heart beat against my rib cage, as if demanding to be let out. I took a deep breath, trying to slow my racing pulse. *Why am I so nervous?* I'd begged Daddy for a chance to catch Miguel. I'd given away the next two and a half years of my life. But now that the time had almost come, I was petrified.

I glanced at the phone again, checking the battery. It was fully charged when I found it and had only lost half of the available power in the hours since. So nothing was wrong with the phone. But what if one of the other phones had died? What if I went out to check and Miguel saw me? I'd ruin the entire setup. Better to sit still and wait. I hate waiting. I'm not very good at being still, either. Not while I'm conscious, anyway.

Brian glanced at me in sympathy. I knew he could hear my heartbeat, and maybe even smell my fear. I smiled back, trying to pretend nothing was wrong, that I wasn't about to take a leisurely stroll down the footpath and into the claws of death.

Melodramatic? Me? Surely not.

The air conditioner clicked off, leaving us in total silence. I hadn't even realized it was running until it stopped, and suddenly I heard nothing but my own pulse.

As I lifted the phone to check the time again, a single warbling yowl of pain pierced the stillness, only to be cut off a second later. It came from the north.

Marc. My head swung toward the backyard. My neck popped but I barely registered the sound. In an instant I was up, running for the back door.

"Faythe, wait!" Brian shouted, stealth all but forgotten. I ignored him. Footsteps pounded on the tile behind me. Plastic crunched as he stepped on Eric's phone where I'd dropped it. I turned the doorknob but nothing happened. I howled in rage, panicked because I couldn't disengage the lock. Why hadn't we unlocked the doors?

Brian grabbed my shoulder. I turned on him, hissing. He let me go, palms raised in front of his chest. I shoved him with both hands. He stumbled backward, tripping down two carpeted steps to land on his ass in the sunken living room. He made no move to get up, and I turned back to the door.

My heart hammering, I gripped the knob with both sweaty hands. I jerked it clockwise. Hard.

Something snapped, and the door swung toward me. I shoved the storm door open. Its lock popped too, the sound faint beneath the roar of my pulse in my ears.

I jumped off the back porch and landed with my legs already pumping. My feet shoved against the earth, fighting gravity itself. All I could think about was that someone on the north side of the path had been hurt, badly. Marc was on the north side.

Thick clouds hid the moon, and I had only what light filtered through the upstairs windows with which to see. It was just enough for me to make out the top of the chain-link fence thirty feet ahead. I sprinted toward it, flying through the yard. As I neared the fence, I sped up. Grabbing the top of the metal frame, I launched myself over, shredding my palms in the process. I landed on my feet, both knees bent. Shock from the impact rippled its way up my legs. I straightened them slowly, my pain eclipsed by fear for Marc and dread of what I might find.

Before the tingle faded from my toes, I was running again, headed for the footpath. Fifteen feet from the fence, I tripped over my too-big shoes and fell face-first into the dirt. I stood quickly, brushing fragrant grass clippings from my forearms with palms caked with blood and dirt. But before I could take another step, a deep feline growl rumbled from the trees to my left. The sound rolled across my skin, raising the hairs on the backs of my arms. I froze.

He stood at the edge of the woods, ten feet down the path. His ears lay flat against his head, the tips pointing to either side. His tail swished slowly against the ground, stirring last years' dead leaves. Reflective pupils flashed at me as he blinked. He growled again, low and threatening. He was growling at *me*.

I frowned at him in confusion. It was Marc. Even half blinded by the dark and with only a moderately enhanced sense of smell, I recognized him. I knew his voice, his purr, his roar, and even his growl. It was definitely Marc, and he was mercifully uninjured. So why was he growling at me?

Grass crunched behind me. Before I could turn, a hand wrapped around my neck, warm and damp, with a grip like iron. I yipped in surprise, my hands flying up automatically to try to pry it loose.

Miguel. I didn't need to see or smell him to know who it was and to realize my mistake. I'd tripped over my own feet, landing within arm's reach of the man I'd meant to catch. *Brilliant, Faythe.*

"*Buenas noches, mi amor,*" he said, using his free hand to pry my fingers from the hand around my neck. "Going incognito tonight?" Clearly uninterested in my answer, he squeezed my neck slowly, as if in warning.

I gasped. Panic flooded my bloodstream. A sharp fluttering sensation consumed my stomach, as if the butterflies in my belly had razor-edged wings. I could still breathe, which meant he didn't mean to kill me. Not yet, anyway.

For a human, his grip might have been good enough to choke me. I could handle being choked. Choking was slow enough that a good elbow to his gut or stomp on his foot might throw him off balance, or at least give Marc a chance to pounce. But Miguel was a werecat, and his grip was good enough to snap my neck with a single sharp twist.

But I'd take a slashed throat over a broken neck any day. At least that way I'd get to bleed all over his shoes. One final fuck-you before I died.

Thirty-One

Marc's tail twitched, a play of shadows in the night, and something heavy thumped to the ground on my right, just ahead of us and out of my view. Marc's eyes slid to the side, peering past me at whoever had dropped from the trees.

Miguel grabbed my left arm with his free hand, tightening his grip on my neck at the same time. He twisted backward and to the side, dragging me with him into the center of the path. From my new position I could see Marc on the left edge of my vision, his tail swishing along the ground slowly, angrily. Parker now stood on the path in front of me.

"Come out!" Miguel shouted almost directly into my ear, and I cringed away from the sudden deafening sound. "I know you're all up there. If you want your tabby to live, come down now!"

While I watched, my left ear still ringing, Vic dropped onto the path fifty feet behind Parker, from Marc's side of the woods.

"There are more, *mi amor,*" Miguel whispered, his lips brushing my hair. "Who are they?"

I shook my head as much as I could with my throat in his grip, refusing to answer.

"Who are they?" His fingers tightened, and my windpipe began to close.

Marc growled in Vic's direction, and Vic stepped forward. "Lucas," he said. "There's only Lucas."

"Lucas, come join us!" Miguel called, loosening his grip on my neck.

A moment passed in silence, then footsteps sounded from around a sharp curve in the direction of the cabin. Lucas stepped into view, walking slowly and carefully, as if afraid that any sudden movement would startle Miguel into killing me. Maybe it would have.

My heart jumped painfully as I watched him approach. *Where's Ethan?* And for that matter, where was Anthony? But as soon as I thought the question, I knew the answer. Anthony was gone. His dying cry was what drew me outside. The Di Carlos had now lost their youngest son, as well as their only daughter, and it was my fault, because this had been my idea. My stupid, stupid idea.

"And the one in the house?" Miguel asked, stroking my cheek with his free hand. "The one who shouted your name?"

He already knew about Brian, so it would do me no good to lie. "Brian," I called, but my voice came out hoarse, so I cleared my throat and tried again. "Brian, come on out."

A soft, low-pitched growl met my ears, and I felt Miguel twist to glance behind us. Brian had Shifted. That's what had taken him so long.

"Over there with your friends," Miguel ordered, and Brian complied, growling as he eased past us to stand between Marc and Parker, just as Lucas joined them. "This is quite a gathering, but I can only think of one thing we have in common." His free hand slid down my left arm, over my waist, and around my hip.

Marc stepped forward, still growling. The hand around my throat tightened even more, making my breaths short and shallow. "Get back," Miguel ordered, and his voice made it clear why Eric and Sean had followed his orders. His was not a voice to be ignored.

But Marc stood his ground. His eyes were spheres of reflected light, focused just above and behind me.

"You wouldn't want anything to happen to your tabby, would you?" Miguel adjusted his grip on my neck, his fingers forcing my chin up. He was no longer choking me. Instead, short, jagged fingernails dug into the skin to the left of my windpipe, his thumb mirroring them on the other side. He wouldn't bother with breaking my neck now. He would just crush my throat. Or rip it out altogether. Of course, if he did, the guys would make short work of him. That wouldn't help me though, would it?

Marc's eyes flashed at me as if in apology, and he stepped back. But he never stopped growling.

"What do you want?" Parker asked, his voice taut with tension.

"Why ask foolish questions?" Miguel's accent was crisp in my ear. "Ask me what happened to your other cat in the woods. Ask me where Sean is. Ask me where Luiz is. Ask how I got this deep into your territory without getting caught. But don't insult your own intelligence by asking for answers you already have."

Unperturbed, Parker tried again. "Where's Luiz?"

"That's better," Miguel said, sounding legitimately pleased by the new inquiry. "Instead of answering, let me ask you a question." He barreled on, without waiting for a reply. "Have you had any trouble with humans? Any women missing? Any bodies found partially consumed? Because Luiz has a…a taste, shall we say?" Delight resonated in his voice, and my chest tightened. He was entirely too happy with his word choice. "Yes, he has a *taste* for human women. He likes them young and pretty. And raw. And three days ago I sent him on a project in your territory."

Project? Was he talking about the girl murdered in Oklahoma? Had Miguel ordered a hit on a human woman? Or women? Why?

Parker and Vic exchanged a glance. They knew about the human murders. We all knew about them. We just hadn't known enough about Luiz.

"He's a friend of yours?" Vic asked, stepping slowly toward the far edge of the path.

Miguel's chin scratched my neck as he spoke. "My brother, and my business partner."

"Who do you work for?" Lucas asked.

"We work for no one. We are…independent dealers."

Independent dealers. Riiiiight. As if what he did could ever be defined by such a benign term.

Lucas frowned. "Who hired you?"

"Our client list is confidential."

What the hell? Was Miguel under the delusion that grand phrasing made his business legitimate? Or honorable? Or valuable? As different as the U.S. Prides were from those in Central and South America, they did have a few things in common.

Like strays. No matter how important Miguel thought he was, the truth was that he was a stray, a second-class citizen. His "clients" might be willing to let him do their dirty work, but they'd never invite him to their table. Never.

"Any idea where we can find Luiz?" This came from Parker.

"Follow the trail of bodies. Each time he fails, there will be a new one."

That was enough for Vic. He didn't care about Miguel's cryptic answers. He didn't care about Luiz and his human women. He only cared about getting me away from Miguel so he could avenge his sister and brother. "You know we won't let you leave with her," he said.

Miguel laughed against my cheek, and my skin crawled with revulsion. "You won't let me leave without her, either, so I'll take my chances with the bitch." His tongue slithered into my left ear, and I tried to jerk my head away, but his grip on my neck stopped me.

"You want the truth?" Vic asked, his voice cold and hard with hatred. "You're right. We won't let you leave. But if you let her go, we'll make it fast and easy. No pain. You have my word." He paused, and I saw the lie in his eyes. He wanted Miguel to suffer, and he was not alone.

When Vic continued, I could barely hear him. "But if you touch her again, I swear we'll rip you apart one piece at a time and show you the bits as they come off."

Miguel laughed again, his chest shaking against my back. "I've already had my hands all over her. Haven't you seen her face?" His right hand tilted my chin toward Vic while his left hand slid beneath Carissa's halter top and across my bruised ribs. I hadn't worn a bra because of the spaghetti straps, so when he cupped my breast, he touched bare skin. He squeezed, and tears blurred my vision. Not from pain, but from humiliation and the first infant flames of true rage.

I snatched his hand out from under my shirt, squeezing his wrist as I pulled. Bones ground together, and Miguel gasped. His right hand tightened around my neck, and suddenly I couldn't breathe.

"Watch yourself, *mi amor*." His breath teased my ear as I tried desperately to suck in one of my own. In my panic, I squeezed his wrist harder, almost horrified to hear a tiny crack as one of his bones fractured.

Miguel flinched but didn't loosen his grip. "You don't breathe again until you let go," he whispered, nudging my earlobe with his nose. His nails bit into my neck, seconds from breaking through my skin.

Marc hissed and took a step forward, but there was nothing he could do until Miguel released my throat. So I let go.

Miguel's left arm dropped out of sight, and his opposite hand relaxed around my neck. I drew in as much air as I could, fighting not to hyperventilate now that I could breathe again.

Marc's tail whipped back and forth across the ground in warning, but Miguel didn't seem to notice. "Is this your tabby?" he asked. "Are you the stray I smelled all over her? And I do mean *all over*."

Marc growled and inched forward, but Miguel only chuckled, dismissing him for the moment to address Vic. "If this tabby belongs to him, which one was yours?"

Vic's teeth gnashed together. He didn't answer, but even in the poor light I saw the muscles of his jaw bulge.

"Well, since the big guy has Abby's pretty, red curls, I'm guessing Sara meant something to you. That little kitty was something special." His accent thickened as his words ran together. "Do you know she spit in my face? And bit me?"

Vic growled. It wasn't the same sound Marc had made, because a human throat couldn't produce such a low pitch. Still, it was a great approximation for someone on two feet.

"Each girl is special, of course," Miguel continued, wrapping his free arm around my rib cage,
heedless of his injured wrist. His thumb brushed the
underside of my breast through the nightshirt, and I
couldn't suppress a shudder.

He liked it. Miguel liked forcing a reaction from
me. He pressed me tighter against him, his breath
brushing my neck. "Yes, they each have their own
style. Some fight up until the very end, like your
Sara. Or I guess she's *our* Sara now, no?"

Fury flashed in Vic's eyes, and Parker put a
warning hand out to calm him. They were waiting
for a shot at Miguel, and were clearly running out
of patience. But then, so was I.

"Some are too scared to resist at all, but those are
mostly the human girls. I think that's why Luiz likes
them. Then others—like little Abby—make a lot of
noise at first, hissing, and crying and trying to crawl
away. But once you get in one good thrust—" he
rammed his hips into me, and I would have lost my
balance if he hadn't been holding me up "—they
kind of give up, like there's nothing left worth
fighting for. And Abby was fresh. Untouched. *Muy
dulce.*" *Very sweet.*

Lucas's arms bulged as his huge hands curled
into fists. His cheeks flushed in outrage.

Marc slipped silently forward while Miguel was

focused on Lucas, but Miguel caught the movement, even on the edge of his vision. "Uh-uh," he said. "Don't come too close. I don't want to have to break your tabby's neck. At least not before I'm done with her." He slid his free hand down my stomach and beneath the low waistband of my borrowed pants, careful with his injured wrist. His fingers hovered just above my pubic bone.

My hands clenched around material from the sides of Carissa's pants, and I took shallow breaths, afraid the slightest movement of my stomach would nudge his hand farther down. Only the memory of fighting to breathe kept me from removing his hand myself.

"She and I have unfinished business. Don't we, *mi amor?*"

Yeah, I thought. *Your death.*

His grip forced my chin even higher as his lips brushed my ear. "But I tell you what," he said, now speaking to Marc. "If I don't like my free sample, I'll return her. Used, of course. But then, we strays are accustomed to secondhand goods, aren't we?"

If Miguel thought he could bait Marc with jabs at his heritage, he was wrong. Marc had long since developed emotional calluses, and remarks like that didn't even faze him. But sticking a hand down my pants did.

Marc hissed, arching his back as his tail swished furiously. He took several gliding steps toward us, his fur glistening in a beam of moonlight shining through a hole in the clouds. He leapt to one side and landed gracefully on all four paws, several feet from the guys on the path.

Miguel turned toward Marc, now keeping all five of them easily in view.

I stared at Marc, confused because his movements seemed pointless and panicked, like a hostage dancing during a bank robbery. But his eyes never left mine. He was up to something. We had come to a standstill. Miguel wasn't going to let me go, and they weren't going to let him take me. So something had to change.

"Skittish, kitty?" Miguel asked, chuckling at what he mistook for nervous indecision on Marc's part. But Marc never did anything without a reason, even if no one else understood his motive. What the hell was he doing?

Marc hissed again, showing off long white canines, both top and bottom. His ears flattened against his head as his whiskers arced forward. Leaves crackled as he pierced them beneath his claws. He was posturing, doing everything he could to keep my attention.

No, wait. Not *my* attention. Miguel's. He was trying to distract Miguel, but from what?

"One move and she's dead," Miguel said, finished playing now that Marc clearly meant business. He pulled his hand from my pants and wrapped it around my upper arm, just beneath my shoulder, squeezing hard enough to bruise, in spite of the pain it must have caused him.

Marc hunkered against the ground. He grew absolutely still, moving nothing but his eyes. He was watching, waiting for the opportunity to pounce.

Marc's tail twitched. Miguel's right hand clenched around my throat. His fingernails sank into my skin with an eerie popping sensation, followed immediately by sharp pain and darkness on the edges of my vision.

But his grip loosened almost immediately, and I could breathe again. It had been a spasm, I was almost sure of it. Marc had spooked Miguel, whose hand inadvertently clenched around my throat. It was good to know Miguel wasn't impervious to fear, and that he wasn't ready to kill me yet. But if Marc pushed him too far, he might do it anyway, by accident.

And dead by accident isn't much different than dead on purpose. They both look pretty much the same in the end.

Blood trickled down my neck, pooling in the hollow above my collarbone. The smell was sharp and immediate. Marc's whiskers wiggled as he sniffed. He smelled my blood.

A moment of stillness enveloped us as Marc and Miguel faced off, neither moving or making a sound.

Leaves crunched behind me. At first I thought Miguel was shuffling his feet, but then someone panted. Someone close to the ground. Marc's distraction had worked.

Miguel froze. His head moved away from mine as he turned, trying to look over his left shoulder. He couldn't do it without turning his back on everyone else, but that didn't matter anymore, because he was surrounded.

The growl began behind me, deep and soft. It rose in a rapid crescendo, ending in a roar of fury that was both familiar and terrifying. It was familiar because it was Ethan, and terrifying because he was enraged.

Miguel whirled us both around, heedless of the un-Shifted cats now that they were clearly the lesser threat. He stiffened against my back and I heard his heart race. He was finally scared. And as his confidence faded, his concentration began to slip, just as it had in the basement cage.

My own pulse sped up. I was going to get a shot at him. I could feel it.

"Nice kitty," Miguel whispered, backing us slowly away from Ethan. His head whipped to the right, then back to the left. He was dividing his attention between Marc, Brian, and Ethan, which left little to focus on me. Perfect.

I glanced at Marc, trying to communicate with him through my eyes. His ears perked up. He knew I was trying to tell him something, but that was as good as it was going to get. As long as I'd known Marc, I'd known Ethan longer.

My fists clenched and unclenched at my sides as I shifted my focus to my brother. I blinked at him twice, resurrecting a signal we'd established as children. He blinked back once. He understood. Just to be safe, I did it again. Again he returned the signal. He would wait for my move. He was ready.

"Open the gate," Miguel said.

What gate? I thought, searching behind Ethan for something I'd missed.

"Open it now, or I'll bite off her ear." Miguel's teeth sank into the top of my left ear and I flinched as he tugged.

Marc nodded to Vic, who took off down the path at a jog, moving quickly out of my sight. Metal screeched behind me, and I understood Miguel's demand. The fence had a gate. Why on earth had I jumped over the fence if there was a gate?

Miguel let go of my ear. "Now go stand by your cat. The stray."

Marc nodded at the edge of my vision, and Vic's footsteps drew closer until he walked into sight and past us. Without taking his eyes from Miguel, he stopped beside Marc, fists clenched, arms bulging, and teeth grinding.

"We're going to back slowly toward the house, and if any one of you gets heroic, I'll tear her head off," Miguel said. I didn't think he could actually carry out such a threat in human form, but even a good attempt would be enough to finish me off, so I kept my opinion to myself.

Miguel tightened his already bruising grip on my throat. I sucked in short, desperate puffs of air. He took a step back, dragging me with him. Gasping, I stumbled. He pulled me up by my neck, completely closing my throat for one terrifying moment.

Adrenaline scorched through my veins, urging me into action. I couldn't let him get me into the house; I knew what would happen then. He'd lock the door, knock me out, drag me to the van, and take off.

I was *not* leaving with Miguel. Not again.

He took another step, and another. The guys watched us go, inching forward with us but not daring to charge while Miguel had me by the throat. Ethan drifted slowly to one side, his fur blending with the darkness of the encroaching forest. Several torturous minutes later, Miguel and I were only feet from the fence. I could see it in Vic's face. In moments, I'd be out of reach. I had to do something, and I had to do it now.

The slant of Miguel's head told me he was watching Marc and the guys instead of Ethan. I gave my brother a short nod. He nodded back.

Seize the day, I thought. But what I actually seized was much more painful—for Miguel.

I grabbed one of the fingers around my throat with my right hand and his crotch with my left. I jerked back with my right hand and squeezed with my left. Miguel howled into my ear an instant before I felt, rather than heard, his finger snap.

Ethan raced toward us, pausing several feet away.

Miguel's still-functioning digits dug into my throat. They reopened the wounds on my neck, cutting off what little air I was receiving.

Desperate to breathe, I broke two more fingers. Miguel's howl rose in pitch, sounding remarkably like a cat's screech. I squeezed his crotch tighter, and felt something pop. His shriek rose into tones beyond the human range of hearing. And finally he let me go.

I threw myself onto the dirt path, gasping for air. Ethan pounced, his fur indistinguishable from the night as he leapt over me. Moonlight flashed in his eyes. Miguel's keening ended in a wet gurgle. Metal crunched and squealed as Ethan drove him to the ground, flattening a lengthy section of the chain-link fence.

For a long moment, I lay still on my stomach. I gulped air through my mouth, gorging like a half-starved child at a banquet. Every breath hurt, like swallowing fire. My neck felt thick and slippery, and I kept touching it to find out what was wrong. It was slick with blood. *My* blood. Other than that, it felt okay from the outside. On the inside, my throat hurt like hell.

But it was over. Finally, it was all over. We had him, and once we had answers, Miguel would find out how the American Prides dealt with their enemies.

A hand appeared in front of my face. Glancing up, I saw Vic's face clearly in the moonlight. I took his hand and he hauled me to my feet. Wrapping my arms around his chest, I clung to him, glad to share my simultaneous grief and relief with someone who clearly understood. He hugged me, rocking me gently. I knew he was thinking of Sara.

"Do you want to watch?" Vic asked, lightly stroking my hair.

"Wha?" My voice came out creaky, like I had laryngitis.

He turned me around gently, slowly, and leaned down to whisper into my ear. "They're going to do it now. Do you want to watch?"

Miguel lay on the ground, not three feet away. Marc stood next to him, his muzzle hovering over the jungle cat's belly. Ethan sat by Miguel's head, his open mouth inches from the criminal's throat, where blood ran from four deep puncture wounds, one set on each side of his Adam's apple.

"No!" I croaked, still clinging to Vic as I stared at Miguel in horror. As I watched, his body shuddered, his legs convulsing. "They can't do it yet." I shifted my gaze to Marc, who was already watching me. "You can't do it yet. We have to question him. We need to know where Luiz is, and who hired them."

Marc shook his head slowly. Deliberately.

"What? What's wrong?" I asked, twisting to look up at Vic.

"His throat's crushed." Satisfaction and regret battled for control of his expression. "He can't talk. He'll be dead soon anyway, but he deserves to suffer before he dies. If they're going to do it, they have to do it now. In a few minutes, it'll be too late."

I turned back to the man on the ground, studying his neck carefully in the moonlight. Vic was right. His throat was dented and misshapen. I wasn't sure how he was even breathing.

Miguel stared up at me, blinking in fear, and I returned his gaze. There he was, the man who'd taken me from my home and beaten me senseless for fighting him. The man who'd killed Sara and left her disfigured and exposed for her brothers to find. The man who'd stolen Abby's innocence and ruined her life.

Now he lay helpless in front of me, his eyes were wide with comprehension. He must have known it would end this way. There was really no other possibility.

"Do you want to watch?" Vic asked again, and Marc turned to look at me, waiting for my answer.

Sara's face flashed in my mind, blue eyes shining at me from within my own memory. I saw Abby, bruised, violated and psychologically scarred. I nodded. I did want to watch. He deserved it. I'd earned it.

Lucas and Vic had wanted a shot at Miguel, but there wasn't time now to beat him to death. Since neither of them had Shifted, the honor went to Marc and Ethan. They shared the kill. We all watched.

I'd grown up with the Pride. I'd eaten more fresh deer than birthday cake, but I'd never seen anything like Miguel's death in my entire life. There wasn't time for prolonged and excruciating, which had been the plan, so the guys settled for just plain excruciating. And disgusting.

Marc roared in victory, standing over the body of his enemy. The sound was triumphant, and aggressive, and primal. It triggered instinctual longings in my own heart, and made my inner cat beg for the privilege of roaring alongside him.

When the last glorious note faded into the forest, Marc growled and swiped one claw across Miguel's stomach.

Miguel's spine bowed, pushing him off the ground as he gurgled and bucked against the pain. Lucas stepped on his fractured left wrist and Parker stood on his right, pinning him down. Four stripes appeared in Miguel's shirt. Blood poured from the wounds, soaking the material almost instantly. The reddish-black rivulets ran over, flowing to nourish the dirt path with his life force.

Marc stepped back, and Ethan took a turn, crossing the fresh wounds with four stripes of his own, at a ninety-degree angle with the first four. It was disturbingly neat, yet undeniably revolting. Miguel jerked again and moaned, choking on his own blood.

Marc tore into Miguel's stomach with his teeth, ripping away shirt and skin together. He dropped the hunk of flesh on the ground beside his victim. It reminded me, in a very surreal way, of my own aversion for chicken skin.

Ethan ripped away another chunk, dropping it on Miguel's other side. They wouldn't consume a single bite. They weren't man-eaters, and Miguel wasn't a meal. He was prey of a different sort. He was a threat eliminated.

I was okay until Marc used his teeth to tug Miguel's intestines from his gaping stomach. But that was all I could take; I'd had enough of torture and revenge. Vic held my hair while I threw up. I heard him talking to the guys over my back. "Wrap it up. I think she needs to rest."

Rest. Yeah, that's what I need. More like shock therapy. I needed to forget the last two days. Have them wiped from my memory altogether. There wasn't room in my brain next to the complete works of Shakespeare for Marc's top five ways to torture your enemy before finally letting him die. I didn't want to have dreams of my boyfriend disemboweling anyone, even Miguel.

"Get me out of here," I whispered.

"What?" Vic leaned toward my face, his gaze still focused on the spectacle behind me.

My fist clenched around a handful of his shirt. "You heard me. Get me out of here. Now."

"Faythe…"

I stood up straight, wiping vomit from my mouth with the front of Carissa's shirt as I looked into Vic's face. His eyes begged me to let him stay. He was crying, and pleading with me not to make him leave until Miguel exhaled his last tortured breath.

"Just put your head on my shoulder and close your eyes," he said, trying to draw me into his arms. I stepped back, refusing. Behind me I heard more gurgling and a slick, sliding sound I had no desire to identify.

"Why would you want to watch this?" I asked Vic, swallowing the bile rising in my throat.

He looked at me with unbearable pain and confusion, as if I shouldn't need to ask. "Because this is what he did to her. He violated her in life, then he mutilated her in death. Now he's paying."

Oh. I couldn't argue his point, but neither could I watch.

Parker took my arm. "Come on, Faythe, I'll take you inside."

I met his eyes and saw in them what I wanted to see in Marc's but knew I would never find. Parker didn't want to watch it either. He didn't want any part of it.

He steered me past Brian, who stood watching in fascination, then around Miguel and the cats, and helped me over the chain-link fence, just to be polite. Ethan had flattened an entire section of it, so I only had to walk across a length of mangled metal. Parker stayed to my left the whole time, keeping his body between me and the sight I would never forget, no matter how hard I tried.

Inside, I took a shower in the downstairs bathroom. I stayed in until the water ran cold, trying to scrub away every last molecule of Miguel's scent. When that was gone, I tried to wash away my memories. But they were sticky little bastards, clinging to me like an emotional odor, no matter how many times I lathered and rinsed.

When I finally stepped out of the shower, Parker was waiting with the clothes he and Abby had bought that morning. I couldn't believe it was even the same day, but a glance at the clock showed me that no matter how long each minute as Miguel's hostage had felt, time continued to tick by at its normal rate. Time was the great constant, eternally measuring my life in the ticks of a hundred second hands, the tocks of a thousand pendulums. It portioned my life into good times and bad times, the former too short, and the latter too long.

And now it told me that less than two hours had passed since we'd pulled into the Taylors' driveway. It was ten-thirty. I'd showered for nearly half an hour.

Parker and I sat at the bar in the kitchen, drinking Mrs. Taylor's gourmet coffee, with imported French cream. It was the middle of June, and I was wearing full-length jeans, but I couldn't stop shaking. I'd added a purple neck and four fresh puncture marks to my assortment of bumps and bruises. I felt about as attractive as Frankenstein's monster. And almost as well loved.

"Shouldn't they be done by now?" I asked, not sure I really wanted to hear the answer.

"They are," Parker said. "They're cleaning up."

"Oh." That made sense. I wondered how one went about cleaning up a disemboweled body but was afraid that if I asked, he'd actually tell me. I didn't want to know that badly. But there was something else I *did* want to know. "Was it Anthony?" I asked, cradling the mug in my hands for warmth.

Parker's eyebrows arched into matching question marks and he opened his mouth, clearly intending to ask what I meant. Then he took a good look at my face and decided I deserved better. He knew what I meant.

"Yeah, it was." He stared down into his coffee, as if hoping to read the future from a cup of tea dregs. "Anthony's gone, and so is Sean. Marc filled me in while you were showering." Parker told me what he knew, and—true gentleman that he was—he gave me the G-rated version out of respect for my exhaustion and encroaching shock.

They'd come at us from the north, Sean on four legs and Miguel on two. Sean pounced on Anthony from a nearby tree branch, knocking him to the ground. Anthony only had time to make a single sound before he died, but without his dying cry as warning, Marc might not have known he was in danger until it was too late.

Marc took Sean out in silence, utilizing years of training and experience. But his effort was wasted on Sean, who made no move to defend himself. By all appearances, he was ready to die, and Marc believed Sean attacked Anthony mostly to secure his own fate. Marc was going after Miguel when I came between them, blocking Marc's pounce and nearly getting myself killed.

I listened with my mug still cupped in both hands, thankful suddenly that Marc was around to do what I wasn't willing to do. If my training involved any of what he'd done to Miguel, I would have to find a way out of my promise. I couldn't do it. I just couldn't.

An hour later, everyone had showered and dressed, and no one said a word about me using up all the hot water.

They'd wrapped Miguel's body and its various detached parts in a sheet of black plastic from the garage. Lucas taped up the bundle with his ubiquitous duct tape and tossed Miguel into the back of his own getaway van, which Vic had found parked down the road. Sean's body got the same treatment.

They took far more pains with Anthony, wrapping him carefully and positioning his limbs as if for comfort. But he had to go in the white van, too. Rule number four for cleaning up at the site of an incident: carry all dead bodies in one vehicle so that if both cars get pulled over, fewer people will be caught with corpses. That was also why no one traveled with the bodies except the driver, who, in this case, was Lucas. Vic wanted to do it, to be with his brother, but Marc and I both vetoed his decision. He seemed to be holding up remarkably well, but at some point his grief would sink in, and he shouldn't be behind the wheel when it did.

After inspecting the scene of the incident one last time—out of habit more than necessity—Marc pronounced us ready to go. Someone had redistributed a pile of leaves to cover up all evidence of violence, including my vomit, and Marc assured me that the first good rain would take care of anything they missed. Then he assured me they didn't miss anything.

Unfortunately, the chain-link fence was history. Daddy offered to pay for it, but the Taylors refused his money. They said a fence was a small price to pay for securing their daughter's safety and ridding us all of the men responsible for so much trouble. I thought the term *trouble* was a bit of an understatement, but the Taylors saw no reason to complicate things with the truth.

And, really, who was I to judge?

Thirty-Two

"Did you really throw up?" Jace asked me.

I smiled. Enough time had passed for me to be able to laugh about it, though there were a couple of weeks following that night when I thought I might never smile again. "Yeah. All over the ground. I think I splashed Vic's shoes."

Jace laughed, then grimaced, clutching his chest. He was able to sit up, and had insisted we play chess while we talked, but I knew it was a ruse. He didn't think I could concentrate on the game if I was busy talking. But I had news for him: I was always busy talking, so for me it was business as usual.

"Check," I said, moving my bishop into place.

He moved a knight in to block my bishop. "I wish I could have been there."

"No, you don't." I eyed my captured pieces, lined up on his side of the board. *If I could just get my other bishop back...* "Trust me, it wasn't pretty."

"Well, considering the alternative..." His sweeping gesture took in his entire body.

"How many times can a girl apologize?" I asked, moving my queen forward to back up my remaining bishop. "I should never have taken your car. But look what you get out of it. I'd love six weeks off."

"Not me." He moved a pawn forward one space to threaten my only remaining knight. "Four weeks down, and two to go."

His nose had healed the fastest, and thanks to Dr. Carver it looked as good as new. It would have been a shame to ruin Jace's face with a crooked nose. His toes hadn't been quite as lucky; the little one on the end would never be the same. Jace had a great attitude about it, though. He said the flaw gave him character.

What it actually gave him was a new pick-up line. He'd already made up a story to try out on poor unsuspecting women next time he and Ethan went barhopping. It involved a runaway train, a damsel in distress and a baby carriage. No one ever said he was original. Luckily, he still had his looks. And two more weeks to work on his pick-up line.

Two of his ribs had been broken quite badly, and

Dr. Carver refused to set him loose on the world again until they healed. Until then, it was my job to keep him company, playing the game of his choice, so long as no clothes came off. It was my punishment for taking his keys. It was also punishment for Marc. Daddy had finally been forced to agree that Marc's temper was out of control.

Marc was handling it well, mostly because one side of my bed smelled like him more often than not. He was happy, and annoyingly chipper. I was waiting for the other shoe to drop. If it didn't happen soon, I'd have to take off one of my own and throw it at him.

"Checkmate," I said, moving my poor over-worked queen to her final resting place, in direct diagonal line with Jace's king.

"Bullshit!" Jace cried. "Give me a minute and I'll find another move."

Fat chance. I had him walled in with my remaining bishop and knight. "Take all the time you need." I leaned back in my chair, lacing my hands behind my head. "Just wake me up when you think of something."

"Who won?"

I spun to find Marc in the doorway, dressed in jeans and a plain black T-shirt. *Work clothes. Great.*

"I did." I unlaced my hands and leaned forward. "What's up?"

"Stray in southern Louisiana. The call just came in."

I froze, my heart pounding in my ears. "Jungle cat?" I asked, but he knew what I really meant. *Is it Luiz?*

Since ridding the world of Miguel, we hadn't seen or heard a thing from Luiz, in spite of doubled-up patrols in every claimed territory. Because there were no known victims after the girl in Oklahoma, the council was convinced that another stray eliminated the problem for us, even before we'd caught Miguel. There was also a rumor circulating among the wildcats that Luiz had fled the country after hearing about what happened to Miguel. I didn't know which was true, and I didn't really care, so long as he never showed up again.

Marc shook his head, keeping his smile easy and light, trying to set me at ease. "Nope, plain old garden-variety American stray. He's ours if we want him." He grinned. "You feel like seeing New Orleans?"

I glanced at Jace. He was frowning, but when he noticed me looking, he smiled. "Go ahead."

"You sure?" I asked. "I can stay and kick your ass in a couple more games if you want."

"Gee, how could I turn that down?" He waved me off with a flick of his hand. "Go on. Bring me back some beads."

I laughed. "Jace, it's July."

"So what?"

"So, Mardi Gras is in February."

He frowned again. "Oh. Then just bring me some jambalaya."

I smiled and rolled my eyes. "Sure, Jace. I'll bring you some jambalaya."

"Thanks." He turned back to the board and began setting up the pieces. "Grab Ethan on your way out and tell him I'm bored, will you?"

"No problem."

Marc followed me to my room and took my suitcase from the closet.

"We're staying overnight?"

"In New Orleans? Hell, yeah." He dropped the hard-shell case on the bed.

"What if we catch him this afternoon?"

He grabbed me around the waist and tossed me onto the bed next to the suitcase, pinning me down before I could get up. "What Daddy doesn't know won't hurt him."

I rolled us over and straddled his waist, staring down at him with a smile. "It'll hurt *you* if you try to bill him for the trip."

"Yeah, yeah." He grinned up at me.

"What?"

"You're beautiful."

I blushed. I'd refused to look into the mirror for weeks, until my face felt normal when I touched it. My cheek healed okay, but my throat had scarred. I had four small white crescents running in a vertical line, just to the left of my esophagus. I wasn't vain enough to think they marred my reflection, but I never once looked at them without remembering that night. So I looked in the mirror less and less.

"You're right," I said, planting my palms on his chest. "And you're very lucky."

"I never denied it." And he hadn't. He pulled me down and kissed me again, then rolled me onto my back. "Get packed." Flashing me one last smile, he left for the guesthouse to pack his own bag.

I stood at the end of my bed and opened the suitcase, surprised to discover that it was already full—of books. *What the hell?* Then my eyes settled on a technical-writing textbook, and I remembered.

After my face healed, I'd gone back to school to pack up my stuff, say goodbye to Sammi, and to try to explain my decision to Andrew. But he wasn't there. He'd withdrawn from school shortly after I left, with no explanation. Confused by his absence, I said a tearful goodbye to Sammi as I tossed my belongings into various suitcases and boxes, paying very little attention to what I took and what I left behind.

Now, staring down into the bag, I realized I'd never bothered to unpack.

With a sigh, I began pulling out books, lining them up on my shelf four at a time, in front of the row already in place. At the bottom of the suitcase, my hand hesitated over the last book. *Walden,* by Thoreau. It was a thin paperback edition—and it wasn't mine. I hated the transcendentalists. I preferred to experience nature on four paws rather than read about it.

I probably packed one of Sammi's books by mistake, I thought, pulling back the front cover. But there at the top, printed in his own neat, all-caps handwriting, was the name Andrew Wallace.

Why would I have Andrew's copy of *Walden?* I'd given away my own copy as soon as I'd finished the survey course requiring it. I was flipping through the book, trying to decide what to do with it, when something stuck between two pages caught my eye. It was a flower. A dried, pressed flower. My best guess was that it was some kind of tropical bloom, maybe an orchid. It had beautiful, pale pink petals, a shade darker in the middle.

Huh. I hadn't known Andrew liked tropical flowers. Maybe there were several things I hadn't known about Andrew…

"What's that?"

I slammed the book shut and whirled around, my heart hammering in my throat. Marc leaned against the door frame, duffel bag in hand.

"Aren't you ready yet?" He shook his head, clucking his tongue in mock disappointment. "What is it about women and luggage? You don't have to bring everything you own, and it shouldn't take this long to throw some clothes into a bag. In fact, if it will save you any time, just leave the underwear out all together. Here, let me help." He dropped his bag on the carpet and leaned down to pick up a bra I'd dropped. "Now, see what I mean? You're just wasting time packing stuff like this." He tossed the bra over his shoulder and shoved a T-shirt into the bag.

I laughed, Andrew's flower already forgotten. "Thanks."

"No problem." He smiled. "But you can't take that either." He plucked the thin volume from my hand, stacking it with the others on my shelf. "You won't have time for reading. You won't even have time for sleeping if I have my way." He headed for the door, then turned back, as if something else had occurred to him. "Don't forget your ID."

I frowned, as his reminder led me to another thought. "Hey, Marc?"

"Yeah?"

"Tell me why you really had my wallet that day in Mississippi."

Marc blushed, just as he had the first time I'd asked, and I was intrigued.

"Come on," I begged, brushing his lips with a kiss as I wrapped my arms around his waist. "Spit it out."

He sighed, his face still red. "I took your wallet because your shirt wouldn't fit in my pocket."

"What?"

"Promise you won't laugh?" he asked, and I nodded. "That first day you were gone, I couldn't think straight. All I could do was yell and hit things."

I nodded again, thinking of poor Jace.

"Later, I found your shirt on the floor in the hall. I carried it with me all day because it smelled like you. But when your dad put me in with the search party, I needed something smaller. I came in here, and your wallet was lying on the dresser. So I took it." He looked up at me, searching my face for scorn or amusement, but there was none to find.

"Because it smelled like me?" I asked.

"Yeah. I know it's stupid, but…"

"Yeah, it is stupid," I said. His eyes widened and his jaw tightened, disappointment filling his face. "Thank you for being stupid for me." I stood on my toes to kiss him, and when I pulled away I met his eyes, preparing to eat my words. "I love you, Marc. You're a huge pain in my ass, but I love you."

He smiled. "You said it."

"I believe the proper response is 'I love you, too.'"

He laughed, and shook me gently by the shoulders. "Yeah, but you already know that. And you said it." He glanced around the empty room, then jumped up and ran into the hall, leaving me staring after him in wonder. "Where the hell is everybody?" he asked from somewhere to the left of my doorway. His footsteps came closer, and he passed by my room on his way to the other side of the house, searching for witnesses. "She finally says it, and there's no one here to hear her."

"I heard her," Jace called from Ethan's room, where he was recovering.

"Ah-ha!" Marc jumped back in front of the door with a thud, and I shook with laughter. "There's a witness. You can't deny it now. You're caught."

"All right." I couldn't control my grin. "You got me. I'm caught." *So long as you don't say the M word,* I thought. But there was no reason to warn him. Five lonely years had taught him a lesson.

He swaggered toward me and kissed me again. It was a good kiss, the kind where, in the movies, the girl always raises her foot. I didn't do that, of course, because I wasn't *stupid* in love. Not yet anyway. But it was a damn fine kiss.

"So what are you going to do with me, now that you've caught me?" I asked, looking up into his eyes.

He grinned. "Put you to work."

My jaw dropped. "That's it?"

He nodded. "Come on, woman! Duty calls."

Yes, duty called, and apparently it had my home number. For the first time in my life, I was answering to someone other than myself, and for the most part, the workaday world sucked. Fortunately, my new responsibility came with one awesome perk: all the ass I could kick.

What self-respecting girl could say no to that?

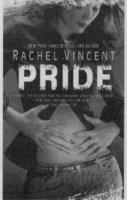

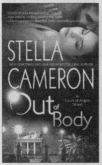

J.T. ELLISON

Homicide detective Taylor Jackson thinks she's seen it all in Nashville—but she's never seen anything as perverse as The Conductor. He captures and contains his victim in a glass coffin, slowly starving her to death. Only then does he give in to his attraction.

Once finished, he creatively disposes of the body by reenacting scenes from famous paintings. And similar macabre works are being displayed in Europe. Taylor teams up with her fiancé, FBI profiler Dr. John Baldwin, and New Scotland Yard detective James "Memphis" Highsmythe, a haunted man who only has eyes for Taylor, to put an end to The Conductor's art collection.

the cold room

Available wherever books are sold.

REQUEST YOUR
FREE BOOKS!

2 FREE NOVELS
FROM THE SUSPENSE COLLECTION
PLUS 2 FREE GIFTS!

YES! Please send me 2 FREE novels from the Suspense Collection and my 2 FREE gifts (gifts are worth about $10). After receiving them, if I don't wish to receive any more books, I can return the shipping statement marked "cancel." If I don't cancel, I will receive 3 brand-new novels every month and be billed just $5.74 per book in the U.S. or $6.24 per book in Canada. That's a saving of at least 28% off the cover price. It's quite a bargain! Shipping and handling is just 50¢ per book in the U.S. and 75¢ per book in Canada.* I understand that accepting the 2 free books and gifts places me under no obligation to buy anything. I can always return a shipment and cancel at any time. Even if I never buy another book, the two free books and gifts are mine to keep forever.

192 MDN E4MN   392 MDN E4MY

Name _____ (PLEASE PRINT) _____

Address _____ Apt. #

City _____ State/Prov. _____ Zip/Postal Code

Signature (if under 18, a parent or guardian must sign)

Mail to **The Reader Service:**
IN U.S.A.: P.O. Box 1867, Buffalo, NY 14240-1867
IN CANADA: P.O. Box 609, Fort Erie, Ontario L2A 5X3

Not valid for current subscribers to the Suspense Collection
or the Romance/Suspense Collection.

Want to try two free books from another line?
Call 1-800-873-8635 or visit www.morefreebooks.com.

* Terms and prices subject to change without notice. Prices do not include applicable taxes. N.Y. residents add applicable sales tax. Canadian residents will be charged applicable provincial taxes and GST. Offer not valid in Quebec. This offer is limited to one order per household. All orders subject to approval. Credit or debit balances in a customer's account(s) may be offset by any other outstanding balance owed by or to the customer. Please allow 4 to 6 weeks for delivery. Offer available while quantities last.

Your Privacy: Harlequin Books is committed to protecting your privacy. Our Privacy Policy is available online at www.eHarlequin.com or upon request from the Reader Service. From time to time we make our lists of customers available to reputable third parties who may have a product or service of interest to you. If you would prefer we not share your name and address, please check here. ☐

Help us get it right—We strive for accurate, respectful and relevant communications. To clarify or modify your communication preferences, visit us at www.ReaderService.com/consumerchoice.

MSUS10

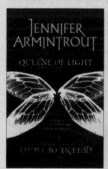
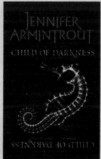
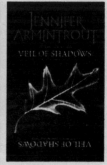

New York Times **bestselling author**

HEATHER GRAHAM

This is the way the world ends....

Not long ago Scott Bryant would have described himself as an ordinary guy. But one act of heroism has changed his life forever—or at least until the apocalypse occurs. Because the end of the world is on its way.

Suddenly and inexplicably possessed of superhuman strength, Scott finds himself allied with the enigmatic and alluring Melanie Regan on a quest to find the mysterious Oracle in hopes of averting the absolute destruction that threatens.

The earth itself will soon turn against its inhabitants, and now mortal and immortal must join forces if any are to survive.

DUST TO DUST

Available now wherever books are sold!

MIRA®

www.MIRABooks.com

MHG2654R